Hippocrene Language and Travel Guide to

RUSSIA

Victoria Andreyeva
and
Margarita Zubkus

HIPPOCRENE BOOKS
New York

For information, address:
HIPPOCRENE BOOKS, INC.
171 Madison Avenue
New York, NY 10016

Library of Congress Cataloging-in-Publication Data
Andreeva, Viktoriia.
  Hippocrene language and travel guide to Russia / [by Victoria
Andreyeva and Margarita Zubkus]. -- 1st ed.
      p.   cm.
  Title on verso t.p.:Language and travel guide to Russia.
  ISBN 0-7818-0047-1 (pbk.) :
  1. Russia (Federation)--Guidebooks.   2.   Russian language--
Conversation and phrase books--English.   I. Zubkus, Margarita.
II. title.   III. Title: Language and travel guide to Russia.
DK510.22.A53   1993
914.704'86--dc20   93-23034
                                                   CIP

Printed in the United States of America.

Contents

Chapter 1 Getting started   7

Chapter 2 Brush up your Russian   16

Chapter 3 Medicine   40

Chapter 4 Money, weights and measures   54

Chapter 5 Accommodations   69

Chapter 6 Communication   88

Chapter 7 Transportation   102

Chapter 8 Sportsmania   126

Chapter 9 Shop smart!   140

Chapter 10 Bon appetit!   157

Chapter 11 Drinks   172

Chapter 12 Russian etiquette   179

Chapter 13 Moscow   193

Chapter 14 St. Petersburg   240

Chapter 15 Other Russian cities   274

Chapter 16 Geographical horizons   286

CHAPTER ONE

GETTING
STARTED

INTRODUCTION

This book will be your best travel companion during your trip to Russia. First of all, it will help you get a firm grasp on the Russian language, so it won't be Greek to you anymore. Then, it will assist you in daily routines and help you to be in good command of situations. By describing some Russian traditions, customs and historical events, it provides you with the information needed to make the most of your trip to Russia.

PRELIMINARY ARRANGEMENTS

Securing the proper documents for your trip far in advance is important. All visitors must have valid passports and visas in order to enter and leave Russia. Your visa can be arranged by an official invitation of a relative or a sponsoring organization or through proof of hotel accommodations. These reservations can be made with your travel agent, who will provide you with a special Intourist number needed to obtain the visa. Some travel agencies will even send your visa application to the Russian Consulate in Washington D.C. or in New York for processing.

The Russian consulates all over the world are renown for inefficiency. Therefore, although visas should be issued within two weeks of their submission, it would be better to send yours in advance. But do not despair if you cannot get it there in advance. Visas have been issued by the consulates in Washington D.C. and in New York within one day or two-four working days for an additional fee.

The visa application is submitted with:

a. the visa application form
b. a xerox copy of your passport
c. your official invitation or Intourist number
d. three passport size photos (black and white or colored, matted or glossy).

Getting there

As is true for all overseas travel, flight plans to Russia should be made in advance to get the best rate. Note that inevitably flight arrangements will have to be made before your visa Intourist validation can be obtained. Visas are extremely precise in their format. Your date of arrival and departure are printed on them and must be observed. No dates will be issued on a traveler's visa that do not conform with the Intourist dates for hotel accommodation. Once you are in the country, visas can be extended with proper authorization.

There are a number of entry ports to Russia. You may enter through the international airports in Moscow, St. Petersburg, Minsk, Kiev, Vladivostok, and Khabarovsk. If you choose not to fly directly to Russia or one of its neighbors, but rather through another city such as Copenhagen, Stockholm or Budapest, you may have to spend the night there either on your flight or on your return. Many travelers prefer to go through Helsinki. You may also travel to Russia from Helsinki by ferry. One scholar who investigated all the possibilities boasts that she was able to get a round trip flight to Helsinki for $500! She then simply took a ferry to St. Petersburg. The ferry goes to St. Petersburg and Tallinn, Estonia. It is also possible to take the train between Helsinki and St. Petersburg. Although this is usually a very inexpensive way to travel, it is inconvenient, especially if you have a lot of luggage.

BEFORE DEPARTING

Immunization and Check-Ups

There are no official immunization requirements for entry into Russia, but check with the US State Department's Health section to learn what immunizations are recommended for general travel to Russia. Do not wait until the last week to take care of your shots. Certain shots are necessarily in pairs with a two week minimal waiting period between them.

It should be noted that since 1987, all foreign travelers who plan to stay in Russia for more than 3 months are required to undergo an AIDS test. If you are a semester student or a long-term visitor you are required to show documentation from your physician (ВРАЧ) [vrach] that you have tested negatively for AIDS (СПИД) [spid]. If you fail to present this documentation when asked, you will have to be tested for the virus while in Russia. Oddly, the emphasis on AIDS testing has diminished greatly since 1990.

If you plan visiting Central Asia, polio, diphtheria and typhoid (БРЮШНОЙ ТИФ) [brush-nóy tif] shots are recommended. Tetnus and gamma gobulin are recommended for travel anywhere in the Commonwealth.

Aside from immunization, it is not a bad idea to get a check-up before traveling if you are due for one.

First-aid Outfit

Take any and every kind of medicine you think you may need during your trip. Medicine, even the most basic, is often difficult to find in Russia, and the problem of shortages of medical supplies has become even more acute in the past few years. Because you may not eat a sufficient amount of vegetables and fruits, it's a very good idea to take a supply of vitamins with you.

The following is a list that you can pick and choose from as you deem appropriate:

Vitamins (especially vitamin C)
Lotions
Band aids
Hydrogen peroxide
Cold/flu medicine
Cough drops
Sore throat lozenges
Tissues
Anti-bacteria spray
Nasal spray
Eye drops
Aspirin
Laxatives and anti-diarrhea remedies
Nail clippers
Antacids
Contraceptives

Many of the above items are now available in some of the foreign cooperative stores. See the chapter on shopping for more information on these stores.

If you are on any sort of prescription medicine (ЛЕКА́РСТВА ПО РЕЦЕ́ПТУ) [le-kárst-va pa re- tsép-tuu], be sure to take enough with you to last your entire stay. You should indicate on your declaration form upon arrival that you are bringing in prescription medication with you.

Travelers with chronic illnesses are advised to get an ID bracelet that contains all the information relevant to their illness.

WHAT TO BRING

Your Wardrobe

While packing, keep in mind that Russia is not overflowing with many of the basic necessities found in the West. Even if you do find the item in a store, it may not be of the same quality you are used to.

Depending on when and where you are traveling, your assortment of clothes will vary. Moscow and St. Petersburg are relatively warm in the summer but can be bitterly cold in the winter. Moscow winters begin in November and run a bitter course through April. It is not uncommon to see snow in Moscow in April. Although St. Petersburg is further north than Moscow, its climate is generally milder than Moscow's because of the warm ocean current of the gulf stream. Yet, is is also often windy and humid. Winters can be very wet and muddy in both cities.

Clothing

General

Sweaters (even in the summer)
A good sturdy raincoat
A good sturdy coat
A pair of sturdy walking shoes or tennis shoes
A pair of boots for wet weather
Hat, scarf, gloves, heavy and regular socks
Undergarments

Men

A suit (Russians generally dress formal for evenings out)
Plenty of shirts that preferably do not require ironing
Sports jacket
Pants

Women

Dresses
Blouses or shirts that require no ironing
Skirts (women wear skirts and dresses in Russia more than in America)

Children

Sweat suit
Sneakers
Nice shirt and slacks (boy)
Skirts and a dress (girl)

Shorts are generally not worn in the cities, but at the resorts and beaches they are very popular. As a general rule bring things that are comfortable, take up little space in your suitcase and do not need ironing. Bring clothing that you can mix and match.

Other More Than Useful Items

Toilet paper (Don't laugh, you will need it!). If you are staying in an Intourist hotel, toilet paper will be readily available. This paper is sometimes the butt of jokes for Western travelers, who say it is so heavy, they can write letters home on it. But even this paper is a rare commodity – not to be found in most public restrooms.

Snacks you cannot live without (peanut butter, granola bars, dried fruits)
Toothpaste

Mouthwash
Bath towel (the ones provided are like American dish towels)
Soap
Shampoo and conditioner
Shaving items
Feminine napkins
Tissues
All supplies and cleaner for contact lenses
Insect repellent
Baby items if traveling with a small child
Diapers
Baby food
Bottle opener/cork screw
Electric converters (voltage 220)
Travel alarm clock
Camera and film
Dictionary or phrase book
Money
Travelers checks
Credit cards
Addresses and phone numbers you will need in Russia
Gifts

Bring gifts for your guides, hosts, and other people you will meet. Gift giving is very common and even expected. The most popular gifts are, naturally, those things that cannot be easily found in Russia. Gifts do not necessarily have to be of great value or uniqueness.

The Following Items Make Good Gifts:

Magazines
Photographs
Postcards
Pens, crayons and magic markers
Music
Pantyhose
Midol

Advil
Chewing gum
Cigarettes, especially Marlboro
Clothing with writing on it (college t-shirts and sweat shirts
are very popular)
Jeans
Lighters
Hair pins, combs etc.
Cosmetics and perfume
Jewelry
Swatch watches
Toys (for children)
Picture books (for children)
All kinds of food and drinks

Do not forget there is a baggage weight limit on inter-national flights. American carriers will charge you a fee if you have more than two suitcases, each weighing up to 70 pounds, and more than one carry on. If the size of your luggage exceeds 80 inches and weighs more than 70 pounds, you may send it by American Customs Service, Inc. (phone: (718) 244-7253, telefax: (718) 244-5529).

Packing Your Film

The metal detectors at Russian airports are notorious for damaging film. To be on the safe side, pack all film in your carry-on luggage.

Bringing in a Computer

Check with the Department of Commerce to find out if you should acquire a "license for temporary export" to bring in a computer. This is only necessary for those high-tech computers which are more advanced than the equipment found in Russia. Upon entering the country, you may be asked to show your computer license. This license insures that you intend to take the computer with you when you leave. Be sure to bring along batteries and proper converters for your lap top computer. You may very well not be able to find them over there.

The Electrical Current

Remember that in Russia, as in most of Europe, the electrical current runs on 220 volts, whereas in the United States it runs on 110 volts. Today many electrical items are available which run on both 110 v and 220 v. If you intend to bring an electric shaver, a blow dryer, iron or anything else that requires electricity you will need to buy a converter. In most cases the electrical sockets are designed for 2-prong round plugs. These types of converters are found in most hardware stores.

CHAPER TWO

BRUSH UP
YOUR RUSSIAN

THE RUSSIAN ABC

Before taking your trip to Russia, let's step into the realm of the Russian language. Believe it or not, you already know some Russian words. Let's prove it. Read a few English words and before learning even one Russian letter you can start building your Russian vocabulary! All these English words are the same in Russian with only a slight difference in pronunciation:

act	АКТ	[akt]
atom	АТОМ	[á-tam]
address	АДРЕС	[ád-res]
America	АМЕ́РИКА	[a-myé-ri-ka]
antagonist	АНТАГОНИ́СТ	[an-ta-ga-níst]
antenna	АНТЕ́ННА	[an-téa-na]
aspect	АСПЕКТ	[as-pyékt]
assonance	АССОНА́НС	[a-sa-náns]
avant-garde	АВАНГА́РД	[a-van-gárt]

These "international words" are mostly of Latin or Greek origin, though some are of English, French, German and, less frequently, Russian origin. In the beginning, these cognates will be the first aid helpers in building your Russian vocabulary.

While pronouncing these words remember that in Russian they sound slightly different. First of all, they should not be slurred over as in English. The Russian language is more melodious than English. You could even say that Russians sing their words. So pronounce the syllables clearly, as if you are pleased to hear every sound, especially if you would like to sound like a Muscovite.

We begin from the very beginning, from the words starting with the letter A, the first letter of the Russian alphabet. And as you know, "In the beginning there was," of course. . . ART. Therefore, the first letter of Russian alphabet, A sounds like the English A in ART.

The second letter of the Russian alphabet Б sounds like English B in BAD.

The third letter of the Russian alphabet B sounds like V in VENT.

Now you know the ABC or "АБВ" of the Russian alphabet:

A for ART and AH!
Б for BAD and BUT
B for VENT and VACANT.

Here are three more Russian letters:

Г like G for GOD
Д like D for DART
E like English YE in YES!

Read these letters one after the other: Г, Д, E.

17

Scan or sing the first Russian letters, now familiar to you, one after the other. The choice of the rhythm and melody is yours: А Б В Г Д Е.

You have already learned almost a fifth of the Russian alphabet, which consists of 33 letters. Most of the Russian letters differ from the English ones, and make up what is known as the Cyrillic alphabet.

A Bit of History

The Cyrillic alphabet was created by two Greek monks, Cyrill and Methodius one thousand years ago for the purpose of translating the Bible into Slavic languages. That is why some of its letters resemble Greek characters. The Russian alphabet is a modified form of that Cyrillic, while for English we use the Latin alphabet.

Graphics of the Russian Letters

The graphics of small and capital printed Russian letters could be both identical or different depending on the letter.
It is the same in the letters Г г and Д д.
It is different in: А а, Б б, Е е

Try to copy the letters next to the printed letters:

Б б
Г г
Д д

Russian Scrabble

Now that you know how some Russian letters are written and pronounced, let us create syllables and words from these letters:

Put Д before A and you will get a syllable ДА [da] which is, in itself, a word. Да [da] means "yes," "sure," "of course," "I am listening to you," "I agree with you."

If you put Д after A you will get a one-syllable word А Д [ad] (hell), a word meaning a state of disorder, struggle, and hatred.

If you put Е between two Д, you will get the one-syllable word ДЕД [dyed] (grandfather). Remember that the Russian Е is a soft sound and should be pronounced like YE in YES.

Put together the three letters Г, Д, and Е and you will get an important question word ГДЕ? [gdye?] (where?). It will help you find out the location of a thing, of a person and/or a place where you are or, perhaps, want to go.

Now you can ask in Russian:

Where is grandfather?
ГДЕ ДЕД? [gdye dyed?]

This is your first Russian sentence. As an inquisitive student, you have begun with a question. As you will soon learn, this book will answer many of your questions.

Let's see what we can get from just six familiar Russian letters.

Put together Б and A and create the syllable БА. Then repeat it and you will get a two-syllable word БÁ-БА [bá-ba] (grandma or colloquial for woman).

If you put together other familiar letters: Д, Е, В, and A, you will get an archaic form of a Russian word for girl ДÉ-ВА [dyé-va]. When you read some of Pushkin's poems, you'll run into this word.

Look at this word carefully and you will find in it the Biblical name É-ВА [yé-va] (Eve) hidden in it like a little matryoshka doll is hidden inside of a big matryoshka.

19

Here are some other Russian words formed with the letters you have already learned:

Д В А [dva] two
Д А Д Á [da-dá] Dada, an artistic movement
Б Е Д Á [be-dá] misfortune, trouble, disaster
Е Д Á [e-dá] food

Each Russian word is read by syllables and has one stress. Remember: the stressed vowel is longer and pronounced more clearly than the unstressed one.

Building Russian Sentences

You already know how to ask some questions in Russian. Put a question word first and then add a subject for which you are looking. The verb "is" is omitted in this kind of Russian sentence:

ГДЕ ЕДÁ [gdye e-dá]? Where is the food?
ГДЕ ÉВА [gdye yé-va]? Where is Eve?
ГДЕ ДÉВА [gdye dyé-va]? Where is a maiden?
ГДЕ БÁБА [gdye bá-ba]? Where is grandma?
ГДЕ ÁДА [gdye á-da]? Where is Ada?
ГДЕ АД? [gdye at]? Where is hell?

Ear training:

A as in ah!
Б as in book
В as in visa
Г as in good
Д as in dip
Е as in year

Add to the first six twelve additional Russian letters:

Ж as in treasure
З as in zeal

20

И as in ear
К as in kid
Л as in lion
М as in milk
Н as in nine
О as in oak
Р as in rosy
С as in soak
Т as in total
У as in truth

Most of these Russian sounds do not present problems to English speakers.

The Russian vowels are comparable to the English vowels:
И might be short like English i in bin, pin, tin, kit, fit and long like English E in eve, peeve, meet, feet.
О is closer to the short English O in dog.
У sounds like English U in tooth, roof.

The Russian consonants are also not too difficult to pronounce. The consonant Ж may look graphically quite ridiculous, like a little beetle, but it sounds very familiar to the English ear. It is pronounced like the English S in the words: leisure, pleasure, and treasure.

The letter З which looks like the number 3, sounds like the English S in bells, goes, pens and the English Z in zigzag and zip.

The letters К, Л, М, Н sound almost like their English counterparts. Pronounce them as you would in English. Only the Russian Л will be slightly different: harder than the English L.
Read them in the following words which are the same in both Russian and English:

К for kaleidoscope
Л for labyrinth

M for Madonna
H for Nobel

The next Russian letter P is pronounced like the English R in car, bar, farm, rabbit.

The Russian C sounds like the English S in the words salt, must, tops.

Two Russian sounds П and T differ little from the English P and T. In Russian they never have the aspiration.

Using your knowledge of the Russian alphabet, read these useful Russian-English words:

passport ПÁСПОРТ [pás-part]
visa ВЍЗА [víi-za].

If you are going to Russia as a tourist you may freely use this English word in Russian, just change the stress: ТУРЍСТ [tuu-ríst].
If you are going to Russia on a business trip, use the Russian words БЍЗНЕС [bíz-nes] and БИЗНЕСМЍН [biz-nes-mén] which have the same meaning. You should, however, pronounce them softer than their English equivalents.

Stressed and Unstressed Vowels

Vowels keep their original sound in the strong position under stress. In the weak position or without stress, vowels should be pronounced shortly. Some vowels even change their quality in a weak position:

O becomes A
E turns into И
Я turns into И

That is why in the word ПРОГРЕ́СС you read the first unstressed syllable "ПРОГ" with "A" [prag-rés] and the word БИЗНЕСС you read like bíz-nes. Some vowels like A, И, etc. do not alter their sounds in a weak position.

Russian Scrabble:

A list of one-syllable words from the letters you already know:

И	and	С О Н	dream
Н Е	not	Н О С	nose
Н Е Т	no	Т Р И	three
Н О	but	П О Л	floor
О Н	he	П И Р	feast
У М	mind	С Т У Л	chair
К Т О	who	С Т О Л	table
Т У Т	here	С Т О П	stop
Т А М	there	З В У К	sound
Т О М	volume	С Т О	hundred

Among these words we can distinguish different parts of speech:

NOUNS: УМ [um] (mind), СОН [son] (sleep), НОС [nos] (nose), ТОМ [tom] (volume), ПОЛ [pol] (floor), ПИР [pir] (feast), СТОЛ [stol] (table), СТУЛ [stul] (chair), ЗВУК [zvuk] (sound).

PRONOUNS: КТО? [kto?] (who?) (interrogative), ОН [on] (he) (personal, 3rd person, singular).

PARTICLES: НЕ [nye] (no), НЕТ [nyet] (not).

ADVERBS: ТУТ [tut] (here), ТАМ [tam] (there).

CONJUNCTIONS: И (and) (connecting), HO [no] (but) (contrasting).

NUMERAL: ТРИ [trii] (three).

The interrogative pronoun KTO? [kto?] is used as a question word in question sentences.

Now using some of these new words ask questions. Give the answer as well.

КТО ТАМ? [kto tám?] Who is over there?
ТАМ ОН. [tam ón] He is over there.

КТО ТУТ? [kto tút?] Who is here?
И ТУТ ОН. [i tút on] He is here also.

КТО ОН? [kto on?] What is he?

The answer is ВЕТЕР [vyé-ter] (wind).

With this word we will move to the next grade and learn two and three-syllable words made with letters you know:

И-Л И [í-lii]	or
О-Н О [a-nó]	it
О Г-Н И [ag-ní]	fires, lights
О К-Н О [ak-nó]	window
О-Д И Н [a-dín]	one
О-Н И [a-ní]	they
О Д-Н И [ad-ní]	(they are) alone
М О Ж - Н О [mózh-na]	may
Н У Ж - Н О [núzh-na]	need
У - Ж И Н [ú-zhin]	supper
П Р О С - Т О [prós-ta]	simple
П О -Т О - Л О К [pa-ta-lók]	ceiling
М О - Л О - Т О К [ma-la-tók]	hammer

24

Here we have the different parts of speech:

NOUNS: У́ЖИН [ú-zhin], ПОТОЛО́К [pa-ta-lók], МОЛО-ТО́К [ma-la-tók]), ОКНО́ [ak-nó], ОГНИ́ [ag-ní].

PRONOUNS: ОНО́ [a-nó] (personal, the 3rd person, neuter] ОНИ́ [a-ní] (personal, 3rd person, plural), ОДИ́Н [a-dín] (sing.), ОДНИ́ [ad-ní] (plur.)

NUMERAL: ОДИ́Н [a-dín] (one)

ADJECTIVE: ПРО́СТО [prós-ta] (easy)

ADVERB: ПРО́СТО [prós-ta] (simply)

VERBS: МО́ЖНО [mózh-na], НУ́ЖНО [núzh-na]

PARTICLE: ПРО́СТО [prós-ta] (just)

CONJUNCTION: И́ЛИ [í-lii].

Parts of Speech

There are nine parts of speech in Russian:

the noun
the verb
the pronoun
the numeral
the adjective
the adverb
the conjunction
the preposition
the particle

The article, the tenth English part of speech, does not exist in Russian.

Dialogues:

Ask the questions with two question words already familiar to you: one is in regard to a person performing an action: K T O [kto]? (who?) and the other ГДЕ [gdye]? refers to the location of a person. Once more, notice that there is no need for verbs in this kind of sentence in Russian.

Use ТУТ [tut] (here) and ТАМ [tam] (there) in your answers to the questions.

КТÓ ТУТ?
ТУТ ДЖОН И МÉРИ.

КТÓ ТАМ?
ТАМ АНТÓН И ВÉРА.

The question КТÓ ТАМ? [who is there?] is asked when somebody knocks on a door.

If you want to be allowed to come in, just tell your name when you hear this question:

(knock-knock)
КТÓ ТАМ?
МÉРИ.

(knock-knock)
КТÓ ТАМ?
ДЖОН.

(knock-knock)
КТÓ ТАМ?
ВÉРА.

(knock-knock)
КТÓ ТАМ?
АНТÓН.

The answer to the question ГДЕ ...? (where is somebody or something?) also may only call for a one-word answer:

ГДЕ БАНК? [gdye bánk?]
ТУТ [tut].

ГДЕ ПАРК? [gdye párk?]
ТАМ [tam].

ГДЕ ОСТАНОВКА? [gdye as-ta-nóf-ka?]
ТУТ [tut].

ГДЕ ОКНО? [gdye ak-nó?]
ТАМ [tam].

THE RUSSIAN ALPHABET REVISITED

You have come to the final part of the Russian alphabet.
Again use English words to learn Russian sounds. After all, the easiest way to the unknown is through the familiar.

Ear Training

Read and repeat:
Ф as in far
Х as in heights
Ц as in tsar
Ч as in child
Ш as in shed
Щ as in shchee (cabbage soup)
Э as in spread
Ю as in unique
Я as in yak
And that's almost it!

In addition, there are letters in the Russian alphabet that are used for marking the softness and hardness of consonants. They are:

Ь ь soft sign
Ъ ъ hard sign

And there is one more letter Ы, which is the hard i.

Two Russian letters resemble Е and И but have diacritical marks. They are Ё and Й and they follow respectively Е and И in the alphabet. They are independent sounds. Ё can be transcribed with diphthong "yo" and й, which is a half sound, with "y".

For example, the name of George Gordon Byron, the English poet who had great influence on Russian literature of the last century, should be written in the Russian transcription with the diphthong including the letter Й: БА́ЙРОН.

The following English words will also help you pronounce these two letters correctly. You should pronounce:

Ё (ё) like diphthongs in yolk and York
Й (й) like the diphthong with "y" in yeast.

Therefore, New York in Russian spelling should be written this way: НЬЮ-ЙОРК [nyu york].

And the well-known exclamation of Hamlet: "Poor Yorick!" should be written in Russian like "БЕ́ДНЫЙ ЙОРИК!"

That brings to mind "БЕ́ДНЫЕ ЛЮДИ" [byéd-nye lú-dii] (*Poor People*), the title of one of Fedor Dostoeyesky's early novels.

But cheer up! НЕ УНЫВА́ЙТЕ! [ne uu-ny-váy-te]

You have already learned the Russian alphabet. Paraphrasing a Russian proverb, you may say that you know it from A to Z (or in Russian: "от А до Я").

Build your Vocabulary:

СОРТ [sort]	sort
КЛАСС [clas]	class
ИДЕЯ [ii–dyé–ya]	idea
ЭЛЕМЕНТ [e–le–myént]	element
СТУДЕНТ [stuu–dyént]	student
ПРЕЗИДЕНТ [pre–zii–dyént]	president
АРИСТОКРАТ [a–ris–ta–crát]	aristocrat
ТЕЛЕФОН [te–le–fón]	telephone
ТЕЛЕГРАФ [te–le–gráf]	telegraph
ТЕАТР [te–átr]	theater
СПОРТ [sport]	sport
АВТОМОБИЛЬ [af–ta–ma–bíl']	automobile
АЭРОПОРТ [a–e–ra–pórt]	airport
ТУАЛЕТ [tuu–a–lyét]	toilet (bathroom, restroom)
БЮРО [bu–ró]	bureau (office)
ЧЕК [chyek]	check
ЦЕНТР [tsyentr]	center
ФИРМА [fír–ma]	firm
МУЗЕЙ [muu–zyéy]	museum
МАВЗОЛЕЙ [mav–za–léy]	mausoleum
ГОСПИТАЛЬ [gós–pii–tal']	hospital
ПОЛИЦИЯ [pa–lí–tsii–ya]	police
СИТУАЦИЯ [sii–tuu–á–tsii–ya]	situation
ЭМОЦИЯ [e–mó–tsii–ya]	emotion
ФАСОН [fa–són]	fashion
МАТЕРИАЛ [ma–te–rii–ál]	material
КАФЕ [ca–fé]	cafe
РЕСТОРАН [res–ta–rán]	restaurant
БАР [bar]	bar
КОФЕ [có–fe]	coffee

Voiced and Voiceless Consonants

While reading this long list of words–cognates you have probably already noticed that the consonant B sounds differently

in two words: АВТОМОБИЛЬ and МАВЗОЛЕЙ. There is a group
of matching consonants in Russian language pronunciation of
which depends on their position in the word. According to it,
they may keep or change their qualities. They are called *voiced
and voiceless consonants* depending on the role of the voice in
their pronunciation. When you pronounce *the voiced
consonants* you use your voice more strongly than for *the
voiceless sounds*. You can even sing them. But you can never sing
their voiceless counterparts. Here are matching groups of the
sounds, both voiced and voiceless, you have already learned.

VOICED: Б В Г Д Ж З
VOICELESS: П Ф К Т Ш С

There are twelve consonants of this kind all together: Б В Г
Д Ж З П Ф К Т Ш С.

Notice that the voiced consonants are concentrated in the
beginning of the alphabet. The voiceless ones are in the end.

Ear training:

If the pronunciation of vowels depends on their position in
regard to stress, the pronunciation of consonants depends on the
sound preceeding or following.

The voiced B transforms into the voiceless F before the
voiceless T as in the word АВТО́БУС [af-tó-bus] (bus). Before the
voiceless consonant K in ПЕРЕСА́ДКА [pe-re-sát-ka] (change) and
in ОСТАНО́ВКА [as-ta-nóf-ka] (stop) the voiced consonants Д
and B change into voiceless ones.

Subsequently the voiceless consonants become voiced before
the voiced ones. That is why you pronounce Г instead of K
before the voiced consonant Z in ВОКЗА́Л [vag-zál] (station).

But neither group of consonants changes its qualities before
vowels and consonants of the same group. That is why you read
the combination of the voiceless consonants KT, CT, НСП and the

voiced consonants ГД, ЗВ, БЛ, ВЗ without changing their qualities. They all are voiceless in the words:

СЕСТРА́ [sest-rá], ПРО́СТО [prós-ta], ГАСТРО-НО́М [gast-ra-nóm], ТРА́НСПОРТ [tráns-part].

They are voiced in the words:

ГДЕ [gdye], ЗВУК [zvuk], ЗВОН [zvon], БИБЛИОТЕ́КА [bib-lii-a-tyé-ka], МАВЗОЛЕ́Й [mav-za-lyéy].

At the end of a word, voiced consonants are transformed into voiceless ones. For example, in the word ПО́ЕЗД [pó-est] (train) the last voiced sound Д becomes the voiceless T.

Note that when the voiced consonants Z, G, and B are paired with the voiced V, N, D, and L they do not change their voiced qualities: ZV, ZN, GD, VZ, BL.

Look carefully at the combinations of consonants while you are reading and pay attention to correct pronunciation.

Here are some questions and answers containing the words with voiced consonants:

ГДЕ БИБЛИОТЕ́КА [gdye bib-lii-a-tyé-ka]?
БИБЛИОТЕ́КА ЗДЕСЬ [bib-lii-a-tyé-ka zdyes'].
ГДЕ МАВЗОЛЕ́Й [gdye mav-za-lyéy]?
МАВЗОЛЕ́Й ЗДЕСЬ [mav-za-lyéy zdyes'].
ГДЕ ЗВОНЯ́Т [gdye zva-nyát]? (Where is it ringing?)
ЗВОНЯ́Т ТАМ [zva-nyát tam].

Now read a proverb with the noun ЗВОН (ringing, clinging):

СЛЫ́ШАЛ ЗВОН, ДА НЕ ЗНА́ЕТ, ГДЕ ОН.
[slý-shal zvon da ne zná-et gdye on].
One doesn't know where the ringing is coming from. (One does not know what it is being talked about).

Of course this is not our case! So let's get back to RUSSIAN GRAMMAR (РУ́ССКАЯ ГРАММА́ТИКА) [rús-ka-ya gra-má-tii-ka].

Nouns: Masculine, Feminine, Neuter

All Russian nouns have gender, like living creatures. And you should be able to distinguish among them "chair-man" and "chair-woman" as well as "chair-it". They might be of the MASCULINE or FEMININE, or NEUTER gender.

It is very important to recognize the gender of the noun in Russian because some forms of verbs and pronouns, as well as some numbers and adjectives, agree in gender with the nouns.

The nouns of the MASCULINE gender (chair-man) generally end with a consonant (СОРТ, sort) or -Й (ТРАМВА́Й [tram-váy] (tram).
Here are some cognates of the MASCULINE gender:

СЕЗО́Н [se-zón]
ФАСО́Н [fa-són]
ТУАЛЕ́Т [tuu-a-lyét]
ПАРК [park]
СТУДЕ́НТ [stuu-dyént]
МУЗЕ́Й [muu-zyéy]
МАВЗОЛЕ́Й [mav-za-lyéy]

The nouns of the FEMININE gender (chair-woman) generally have the endings -A (-Я) and -ИЯ (-ЯЯ):

МА́МА [má-ma]
ИДЕЯ́ [ii-dyé-ya]
ПОЛИ́ЦИЯ [pa-lí-tsii-ya]
СИТУА́ЦИЯ [sii-tuu-á-tsii-ya]
ЭМО́ЦИЯ [e-mó-tsii-ya]

There are a few words with the endings -A (-Я) which indicate persons of MASCULINE gender (ПА́ПА [pá-pa] dad, ДЯ́ДЯ [dyá-dya]) uncle.

32

A group of nouns ending with a soft sign and soft hissing consonants might be either MASCULINE or FEMININE. Check their gender in a dictionary.

(masc.) ПИСА́ТЕЛЬ [pii-sá-tel'] writer
(fem.) МЕТЕ́ЛЬ [me-tyél'] snowstorm
(masc.) ДОЖДЬ [dosht'] rain
(masc.) КОНЬ [kon'] horse, steed
(fem.) ЛО́ШАДЬ [ló-shat'] horse

The nouns which end with a hissing sounds are usually of the MASCULINE gender, if they don't have "Ь" (МУЖ [músh] husband). They are of the FEMININE gender, if they have "Ь": (РОЖЬ [rosh'] rye).

The nouns of the NEUTER gender have the endings -О (-Е), -ЬЕ, -ИЕ:

МЕТРО́ [met-ró] metro
ПАЛЬТО́ [pal'-tó] coat
ПО́ЛЕ [pó-lye] field
БЮРО́ [bu-ró] bureau, office
ПЛА́ТЬЕ [plát'ye] dress
ЗДА́НИЕ [zdá-nii-e] building

Personal pronouns ОН [on] (he), ОНА́ [a-ná] (she), ОНО́ [a-nó] (it) replace nouns according to the gender.

In the plural, nouns of all the genders might be replaced with the personal pronoun ОНИ́ [a-ní] (they).

Notice that in Russian the personal pronouns ОН, ОНА, ОНО, ОНИ may replace any noun whether it is a person or thing.

As we already know, the pattern of a question sentence with an interrogative word includes the question word ГДЕ + the following noun or pronoun in the nominative (the singular or the plural).

"МИСЮСЬ! ГДЕ ТЫ?" [mii-syús', gdye ty?] ("Misus', where are you?"), the question at the end of Chekhov's story "The House with a Mezonine" ("ДОМ С МЕЗОНИНОМ" [dom s me-za-ní-nam]), is a good example of this question pattern.

Use the personal pronouns for the given nouns + the words ЗДЕСЬ [zdyés'], ТУТ [tut] (here) or ТАМ [tam] (there) when answering the ГДЕ questions.

Use the pattern: ГДЕ МЕТРО́ [gdyé met-ró]? ОНО (neut.) ТАМ.

ГДЕ ОСТАНО́ВКА [gdyé as-ta-nóf-ka]? (fem.). . . ТУТ.

ГДЕ МУЗЕ́Й [gdye muu-zyéy]? (masc.). . . ЗДЕСЬ.

ГДЕ ТЕЛЕГРА́Ф [gdye te-le-gráph]? (masc.). . . ТУТ.

ГДЕ ПО́ЧТА [gdye póch-ta]? (fem.). . . ЗДЕСЬ.

ГДЕ ТЕЛЕФО́Н [gdye te-le-fón]? (masc.). . . ТАМ.

ГДЕ БАНК [gdye bank]? (masc.). . . ЗДЕСЬ.

ГДЕ КАФЕ́ [gdye ca-fé]? (neut.). . . ТАМ.

ГДЕ ТУАЛЕ́Т [gdye tu-a-lyét]? (masc.). . . ТУТ.

ГДЕ ПОЛИ́ЦИЯ [gdye pa-lí-tsii-ya]? (fem.). . . ТАМ.

The Word-doubles

In your answers, you can also use for ЗДЕСЬ the word БЛЍЗКО [blís-ka] (nearby) and for ТАМ you can say ДАЛЕКӦ [da-le-kó] (far away).

ПАРК ТАМ, ДАЛЕКӦ.
ПӦЧТА ЗДЕСЬ, БЛЍЗКО.

One can use as well the adverbs very (ӦЧЕНЬ [ó-chen']), not very (НЕ ӦЧЕНЬ [ne ó-chen']) in the short answers to the ГДЕ [gdyé] questions:

Far—very far—not very far
ДАЛЕКӦ — ӦЧЕНЬ ДАЛЕКӦ — НЕ ОЧЕНЬ ДАЛЕКӦ
[da-le-kó — ó-chen' da-le-kó — ne ó-chen' da-le-kó]

Near—very near—not very close
БЛЍЗКО — ӦЧЕНЬ БЛЍЗКО — НЕ ОЧЕНЬ БЛЍЗКО
[blís-ka - ó-chen' blís-ka — ne ó-chen' blís-ka]

ГДЕ МЕТРӦ [gdyé met-ró]?
МЕТРӦ ТАМ [met-ró tam]. ДАЛЕКӦ [da-le-kó].

ГДЕ БАНК [gdyé bank]?
ЗДЕСЬ, БЛЍЗКО [zdyés', blís-ka].

ГДЕ ПАРК [gdye park]?
ПАРК ТАМ [park tam].
ЭТО ДАЛЕКӦ [éa-ta da-le-kó]?
ДАЛЕКӦ [da-le-kó].

ГДЕ УНИВЕРМӒГ [gdyé uni-ver-mák]?
ТАМ [tam].
ЭТО ДАЛЕКӦ [éa-ta da-le-kó]?
НЕ ӦЧЕНЬ [ne ó-chen'].

Give a short answer, the positive (ДА [daa] yes) or the negative (НЕТ [nyet] no):

ГДЕ ГОСТИ́НИЦА [gdye gas-tíi-nii-tsa]?
ГОСТИ́НИЦА ТАМ [gas-tí-nii-tsa tam].
ЭТО ДАЛЕКО́ [éa-ta da-le-kó]?
ДА [da].

ГДЕ РЕСТОРА́Н [gdye res-ta-rán]? РЕСТОРА́Н
ТАМ [res-ta-rán tam].
ЭТО ДАЛЕКО́ [éa-ta da-le-ko]?
НЕТ [nyet].

ГДЕ ГО́СПИТАЛЬ [gdye gós-pii-tal']?
ГО́СПИТАЛЬ ТАМ [gós-pii-tal' tam]. ЭТО ДАЛЕКО́ [éa-ta
da-le-kó]?
ДА [da].

Use the adjectives: *much–not very much* in your answers:

О́ЧЕНЬ [ó-chen'] — НЕ О́ЧЕНЬ [ne ó-chen']

ГДЕ АЭРОПО́РТ [gdye a-e-ra-pórt]?
АЭРОПО́РТ ДАЛЕКО́ [a-e-ra-pórt. da-le-kó]
О́ЧЕНЬ [ó-chen']?
О́ЧЕНЬ [ó-chen'].

ГДЕ СТОЯ́НКА ТАКСИ́ [gdye sta-yán-ka taxí]?
СТОЯ́НКА ТАКСИ́ ТАМ [sta-yán-ka taxí tam].
ЭТО ДАЛЕКО́ [éa-ta da-le-kó]?
НЕ О́ЧЕНЬ [ne ó-chen'].

ГДЕ МОСКВА́ [gdye mas-kvá]? ДАЛЕКО́ [da-le-kó]?
О́ЧЕНЬ [ó-chen'].

Communicating with Russians you will probably need to know some Russian words for relatives. Russians have strong family ties and they might be very pleased if you send your regards to their relatives.

Here are the words for the near ones:
МА́МА [má-ma] mom
ПА́ПА [pá-pa] dad
БРАТ [brat] brother
СЕСТРА́ [sest-rá] sister
МУЖ, СУПРУ́Г [mush, sup-rúk] husband
ЖЕНА́, СУПРУ́ГА [zhe-ná, sup-rú-ga] wife

Grammar: The Dative Case

In order to send your regards in Russian the proper way, you have to change the case of the nouns you just learned. Russian nouns are declined. They change their endings through a system of cases. There are SIX cases in the Russian language. The NOMINATIVE is used for indicating or addressing somebody or something. The words МА́МА [má-ma], ПА́ПА [pá-pa], БРАТ [brat], СЕСТРА́ [sest-rá], МУЖ [mush], ЖЕНА́ [zhe-ná] are given in the NOMINATIVE.

There are five other cases, which show the role of a noun in connection to the other parts of a sentence. They are: the GENITIVE, DATIVE, ACCUSATIVE, INSTRUMENTAL and PREPOSITIONAL. Every case reflects the special character of relations among the words in a sentence. It can denote either possession like the GENITIVE, or an object to which the action passes over, like the ACCUSATIVE, or it may denote an instrument of performing the action, like the INSTRUMENTAL. The DATIVE case is mostly used to denote persons or things toward whom (or which) action is directed.

When you send your regards to people, you have to use the following pattern: you say the word ПРИВЕ́Т [prii-vyét] (regard) + a noun in the DATIVE. The endings for feminine, masculine and neuter nouns are different: -E for fem., -У (-Ю) for masc. and neut.

37

ПРИВЕ́Т МА́МЕ [prii-vyét má-me] (fem.)
Hello to your mother.

ПРИВЕ́Т СУПРУ́ГУ [prii-vyét sup-rú-guu] (masc.)
Hello to your husband.

ПРИВЕ́Т СУПРУ́ГЕ [prii-vyét sup-rú-ge] (fem.)
Hello to your wife.

ПРИВЕ́Т БРА́ТУ [prii-vyét brá-tuu]] (masc.)
Hello to your brother.

ПРИВЕ́Т СЕСТРЕ́ [prii-vyét sest-ryé] (fem.) Hello to your sister.

It would be more proper if you use personal names when sending your regards. You may have already noticed that most masculine Russian last names end with -ОВ (-ЕВ) or -ИН (-ЫН). Most feminine names end with -А.

When addressing people, the word ТОВА́РИЩ [ta-vá-rishch] was used a while back. Before the revolution, it was proper to use the word ГОСПОДИ́Н [gas-pa-dín] in front of the last name of a man whom you were addressing. It has recently come back into use. When addressing a woman, one should say the feminine form of this word, ГОСПОЖА́ [gas-pa-zhá].

Practice putting Russian names into the DATIVE:

ПРИВЕ́Т [prii-vyét] ГОСПОДИ́НУ [gas-pa- dí-nuu] ОНЕ́ГИНУ [a-nyé-gii-nuu]
ПРИВЕ́Т [prii-vyét] ГОСПОДИ́НУ [gas-pa - dí-nuu] КОЗЛО́ВУ [kaz-ló-vuu]
ПРИВЕ́Т [prii-vyét] ГОСПОЖЕ́ [gas-pa-zhyé] КАРЕ́НИНОЙ [ka-ryé-nii-nay]
ПРИВЕ́Т [prii-vyét] ГОСПОЖЕ́ [gas-pa-zhyé] РОСТО́ВОЙ [ras-tó-vay]

And we will leave this chapter with the words of Hamlet to Rosenkrantz and Gilderstern from a modern Russian translation of Shakespeare's *Hamlet:*

ПРИВЕ́Т ВАМ, ГОСПОДА́!

CHAPTER THREE

MEDICINE

TRAVELERS' PRECAUTIONS

Build your medical vocabulary:

ГÓСПИТАЛЬ [gós-pii-tal']
ПОЛИКЛИ́НИКА [pa-lik-lí-nii-ká]
АДМИНИСТРÁТОР [ad-mii-nii-strá-tar]
ДÓКТОР [dóc-tar]
ДАНТИ́СТ [dan-tíst]
АСПИРИ́Н [as-pii-rín]
ВИТАМИ́Н [vii-ta-mín]
СИМПТÓМ [simp-tóm]
ВИ́РУС [ví-rus]
ТЕМПЕРАТУ́РА [tem-pe-ra-tú-ra]
ДÓЗА [dó-za]
ПРОБЛÉМА [prab-lyé-ma] problem
ИНФÉКЦИЯ [in-fyék-tsii-ya] infection
ИММУНИТÉТ [ii-muu-nii-tyét] immunity
РЕЗУЛЬТÁТ [re-sul'-tat] result
ТАБЛÉТКА [tab-lyet-ka] tablet
ДИЭТА [dii-éa-ta] diet

Note that the English word "medicine" may be translated in Russian with two words, МЕДИЦИ́НА [me-dii-tsí-na] and ЛЕ-КА́РСТВО [le-kár-stva] The translation of the phrase "medicine in Russia" requires use of the word МЕДИЦИ́НА. While the expression for "to take medicine" requires the word ЛЕКА́РСТВО and should be translated: ПРИНИМА́ТЬ ЛЕКА́РСТВО [prii-nii-mát' le-kár-stva] or ПИТЬ ЛЕКАРСТВО [pit' le-kár-stva] no matter whether it is liquid, pill, tablet or powder.

Giardia

What is the connection between the Tropics and Moscow or St. Petersburg? Well, about the only thing they have in common is Giardia Lumblia, an intestinal parasite (ГЛИСТЫ́ [glis-tý]). Symptoms of Giardia often do not appear for weeks after infection. You may not be aware of the fact that you have been infected until weeks after you have returned home. Standard symptoms are nausea, diarrhea, fatigue, and weight loss. Most cases originate in St. Petersburg, but since 1988 Giardia has been showing up in visitors that went only to Moscow. One becomes infected with Giardia from drinking tap water (ВОДА́ ИЗ КРА́НА) [va-dá is krá-na]. Therefore, it has become the rule for visitors to St. Petersburg, and now Moscow as well, to avoid all tap water. Boiling the water will kill the parasite.

Tea is safe because the water is boiled. To receive a satisfactory supply of liquids, your best bet is to drink bottled mineral water. Mineral water is plentiful and is served in practically every restaurant. Another possibility is to chemically treat the unboiled tap water. This can be done with iodine (ЙОД). You should check with your doctor or the Center for Disease Control to learn more about this form of treatment. There is also a relatively new product that is available in many camping stores that purifies water and eliminates from the infecting Giardia parasite.

Word-doubles:

The words ДÓКТОР (doctor) and ВРАЧ (physician) are interchangeable in Russian.

As in English, in Russian the expressions "tap water" (ВОДА ИЗ КРÁНА) and "unboiled water" (СЫРÁЯ ВОДÁ) can be used interchangeably.

Food

What about the food? Eat to your heart's content. Besides the fact that your body may not be accustomed to certain rich foods, there is nothing harmful about the food. If you have high cholesterol, you may have to be a bit more conscientious about your dietary requirements and may want to consider eating less at restaurants and buying more fresh fruits and vegetables at the markets. As is true anywhere, including the United States, it is not a good idea to eat in cheap, dingy restaurants. Eating pirozhki sold by the street vendors is like playing a game of Russian roulette. You may or may not get sick from eating them, yet the stories about what goes into making them are themselves quite nauseating, trust us.

Medical Service in Russia

Medical service in Russia has always been free for citizens as well as foreigners. Recent dramatic events have resulted in many major changes, but as of today, state medical service is still free. Private practices, which have become quite popular, and hospitalization both require a fee, but it is much less than in the West.

In the unfortunate case of a serious illness or accident, you will be happy to know that many doctors are very competent. In the large cities the facilities are usually good. One exchange student fell ill with appendicitis and spent weeks in a hospital in Russia. As a result, he returned home (healthy, by the way) with a very advanced vocabulary of Russian medical terms.

Expressions of Complaint and Need:

I am not well, I feel bad. МНЕ ПЛÓХО [mnye pló-kha].
Help. ПОМОГИ́ТE [pa-ma-gíi-te]
I need a doctor. МНÉ НУ́ЖЕН ДÓКТОР [mnye nú-zhen dóc-tar].

You need to know these relative words in order to express your bad condition:
the noun: ache БОЛЬ [bol']
the verb: БОЛИ́Т (hurts, ails)
the adjective: БОЛЬНÓЙ (-АЯ, -ОЕ, -ЫЕ) (sick, ill) which can be a noun as well (a patient).

Answer the doctor's question: "ЧТО У ВАС БОЛИ́Т?" ("What hurts you?", "What is the problem?")

The English grammar pattern "I have an ache" is formed in Russian by the pattern: У МЕНЯ́ БОЛИ́Т [uu me-nyá ba-lít].
Use in answering the pattern:
"У МЕНЯ́ БОЛИ́Т" [uu me-nyá ba-lít] + the noun in the NOMINATIVE:

head	ГОЛОВÁ	[ga-la-vá]
throat	ГÓРЛО	[gór-la]
tooth	ЗУБ	[zuup]
ear	У́ХО	[úu-cha]
chest	ГРУДЬ	[grut']
back	СПИНÁ	[spii-ná]
stomach	ЖЕЛУ́ДОК	[zhe-lúu-dak]
muscles	МЫ́ШЦЫ	[mýsh-tsii]
neck	ШÉЯ	[shyé-ya]
leg	НОГÁ	[na-gá]
foot	СТУПНЯ́	[stup-nyá]
hand	РУКÁ	[ruu-ká]
finger	ПÁЛЕЦ	[pá-lets]
toe	ПÁЛЕЦ	[pá-lets]

Answer the doctor's question:
"ЧТО У ВАС БОЛЍТ?"

У МЕНЯ́ БОЛЍТ ГО́РЛО.
У МЕНЯ́ БОЛЍТ ГОЛОВА́.
У МЕНЯ́ БОЛЍТ У́ХО.
У МЕНЯ́ БОЛЍТ ЖИВО́Т.
У МЕНЯ́ БОЛЍТ ЗУБ.

The other ways of asking the question: "What hurts you?"
"ЧТО У ВАС БОЛЍТ?"

ЧТО ВАС БЕСПОКО́ИТ [shto vas bes-pa-kó-it]? ("What bothers you?")

КАК ВЫ СЕБЯ́ ЧУ́ВСТВУЕТЕ [kak vy se-byá chúst-vuu-e-te]? (How do you feel?)

Answer the doctor's question:
"ЧТО ВАС БЕСПОКО́ИТ?", "КАК СЕБЯ́ ЧУ́ВСТВУЕТЕ?" using the pattern: "I have" + a noun in the NOMINATIVE:
flu ГРИПП [grip]
cold ПРОСТУ́ДА [pras-tú-da]

I have a flu. У МЕНЯ́. . .
I have a cold. У МЕНЯ́. . .

The other forms of answering the question: КАК СЕБЯ́ ЧУ́ВСТВУЕТЕ [kak se-byá chúst-vuu-e-te]?

I got sick. Я ЗАБОЛЕ́Л (-А) [ya za-ba-lyél(a)].

Not very well. НЕ О́ЧЕНЬ ХОРОШО́ [ne óchen' kha-ra-shó], НЕВА́ЖНО [ne-vázh-na].

I don't feel well. МНЕ НЕХОРОШО́ [mnye ne-kha-ra-shó].
Bad. ПЛО́ХО [pló-kha].

Very bad. ÓЧЕНЬ ПЛÓХО [ó-chen' pló-kha].

Not bad. НЕПЛÓХО [ne-pló-kha].

Better. ЛÝЧШЕ [lúch-she].

Fine. ХОРОШÓ [kha-ra-shó].

I am all right. Everything is under control. ВСЁ В ПО-
РЯ́ДКЕ [fsyo f pa-ryát-ke].

Very well. ÓЧЕНЬ ХОРОШÓ [ó-chen' kha-ra-shó].

Wonderful. ПРЕКРÁСНО [pre-krás-na].
Perfect, terrific. ПРЕВОСХÓДНО [pre-vas-khód-na].

The Expressions You Hopefully Won't Need:

У МЕНЯ́ ПОВЫ́ШЕННОЕ ДАВЛÉНИЕ [uu me-nyá pa-
vý-she-na-e dav-lyé-nii-e].
I have high blood pressure.

У МЕНЯ́ КРÝЖИТСЯ ГОЛОВÁ [uu me-nyá krúu-zhi-tsya
ga-la-vá].
I am dizzy.

МЕНЯ ТОШНИ́Т [me-nyá tash-nít].
I have nausea.

Here is a Russian proverb with the grammar construction
you have just learned:
У КОГÓ ЧТО БОЛИ́Т, ТОТ О ТÓМ И ГОВОРИ́Т [uu ka-vó
shto ba-lít tot a tom ii ga-va-rít].
(If you have a pain, that is what you always talk about).

AT THE PAID POLICLINIC

At The Registrar

A. I want to make an appointment with a physician.
ЗАПИШИ́ТЕ МЕНЯ́ К ТЕРАПЕ́ВТУ [za-pii-shíi-te me-nyá k te-ra-pyéf-tuu]

B. Do you have documents?
У ВАС ЕСТЬ ДОКУМЕ́НТЫ? [uu vas yest' da-kuu-myén-ty]

A. Here is my passport.
ВОТ МОЙ ПА́СПОРТ [vot moy pás-part]

B. Fill out the registration card.
ЗАПО́ЛНИТЕ РЕГИСТРАЦИО́ННУЮ КА́РТУ [za-pól-nii-te re-gist-ra-tsii-ó-nuu-yu kár-tuu]

A. Could you please help me. My written Russian is not good enough.
НЕ МОГЛИ́ БЫ ВЫ МНЕ ПОМО́ЧЬ [ne mag-lí by vy mnye pa-móch]
Я ПЛО́ХО ПИШУ́ ПО-РУ́ССКИ [ja pló-kha pii-shúu pa rúus-kii]

B. Your name?
ВА́ШЕ И́МЯ [vá-she íi-mya]?

A. Mary Johnson.
МЭРИ ДЖОНСОН

B. The day, year and place of your birth.
ДЕНЬ, ГОД И МЕ́СТО РОЖДЕ́НИЯ [dyen', gót ii myés-ta razh-dyé-nii-ya]

A. April 1, 1960, Chicago, USA.
1 АПРЕЛЯ, 1960, ЧИКА́ГО, США.

B. Where are you staying in Moscow?

ГДЕ ОСТАНОВИЛИСЬ В МОСКВЕ [gdyé as-ta-na-ví-lis' v mask-vyé]?

A. At the hotel "Intourist", Tverskaya, 3 room 21.

ГОСТИНИЦА "ИНТУРИСТ", ТВЕРСКАЯ, 3, КОМНАТА НОМЕР 21 [gas-tí-nii-tsa in-tuu-ríst tver-ská-ya three kóm-na-ta nó-mer 21].

B. What is the problem?

ЧТО С ВАМИ [shtó s vá-mii]?

A. I have nausea. I am dizzy.

МЕНЯ ТОШНИТ [me-nyá tash-nít].

У МЕНЯ КРУЖИТСЯ ГОЛОВА [uu me-nyá krú-zhi-tsya ga-la-vá].

B. Pay 40 rubles at the cashier's and bring me the receipt.

ЗАПЛАТИТЕ В КАССУ СОРОК РУБЛЕЙ И ПОДОЙДИТЕ КО МНЕ С ЧЕКОМ [za-pla-tí-te f ká-suu só-rak rub-léy ii pa- day-dí-te ka mnye s chyé-kam].

A. Where is the cash register?

ГДЕ КАССА [gdye ká-sa]?

B. Over there.

КАССА ТАМ [ká-sa tam].

A. Here is the receipt.

ВОТ ЧЕК [vot check].

B. Here is your card. Here is your slip. Your doctor is in room No. 8. Go to the second floor and turn left.

ВОТ ВАША РЕГИСТРАЦИОННАЯ КАРТОЧКА [vot vá-sha re-gist-ra-tsii-ó-na-ya kár-tach-ka].

ВОТ ТАЛОН К ВРАЧУ [vot ta-lón k vra-chú].

ВАШ ВРАЧ ПРИНИМАЕТ В ВОСЬМОМ КАБИНЕТЕ [vash vrach prii-nii-má-et v vas'-móm ka-bii-nyé-te].

ВТОРОЙ ЭТАЖ НАЛЕВО [fta-róy ea-tásh na-lyé-va].

A. Where are the stairs?
ГДЕ ЛЕСТНИЦА [gdye lés-nii-tsa]?

B. The stairs are over there.
ЛЕСТНИЦА ВОН ТАМ [lés-nii-tsa von tam].

A. Thank you.
СПАСИБО [spa-sí-ba].

At the Doctor's Office

A. May I come in?
МОЖНО ВОЙТИ [mózh-na vay-tí]?

B. One moment. I will be with you in a moment. Yes, how can I help you? Have a seat, please. What is bothering you?
МИНУТОЧКУ [mii-nú-tach-kuu].
Я СЕЙЧАС ОСВОБОЖУСЬ [ya se-chás as-va-ba-zhús'].
ДА, СЛУШАЮ ВАС [da slú-sha-uu vas]. САДИТЕСЬ, ПОЖАЛУЙСТА [sa-dí-tes' pa-zhá-lus-ta].
НА ЧТО ЖАЛУЕТЕСЬ [na shto zhá-luu-e-tes']?

A. Doctor, I don't feel well. I have nausea. I am dizzy.
ДОКТОР, Я ПЛОХО ЧУВСТВУЮ СЕБЯ [ya pló-kha chúst-vuu-yu se-byá].
МЕНЯ ТОШНИТ [me-nyá tash-nít].
У МЕНЯ КРУЖИТСЯ ГОЛОВА [uu me-nyá krú-zhii-tsya ga-la-vá].

B. How long have you been sick?
ДАВНО ЭТО [dav-nó éa-ta]?

A. For the past two days.
ДВА ПОСЛЕДНИХ ДНЯ [dva pas-lyéd-nikh dnya].

PHARMACY

Names of some of the Russian medicine for the following ailments:

for heart problems – ВАЛИДÓЛ [va-lii-dól]
for a cold and headache – АНАЛЬГИ́Н [a-nal'-gíin]
for a headache – ЦИТРАМÓН [tsit-ra-món]

Most likely, you will not find yourself in a policlinic, but you may need to take a trip to the pharmacy (АПТÉКА). In Russia, the pharmacy is not a place to buy birthday cards, film or laundry detergent. It is serious business—a place to buy over-the-counter drugs (ГОТÓВЫЕ ЛЕКÁРСТВА) and have your prescription (РЕЦÉПТ) [re-tsyépt] filled. For common drugs you will most likely only need to wait an hour or two. Some prescriptions, however, will only be available up to a few days after you put in your order.

Your conversation with the pharmacist (АПТÉ-КАРЬ) [ap-tyé-kar'] may sound something like this:

A. Do you have this medicine?
У ВАС ЕСТЬ ЭТО ЛЕКÁРСТВО [uu vas yest' éa-ta le-kár-stva]?

P. No, we don't. We have only ready-made medicine here.
НЕТ [nyet]. У НАС ЗДЕСЬ ТÓЛЬКО ГОТÓВЫЕ ЛЕКÁРСТВА [uu nas zdyes' tól'-ka ga-tó-vy-e le-kárst-va].

A. Where can I get this medicine? ГДЕ Я МОГУ́ ДОСТÁТЬ ЭТО ЛЕКÁРСТВО [gdye ya ma-gú das-tát' éa-ta le-kárst-va]?

P. You have to check in window No. 2. See, there is the sign: Orders for Prescription Medicine.
УЗНÁЙТЕ ВО ВТОРÓМ ОКÓШКЕ [uz-náy-te va fta-róm a-kósh-ke].

ВИ́ДИТЕ, ТАМ НАПИ́САНО "ПРИЁМ РЕЦЕ́ПТОВ" [ví-dii-te tam na-pí-sa-na prii-yóm re-tsyép-taf].

A. Can you tell me whether they have this medicine? There is a long line over there.
ВЫ НЕ СКА́ЖЕТЕ, ЕСТЬ ЛИ У НИХ ЭТО ЛЕКА́РСТВО [vy ne ská-zhe-te yest' lii uu nikh éa-ta le-kárst-va]?
ТАМ БОЛЬША́Я О́ЧЕРЕДЬ [tam bal'-shá-ya ó-che-ret'].

P. No, I can't. I know nothing about that section. Everybody waits in the line and you wait too.
НЕТ [nyet]. Я НЕ ЗНА́Ю, ЧТО ЕСТЬ В ЭТОМ ОТДЕ́ЛЕ [ya ne zná-yu shto yest' v ea-tam o-dyé-le].
ВСЕ СТОЯ́Т В О́ЧЕРЕДИ, И ВЫ СТО́ЙТЕ [fsye sta-yát v ó-chye-re-dii ii vy stóy-te].

A. Thank you.
СПАСИ́БО [spa-sí-ba].

The dialogue in front of the window: Orders for Prescription Medicine (ПРИЁМ РЕЦЕ́ПТОВ):

An unlucky case:

A. Do you have this medicine?
У ВАС ЕСТЬ ЭТО ЛЕКА́РСТВО [uu vas yest' éa-ta le-kárst-va]?

P. No.
НЕТ [nyet].

A. May I order it?
МОГУ́ Я ЗАКАЗА́ТЬ ЕГО́ [ma-gú ya za-ka-zát' e-vó]?

P. No. We don't have the ingredients to make it.
НЕТ [nyet].
У НАС НЕТ КОМПОНЕ́НТОВ ДЛЯ НЕГО́ [uu nas nyet cam-pa-nyén-taf dlya ne-vó].

50

A. When will you have them?

КОГДА́ ОНИ́ БУ́ДУТ [kag-dá aní bú-dut]?

P. I don't know. We have not had them since last year.

Я НЕ ЗНА́Ю [ya ne zná-u].

МЫ ИХ НЕ ПОЛУЧА́ЛИ С ПРО́ШЛОГО ГО́ДА [my ikh ne pa-luu-chá-lii s prósh-la-va gó-da].

A. Can you recommend something comparable?

МО́ЖЕТЕ ЛИ ВЫ ПРЕДЛОЖИ́ТЬ ЧТО-НИБУ́ДЬ ВЗАМЕ́Н [mó-zhe-te lii vy pred-la-zhít' shto nii-bút' vza-myén]?

P. No we have nothing of this kind. It is in deficit.

НЕТ, У НАС БО́ЛЬШЕ НИЧЕГО́ НЕТ [nyet uu nas ból'-she ni-che-vó nyet].

ЭТО - ДЕФИЦИ́Т [éa-ta de-fii-tsít].

A lucky case:

A. Do you have this medicine?

У ВАС ЕСТЬ ЭТО ЛЕКА́РСТВО [uu vas yest' éa-ta le-kár-stva]?

P. You may order it.

ВЫ МО́ЖЕТЕ ЗАКАЗА́ТЬ ЕГО́ [vy mó-zhe-te za-ka-zát' e-vó].

A. When will it be ready?

КОГДА́ ОНО́ БУ́ДЕТ ГОТО́ВО [kag-dá aa-nó bú-det ga-tó-va]?

P. Next Monday at 2 pm.

В СЛЕ́ДУЮЩИЙ ПОНЕДЕ́ЛЬНИК В ДВА ЧАСА́ [f slyé-duu-shchiy pa-ne-dyél'-nik v dva che-sá].

A. Can it be ready sooner? I need it badly.

МО́ЖНО ЛИ ПОБЫСТРЕ́Й? ОНО́ МНЕ О́ЧЕНЬ НУ́Ж-НО [mózh-na lii po-byst-ryéy aa-nó mnye ó-chen' núzh-na].

51

P. Let me check. I will be back in a moment.... Yes, you may have it tomorrow at 4 pm.

СЕЙЧА́С УЗНА́Ю. [se-chás uz-ná-yu]

Я БУ́ДУ ЧЕ́РЕЗ МИНУ́ТУ [ya bú-duu ché-res mii-nú-tuu]

ПРИХОДИ́ТЕ ЗА́ВТРА В ЧЕТЫ́РЕ ЧАСА́ [prii-kha-dí-te záft-ra f che-tý-re che-sá]

A. Thank you very much.

БОЛЬШО́Е СПАСИ́БО [bal'-shó-e spa-sí-ba]

Dosage

The pattern of the dosage (ДОЗИРО́ВКА [da-zii-róf-ka]) requires use of the preposition ПО and the DATIVE case:

One tablet three-four times a day.

ПО ОДНО́Й ТАБЛЕ́ТКЕ ТРИ-ЧЕТЫ́РЕ РА́ЗА В ДЕНЬ [pa ad-nóy tab-lyét-ke trí-che-tý-re rá-za v dyen']

One teaspoonful three-four times a day.

ПО ЧА́ЙНОЙ ЛО́ЖКЕ ТРИ-ЧЕТЫ́РЕ РА́ЗА В ДЕНЬ [pa cháy-nay lósh-ke trí-che-tý-re ráza v dyen']

By the way, there is a Russian expression В ЧАС ПО ЧА́ЙНОЙ ЛО́ЖКЕ

[f chas pa cháy-nay lósh-ke] (One teaspoonful an hour) meaning to do something very slow.

Grammar: The Unpronounced Sounds

The word СЕЙЧАС is not read as it is written, but rather [sii-chás] where a diphthong -ЕЙ is pronounced like the vowel -И. Similarly, the word ПОЖА́ЛУЙСТА (please) should be pronounced [pa-zhá-lus-ta] where a diphthong -УЙ is pronounced like -У. In the word ЛЕСТНИЦА (staircase), the combination of consonants -СТН is pronounced like -СН [lyés-nii-tsa]. In the word ЧУ́ВСТВУЕТЕ (feel) the combination of consonants

52

-ВСТВ should be read like -СТВ. This cluster of consonants in the word ЗДРАВСТВУЙТЕ is pronounced the same way [zdrást-vuy-te]. Learn this word well, you will start every day in Russia with it. It literally means "be healthy" or "be prosperous" at the same time.

This is the right point to finish our discussion on medicine in Russia.

CHAPTER FOUR

MONEY, WEIGHTS AND MEASURES

Build your vocabulary with words which are in your pocket:

ДО́ЛЛАР
ЦЕНТ
КОПЕ́ЙКА
РУ́БЛЬ
ФРАНК
МА́РКА
ЭКВИВАЛЕ́НТ

Money, Money, Money

Who can say what the exchange rate will be when you set out for your journey to Russia? In 1992 the official rate was up to 400 rubles to $1. You might find that a three course meal with a bottle of champagne will cost each individual about $1. If that isn't incentive enough to make Russia you next destination, we don't know what is!

The Ruble

Because the ruble is presently still not convertible, it is worthless outside of Russia. However, it is illegal to take in or bring out rubles from the country. You will be permitted to take only a few rubles out as souvenirs.

The Dollar - the Ruble
The Cent - the Kopeck

The equivalent of dollars and cents in Russia is rubles and kopecks. Rubles come in notes of 1, 3, 5, 10, 25, 50, 100, 500, 1000, and 5000.

The supply of kopeck currency is now dwindling and many cashiers will not have any kopecks left to give change. You won't have to concern yourself much with kopecks —inflation has rendered them almost worthless. But there are two coins which remain valuable in Russia. The two-kopeck coin (две копе́йки [dvye ka-pе́y-kii]) is used for telephones, alternating with the fifteen kopeck coin (пятна́дцать копе́ек [pet-ná-tsat' ka-pе́-ek]) to meet the raised phone fare (many phones have been remade to accept the new fare of fifteen kopecks while some of them are still not fixed, and require the two kopeck coin).

The kopeck coins come in 1, 2, 3, 5, 10, 15, 20 and 50 kopecks. There are also 1 ruble coins. Now 10, 25 and 50 ruble coins are on their way to being introduced.

Cash: Domestic and Hard Currency

Due to the devaluation of the ruble, and the fact that the ruble is not yet convertible, hard currency (ВАЛЮТА) nowadays arouses much more interest among Russians.

Cash, that is dollars, is always handy to have around in Russia just as it is in America. You may want to pay for a taxi with a few dollars, leave a dollar tip somewhere, or purchase something from a hard currency shop called the "Beriozka".

Credit cards

Russia readily welcomes Western credit cards. With the entrance of many Western businesses the country, credit card purchases have become a routine in Moscow and St. Petersburg. Even Aeroflot tickets may be purchased by credit card. The most widely accepted have been American Express and Diner's Club in the past, but Visa and Mastercard are becoming increasingly popular.

Exchanging Currency

You can exchange dollars for rubles at Intourist exchange bureaus located in international airports, certain hotels and banks. You will doubtless be pursued by Russian money changers on the streets who, noticing that you are a foreigner, will call after you, "Change money, change money?" Or you may encounter these upstart bankers in the small booths that sell alcohol, newspapers, and miscellaneous goods. They advertise their rates in the windows, conveniently offering both $ and Deutshe marke rates. You might consider changing up to $20 with them, but heavy trade is not advised. Some tourists report being followed and mugged by these traders after their transactions. Robberies in general are on the rise in Russia—so do not carry around wads of bills!

Useful monetary words and expressions:

ПОЛУЧИТЬ ДЕНЬГИ [pa-luu-chít' dyén'-gii] get money
ЗАПЛАТИТЬ [za-pla-tít'] pay
МЕЛОЧЬ [myé-lakh'] change
ПОЛУЧИТЬ СДАЧУ [pa-luu-chít' zdá-chuu] receive change
ДАТЬ СДАЧУ [dat' zdá-chuu] give change
КОШЕЛЁК [ka-she-lyok] wallet
КАССИР [ka-sír] cashier
КÁССА [ká-sa] cash register
КВИТАНЦИЯ [kvi-tán-tsii-ya] receipt

ОБМЕНЯ́ТЬ ДЕ́НЬГИ [ab-me-nyát' dyén'-gii] change money

ОБМЕНЯ́ТЬ ДО́ЛЛАРЫ НА РУБЛИ́ [ab-me-nyat' dó-la-ry na rub-lí] exchange dollars for rubles

ОБМЕНЯ́ТЬ РУБЛИ́ НА ДО́ЛЛАРЫ [ab-me-nyt' rub-lí na dó-la-ry] the reverse transaction

Here is a sample conversation with a bank teller in an exchange bureau:

ТУРИ́СТ: I need to change money.
МНЕ НУ́ЖНО ОБМЕНЯ́ТЬ ДЕ́НЬГИ
[mnye núzh-na ab-me-nyát' dyén'-gii].

КАССИ́Р: What currency?
КАКА́Я ВАЛЮТА [ka-ká-ya va-lú-ta]?

ТУРИ́СТ: Dollars.
ДО́ЛЛАРЫ [dó-la-ry].

КАССИ́Р: How much?
СКО́ЛЬКО [skól'-ka]?

ТУРИ́СТ: 10 dollars
10 ДО́ЛЛАРОВ [dyé-sit' dó-la-raf].

КАССИР: Here is your money and receipt.
ВОТ ВА́ШИ ДЕ́НЬГИ [vot vá-shii dyén'-gii].
ВОТ ВА́ША КВИТА́НЦИЯ [vot vá-sha kvii-tán-tsii-ya].

ТУРИ́СТ: Thank you.
СПАСИ́БО [spa-sí-ba].

RUSSIAN WEIGHTS AND MEASURES

ВЕС – weight   МЕРА – measure
Lengthen your vocabulary list with these cognates:

ЛИТР [litr]
ГРАММ [gram]
КИЛОГРАММ [kii-la-grám]
КИЛОМЕ́ТР [kii-la-myétr]
САНТИМЕ́ТР [san-tii-myétr]
ТЕМПЕРАТУ́РА [tem-pe-ra-tú-ra]
СПИДО́МЕТР [spii-dó-metr]
АДА́ПТЕР [a-dáp-ter]

Russia uses the metric system (МЕТРИ́ЧЕСКАЯ СИСТЕ́МА ИЗМЕРЕ́НИЯ) and therefore, unless you are skillful at judging weights in kilograms (КИЛОГРА́ММЫ) and liters (ЛИ́ТРЫ), you may have to do some quick conversions when shopping for food.

The following list provides you with some of the weight equivalencies:

1 liter = 1 3/4 pint
1 gram = .035 ounces
28.6 grams = 1 ounce
1 kilogram = 2 pounds, 2 ounces

Kilometers are used instead of miles. Keep this in mind if you decide to rent a car (ВЗЯТЬ МАШИ́НУ НАПРОКА́Т). When you glance down at the speedometer and read 96, do not attribute it to the excellent road conditions which make your ride seem so smooth! You are really only traveling at about 60 miles per hour. Distances and heights are always given in metric.

Prepare yourself for the new system of measurement. You will be surprised by how often issues of size and measurement will arise in everyday life.

'Remember–remember':

1 centimeter (САНТИМЕ́ТР) = .39 inches
1 meter (МЕТР) = 39.37 inches
1.6 kilometers (КИЛОМЕ́ТР) = 1 mile

You probably intend to spend a lot of time outdoors traveling and sightseeing and thus you'll want to keep abreast of weather conditions. Every day you will hear the weather report (ПРОГНО́З ПОГО́ДЫ [prag-nós pa-gó-dy]) announced either by a guide or on the radio. The temperature will be in Celsius (ПО ЦЕ́ЛЬСИЮ) rather than Fahrenheit (ПО ФАРЕНГЕ́ЙТУ). If the temperature is below zero, the number will be followed by minus (МИ́НУС).

Here are some equivalencies:

Fahrenheit ФАРЕНГЕ́ЙТ	Celsius ЦЕ́ЛЬСИЙ
32°	0°
50°	10°
75°	23.9°
90°	32.2°

To convert Fahrenheit degrees into Celsius subtract 32 from the Fahrenheit measurement, multiply by 5 and divide by 9.

Numbers, numbers, numbers...

Here are your first dozen (ДЮ́ЖИНА) Russian numerals:

ОДИ́Н [a-dín] 1
ДВА [dva] 2
ТРИ [trí] 3
ЧЕТЫ́РЕ [che-tý-re] 4
ПЯТЬ [pyat'] 5
ШЕСТЬ [shyést'] 6

59

СЕМЬ [syem'] 7
ВÓСЕМЬ [vó-sem'] 8
ДÉВЯТЬ [dyé-vet'] 9
ДÉСЯТЬ [dyé-set'] 10
ОДИ́ННАДЦАТЬ [a-dí-na-tsat'] 11
ДВЕНÁДЦАТЬ [dve-ná-tsat'] 12

Grammar: The Gender of Some Numerals

The numerals ОДИ́Н and ДВА change for gender.
The main form ОДИ́Н is used for the masculine, ОДНÁ for the feminine, and ОДНÓ for the neuter:

ОДИ́Н КОНВÉРТ envelope
ОДНÁ БУ́ЛОЧКА bun
ОДНÓ ПИСЬМÓ letter

The numeral ДВА has two forms: ДВА for the masculine and neuter and ДВЕ for the feminine:

ДВА КОНВÉРТА (КОНВÉРТ, masc., envelope)
ДВА ПИСЬМÁ (ПИСЬМÓ, neut., letter)
ДВЕ БУ́ЛОЧКИ (БУ́ЛОЧКА, fem., bun)

The other numerals do not change according to the gender:

ТРИ КОНВÉРТА
ТРИ ПИСЬМÁ
ТРИ БУ́ЛОЧКИ

So when you buy something and you are not sure about the gender of a numeral, buy more than two things and use the main form of the numeral without any doubts.

How much? How many? СКÓЛЬКО?

The first word you need to know when talking about amount is СКÓЛЬКО? How much? How many?

The most common СКÓЛЬКО phrase is:
How much does it cost?
СКÓЛЬКО СТÓИТ? [skól'-ka stó-it],
where the verb follows the question word.

Grammar: The Genitive Case

The question СКÓЛЬКО followed by a noun requires the genitive case (singular or plural).
The genitive case is always used when we speak of the parts of the whole.

СКÓЛЬКО ГРÁДУСОВ? (plur.) What is the temperature?
СКÓЛЬКО КНИГ? (plur.) How many books?
СКÓЛЬКО СÁХАРУ? (sing.) How much sugar?
СКÓЛЬКО СÓЛИ? How much salt?

The Genitive Singular

ХЛЕБ (masc.) bread: СКÓЛЬКО ХЛÉБА? How much bread?
КОЛБАСÁ (fem.) sausage: СКÓЛЬКО КОЛБАСЫ́?
МÁСЛО (neuter) butter: СКÓЛЬКО МÁСЛА?

The genitive singular has the following endings:
-А (-Я) for the masculine and neuter
-Ы (-И) for the feminine.

61

The Genitive Plural

The genitive plural has no endings for the feminine and neuter (the final vowel drops off) and ends with -ОВ (-ЕВ) and -ЕЙ for the masculine:

candy КОНФЕ́ТА (fem.): СКО́ЛЬКО КОНФЕ́Т?
berry Я́ГОДА (fem.): СКО́ЛЬКО Я́ГОД?
mirror ЗЕ́РКАЛО (neut.) СКО́ЛЬКО ЗЕРКА́Л
month МЕ́СЯЦ (masc.): СКО́ЛЬКО МЕ́СЯЦ-ЕВ?
day ДЕНЬ (masc.): СКО́ЛЬКО ДН-ЕЙ?

In the answers as well as in the questions, numbers will be followed by nouns in the genitive case. Numbers that end from one to four are followed by the genitive singular. Numbers that end in five and further are followed by the genitive plural.

After words denoting quantity such as МНО́ГО (a lot) and МА́ЛО (a little), the genitive singular or plural is used. After the word НЕ́СКОЛЬКО (a few) only the GENITIVE plural is used.

Questions and Answers:

СКО́ЛЬКО ДЕ́НЕГ? [skó-l'ka dyé-nek] (plur.)

Possible responses:
МА́ЛО. [má-la]
МА́ЛО ДЕ́НЕГ. [má-la dyé-nek] (plur.)
МНО́ГО. [mnó-ga]
МНО́ГО ДЕ́НЕГ. [mnó-ga dyé-nek] (plur.)
НЕ́СКОЛЬКО РУБЛЕ́Й. [nyés-kal'-ka rub-lyéy] (plur.)

СКО́ЛЬКО ВРЕ́МЕНИ? [skól'-ka vryé-me-nii] (sing.)

Possible responses:

МА́ЛО ВРЕ́МЕНИ. [má-la vryé-me-ni] (sing.)
МНО́ГО ВРЕ́МЕНИ. [mnó-ga vryé-me-nii] (sing.)
НЕ́СКОЛЬКО ЧАСО́В. [nyés-kal'-ka che-sóf] (plur.)
НЕ́СКОЛЬКО МИНУ́Т. [nyés-kal'-ka mii-nút] (plur.)
НЕ́СКОЛЬКО СЕКУ́НД. [nyés-kal'-ka sii-kúnt] (plur.)

To find out the time, ask:

КОТО́РЫЙ ЧАС [ka-tó-ry chas]?

Dialogue:

A. КОТО́РЫЙ ЧАС? What time is it?
B. ТРИ ЧАСА́ [trii che-sá]. It is three o'clock.

The pattern for an answer includes a numeral + noun in the genitive (singular or plural). When the answer is "one o'clock" one should use just the nominative case of the noun "ЧАС" without the number "one".

A. КОТО́РЫЙ ЧАС?
B. ЧАС. It is one o'clock.

Here is the Russian version of the "Mother Goose" children's poem:

КОТО́РЫЙ ЧАС?
ДВЕНА́ДЦАТЬ БЬЁТ.
КТО ВАМ СКАЗА́Л?
ЗНАКО́МЫЙ КОТ.
What time is it now?
It's 12 o'clock.
Who told you that?
My friend the cat.

Moscow Radio Speaks

Don't be shocked when you hear on Moscow radio РА́ДИО [rá-dii-a]: "It is 22 o'clock in Moscow now." Russians, like many other Europeans, use the 24 hour clock. They say 13 o'clock instead of 1 p.m., 19 o'clock instead of 7 p.m., etc.

In order to be in tune with European time, take the next dozen numerals.

11 ОДИ́ННАДЦАТЬ [a-dí-na-tsat']
12 ДВЕНА́ДЦАТЬ [dve-ná-tsat']
13 ТРИНА́ДЦАТЬ [trii-ná-tsat']
14 ЧЕТЫ́РНАДЦАТЬ [che-týr-na-tsat']
15 ПЯТНА́ДЦАТЬ [pet-ná-tsat']
16 ШЕСТНА́ДЦАТЬ [shes-ná-tsat']
17 СЕМНА́ДЦАТЬ [sem-ná-tsat']
18 ВОСЕМНА́ДЦАТЬ [va–sem-ná-tsat']
19 ДЕВЯТНА́ДЦАТЬ [de–vet-ná-tsat']
20 ДВА́ДЦАТЬ [dvá-tsat']

In counting from 20 to 30 a subsequent number is added:

21 ДВА́ДЦАТЬ ОДИ́Н [dvá-tsat' a-dín]
22 ДВА́ДЦАТЬ ДВА [dvá-tsat' dva]
23 ДВА́ДЦАТЬ ТРИ [dvá-tsat' trii]
24 ДВА́ДЦАТЬ ЧЕТЫ́РЕ [dvá-tsat' che-tý-re]

Count from 30 (ТРИ́ДЦАТЬ) to 40 (СО́РОК) by yourself:

31 ТРИ́ДЦАТЬ ОДИ́Н [trí-tsat' a-dín]
32 ТРИ́ДЦАТЬ ДВА [trí-tsat' dva]
33 ТРИ́ДЦАТЬ ТРИ [trí-tsat' tri]
34 ТРИ́ДЦАТЬ ЧЕТЫ́РЕ [trí-tsat' che-tý-re]

Count to 50 (ПЯТЬДЕСЯТ) [pet'-de'-syát]:

41 СО́РОК ОДИ́Н [só-rak a-dín]
42 СОРОК ДВА [só-rak dva]

Now for a change, sing a children's counting song by Daniel Kharms:

ЖИ́ЛИ В КВАРТИ́РЕ [zhí-li f kvar-tí-re]
СО́РОК ЧЕТЫ́РЕ [só-rak che-tý-re]
СО́РОК ЧЕТЫ́РЕ [só-rak che-tý-re]
ВЕСЁЛЫХ ЧИЖА́ [ve-syo-lykh chi-zhá]

In one appartment lived
forty four
forty four
merry finches.

Revisiting Numbers

Count to 60 (ШЕСТЬДЕСЯТ) [shest'-de-syát]:

51 ПЯТЬДЕСЯТ ОДИ́Н [pet'-de'-syát a-dín]
52 ПЯТЬДЕСЯТ ДВА [pet'-de'-syát dva]

Then to 70 (СЕ́МЬДЕСЯТ) [syém'-de-syat]:

61 ШЕСТЬДЕСЯТ ОДИ́Н [shest'-de-syát a-dín]
62 ШЕСТЬДЕСЯТ ДВА [shest'-de-syát dva]

To 80 (ВО́СЕМЬДЕСЯТ) [vó-syem'-de-syat]:

71 СЕМЬДЕСЯТ ОДИ́Н [syém'-de-syat a-dín]
72 СЕМЬДЕСЯТ ДВА [syém'-de-syat dva]

To 90 (ДЕВЯНÓСТО) [de-ve-nós-ta]:

ВÓСЕМЬДЕСЯТ ОДЍН [vó-syem'-de-syat a-dín]
ВÓСЕМЬДЕСЯТ ДВА [vó-syem'-de-syat dva]

To 100 (СТО) [sto]:

ДЕВЯНÓСТО ОДЍН [de-ve-nós-ta a-dín]
ДЕВЯНÓСТО ДВА [de-ve-nós-ta dva]

Tell the time the Russian way:

Answer the question: КОТÓРЫЙ ЧАС?
Be sure to use the correct form of o'clock (plural or singular):
12 noon, 2 a.m., 8 a.m., midnight, 1 a.m., 2 p.m., 5 p.m., 9 p.m.

Words for the measurement of time:

ГОД [got] year
МÉСЯЦ [myé-sets] month
НЕДÉЛЯ [ne-dyé-lya] week
ДЕНЬ [dyen'] day
ЧАС [chas] hour
МИНÝТА [mii-nú-ta] minute
СЕКÝНДА [se-kún-da] second

Answer these questions paying attention to the case of nouns
after the numbers:

How many months are in one year?
СКÓЛЬКО МÉСЯЦЕВ В ГОДÝ [skól'-ka myé-se-tsef v ga-dú]?
В ГОДÝ 12 . . .

How many weeks are in one month?
СКÓЛЬКО НЕДÉЛЬ В МÉСЯЦЕ [skól'-ka ne-dyél' v
myé-se-tse]?
В МÉСЯЦÉ 4 . . .

66

How many days are in a week?
СКО́ЛЬКО ДНЕЙ В НЕДЕ́ЛЕ [skól'-ka dnyey v ne-dyé-le]?
В НЕДЕ́ЛЕ 7 . . .

How many hours are in a day?
СКО́ЛЬКО ЧАСО́В В ОДНО́М ДНЕ [skól'-ka che-sof v ad-nóm dnye]?
В ОДНО́М ДНЕ 24 . . .

How many minutes are in one hour?
СКО́ЛЬКО МИНУ́Т В ОДНО́М ЧА́СЕ [skól'-ka mii-nút v ad-nóm chá-se]?
В ОДНО́М ЧА́СЕ 60 . . .

How many seconds are in one minute?
СКО́ЛЬКО СЕКУ́НД В ОДНО́Й МИНУ́ТЕ [skól'-ka se-kúnt v ad-nóy mii-nú-te]?
В ОДНО́Й МИНУ́ТЕ 60 . . .

Speaking of the time, remember the American saying:
ВРЕ́МЯ – ДЕ́НЬГИ [vryé-mya – dyén'-gii] Time is money.
Compare it with the Russian saying:
МИНУ́ТА ЧАС БЕРЕЖЁТ [mii-nú-ta chas be-re-zhyot].
A minute saves an hour.

The Prepositional Case with the Preposition "B"

In the prepositional singular with the preposition "B", there are two kinds of endings: stressed -У́, -Е́; unstressed -Е:
В ГОДУ́, В МЕ́СЯЦЕ, В НЕДЕ́ЛЕ, В ДНЕ́, В МИНУ́ТЕ, В СЕКУ́НДЕ

The 7 Days of the Week

ПОНЕДЕ́ЛЬНИК [pa-ne-dyél'-nik] Monday
ВТО́РНИК [ftór-nik] Tuesday
СРЕДА́ [sre-dá] Wednesday
ЧЕТВЕ́РГ [khet-vyérk] Thursday
ПЯ́ТНИЦА [pyát-ni-tsa] Friday

СУББОТА [suu-bó-ta] Saturday
ВОСКРЕСЕНЬЕ [vas-kre-syé-nye] Sunday

Some Numerology and Folklore around the Magic Number 7:

7 ДНЕЙ НЕДЕЛИ [syem' dnyey ne-dyé-lii] 7 days of week
7 ДНЕЙ ТВОРЕНИЯ [syem' dnyey tva-ryé-nii-ya] 7 days of creation
7 ЦВЕТÓВ РÁДУГИ [syem' tsve-tóf rá-duu-gii] 7 colors of the rainbow
7 НОТ В ГÁММЕ [syem' not v gá-me] 7 notes in the scale
7 ЧУДЕС СВЕТА [syem' chuu-dyés svyé-ta] 7 wonders of the world

Here are some Proverbs :

У НЕГО СЕМЬ ПЯТНИЦ НА НЕДЕЛЕ [uu ne-vó syem' pyát-nits na ne-dyé-le].
He has seven Fridays in one week/ he is an irresponsible person/ he never keeps his promises.

СЕМЬ БЕД ОДИН ОТВЕТ [syem' bet aa-dín at-vyét].
Seven faults one punishment.

Here is a Riddle:

СЕМЬ БРАТЬЕВ [syem' brát'-ef]
ГОДАМИ РАВНЫЕ [ga-dá-mii ráv-ny-ye]
ИМЕНАМИ РАЗНЫЕ [ii-me-ná-mii ráz-ny-e].
(дни недéли)

There are seven brothers
of the same age
but with different names.
Who are they?
(days of the week)

CHAPTER FIVE

ACCOMMODATIONS

IN SEARCH OF COMFORT

Build your vocabulary with these comfort-related cognates:

КЛАСС
СТАНДА́РТ
КОМФО́РТ
ОТЕЛЬ
ПЕРСОНА́Л
ОПЕРА́ТОР
АДМИНИСТРА́ТОР
ТЕЛЕВИ́ЗОР
А́РИЯ
БЮРО́
БУ́НГАЛО

Your accommodation (ВАШЕ УСТРО́ЙСТВО) in Russia will probably be quite comfortable and everything will be just as you expected. . . if you stay in certain Intourist hotels or in one of the new foreign hotels that have opened up recently as joint ventures (СОВМЕ́СТНЫЕ ПРЕДПРИЯ́ТИЯ). As is true in most countries, hotel quality varies from place to place. In general,

69

you should avoid anything rated lower than deluxe or first class by Intourist standards. Keep in mind that second rate hotels in Russia are considered to be of much poorer quality than second rate hotels in the West. But they may suit your needs just fine – especially if you don't mind small inconveniences.

The names and the addresses of some Moscow hotels:

1. *Aeroflot* ГОСТИ́НИЦА "АЭРОФЛО́Т" Leningrádsky prospéct, 37, building 5
2. *Intourist* ГОСТИ́НИЦА "ИНТУРИ́СТ" úlitsa Tverskáya, 3
3. *Tsentral'naya* ГОСТИ́НИЦА "ЦЕНТРА́ЛЬНАЯ" úlitsa Tverskáya, 10
4. *Minsk* ГОСТИ́НИЦА "МИНСК", úlitsa Tverskáya, 22
5. *Metropol'* ГОСТИ́НИЦА "МЕТРОПО́ЛЬ" prospéct Marxa, 1
6. *Moskva* ГОСТИ́НИЦА "МОСКВА́" Okhótny ryad, 7
7. *Natsional* ГОСТИ́НИЦА "НАЦИОНА́ЛЬ" Okhótny ryad, 14/1
8. *Peking* ГОСТИ́НИЦА "ПЕКИ́Н" Bol'shaya Sadóvaya, 5/1
9. *Savoy* ГОСТИ́НИЦА "САВО́Й" úlitsa Rozhdéstvenka, 3
10. *Budapest* ГОСТИ́НИЦА "БУДАПЕ́ШТ" Petróvskie línii, 2/18
11. *Bucharest* ГОСТИ́НИЦА "БУХАРЕ́СТ" úlitsa Bálchug, 1
12. *Rossiya* ГОСТИ́НИЦА "РОССИ́Я" úlitsa Rázina, 6
13. *Mezhdunarodnaya* ГОСТИ́НИЦА "МЕЖДУНАРО́Д-НАЯ" Krasnoprésnenskaya náberezhnaya, 12
14. *Kievskaya* ГОСТИ́НИЦА "КИ́ЕВСКАЯ" Kíevskaya úlitsa, 2
15. *Belgrade* ГОСТИ́НИЦА "БЕЛГРА́Д" Pérvaya Smolénskaya úlitsa, 5
16. *Cosmos* ГОСТИ́НИЦА "КО́СМОС" prospect Mira, 150
17. *Ural* ГОСТИ́НИЦА "УРА́Л" úlitsa Chernyshévskogo, 40
18. *Molodyozhnaya* ГОСТИ́НИЦА "МОЛОДЕЖНАЯ" Dmítrovskoye schaussee, 27
19. *Yúnost'* ГОСТИ́НИЦА "ЮНОСТЬ" Khamóvnichesky val, 34
20. *Tourîst* ГОСТИ́НИЦА "ТУРИ́СТ" Sel'skokhozyáystvennaya úlitsa, 17/2.

The names and the addresses of some St. Petersburg's hotels:

1. *Astoria* ГОСТИ́НИЦА "АСТО́РИЯ" úlitsa Gértsena, 39
2. *Baltiyskaya* ГОСТИ́НИЦА "БАЛТИ́ЙСКАЯ" Névsky prospéct, 57
3. *Evropeyskaya* ГОСТИ́НИЦА "ЕВРОПЕ́ЙСКАЯ" úlitsa Bródskogo, 1/7
4. *Moskva* ГОСТИ́НИЦА "МОСКВА́" plóshchad' Alexándra Névskogo, 2
5. *Neva* ГОСТИ́НИЦА "НЕВА́" úlitsa Tchaykóvskogo, 2
6. *Rossiya* ГОСТИ́НИЦА "РОССИ́Я" úlitsa Chernyshévskogo, 11
7. *Sportivnaya* ГОСТИ́НИЦА "СПОРТИ́ВНАЯ" Deputátskaya úlitsa, 34
8. *Sputnik* ГОСТИ́НИЦА "СПУ́ТНИК" prospéct Morísa Torésa, 34
9. *Tourist* ГОСТИ́НИЦА "ТУРИ́СТ" úlitsa Sevastiánova, 3.

The favorite word of all travelers: "Where???"

Where are we?, ГДЕ МЫ?, you may ask, seeing yourself in an unfamiliar place. In the answer a noun will be in the prepositional case with the preposition "В" denoting the location of a person or an object:

МЫ В МОСКВЕ́.
МЫ В ПЕТЕРБУ́РГЕ.
МЫ В ОРЛЕ́.
МЫ В ОТЕ́ЛЕ.

You may be asked:
ГДЕ ДЖОН? ГДЕ МЭРИ? ГДЕ ОНИ́?

Answer using the pronoun ОНИ and the noun in the prepositional case with the preposition "В":

ОНИ́ В ВАШИНГТОНЕ.
ОНИ́ В МЕЛЬБУРНЕ.
ОНИ́ В ЛОНДОНЕ.

The main concerns of every traveler:

Where is my suitcase?
ГДЕ ЧЕМОДА́Н [gdye che-ma-dán]?!

Where is my passport?
ГДЕ ПА́СПОРТ [gdye pás-part]?!

Where is my visa?
ГДЕ ВИ́ЗА [gdye ví-za]?!

The answer can be:

The suitcase is on the plane.
ЧЕМОДА́Н В САМОЛЁТЕ. [che-ma-dán f sa-ma-lyo-te]
The visa is in the suitcase.
ВИ́ЗА В ЧЕМОДА́НЕ. [ví-za f che-ma-dá-ne]
The passport is in the pocket.
ПА́СПОРТ В КАРМА́НЕ. [pás-part f kar-má-ne]

Notice, that in this kind of sentence the verb "is" (ЕСТЬ) is always omitted.

If you lose your friend in a crowd, you may call her:

МА́ША! ГДЕ́ ТЫ [má-sha gdyé ty]?
Masha! Where are you?

And you may get the answer:

Я ЗДЕСЬ. [ya zdyes']
I am here. (if she is around)

Or somebody may point towards her:

ОНА ТАМ. [a-ná tam]
She is there. (if she is far away)

If you don't see John around, you might ask:

ГДЕ ДЖОН [gdye John]?

And you might get the answer:

ОН В ГОСТИНИЦЕ [on v gas-tí-nii-tse].
He is at the hotel.

Or if he is not far away he might respond himself:

ЗДЕСЬ [zdys']. Here I am.

In some cases dialogue might be reduced to the calling a person by name and his short answer, like in the aria of Figaro:

ФИГАРО! ФИГАРО! ФИГАРО!
ФИГАРО ЗДЕСЬ! ФИГАРО ТАМ!

CHECKING IN

As travelers to foreign lands often are, you may be lost and confused the second you step off the plane. However, once you meet your tour leader (РУКОВОДИТЕЛЬ ГРУППЫ) or whomever is there meeting you, things should go smoothly. For those not

73

being met at the airport (АЭРОПО́РТ) there should be plenty of reliable official taxis (ТАКСИ́). Settle the price before climbing aboard. Recently, a tourist who failed to do this found herself paying $20 for a fifteen minute trip, which is a lot for the current exchange rate.

If you are part of a tour, your guide (ГИД) will do all of the work in checking in. However, if you are traveling alone or are joining the group later, this burden will fall upon you. As you arrive at the hotel, proceed to the check-in counter. If the person does not speak English, you will need to communicate in Russian, and even limited knowledge of Russian might be very helpful. You will have to be able to answer questions about yourself.

Your name? ВА́ШЕ ИМЯ [vá-she i-mya]?
ЭДГАР ДЖОНСОН.

Where are you from? ОТКУ́ДА ВЫ [at-kú-da vy]?
ИЗ АМЕ́РИКИ (КАНА́ДЫ, ЮЖНОЙ А́ФРИКИ, А́НГЛИИ, АВСТРА́ЛИИ, НО́ВОЙ ЗЕЛА́НДИИ).

Place of birth? МЕ́СТО РОЖДЕ́НИЯ [myés-ta razh-dyé-nii-ya]?
Date of birth? ДА́ТА РОЖДЕ́НИЯ [dá-ta razh-dyé-nii-ya?]?
ФИЛАДЕ́ЛЬФИЯ, США. 23 МАЯ, 1960 ГО́ДА.

Permanent address? ГДЕ ЖИВЁТЕ [gdye zhii-vyo-te]?
15 Spring Street, #2B, New York.
НЬЮ-ЙОРК, СПРИНГ СТРИТ, ДОМ 15, КВАРТИ́РА 2Б.

Taking a Room

Can you show me an inexpensive room for two?
ВЫ МО́ЖЕТЕ ПОКАЗА́ТЬ МНЕ НЕДОРО́ГОЙ НО́МЕР НА ДВОИ́Х [vy mó-zhe-te pa-ka-zát' mnye ne-da-ra-góy nó-mer na dva-íkh]?

How much does it cost?
СКÓЛЬКО СТÓИТ ЭТОТ НÓМЕР [skól'-ka stó-it éa-tat nó-mer]?

I will stay here for one week.
МНЕ НÝЖЕН НÓМЕР НА ОДНÝ НЕДÉЛЮ [mnye nú-zhen nó-mer na ad-nú ne-dyé-lu].

What else do you have?
ЧТО ЕЩЁ У ВАС ЕСТЬ [shto e-shchó uu vas yést']?

On what floor?
НА КАКОМ ЭТАЖЕ [na ka-kóm e-ta-zhé]?

Where do the windows face?
КУДА ВЫХОДЯТ ÓКНА [kuu-dá vy-khó-dyat ók-na]?

How much does it cost?
СКÓЛЬКО СТÓИТ ЭТОТ НÓМЕР [skól'-ka stó-it éa-tat nó-mer]?

What does it include?
ЧТО ВХÓДИТ В ЭТУ ЦÉНУ [shto fkhó-dit v éa-tuu tsyé-nuu]?

May I look at this room?
МОГÝ Я ПОСМОТРÉТЬ ЭТУ КОМНАТУ [ma-gú ya pa-smat-ryét' éa-tuu kóm-na-tuu]?

I will take this room.
Я БЕРÝ ЭТОТ НОМЕР [ya be-rú éa-tat nó-mer].

Receiving Your Hotel Card and Key

After completing all the formal procedures, you will receive your hotel card (ПРÓПУСК) and possibly your key (КЛЮЧ). In most cases the key will be obtained on the floor (ЭТÁЖ) where your room is. You will be asked to show your passport

(ПА́СПОРТ) and visa (ВИ́ЗА). You may choose to use your knowledge of Russian when speaking with the hotel personnel (ПЕРСОНА́Л). This may not be the case when speaking with the administrator (АДМИНИСТРА́ТОР) or receptionist (ДЕЖУ́РНАЯ-РЕГИСТРА́ТОР) but, as you will see later, there will be some very handy people who work at these hotels with whom conversations may become a daily affair; usually they will not speak English.

The hotel card (ПРО́ПУСК) identifies you as a guest of the hotel. When you leave, you hand over the key (КЛЮЧ) to the floor administrator and she (the administrator is almost always a woman) will give you your hotel card (ПРО́ПУСК). When you return the opposite exchange is done. This may seem a tedious process, but carrying a little piece of paper around with you rather than a key attached to an enormous key chain is actually preferable.

Grammar: Personal Pronouns

"Я" is the last letter of the Russian alphabet and the first person of the personal pronoun at the same time.

With "ТЫ" one may address only one's close friends, to John, or to Mary.

"ВЫ" might be addressed to both, John and Mary.

And "ВЫ" is the polite form of "ТЫ". When you speak formally you always use "ВЫ".

John is ОН.
Mary is ОНА́.
John and Mary are ОНИ́.

"МЫ" means Mary and I.

I	Я
we	МЫ
you	ТЫ
you	ВЫ (polite form and plural)
he	ОН
she	ОНА́
it	ОНО́
they	ОНИ́

The Genitive Case of Personal Pronouns

I − the genitive МЕНЯ́ [me-nyá]

we − the genitive НАС [nas]

you − the genitive singular ТЕБЯ́ [te-byá], the genitive plural ВАС [vas]

A Form of Inquiry: "Do you have?"

1. The expression "Do you have?" is translated into Russian as: "У ВАС ЕСТЬ?" The personal pronoun "ВЫ" is used here with the preposition "У" which requires the genitive case.

The positive answer will be:

У НАС ЕСТЬ СВОБО́ДНЫЕ НОМЕРА́.

[uu nas yest' sva-bód-ny-e na-me-rá]

We have rooms free.

For the genitive singular of the first person the positive answer will be: I have (У МЕНЯ́ ЕСТЬ) + a noun in the nominative.

У МЕНЯ́ ЕСТЬ СВОБО́ДНЫЕ НОМЕРА́. [uu me-nyá yest' sva-bód-ny-e na-me-rá] I have rooms free.

The negative answer will be: "I have no" (У МЕНЯ́ НЕ́Т) + a noun in the genitive.

Answer the questions: "Do you have?" using this pattern:

77

Do you have a towel?
У ВАС ЕСТЬ ПОЛОТЕ́НЦЕ (neut.)?
[uu vas yést' pa-la-tyén-tse]?
У МЕНЯ́ НЕТ (gen.) ПОЛОТЕ́НЦА [uu- mye-nyá nyét pa-la-tyén-tsa].

Do you have a book?
У ВАС ЕСТЬ (acc.) КНИ́ГА (fem.) [uu vas yést' kní-ga]?
У МЕНЯ́ НЕТ (gen.) КНИГИ [uu- mye-nyá nyét kní-gii].

У ВАС ЕСТЬ (acc.) МАШИ́НА (fem.) [uu vas yést' ma-shí-na]?
У МЕНЯ́ НЕТ (gen.) МАШИ́НЫ [uu me-nyá nyet ma-shí-ny].

Do you have cheese?
У ВАС ЕСТЬ (acc.) СЫР (masc.)?
У МЕНЯ́ НЕТ (gen.) СЫ́РА [uu me-nyá nyét sý-ra].

About Tipping

Whereas before only taxi drivers and sometimes waiters were tipped a very nominal amount, today tips (ЧАЕВЫ́Е) [che-ii-vý-ii] are the norm rather than the exception. Although it is still not outrageously offensive if you fail to tip (ДАТЬ НА ЧАЙ) [dat' na chay] you should tip the taxi drivers, porters, and waiters. Because tipping was previously disapproved of, it became a tradition to leave gifts (ПОДАРКИ) [pa-dár-kii] for some of the Intourist employees. This is especially true of the maids, interpreters, and guides.

Grammar: Words with the Same Roots.

The words ЧАЙ [chay] (tea), ЧА́ЙНИК [chay-nik] (tea-cattle) and ЧАЕВЫ́Е [che-ii-vý-ii] (tipping) have the same root. They differ by the suffixes. The word ЧАЕВЫ́Е literally means the small change which is left in addition to payment "for a cup of tea".

The word tipping is translated with the idiomatic expression: ДАТЬ НА ЧАЙ [dat' na chay] where after the verb, the preposition "НА" is used.

The verb ДАТЬ without prepositions takes the accusative denoting an object of an action.

Idiomatic Expressions with the Verb ДАТЬ:

ДАТЬ РУ́КУ [dat' rú-kuu] give one's hand

ДАТЬ МИ́ЛОСТЫНЮ [dat' mí-las-ty-nu] give alms

ДАТЬ ПРИМЕ́Р [dat' prii-myér] give an example

ДАТЬ ОТВЕ́Т [dat' at-vyét] give an answer

ДАТЬ СДА́ЧИ [dat' zdá-chii] get even with somebody

ДАТЬ ПОЩЁЧИНУ́ [dat' pa-shchyo-chii-nuu] slap somebody in the face

ДАТЬ ПО ШЕ́Е [dat' pa shyé-e] slap one in the neck

ДАТЬ РАЗГОВО́Р [dat' raz-ga-vór] connect someone on the phone line

ДАТЬ НЬЮ-ЙОРК connect one with New York (on the phone)

The Imperative Mood of Verbs

In the singular, the verbs of the imperative mood are formed with the ending -И (ПРИНЕСИ́ [prii-ne-sí] bring), -Й (ДАЙ) or -Ь (ВСТАНЬ [fstan'] (stand up). In the plural, all imperative verbs end with -ТЕ.

During your trip, the verb ДАТЬ will probably be the most useful in this form which denotes request or order. It is used at the hotels, at the stores, at the booking and box-offices.

ДА́ЙТЕ МОЙ БАГА́Ж [dáy-te moy ba-gásh].

ДА́ЙТЕ МОЙ ЧЕМОДА́Н [dáy-te moy che-ma-dán].

ДА́ЙТЕ МОЙ ПРО́ПУСК [dáy-te moy pró-pusk].

ДА́ЙТЕ МОЙ ПА́СПОРТ [dáy-te moy pás-part].

ДА́ЙТЕ МНЕ БИЛЕ́Т ДО МОСКВЫ́ [dáy-te mnye bii-lyét da mas-kvý] (give me a ticket to Moscow)

At the restaurants the verb ПРИНЕСИ́ТЕ [prii-ne-síi-te] (bring) will be employed as often.

Both verbs take the accusative without prepositions.

Transitive Verbs

Verbs which require use of nouns in the accusative denoting an objects of an action are called the TRANSITIVE verbs (ПЕРЕХО́ДНЫЕ ГЛАГО́ЛЫ).

Most Russian verbs are TRANSITIVE. The transitive verbs require the questions: what? ЧТО? or whom? КОГО́?

The given verbs are used in the polite form of the IMPERATIVE mood:
ПРИНЕСИ́ТЕ, ПОЖА́ЛУЙСТА, КО́ФЕ [prii-ne-sí-te pa-zhá-lus-ta có-fe].
Bring me coffee please.

ДА́ЙТЕ, ПОЖА́ЛУЙСТА, БАТО́Н [dáy-te pa-zsá-lus-ta ba-tón]
Give me a loaf of bread please.

Your Room

Depending upon the hotel and the class of tour you are on, the amenities of the hotel room will vary. Any room that is rated first class or deluxe will include a telephone (ТЕЛЕ-ФО́Н) [te-le-fón] and a private bath. You will probably have a television set (ТЕЛЕВИ́ЗОР) [te-la-ví-zar] and radio as well, and even possibly a refrigerator (ХОЛОДИ́ЛЬНИК) [kha-la-díl'-nik].

The first thing you should do when you enter your room is check to see if you have linens (ПРÓСТЫНИ) [prós-ty-nii], soap (МЫ́ЛО) [mý-la], and toilet paper (ТУАЛÉТНАЯ БУМÁГА) [tuu-a-lyét-na-ya buu-má-ga] in the bathroom (ТУАЛÉТ) [tuu-a-lýet]. If not, catch one of the maids (ГОРНИЧНАЯ) [gór-nish-na-ya] and inform her immediately upon arrival. It becomes much more difficult to take care of these matters at night after key personnel have already gone home for the day. As you venture away from the larger cities, you will notice a substantial difference in the quality of service and facilities in the Intourist hotels. However, one suggestion will be useful for all. Bring your own bath towel (БÁННОЕ ПОЛОТÉНЦЕ) [bá-na-e pa-la-tyén-tse]. The towels (ПОЛОТÉНЦА) [pa-la-tyén-tsa] provided are very small and thin by Western standards.

One final word should be made about your room. You may be in for a rude awakening the morning after you arrive, when you hop into the shower (ДУШ) [dush] and discover there is no hot water (ГОРЯ́ЧАЯ ВОДÁ) [ga-ryá-che-ya va-dá]. Unfortunately, the lack of hot water in the hotel rooms in Russia is quite typical. Do not be too alarmed; this is not a permanent condition. You may find that the morning rush for hot water is too much for the system to handle and that waiting until evening to bathe will guarantee hot water. If this is not the case, you can still be pretty sure the hot water will reappear within one or two days.

The Floor Attendants

In the past, the floor attendant (ДЕЖУ́РНАЯ) [de-zhúr-na-ya] was the distinguishing feature in Russian hotels. Today, however, fewer and fewer hotels have these typically militant floor ladies. Although known to be very tough and frightening, the attendant can also be very motherly and watchful. If it's cold outside and you are seen leaving your room without the proper headwear, you can be sure your ДЕЖУ́РНАЯ will scold you. On the other hand, if you come back with a cold she will put the kettle (ЧА́ЙНИК) on to boil and will make you some tea. In the present day, such instances are rare. Todays ДЕЖУ́РНАЯ, if there is one at all at the hotel, may still make tea for you upon request but will do little else other than collect and give out room keys.

You may address the ДЕЖУ́РНАЯ [de-zhúr-na-ya] with the following:

ГДЕ ЗДЕСЬ РЕСТОРА́Н [gdye zdyes' res-ta-rán]?
Where is the dining room?

В КАКО́Е ВРЕ́МЯ ЗА́ВТРАК, ОБЕ́Д, У́ЖИН [f ka-kó-e vryé-mya záft-rak, a-byét, ú-zhin]?
At what time are the meals served?
Я УХОЖУ́ [ya uu-kha-zhúu].
I am going out.

Я ВЕРНУ́СЬ В 7 ЧАСО́В [ya ver-nús' f syem' che-sòf].
I will be back at . . . o'clock.

ВОТ МОЙ КЛЮЧ [vot moy kluch].
Here is my key.

ПОЖА́ЛУЙСТА, ДА́ЙТЕ КЛЮЧ ОТ КО́МНАТЫ No.2
[pa-zhá-lus-ta dáy-te kluch at kóm-na-ty nó-mer dva].
Please give me the key from the room No. 2.

ПОЖА́ЛУЙСТА, РАЗБУДИ́ТЕ МЕНЯ́ В . . . ЧАСО́В [pa-zhá-lus-ta raz-buu-dí-te me-nyá v . . . che-sóf].
Please wake me at . . . o'clock.

Я ХОТЕ́Л(А) БЫ ПОЛУЧИ́ТЬ ЕЩЁ ОДНО́ ОДЕЯ́ЛО [ya kha-tyél(a) by pa-luu-chít' e-shchyo ad-nó a-de-yá-la].
I would like another blanket.

ПРИНЕСИ́ТЕ, ПОЖА́ЛУЙСТА, ЧА́ШКУ ЧА́Я [prii-ne-sí-te pa-shá-lus-ta chásh-kuu cha-ya]
Please bring me a cup of tea.

The Maid Service

The maid service varies greatly from one hotel to another. Although you may see the maids only when they are chatting and drinking tea, your bed will always be made. Your wallet may increase the quality and speed of maid service. If you need your suits cleaned and pressed quickly, trying using some monetary incentive.

When you check out of a hotel, it is customary to leave a tip for the maids. Some of the best tips are pantyhose, bic lighters, cigarettes, and other similar small items.

Use of transitive verbs at the hotel:

ПОЗВА́ТЬ ГО́РНИЧНУЮ [pa-zvát' gór-nish-nuu-u] call the maid

УБРА́ТЬ КРОВА́ТЬ [ub-rát' kra-vat'] make the bed

УБРА́ТЬ КО́МНАТУ [ub-rat' kóm-naa-tuu] clean the room

Hotel Services

Most hotels have the basics: a restaurant, souvenir shops, a newsstand (ГАЗЕ́ТНЫЙ КИО́СК) [ga-zyét-ny kii-ósk], a snack bar (БУФЕ́Т) [buu-fyét] on certain floors, laundry (ПРА́ЧЕЧНАЯ) [prá-chesh-na-ya] and foreign currency exchange booths.

If you are part of a tour or have a package deal with Intourist, most of your meals will be provided in the main restaurant. The snack bars are typically poorly stocked, badly run, open odd hours and crowded. If they are not out of everything, they serve coffee, tea, juices (СО́КИ) [só-kii], prepared salad (ГОТО́ВЫЕ САЛА́ТЫ) [ga-tó-vy-ye sa-lá-ty], small open-faced sandwiches (БУТЕРБРО́ДЫ) [buu-ter-bró-dy], cheese (СЫР) [syr], boiled eggs (ВАРЁНЫЕ ЯЙЦА) [va-ryó-ny-ye yáy-tsa], bread (ХЛЕБ) [khlep], buns (БУ́ЛОЧКИ) [búu-lach-kii] and pastries (ПИРО́ЖНЫЕ) [pii-rózh-ny-e] in the mornings. Other than being conveniently located, they have little else going for them.

83

Hotel "Beriozkas" are often well stocked. There is usually a larger food and drink section where you can buy your own snacks and alcohol.

Calling a Cab

In your hotel room there should be a list of numbers to call for various hotel services. You will have to pay a fee for this service. If you need a taxi to take you to the airport in the afternoon, call and reserve on the day before.

If you order a taxi by phone while staying in Moscow, the number you need is: 927-00-00 or 927-00-40. If you get through, you may try to order the taxi as follows:

A. Hello, I need a cab for tomorrow.
АЛЛЁ! МНЕ НУ́ЖНО ТАКСИ́ НА ЗА́ВТРА. [alyo mnye núzh-na taxí ha záft-ra]

B. Where do you want to go?
КУДА́ ВАМ НУ́ЖНО Е́ХАТЬ? [kuu-dá vam núzh-na yé-khat']

A. Sheremetyevo-2 Airport.
В АЭРОПО́РТ ШЕРЕМЕ́ТЬЕВО-2. [v a-e-ra-pórt she-re-myé-tye-va]

B. When do you need a car?
КОГДА́ ВАМ НУЖНА́ МАШИ́НА? [kag-da vam nuzh-ná ma-shí-na]

A. At 1 p.m.
В ЧАС ДНЯ [v khas dnya].

B. No taxis for that time. We have one taxi available at 11 a.m.
НА ЧАС НИЧЕГО́ НЕТ. [na chas nii-che-vó nyet] ЕСТЬ ТО́ЛЬКО ОДНА́ МАШИ́НА НА ОДИ́ННАДЦАТЬ УТРА́. [yest' tól'-ka ad-ná ma-shíi-na na adí-na-tsat' ut-rá]

A. But that is too early for me. My flight is at 5 p.m.
НО ЭТО СЛИ́ШКОМ РА́НО ДЛЯ МЕ́НЯ [no é-ta slísh-kam

84

rá-na dlya me-nyá]. МОЙ САМОЛЁТ ВЫЛЕТА́ЕТ В ПЯТЬ
ВЕ́ЧЕРА [moy sa-ma-lyot vy-le-tá-et f pyat' vyé-che-rá].

B. Will you take this taxi or not?
ТАК ВЫ БЕРЁТЕ ЭТО ТАКСИ И́ЛИ НЕТ [tak vy be-ryo-te
éa-ta taxí í-lii nyet]?

A. All right. I have no choice. Book me in.
ХОРОШО́. [kha-ra-shó] У МЕНЯ́ НЕТ ВЫ́ХОДА. [uu me-nyá
nyet vý-kha-da] ПРИМИ́ТЕ ЗАКА́З. [prii-míi-te za-kás]

B. Your name? ВА́ШЕ ИМЯ? [vá-she íi-myá] Your address
and telephone? ВАШ А́ДРЕС И ТЕЛЕФО́Н? [vash ád-res ii
te-le-fón]

A. Edgar Johnson, hotel "Intourist", Tverskaya, 3, room No.
28. The phone number is 228-12-18.
ЭДГАР ДЖОНСОН, ГОСТИ́НИЦА "ИНТУРИ́СТ", ТВЕРСКА́Я, 3,
КО́МНАТА НО́МЕР 28. ТЕЛЕФО́Н: 128-12-18.
[gas-tí-nii-tsa in-tuu-ríst tver-ská-ya trí, kóm-na-ta nó-mer
dvá-tsat' vó-sem' te-le-fón sto dvá-tsat' vó-sem' dve-ná-tsat'
va-sem-ná-tsat'].

B. The taxi will arrive at 1 p.m. ТАКСИ ПРИЕ́ДЕТ В ЧАС
ДНЯ [taxi prii-yé-det f chas dnya].

Grammar: Expression of Need

1. The impersonal expressions МНЕ НУ́ЖНО [mnye núzh-na]
(I need), ВАМ НУ́ЖНО [vam núzh-na] (you need) are very useful.
They are followed by a noun in the accusative case or by a verb
in the infinitive.

МНЕ НУ́ЖНО ПОЗВОНИ́ТЬ [mnye núzh-na pa-zva-nít']
I need to make a call.

МНЕ НУ́ЖНО КУПИ́ТЬ БИЛЕ́Т [mnye nŭzh-na kuu-pit' bii-lyét].
I need to buy a ticket.

МНЕ НУ́ЖНО ТАКСИ́ [mnye nŭzh-na taxí].
I need a taxi.

МНЕ НУ́ЖНО БЫТЬ У ТЕЛЕФО́НА [mnye nŭzh-na byt' uu te-le-fó-na].
I need to be by the telephone

Dormitories

Students are often housed in less than exquisite hotels, but generally their hosts try their best to find satisfactory accommodations for their guest students. Many students end up in dormitories (ОБЩЕЖИ́ТИЯ). Dormitories in Russia have never been praised as top notch by foreign students, yet most agree that their experience in a Russian dormitory was quite educational. At the very least it teaches tolerance! Security is not always good in dormitories, and many students have reported stolen articles. Students who bring with them valuable items should also take along a lock.

Camping

Intourist also arranges camping trips for those prefering the great outdoors and cheap rates. Most are pre-arranged tours where you travel by bus from site to site. You also have the option of taking your own camping trip by car, but even these trips must be arranged through Intourist and the routes must be strickly adhered to. Camping spots are only open in the summer for reasons you can well imagine. The degree of roughing it can be specified. Some camp sites (ПАЛА́ТОЧНЫЕ ГОРОДКИ́ [pa-lá-tach-ny-e ga-rat-kí]) provide bungalows (БУ́НГАЛО), others just a spot of ground. All Intourist campgrounds provide showers (ДУ́Ш) and cooking facilities. You can rent linens as well. In theory grocery stores are also there. In practice, bring all the food your arms can carry! Camping can be great fun but it does limit your traveling power. The quality campground network in Russia is very small and you will have little choice or flexibility as to your tours or city visits.

Recently Russia has been promoting tourism more than in years past, and the number of people traveling through Russia has increased immensely. As a result, a great effort is being made to improve accommodations and facilities to better serve guests.

CHAPTER SIX

COMMUNICATION

AT THE POST OFFICE

Cognates for better communication:

ТЕЛЕФÓН [te-le-fón]
ТЕЛЕГРÁФ [te-le-gráf]
ТÉЛЕКС [té-lex]
ТЕЛЕФАКС [te-le-fáx]
ТЕЛЕГРÁММА [te-le-grá-ma]
ЭКСПРЕСС [ex-prés]
ИНФОРМÁЦИЯ [in-far-má-tsii-ya]
АДРЕС [ad-ryes]

Before departing for your Russian adventure, be sure to warn your family and friends that they should not plant themselves by the telephone or mailbox eagerly expecting day-to-day updates from you. Communication (СВЯЗЬ [svyas']) from Russia to the West is low quality and unreliable.

At some point, however, you may want to brave the system and telephone, telefax, telex or telegram home or send packages

(БАНДЕРО́ЛЬ [ban-de-ról']), postcards (ОТКРЫ́ТКИ [at-krýt-kii])
or letters (ПИ́СЬМА [pís'-ma]) to your family and friends.

The Main Post Office & The Central Telegraph

If you are not staying at an Intourist hotel, where many postal
services are available and where many attendants speak English,
your best bet in Moscow is the Main Post Office (ГЛАВПОЧТА́МТ
[glaf-pach-támt] (úlitsa Myasnítskaya, 42, ph. 926-26-57) or the
Central Telegraph (ЦЕНТРА́ЛЬНЫЙ ТЕЛЕГРА́Ф) [tsent-rál'-nyi
te-le-gráf] (úlitsa Tverskáya, 9, ph. 927-20-02) (24-hour service). In
St. Petersburg, Central Post Office (úlitsa Soúsa Svyázi, 9; Central
Telegraph Office (úlitsa Soúza Svyázi, 15 (24-hour service).

There you may buy stamps, envelopes and postcards, send
telegrams, letters, small packages and make international phone calls.
Large packages or parcels (ПОСЫ́ЛКИ) [pa-sýl-kii] can be sent
from the International Post Office (МЕЖДУНАРО́ДНЫЙ
ПОЧТА́МТ [mezh-duu-na-ród-ny pach-támt] (Moscow,
Varshávskoye shaussee, 7, ph. 114-46-45).

You should be able to explain to the clerk at the post office
what you need:

I need envelopes.
МНЕ НУЖНЫ́ КОНВЕ́РТЫ [mnyé nuzh-ný kan-vér-ty].

I want to buy stamps.
Я ХОЧУ́ КУПИ́ТЬ МА́РКИ [ya kha-chú kuu-pít' már-kii].

Please give me envelopes and stamps.
ДА́ЙТЕ МНЕ, ПОЖА́ЛУЙСТА, КОНВЕ́РТЫ И МА́Р-
КИ [dáy-te mnyé, pa-zhá-lus-ta, kan-vér-ty ii már-kii].

I want to buy envelopes with stamps.
Я ХОЧУ́ КУПИ́ТЬ КОНВЕ́РТЫ С МА́РКАМИ
[ya kha-chú kuu-pit' kan-vyér-ty s már-ka-my].

I need post cards.
МНЕ НУЖНЫ́ ОТКРЫ́ТКИ [mnyé nuzh-ný at-krýt-kii].

A. I want to buy post cards with stamps.
Я ХОЧУ́ КУПИ́ТЬ ОТКРЫ́ТКИ С МА́РКАМИ
[ya kcha-chú kuu-pít' at-krýt-kii s már-ka-mii]

Mailing: To Where? To Whom? From Whom?

Mail from Russia to foreign lands (ЗА ГРАНИ́ЦУ [za graa-ní-tsuu]) can take anywhere from ten days to four weeks. But who knows? Your letters may even arrive four months later! For mail within Russia you may buy envelopes with stamps already printed on them (КОНВЕ́РТЫ С МА́РКАМИ [kan-vyér-ty s már-ka-mii]).

Don't forget that envelopes in Russia are addressed exactly opposite from those in the West. On the top line, where you will find the word "КУДА́" (to where), enter the city and city code. Then write the name of the street, the number of the building and the apartment number. On the last line, where you will see the word "КОМУ́" (to whom, takes the dative), write the surname followed by the first name and patronymic of the addressee. The return address is put below the mailing address where you find the words: "ОТ КОГО́" (from whom). This inconsequential detail should not be overlooked. You can just imagine what would happen to your letters mailed in Russia if you address them as you would in the West. Yes, your letters would be delivered . . . right back to you!

In general, mail sent to Russia from the West finds its way to the right person because the employees in the main post offices are familiar with the Western way of addressing mail. However, westerners in Russia sending mail to other addresses in Russia cannot expect their letters to reach their destination if not labelled in the customary Russian manner.

An envelope looks like this:

Куда _____

_____

Кому _____

| Индекс предприятия связи | и адрес отправителя |

Пишите индекс предприятия связи места назначения

Explain to the postal clerk what you want to send:

I want to send a registered letter.
Я ХОЧУ ПОСЛА́ТЬ ЗАКАЗНО́Е ПИСЬМО́.
[ya kha-chú pas-lát' za-kaz-nó-e pis'-mó]

I want to send a money order.
Я ХОЧУ ПОСЛА́ТЬ ДЕ́НЕЖНЫЙ ПЕРЕВО́Д.
[ya kha-chú pas-lát' dyé-nezh-ny pe-re-vót]

I want to send a small package.
Я ХОЧУ́ ПОСЛА́ТЬ БАНДЕРО́ЛЬ.
[ya kha-chú pas-lát' ban-de-ról]

I want to send a package.
Я ХОЧУ́ ПОСЛА́ТЬ ПОСЫ́ЛКУ.
[ya kha-chú pas-lát' pa-sýl-kuu]

There are different forms of mailing letters in Russia:

regular ОБЫ́ЧНОЕ [a-bých-na-e]

registered ЗАКАЗНО́Е [za-kaz-nó-e]

91

registered with return notice ЗАКАЗНОЕ С УВЕДОМЛЕ́-
НИЕМ [za-kaz-nó-ye s u-ve-dam-lyé-nii-em]

air mail АВИАПОЧТА [a-vii-a-póch-ta]

express ЭКСПРЕСС [ex-prés]
It takes about two weeks to receive the express mail from Russia to
the States.

At the International Post Office (МЕЖДУНАРО́ДНЫЙ
ПОЧТАМТ) there is УСКОРЕННАЯ ПОЧТА [us-kó-re-na-ya
póch-ta] or express mail. It is the most expensive and most reliable mail.
It promises delivery within three days, but actually takes from 4 to 6
days.

Sending packages in and out of Russia is slow, expensive and
unreliable. Sending printed materials is less expensive. Never pack your
parcel yourself. The post office attendant first inspects it and then packs
it for you. The packing cases for parcels are sold at the post offices.

Telegrams

You can send telegrams inside the country from any post office.
Telegrams abroad (МЕЖДУНАРО́ДНЫЕ ТЕЛЕГРА́М-
МЫ [mezh-duu-na-ród-ny-e te-le-grá-my]) should be sent from the
Main Post Office ГЛАВПОЧТА́МТ [glaf-pach-támt], the Central
Telegraph ЦЕНТРА́ЛЬНЫЙ ТЕЛЕГРАФ [tsen-trál'-ny te-le-gráf]
and the International Post Office МЕЖДУНАРО́ДНЫЙ ПОЧ-
ТАМТ [mezh-duu-na-ród-ny pach-támt]. Whereas express mail abroad
can take up to four-six weeks, a telegram should arrive in one to two
days, and has been recommended by many visitors as a relatively quick,
reliable, and inexpensive means of communication.
Telegrams are taken at a window with the sign: ПРИЁМ
ТЕЛЕГРАММ [prii-yom te-le-grám] which literally means "acceptance
of telegrams."

You need to know just one phrase:

A. I want to send a telegram.
Я ХОЧУ ПОСЛА́ТЬ ТЕЛЕГРА́ММУ [ya kha-chú pas-lát'
te-le-grá-muu].

Don't forget the word "international": МЕЖДУНАРО́ДНАЯ
[mezh-duu-na-ród-na-ya]. It will direct you to the right window at
the post office.

Telephoning abroad

Telephoning abroad (МЕЖДУНАРО́ДНЫЕ ПЕРЕГО-
ВО́РЫ) [mezh-duu-na-ród-ny-e pe-re-ga-vó-ry] can be rather
frustrating. It is best to order the call from the post office one day
in advance. The International Telephone Call Office in Moscow is at
úlitsa Tverskaya, 9 (24-hour-service); in Petersburg, úlitsa Gértsena,
3/5 (24-hours service). If you choose to wait for a call, it is best to
arrive at the post office first thing in the morning. Emphasize that
your call is urgent (СРО́ЧНЫЙ) [sróch-ny] and you may have more
luck. Before you leave home, set the time when you will be regularly
calling your family and friends. Keep in mind that it is 8 hours
earlier in New York than in Moscow.

To place an international call you say:

I want to place an international phone call.
Я ХОЧУ ЗАКАЗА́ТЬ МЕЖДУНАРО́ДНЫЙ РАЗГОВО́Р [ya
kha-chù za-ka-zát' mezh-duu-na-ród-nyi raz-ga-vór].

Local calls can be made from any phone booth (ТЕЛЕФО́ННАЯ
БУ́ДКА) [te-le-fó-na-ya bút-ka] in the city. Be sure to have 1 or 2 or
15 kopeck pieces with you; those are the only coins these machines will
accept. With 2 or 15 kopecks you may make a local call. Place your
coins in the slots before dialing. Only if your call is answered will the

coins fall in. Therefore there is no need for a coin return lever. As your time runs out, additional coins, which you should place in the upper slot, will drop in. Quick short beeps mean the line is busy (НÓМЕР ЗÁНЯТ) [nó-mer zá-net]; longer beeps indicate the line is ringing (НÓМЕР СВОБÓДЕН) [nó-myer sva-bó-den]

Out-of-City Calls

To make non-local calls to other cities of the country, you will need to find an inter-city pay phone (МЕЖДУГОРÓДНИЙ ТЕЛЕФÓН [mezh-duu-ga-ród-ny te-le-fón]). For the inter-city calls by pay phone you will need only 15 kopeks (ПЯТНÁДЦАТЬ КОПÉЕК [pet-na-tsat' ka-pyé-ek]). Have plenty of them on hand when you want to make your call. At each inter-city phone there is a list of area and city codes.

The number to call for information throughout Russia is 09. Additional numbers vary from city to city. Anyone at the hotel or post office should know it. As in most Western nations, local information is free. You can also use the Russian equivalent of the Yellow Pages "СПРÁВОЧНАЯ ТЕЛЕФÓННАЯ КНИ́ГА" [sprá-vach-na-ya te-le-fó-na-ya kní-ga] and the White Pages "КНИ́ГА ТЕЛЕФОНОВ И АДРЕСОВ" [kní-ga te-le-fó-nof ii ad-re-sóf] You can find these books in some post offices and hotels.

The information bureau (СПРÁВОЧНЫЕ БЮРÓ [sprá-vach-ny-y bu-ró]) can provide you with phone numbers and addresses of offices and private people. In the very large major cities you will find these kiosk-type centers throughout the city streets. In other cities you will find them at the railroad stations (ВОКЗÁЛЫ [vag-zá-ly]), seaports (МОРСКИЕ ВОКЗÁЛЫ [mars-kí-e vag-zá-ly]) and airports (АЭРОПОРТЫ [a-ea-ra-pór-ty]).

The list of the phone numbers in Moscow you might need:

1. General Information (operator)   09
СПРА́ВОЧНАЯ [sprá-vach-na-ya]
If there is no information available, the operator will suggest that you call a special service "Moscow for You" ("МОСКВА́ ДЛЯ ВАС" [mask-vá dlya vas]), a charge number 927-00-09. This service is relatively expensive but much more efficient than the general information.

2. Fire: 01
ПОЖА́РНАЯ [pa-zhár-na-ya]

3. Police   02
МИЛИ́ЦИЯ [mii-líi-tsii-ya]

4. Ambulance   03
СКО́РАЯ ПО́МОЩЬ [skó-ra-ya pó-mashch]

5. Check the Time
ВРЕ́МЯ   100

6. Out-of-City Calls   07
МЕЖДУГОРО́ДНЯЯ

7. International Operator   МЕЖДУНАРО́ДНАЯ
Dial 8, wait for a beep, and dial 194

8. Intourist Information :   203-69-62
СПРА́ВОЧНАЯ "ИНТУРИ́СТА"

9. Emergency Number: 925-55-10
О НЕСЧА́СТНЫХ СЛУ́ЧАЯХ

10. Lost and Found:
СПРА́ВКИ О ЗАБЫ́ТЫХ ВЕЩА́Х:

      In a taxi   233-42-25
      В ТАКСИ́

In the subway   222-20-85
В МЕТРО́

In a train, bus, trolley, tram 923-87-53
В ПО́ЕЗДЕ, АВТО́БУСЕ, ТРОЛЛЕ́ЙБУСЕ, ТРАМВА́Е

Lost ID   200-99-57
ПОТЕ́РЯННЫЕ ДОКУМЕ́НТЫ

The numbers 1,2,3,10 on the list are the same throughout Russia.

A Telephone Conversation:

B. Hello.
АЛЛЁ [aa-lyó].

A. May I talk to Peter Ivanovich?
МО́ЖНО ПЕТРА́ ИВА́НОВИЧА [mózh-na pet-rá ii-vá-na-vii-cha]?

B. One moment. Peter Ivanovich, there is a phone call for you.
МИНУТКУ. ПЁТР ИВА́НОВИЧ, ВАС К ТЕЛЕФО́НУ [mii-nút-kuu pyotr ii-vá-na-vii-ch vas k te-le-fó-nuu].

C. Hello.
АЛЛЁ. [aa-lyó]

A. Is this Peter Ivanovich?
ЭТО ПЁТР ИВА́НОВИЧ [é-ta pyotr ii-vá-na-vich]?

C. Yes, it is.
ДА, ЭТО Я [da éa-ta ya].

A. Good Morning. My name is Peter Johnson.
ЗДРА́ВСТВУЙТЕ. МЕНЯ́ ЗОВУ́Т ПИ́ТЕР ДЖО́НСОН [zdrást-vuy-te me-nyá za-vút . . .].

If the person is not available, you will get either of these answers:

B. He is not here right now. Can you call later? He should be here in 15 minutes.

ЕГО СЕЙЧАС НЕТ [e-vó se-chás nyet]. МО́ЖЕТЕ ПО-ЗВОНИ́ТЬ ПОПО́ЗЖЕ [mó-zhee-te paz-va-nit' pa-pó-zhe]? ОН ДО́ЛЖЕН БЫТЬ ЧЕ́РЕЗ 15 МИНУ́Т [on dól-zhen byt' che-res pet-ná-tsat' mii-nút].

Or:

B. He left already. Would you like to leave a message?

ОН У́ЖЕ УШЁЛ [on uu-zhé uu-shól].
ЧТО-НИБУ́ДЬ ПЕРЕДА́ТЬ [shto nii-but' pe-re-dát']?

A. Tell him that Peter Johnson called him. I will call him tomorrow.

СКАЖИ́ТЕ ЕМУ́, ЧТО ПИ́ТЕР ДЖО́НСОН ЗВОНИ́Л [ska-zhí-te e-muú shto . . . zva-níl]. Я БУ́ДУ ЗВОНИ́ТЬ ЕМУ́ ЗА́ВТРА [ya bú-duu zva-nít' e-mú záft-ra].

B. Fine, I will tell him when he returns.

ХОРОШО́, Я ПЕРЕДА́М ЕМУ, КОГДА́ ОН ВЕРНЁТСЯ [kha-ra-shó ya pe-re-dám e-mú kag-dá on ver-nyo-tsya].

Long Distance Calls

You have to dial the number of an international operator and tell the country, the city, the time of your call, the number of a person you want to call, your name and number. The reservation is made a day in advance:

O. International operator.
МЕЖДУНАРО́ДНАЯ.

A. Can you give me New York tomorrow at 5 p.m.? В Ы МО́ЖЕТЕ ДАТЬ МНЕ НЬЮ-ЙОРК ЗА́ВТРА В ПЯТЬ ЧАСО́В [vy mó–zhe–te dat' mnye nyu yórk záft–ra f pyat' che–sóf] ?

O. What is the number in New York? КАКО́Й НО́МЕР В НЬЮ-ЙО́РКЕ [ka–kóy nó–mer v nyu yór–ke] ?

A. The number in New York is (212) 575-2839. НО́МЕР В НЬЮ-ЙО́РКЕ . . . [nó–mer v nyu yór–ke. . .]

O. Whom do you want to talk to? КОГО́ ВЫЗЫВА́ЕТЕ [ka–vó vy–zy–vá–ye–te] ?

A. Just call the number. This is a home phone number. КТО ПОДОЙДЁТ. ЭТО ДОМА́ШНИЙ ТЕЛЕФО́Н [kto pa–dai–dyot éa–ta da–másh–ny te–le–fón].

O. Your name. ВА́ШЕ ИМЯ [vá–she í–me] ? Your number? ВАШ ТЕЛЕФО́Н [vash te–le–fón] ?

A. My name is ПИТЕР ДЖОНСОН. My number is . . . МОЙ ТЕЛЕФО́Н [moy te–le–fón ...]

O. I have made a reservation for tomorrow 5 p.m. ВАШ ЗАКА́З ПРИ́НЯТ [vash za–kás prí–nyat].

Faxing and Telexing

Fax machines are not readily available in Russia but can be found at the Central Telegraph Office in certain large cities. In Moscow a Western company called AlphaGraphics provides fax and telex services for hard currency (Pérvaya Tverskáya-Yamskáya, ph. 251-12-15; Cosmos hotel, ph. 288-95-51). It is expected that many more of these types of service stores will open up in Moscow and in other Russian cities in the near future.

If you are staying at the Intourist hotel, telephoning from your hotel room within the city is free. However, long distance calls (МЕЖДУГОРÓДНИЕ ПЕРЕГОВÓРЫ [mezh-duu-ga-ród-nii-e pe-re-ga-vó-ry]) from your room will be recorded by the telephone attendant in the hotel. Although the readings are printed out, they are often not readily available on computers. The telephone administrator sometimes scroll through a whole role of paper print outs listing phone calls made from the entire hotel. Try to remember on which days you placed your calls; often these stacks of paper cover a long period of time.

Calls to the United States, which will have to be ordered through the operator (ТЕЛЕФОНИ́СТКА [te-le-fa-níst-ka]) ahead of time (ЗАРÁНЕЕ [za-rá-ne-e), are substantially more expensive (ДОРÓЖЕ [da-ró-zhe]). To avoid all of the above, you can always call from a pay phone (ТЕЛЕФÓН-АВ- ТОМАТ [te-le-fón-af-ta-mát]) in the lobby. However, you may have to go to the Central Telegraph Office (ЦЕНТРÁЛЬНЫЙ ТЕЛЕГРÁФ) or Central Post Office (ГЛАВПОЧТÁМТ).

Grammar: Words with the Same Roots

The words-relatives:

ТЕЛЕФÓН
ТЕЛЕФОН-И́СТК-А
ТЕЛЕФÓН-НЫЕ ПЕРЕГОВÓРЫ
ТЕЛЕФÓН-НЫЙ СЧЁТ
ТЕЛЕФÓН-НАЯ СТÁНЦИЯ

The feminine noun ТЕЛЕФÓНИСТКА is formed from the word ТЕЛЕФÓН by adding the suffix -ИСТК and the ending -А.
The same way words denoting certain professions are formed from the following nouns:
МАССÁЖ - МАССАЖИ́СТКА
ПИАНИ́(НО) - ПИАНИ́СТКА

99

The masculine counterparts of these words:
ТЕЛЕФО́НИСТ
МАССАЖИ́СТ
ПИАНИ́СТ

The adjectives ТЕЛЕФО́Н-Н-ЫЙ (-ЫЕ) are formed by adding to the noun ТЕЛЕФО́Н the suffix of the adjectives -Н and the endings of the adjectives: -ЫЙ (for the masculine), -АЯ, (for the feminine), -ОЕ, (for the neuter), -ЫЕ (for the plural).

Useful Expressions:

The expression "to pay for" "ПЛАТИ́ТЬ ЗА" [pla-tít' za] requires the accusative:

ПЛАТИ́ТЬ ЗА ТЕЛЕФО́Н [pla-tít' za te-le-fón]
ПЛАТИ́ТЬ ЗА ТЕЛЕГРА́ММУ [pla-tít' za te-le-grá-muu]
ПЛАТИ́ТЬ ЗА НО́МЕР [pla-tít' za nó-mer]
ПЛАТИ́ТЬ ЗА УСЛУ́ГИ [pla-tít' za uus-lú-gii]

Here are some other useful expressions with the preposition "ЗА":

thank for БЛАГОДАРИ́ТЬ ЗА [bla-ga-da-rít' za],
praise for ХВАЛИ́ТЬ ЗА [chva-lít' za].

The lines from Lermontov's sarcastic poem "Gratitude" will help you better remember this form:

ЗА ВСЁ, ЗА ВСЁ ТЕБЯ́ БЛАГОДАРЮ́ Я...
[za fsyo, za fsyo te-byá bla-ga-da-ryú ya]
ЗА ЖАР ДУШИ́, РАСТРА́ЧЕННЫЙ В ПУСТЫ́НЕ,
[za zhar duu-shí rast-ra-chye-ny f pus-tý-ne]
ЗА ВСЁ, ЧЕМ Я ОБМА́НУТ В ЖИ́ЗНИ БЫЛ...
[za fsye chem ya ab-má-nut v zhíz-nii byl]
УСТРО́Й ЛИШЬ ТАК, ЧТО́БЫ ТЕБЯ́ ОТНЫ́НЕ
[us-tróy lish tak shtó-by te-byá at-ný-ne]
НЕДО́ЛГО Я ЕЩЁ БЛАГОДАРИ́Л
[ne-dól-ga ya e-shchó bla-ga-da-ríl].

100

I am grateful to you for everything, for everything...
For the fire of soul wasted in the desert,
For everything with which I was deceived...
Grant only that
I will not be grateful to you much longer.

You may need to know some other verbs which require use of the accusative with the preposition "З А" such as:

ВОЛНОВА́ТЬСЯ ЗА worry for
ШТРАФОВА́ТЬ ЗА fine for
РУГА́ТЬ ЗА scold

But we don't want to finish this chapter on a grave note.

Remember that Russia is a place of vivid social and cultural activities. Don't waste your time at the post offices. Enjoy your trip!

CHAPTER SEVEN

TRANSPORTATION

From now on you will have to walk in the land of Cyrillic letters without Latin crutches. We will provide you with Latin transcription of some Russian words only when you might need this help.

Welcome!

Welcome! (ДОБРО́ ПОЖА́ЛОВАТЬ!) This is probably the first phrase you will hear upon your arrival in Russia.

Then you may hear:

КАК ДОЛЕТЕ́ЛИ? How was the flight?

КАК ДОЕ́ХАЛИ? How was your trip?

КАК СЕБЯ́ ЧУ́ВСТВУЕТЕ? How do you feel?

ГДЕ ВА́ШИ ВЕ́ЩИ? Where is your luggage?

ВАМ ПОМО́ЧЬ? Do you need help?

ВАМ КУДА́ Е́ХАТЬ? Where are you going?

You already know the difference between interrogative words ГДЕ? (where) and КУДА? (to where).

Besides ГДЕ and КУДА questions you often hear КАК and КАКО́Й questions:

The interrogative word КАК? is used in questions such as: How are you? How do you feel? How are things going?

You may use the following nouns and verbs after this question word:

КА́К ТЫ?
How are you?

КАК ЖИВЁШЬ?
КАК ЖИ́ЗНЬ?
How is your life?

КАК ДЕЛА́?
How are things going?

КАК ДЕ́ТИ?
How are the children?

КАК МА́МА?
How is your mother?

КАК ЗДОРО́ВЬЕ?
How is your health?

КАК РАБО́ТА?
How is your job?

КАК ПОЕ́ЗДКА?
How is your journey?

КАК УЧЁБА?
How are your studies?

The КАКО́Й question supposes in its answer the characteristic of an object, describing what kind of thing, person, etc. it is. It keeps the gender of the object it describes and has the ending –АЯ (–ЯЯ) for the feminine, –ОЕ (–ЕЕ) for the neuter, and –ОЙ for the masculine.

Answer the ГДЕ, КУДА́, СКО́ЛЬКО, КАКО́Й (–АЯ, –ОЕ, –ИЕ) questions. Choose the proper answer:

ГДЕ ВА́ШИ ВЕ́ЩИ?
Where is your luggage?

ВОТ ОНИ́. Here.
ТАМ. Over there.

У МЕНЯ́ НЕТ ТЯЖЁЛОГО БАГАЖА́.
I have no luggage.

Я ЕЩЁ НЕ ПОЛУЧИ́Л БАГА́Ж.
I haven't gotten it yet.

МОЙ БАГА́Ж В КА́МЕРЕ ХРАНЕ́НИЯ.
My luggage is in the check-room.

У МЕНЯ́ МНО́ГО ВЕЩЕ́Й. МНЕ НУ́ЖЕН НОСИ́ЛЬЩИК.
I have a lot of luggage. I need a porter.

МОЙ БАГА́Ж ПОТЕ́РЯН. ЧТО МНЕ ДЕ́ЛАТЬ? МО́ЖЕТЕ МНЕ ПОМО́ЧЬ?

My luggage has been lost. What should I do? Can you help me?

КАКО́Й У ВАС ЧЕМОДА́Н?

What kind of suitcase do you have?

НОСИ́ЛЬЩИК! ВОЗЬМИ́ТЕ МОЙ ВЕ́ЩИ!

Porter! Take my luggage.

СКО́ЛЬКО Я ВАМ ДО́ЛЖЕН?

How much do I owe you?

Choose the proper answer to the question:
ВАМ ПОМО́ЧЬ?
Do you need help?

ДА, КОНЕ́ЧНО.

Yes, of course.

НЕТ, СПАСИ́БО.

No, thank you.

СПАСИ́БО. Я СПРА́ВЛЮСЬ САМ (masc.), САМА́ (fem.).

Thank you. I will manage.

О́ЧЕНЬ ЛЮБЕ́ЗНО С ВА́ШЕЙ СТОРОНЫ́.

That's very kind of you.

СПАСИ́БО. МНЕ УЖЕ́ ПОМОГА́ЮТ.

I am taken care of already.

Public Transportation

The first time you enter the Moscow or St. Petersburg subway station (МЕТРО́), you may feel like you've stepped into the foyer of a museum. In general, public transportation in Russia is reliable, inexpensive and clean. It is so extensively used that during rush hour "ЧАСЫ ПИК" you may want to take a taxi instead of the metro to avoid feeling like a sardine in a can. The metro is only found in the large cities: Moscow, St. Petersburg, and Novosibirsk. It runs from daybreak to 1 a.m. The maps of the routes are very easy to follow, but you do need to be able to read Russian in order to use them.

Trams, Trolleys, Buses

These services also run from daybreak to midnight or 1 a.m. and run regularly. They are designated by numbers. Their stops (ОСТАНОВКИ) are marked with special signs on the street.

Try to ride the trams simply for the sake of amusement. All too often the electric rod from the tram disconnects from the wires above. The driver, usually a strong, hearty woman, will diligently hop out of the tram with her long pole and fight with the electric rod until she manages to get it back in place. Of course, the scene may be funnier from the street rather than from inside the tram. Inevitably you will witness such an occurrence at least once during your visit.

The trams may be less expensive in some cities though none of the transportation fares run over a few rubles. All services operate on a sort of honor principle. You buy packets of 10 tickets called "ТАЛО́НЫ" from either street kiosks or the drivers. Try to have exact change when purchasing from the drivers. Once you have your tickets, you must punch them in the little boxes located throughout the vehicle. If you fail to punch your tickets, you may be caught and hit with a fine. If you cannot reach the little punch box, ask the person next to you to pass your tickets along (ПЕРЕДÁЙТЕ, ПОЖÁЛУЙСТА, МОЙ БИЛÉТ) to the person near the box.

Because of the frequent crowding in public transportation, getting off may be more difficult than you think. Ask in advance for your stop:

Excuse me, what stop is this?
ПРОСТИ́ТЕ, КАКÁЯ ЭТО ОСТАНÓВКА?

Sokolniki.
СОКÓЛЬНИКИ.

What is the next stop?
КАКÁЯ СЛÉДУЮЩАЯ ОСТАНÓВКА?

Are you getting off at the next stop?
ВЫ ВЫХÓДИТЕ НА СЛÉДУЮЩЕЙ ОСТАНÓВКЕ?

No, please pass through.
НЕТ, ПРОХОДИ́ТЕ, ПОЖÁЛУЙСТА.

When someone is giving you directions they may indicate what form of transportation is the best and what number of tram, trolley or bus you should take:

A. Where is the closest metro station?
ГДЕ ЗДЕСЬ БЛИЖÁЙШАЯ СТÁНЦИЯ МЕТРÓ?

B. Where are you going?
ВАМ КУ́ДА НУ́ЖНО ÉХАТЬ?

A. To the Hermitage Museum.
ЭРМИТÁЖ.

B. From here it is best to go by tram. ОТСЮДА ЛУ́ЧШЕ
Е́ХАТЬ НА ТРАМВА́Е.

By metro you will have to transfer trains.
НА МЕТРО́ ВАМ ПРИДЁТСЯ ПЕРЕСА́ЖИВАТЬСЯ.

You can catch the tram a block down the street.
ТРАМВА́ЙНАЯ ОСТАНО́ВКА КВАРТА́ЛОМ НИ́ЖЕ.

Take the number 4.
САДИ́ТЕСЬ НА ТРАМВА́Й НО́МЕР 4.

Ediny Bilet

If you are staying in one city for a long time and will be
using public transportation regularly, purchase a ЕДИ́ННЫЙ
БИЛЕ́Т. This pass, available at metro stations and kiosks, allows
you to travel as much as you want on the metro, trams, buses
and trolleys for one month. You simply show the metro attendant
your ЕДИ́ННЫЙ БИЛЕ́Т when entering the station. Always carry
it with you on all forms of transportation as you may be asked
to present it to the controller.

Public Transportation Etiquette

It is expected that riders give up their seats to the elderly,
to pregnant women and to mothers with small children if there
are no empty seats. Failing to do so may get not only evil looks
but probably nasty remarks as well.

Taxis

There are three types of taxis in Russia: official taxis,
"marshrutnyi" taxis and non-official or gypsy cabs.

Official Taxis

Official taxis (ГОРОДСКЍЕ ТАКСЍ) usually have checkered patterns on their doors. When free, they illuminate a green light in the window. Taxi drivers, as in many countries, often take advantage of foreigners. Although official taxis have set rates per kilometer, they may still ask for exorbitant sums for short trips. You may want to ask your guide or friends what the going official rate is and what would be a reasonable fare for a particular ride. In Moscow, you can order a taxi by dialing 927-00-00 or 927-00-40 or by ordering one through the hotel taxi attendant. You can catch a taxi at a taxi stand or simply on the street. Since official taxis are in short supply, many unofficial taxis operate in Russia.

Unofficial or Gypsy Cabs

Unofficial taxis (ЧАСТНЫЕ МАШЍНЫ) are simply private drivers trying to make some extra money. When you stick your hand out, you never know what may stop. One tourist reports being driven around in an ambulance, a very efficient ride since the driver was experienced at speeding around the streets of Moscow. You may be in danger of paying too much for your trip, especially if you are a foreigner. Depending on the exchange rate and how much the driver requests, you may or may not want to take up the offer. In any case, the rates will probably be lower than in America.

Unofficial taxis are also known to be selective. The first thing they will ask is "Where are you going?" "ВАМ КУДА?" For their own personal reasons they may decide not to take you. If you begin feeling comfortable with the system, you may want to do some bargaining. It is very important to note, however, that traveling by unofficial taxi has become riskier over the years. Incidents of robbery and abandonment of those traveling to and from airports by way of gypsy cabs have increased. Acts of violence have been reported as well. Yet, within the city, unofficial taxi travel is still considered quite safe.

The question: ВАМ КУДА́? (to where?) is the short form of a question: Where do you want to go?)
In the answer you might just say the name of the place you want to go:

Hotel "Rossiya"
ГОСТИ́НИЦА "РОССИ́Я"

Hotel "Metropol"
ГОСТИ́НИЦА "МЕТРОПО́ЛЬ"

Hotel "Cosmos"
ГОСТИ́НИЦА "КО́СМОС"

Tverskaya
ТВЕ́РСКАЯ У́ЛИЦА

Belorussian Railroad Station
БЕЛОРУ́ССКИЙ ВОКЗА́Л

A conversation with a taxi driver may sound like this:

A. Is this taxi free? ВЫ СВОБО́ДНЫ?

T. Where are you going? ВАМ КУДА́?

A. I am going to the Bolshoi Theater. Please hurry. I am late.
БОЛЬШО́Й ТЕА́ТР. ПОЖА́ЛУЙСТА, ПОБЫСТРЕ́Й. Я ОПА́ЗДЫВАЮ.

T. It will take 20 minutes.
ЧЕ́РЕЗ 20 МИНУ́Т БУ́ДЕМ ТАМ.

A. How much will that be?
СКО́ЛЬКО ЭТО БУ́ДЕТ СТО́ИТЬ?

T. Coefficient 50
КОЭФФИЦИЕ́НТ 50.

A. What does it mean?
ЧТО ЭТО ЗНА́ЧИТ?

T. Did you never see a taxi? It means that you have to multiply the amount shown on the meter by 50, add tips and pay. Are you coming?
ТЫ ЧТО ТАКСИ́ В ГЛАЗА́ НЕ ВИ́ДЕЛ? ЭТО ЗНАЧИ́Т, ЕСЛИ НА СЧЁТЧИКЕ 10 РУБЛЕ́Й, УМНО́ЖЬ НА 50, ПРИБА́ВЬ ЧАЕВЫ́Е И ПЛАТИ́. НУ ЧТО, Е́ДЕШЬ?

A. Fine.
ХОРОШО́.

Route Taxis

Route Taxis (МАРШРУ́ТНЫЕ ТАКСИ́) are really vans that carry about 10 people back and forth along certain routes. They have only final stops but may stop when someone indicates the desire to get off. They are very inexpensive and the price is the same no matter how far one travels. Their stops are generally bus, metro and train stations.

Car Rentals

Not very common among tourists, car rentals (МАШИ́НЫ НА ПРОКА́Т) are available through Intourist. You may be scared away from the steering wheel by the extremely long gas lines, the poor conditions of the roads and the renegade driving style of others on the road.

Trains

Trains, buses, boats, and planes run between cities. Although recent changes have made traveling for foreigners more expensive through the introduction of hard currency fares for non–citizens, it is still reasonable, especially on trains. If you are comfortable with the language, it is possible to travel by train on rubles.

Travel by rail is probably the best way to get from one city to another when the two are relatively close. Trains (ПОЕЗДА́) are quite inexpensive and convenient. Many trains operate overnight and are equipped with sleeping compartments for 2 or 3 people; 4 is standard. The overnight between Moscow and St. Petersburg takes about 7 hours. There is usually a small buffet on the trains where snacks and tea are served. It is not a bad idea to bring your own snacks and sugar for the tea. Drinking and merrymaking are common on trains. The restroom facilities on Russian trains leave something to be desired. This is one of those times you don't want to forget your toilet paper, soap and towel. You may be able to buy tickets the day of travel at the train station. However, if you are traveling between major cities or during the summer season, it is best to make reservations two weeks in advance. Revervations can be made at the hotel or at the "Zheleznodoró́zhnaya Ká́ssa Predvarítelnoi Prodá́zhi Biletov". They will take reservations up to 3 days before your trip. Usually this office if located near the train station. The phone numbers of the general information in Moscow are: from 266-90-00 to 266-9009, of the general booking office (БЮРО́ ЗАКА́ЗОВ) 266-83-33.

Train Stations

As in the United States, train stations (ВОКЗА́ЛЫ) in Russia are very busy places. Large arrival and departure information boards indicate the train number and name, from where it is arriving, its time of arrival, the track it is arriving on, and its status. Arrivals are called "ПРИБЫ́ТИЕ" and departures are called "ОТПРАВЛЕ́НИЕ".

A conversation with the ticket window attendant at the "ЖЕЛЕЗНОДОРÓЖНАЯ КÁССА ПРЕДВАРЍТЕЛЬНОЙ ПРОДÁЖИ БИЛÉТОВ" may sound something like this:

A. I would like to make a train reservation for August 3rd to Sochi.
Я ХОЧÝ ЗАРЕЗЕРВЍРОВАТЬ БИЛÉТ НА ТРÉТЬЕ ÁВГУСТА НА СÓЧИ.

B. Round trip or one way?
ТУДÁ И ОБРÁТНО?

A. One way.
ТÓЛЬКО ТУДÁ.

B. There are 3 trains going to Sochi that day. A 4:30, 5:30 and 7:30. Which one would you like?
В ЭТОТ ДЕНЬ ТРИ ПÓЕЗДА ДО СÓЧИ: В 16:30, 17:30 И 19:30. ВАМ КАКÓЙ?

A. The earliest one.
МНЕ НА СÁМЫЙ РÁННИЙ.

B. Which car type?
КАКÓЙ ВАГÓН?

A. The coupee.
КУПÉ.

B. Your train number is 12, your car number is 24, your space is 4. ВАШ ПÓЕЗД 12, ВАШ ВАГÓН 24, ВÁШЕ МÉСТО 4.

A. How much will it cost?
СКÓЛЬКО СТÓИТ БИЛÉТ?

B. 1300 rubles.
1300 РУБЛÉЙ.

A. Here it is.
ВОТ ДЕ́НЬГИ.

B. Here is your ticket. And here is the change.
ВОТ ВАШ БИЛЕ́Т. ВОТ СДА́ЧА.

A. Thank you.
СПАСИ́БО.

Moscow Railroad Stations:

1. Belorússky Railroad Station (БЕЛОРУ́ССКИЙ ВОКЗА́Л) plóshchad' Belorússkogo vokzála (subway station "Belorússkaya")
2. Saviólovsky Railroad Station (САВЁЛОВСКИЙ ВОКЗА́Л) plóshchad' Butýrskoy zastávy (subway station "Saviólovskaya"
3. Rízhsky Railroad Station (РИ́ЖСКИЙ ВОКЗА́Л) Rízhskaya plóshad' (subway station "Rízhskaya")
4. Kazánsky Railroad Station (КАЗА́НСКИЙ ВОКЗА́Л) Komsomól'skaya plóshchad', 2 (subway station "Komsomol'skaya")
5. Leningrádsky Railroad Station (ЛЕНИНГРА́ДСКИЙ ВОКЗА́Л) Komsomól'skaya plóshchad', 2 (subway station "Komsomol'skaya")
6. Yaroslávsky Railroad Station (ЯРОСЛА́ВСКИЙ ВОКЗА́Л) Komsomól'skaya plóshchad', 2 (subway station "Komsomol'skaya")
7. Kíevsky Railroad Station (КИ́ЕВСКИЙ ВОКЗА́Л) plóshchad' Kíevskogo vokzála (subway station "Kíevskaya")
8. Kúrsky Railroad Station (КУ́РСКИЙ ВОКЗА́Л) úlitsa Chkálova, 29 (subway station "Kúrskaya")
9. Pavelétsky Railroad Station (ПАВЕЛЕ́ЦКИЙ ВОКЗА́Л) Léninskaya plóshchad', 1 (subway station "Pavelyétskaya).

St. Petersburg Railroad Stations:

1. Moskóvsky Railroad Station (МОСКО́ВСКИЙ ВОКЗА́Л) ploshcháď Vosstániya, 2.
2. Baltíysky Railroad Station (БАЛТЍЙСКИЙ ВОКЗА́Л) náberezhnaya Obvodnógo kanála, 120.
3. Varshávsky Railroad Station (ВАРША́ВСКИЙ ВОКЗА́Л) náberezhnaya Obvodnógo kanála, 118.
4. Finlándsky Railroad Station (ФИНЛЯ́НДСКИЙ ВОКЗА́Л) ploshcháď Lénina, 6.
5. Vítebsky Railroad Station (ВЍТЕБСКИЙ ВОКЗА́Л) Zágorodny prospéct, 52.

Airplanes

You may have been warned not to fly on Aeroflot by those who have experienced the bumpy take-offs and abrupt landings for which this airline is notorious. In the past, however, its safety record was quite good, and this remains the case for international travel. Unfortunately, due to the recent oil shortages and the deficit of spare machine parts, the number of accidents has increased in domestic Aeroflot travel. This is not to say that flying on Aeroflot means taking a big risk. However it is a good idea to keep yourself informed about the recent developments in air travel in Russia when making travel arrangements.

Aeroflot flies to all major cities in the country and abroad. Although it now charges hard currency to foreigners for domestic flights, the rates are still reasonable. You must present your passport when purchasing a ticket. You can buy tickets at most Intourist hotels, even if you are not staying at the hotel. Do not be discouraged by the long lines that form outside of the offices; there is a special window just for foreigners which is generally empty. Tickets can be purchased by credit card. Reservations should be made at least a week in advance. There are Aeroflot offices in all major cities. The phone number of the Central International Agency of Aeroflot in Moscow (ЦЕНТРА́ЛЬНОЕ МЕЖДУНАРО́ДНОЕ АГЕ́НСТВО АЭРОФЛО́ТА): 245-00-02, of the City Airport (ГОРОДСКО́Й АЭРОВОКЗА́Л): 155-09-02.

115

The address of the Agency of Air Connections (АГÉНСТВО ВОЗДУ́ШНЫХ СООБЩÉНИЙ) in St. Petersburg: Nevsky prospect 7/9.

Moscow Airports:

Vnúkovo: there are flights to the Northern, Western, and Southern directions.

Domodédovo: flights to Siberia, the Far East, the Middle Asia

Sheremétievo-1: flights to the North-Western direction.

Sheremétievo-2, the International airport.

Bykóvo, a small airport.

St. Petersburg Airports:

Púlkovo
Púlkovo-2
Rzhevka

Travel by Boat

Although travel by boat is quite limited, travelers can take advantage of some very pleasant trips to the north and the south of Russia. Within St. Petersburg, boats, including the speedy hydrofoil, regularly travel from the city center to one of the most popular tourist and non-tourist attractions, Petrodvorets, a large park covered with fountains and pavilions. Trips along the Neva River are especially pleasant in the evenings during its White Nights. Trips down the Moscow and Volga rivers are also a must.

Moscow River Ports:

The North River Port (СÉВЕРНЫЙ РЕЧНÓЙ ВОК-ЗÁЛ) Leningrádskoye shaussee, 89

The South River Port (ЮЖНЫЙ РЕЧНÓЙ ВОКЗАЛ) Nogátinskaya náberezhnaya

St. Petersburg River Ports:

The River Port (РЕЧНО́Й ВОКЗА́Л) prospéct Obukhóvskoy oboróny, 195)
The Sea Port (МОРСКО́Й ВОКЗА́Л) plóshchad' Morskóy slávy, 1

Your transport vocabulary:

car МАШИ́НА
tram stop ОСТАНОВКА ТРАМВАЯ
bus stop ОСТАНОВКА АВТОБУСА
metro station СТАНЦИЯ МЕТРО
train station ВОКЗАЛ
bus station АВТОБУСНАЯ СТАНЦИЯ
ticket БИЛЕТ
fine ШТРАФ
airplane САМОЛЁТ
train ПОЕЗД
track ПУТЬ
platform ПЛАТФОРМА
waiting room ЗАЛ ДЛЯ ПАССАЖИРОВ
local train ЭЛЕКТРИ́ЧКА
express train СКОРЫЙ ПОЕЗД
low (passenger) train ПАССАЖИ́РСКИЙ ПОЕЗД
direct train ПОЕЗД ПРЯМОГО СООБЩЕНИЯ
sleeping compartment СПАЛЬНОЕ КУПЕ
car (of a train) ВАГОН
first-class carriage МЯГКИЙ ВАГО́Н
reserved-seat carriage ПЛАЦКАРТКАРТНЫЙ ВАГОН
dining car ВАГОН-РЕСТОРАН
conductor ПРОВОДНИ́К
lavoratory УБОРНАЯ
occupied ЗАНЯТО
vacant СВОБОДНО
boat ПАРОХОД

117

arrival ПРИБЫТИЕ
departure ОТПРАВЛЕНИЕ
go (by means of vehicle) ЕХАТЬ
fly ЛЕТЕТЬ
go by boat ПЛЫТЬ (НА КОРАБЛЕ)
transfer ПЕРЕСАЖИВАТЬСЯ

The Conducting Phrases:

How do I reach?
КАК МНЕ ПОПАСТЬ НА. . .

Which bus/tram/trolley should I take?
КАКОЙ АВТО́БУС (ТРАМВАЙ, ТРОЛЛЕ́ЙБУС) МНЕ НУЖЕН?

I need to go to. . .
МНЕ НУЖНО ПОЕХАТЬ В. . .

What subway station?
КАКОЕ МЕТРО?

How long does the trip take? СКОЛЬКО ВРЕ́МЕНИ ЗАЙМЁТ
ЭТА ПОЕЗДКА?

Are you getting off?
ВЫ ВЫХОДИТЕ?

When does is leave?
КОГДА ОТПРАВЛЯЕТСЯ?

When does it arrive?
КОГДА ПРИБЫВАЕТ?

I have missed my train.
Я ОПОЗДА́Л(А) НА СВОЙ ПОЕЗД.

When is the next train?
КОГДА СЛЕДУЮЩИЙ ПОЕЗД?

Grammar: Verb ЕХАТЬ. Aspect of the Verb.

You probably have heard or will hear some of the Russian "romances" (РУ́ССКИЕ РОМА́НСЫ) [rús-kii-e ra-mán-sy]. This is the word used for lyrical songs for one voice and an instrument. Some of them were performed by gypsy singers and were sung all over the world. "О́ЧИ ЧЁРНЫЕ" [ó-chii chyor-ny-e] ("Black eyes, passionate eyes") is one of these kinds of songs. "Я Е́ХАЛА ДОМО́Й, Я ДУ́МАЛА О ВАС" [ya yé-kha-la da-móy ya dú-ma-la a vás] ("I was going home, I was thinking about you") is the other, which is just as popular a romance. The verb Е́ХАТЬ is used here in the past tense of the imperfective aspect. This concept of aspect is a unique feature of Russian verbs.

The imperfective aspect defines an action in a process and does not specify whether it is completed or not.

The perfective aspect denotes completed action. Most of verbs of the perfective aspect have either prefixes or suffixes:

ПО-Е́ХАТЬ [pa-yé-khat'] go
ПРИ-Е́ХАТЬ [prii-yé-khat'] come, arrive
У-ЕХАТЬ [uu-ye´-khat'] leave

The Conjugation of the Verb Е́ХАТЬ. The Present Tense

In the present tense of the verb ЕХАТЬ there is alternation of the   consonants: Х and Д in the stem: Е́Х-АТЬ [ye-khat'] - Е-Д У́ [yé-duu]

The Singular:

I go Я Е́ДУ [ya yé-duu]
You go   ТЫ Е́ДЕШЬ [ty yé-desh]
He (she, it) goes ОН (ОНА́, ОНО́) Е́ДЕТ [on, a-ná, a-nó yé-det]

119

The Plural:

We go   МЫ ЕДЕМ [my yé-dem]
You go   ВЫ ЕДЕТЕ [vy yé-de-te]
They go ОНИ ЕДУТ [a-ní yé-dut]

There is a popular song of good cheer which uses this verb:

МЫ Е́ДЕМ, Е́ДЕМ, Е́ДЕМ [my yé-dem...
В ДАЛЁКИЕ КРАЯ [v da-lyo-ki-e kra-yá]
ВЕСЁЛЫЕ СОСЕ́ДИ [ve-syo-ly-e sa-syé-dii]
СЧАСТЛИ́ВЫЕ ДРУЗЬЯ [sches-lí-vy-e dru-zyá].

We are riding, riding, riding
To far away lands
The merry neighbors,
The happy friends.

The Past Tense of the Verb ЕХАТЬ

The form of the past singular you already know from the romance: "Я ЕХАЛА ДОМОЙ".

There is no alternation of consonants in the past tense. There are different endings: no ending for the masculine ЕХАЛ; -А for the feminine ЕХАЛА and -О for the neuter ЕХАЛО. In the plural, there is one form for all genders: ЕХАЛИ.

Questions with КУДА́? КОГДА́? КАКО́Й?

The grammar pattern of an answer to a КУДА́ question with the verb ЕХАТЬ is: "Я ЕДУ В" or "Я ЕДУ НА" + the noun in the accusative.

In a short answer the verb may be omitted:

Downtown
В ЦЕНТР

the Arbat Street
НА АРБА́Т

Kutuzov prospect
НА КУТУ́ЗОВСКИЙ ПРОСПЕ́КТ

the Solyanka Street
НА СОЛЯ́НКУ

Ask questions when speaking about a trip to Russia:

КУДА ОНИ́ ЕДУТ? Where are they going?
ОНИ́ Е́ДУТ В РОССИ́Ю. [a-ní yé-dut v ras-sí-u] They are going
to Russia.

КУДА. . . Where he is going?
ОН Е́ДЕТ В ПОВО́ЛЖЬЕ. [on yé-det f pa-vólzhye] He is going
to Povolje.

КУДА. . . Where are you going?
МЫ Е́ДЕМ НА СЕ́ВЕР. [my yé-de-m na syé-ver] We are going
to the North.

КУДА. . . Where are you going?
Я Е́ДУ В ПЕТЕРБУ́РГ. [ya yé-duu f pe-ter-búrk] I am going to
Petersburg.

КУДА. . . Where are we going?
МЫ Е́ДЕМ В АМЕ́РИКУ. [my yé-dem v a-myé-rii-kuu] We are
going to America.

КУДА. . . Where am I going?
Я Е́ДУ НА ЗА́ПАД. [ya yé-duu na sá-pat] I am going to the West.

КУДА . . . Where are you going?

МЫ Е́ДЕМ НА ЮГ [my yé-dem na yuk]. You are going to the South.

КУДА. . . Where is he going?
ОН Е́ДЕТ НА ВО́ЛГУ. [on yé-det na vól-guu] He is going to Volga.

Ask and answer the following question with the question word КУДА?

ВАМ КУДА́? or КУДА́ ВЫ Е́ДЕТЕ?
Where are you going?

Я Е́ДУ В МОСКВУ́.
I am going to Moscow.

Я Е́ДУ В ЦЕНТР.
I am going downtown.

Я Е́ДУ НА АРБА́Т.
I am going to the Arbat.

The other pattern is:
МНЕ НУ́ЖНО (I need) + "В" or "НА" with a noun in the accusative:

МНЕ НУ́ЖНО В ЦЕНТР (downtown).
МНЕ НУ́ЖНО НА АРБА́Т (street).
МНЕ НУ́ЖНО НА ТВЕРСКУ́Ю (street).
МНЕ НУ́ЖНО НА ПЛО́ЩАДЬ ПУ́ШКИНА (plaza).

To answer the question: КАКО́Й ТРАМВА́Й? [ka-kóy tram-váy?]

. . . АВТОБУС? [af-tó-bus?], . . . ТРОЛЛЕЙБУС? [tra-léy-bus?] you should give the number of your transport and then the name of the stop you need:

ТРАМВА́Й НО́МЕР 24 [tram-váy nó-mer 24]. ОСТАНО́ВКА "ШОССЕ́ ЭНТУЗИА́СТОВ" [as-ta-nóf-ka sha-sé ean-tu-zii-ás-taf].

АВТО́БУС НО́МЕР 5 [af-tó-bus nó-mer 5]. ОСТАНО́ВКА "ГОСТИ́НИЦА́ "МЕЖДУНАРО́ДНАЯ" [as-ta-nóf-ka gas-tí-nii-tsa mezh-du-na-ród-na-ya]

ТРОЛЛЕ́ЙБУС НО́МЕР 10 [tra-léy-bus nó-mer 10]. ОСТАНО́ВКА "МА́ЛАЯ БРО́ННАЯ" [as-ta-nóf-ka má-la-ya bró-na-ya]

Prepare yourself for a long stroll through St. Petersburg. Excercise by asking and answering questions:

A. Excuse me, how do I get to the Kunstkammer?
ПРОСТИ́ТЕ, КАК МНЕ ПОПА́СТЬ В КУНСТКА́МЕРУ?

B. It is on Universitetskaya Naberezhnaya.
ОНА́ НА УНИВЕРСИТЕ́ТСКОЙ НАБЕ́РЕЖНОЙ.

A. How do I get there from here?
КАК ТУДА́ ДОБРА́ТЬСЯ?

B. By bus.
НА АВТО́БУСЕ.

A. Which bus should I take?
КАКОЙ АВТО́БУС МНЕ НУ́ЖЕН?

B. Take the number 6, 13, or 22. They all go there. You can catch the bus across the street.
НО́МЕР 6, 13 ИЛИ 22. ОНИ ВСЕ ТУДА́ ИДУ́Т. САДИ́ТЕСЬ НА ТОЙ СТОРОНЕ́.

Thank you.
СПАСИ́БО.

The verb ЕХАТЬ with a prepositional "НА" is often used with the noun denoting a means of transportation:

"Я Е́ДУ НА" + the noun in the prepositional case (the ending - Е or -И for singular -АХ for plural)

Я Е́ДУ НА ПО́ЕЗДЕ (masc.) [ya yé-duu na pó-ez-de] .
I am going by train.

ОН Е́ДЕТ НА ВЕРБЛЮ́ДЕ (masc.) [on yé-det na ver-blú-dii].
He is riding on a camel.

ОНИ́ Е́ДУТ НА СОБА́КАХ (plur.) [a-ní yé-dut na sa-bá-kakh].
They are riding on dogs.

МЫ Е́ДЕМ НА ОЛЕ́НЯХ (plur.) [my yé-dem na a-lyé-nekh].
We are riding on reindeer.

Yesterday, Today, Tomorrow ВЧЕРА́, СЕГО́ДНЯ, ЗА́ВТРА
[ʃche-rá, se-vód-nya, záft-ra]

КОГДА́ ОНИ́ Е́ДУТ? [kag-dá a-ní yé-dut?] When are they going?

Я Е́ДУ СЕГО́ДНЯ [ya yé-duu se-vód-ne].
I am going today.

ТЫ Е́ДЕШЬ ЗА́ВТРА [ty yé-desh záft-ra].
You are going tomorrow.

ВЫ Е́ДЕТЕ СЕГО́ДНЯ [vy yé-de-te se-vód-ne].
You are going today.

МЫ ÉДЕМ ЗÁВТРА [my yé-dem záft-ra].
We are going tomorrow.

Notice that in conversational Russian one can use the present tense speaking about the near future (tomorrow ЗАВТРА [záft-ra]).

Idiomatic Expressions for Long-Distance Travel:

There are two idiomatic expressions meaning to go far away:

1. ЕХАТЬ НА КРАЙ СВÉТА go to the end of the earth

2. The expression ДÁЛЬШЕ ЕХÁТЬ НÉКУДА literally means "there is no other place to go." Its second, figurative meaning is "this is the limit (of one's patience)."

CHAPTER EIGHT

SPORTSMANIA

Exercise your mind with these cognates:

СПОРТ
АЭРО́БИКА
БЕЙЗБО́Л
БАСКЕТБО́Л
ВОЛЕЙБО́Л
ХОККЕЙ
ГИМНА́СТИКА
ТЕ́ННИС
КОРТ
СЛА́ЛОМ
КО́МПЛЕКС
ПРОГРА́ММА
ТУРИ́СТ
ЭНТУЗИА́СТ
ФАНА́ТИК
МАССА́Ж
ХО́ББИ

Aerobics АЭРО́БИКА have become quite a fad in Russia. Jane Fonda look-alikes are popping up everywhere in the sports complexes (СПОРТИ́ВНЫЕ КО́МПЛЕКСЫ) and television programs (ТЕЛЕВИЗИО́ННЫЕ ПРОГРА́ММЫ).

Russia has discovered baseball (БЕЙЗБО́Л), but it seems that it will take some time before it really catches on. Basketball (БАСКЕТБО́Л) is going strong, and American football (ФУТБО́Л) has even hit the fields in Russia.

While in Russia, you can enjoy almost all the same activities you do at home and more.
You may find yourself going ice swimming in the winter or taking a mud bath. Russia offers many opportunities for sports enthusiasts. Russians are very active people and enjoy many sports.

Sports Stadiums and Health Centers

The two major places to exercise are the sports stadiums (СТАДИО́Н) and the sport health center complexes (СПОРТИ́ВНЫЙ ОЗДОРОВИ́ТЕЛЬНЫЙ КО́МПЛЕКС). Many of the nicer and better equipped facilities are found near major hotels.

The stadiums are outdoor fields for soccer, track, volleyball (ВОЛЕЙБО́Л) and tennis (ТÉННИС). There is also equipment (ОБОРУ́ДОВАНИЕ) for some limited gymnastics (ГИМНА́СТИКА). Except for the olympic stadiums, they are free and open to all. For tennis (ТÉННИС) you may have to sign up for a court (КОРТ), but if no one is there feel free to play. Because volleyball courts, basketball courts and tennis courts are indoors and in great demand, you will want to reserve a spot for yourself a few days in advance. If you are planning to play tennis, bring your own balls and racket.

Some stadiums have lights for evening play as well. At the nicer stadiums there will be rental offices where you can rent goal nets (СЕ́ТКИ ДЛЯ ВОРО́Т) and volleyball nets (ВОЛЕЙБО́ЛЬНЫЕ СЕ́ТКИ). If you are looking to play some soccer but do not have a whole team together, it is possible to join in on a game already in progress. Don't be shy, it is a great way to make new friends.

In the winter, most tennis courts and stadiums are converted into rinks for ice skating and ice hockey (КАТКИ́). You can rent skates at the rental office. The sport health centers are indoor facilities. Most are owned by a large factory and membership for the employees is free. Others must pay a nominal fee. At these centers you will find a weight room, pool (БАССЕ́ЙН), sauna (СА́УНА), massage specialists (МАССАЖИ́СТЫ), indoor "mini" soccer, indoor tennis, volleyball, basketball, gymnastics equipment, indoor track, wrestling rooms, table tennis (НАСТО́ЛЬНЫЙ ТЕ́ННИС), aerobic classes, equipment rental office (ПУНКТ ПРОКА́ТА) and shower facilities (ДУШ). Most of the centers are open from 9 a.m. to 8 p.m. Some of them provide the guests with a towel (ПОЛОТЕ́НЦЕ) and sometimes even a swimming cap (КУПА́ЛЬНАЯ ША́ПОЧКА) and goggles (ЗАЩИ́ТНЫЕ ОЧКИ́). To be on the safe side though, bring you own towel and soap (МЫ́ЛО).

Massage

In most sport health centers you will find saunas where you can order a massage (МАССА́Ж). The masseurs (МАССАЖИ́СТЫ) and masseuses (МАССАЖИ́СТКИ) are real professionals. But be prepared, Russian massages are as invigorating as they are relaxing!

Some of these centers have a small buffet area. There you will find snacks (ЗАКУ́СКИ), drinks (НАПИ́ТКИ) and sometimes beer (ПИ́ВО).

128

Other Fitness Centers

In the middle of the cities you will always be able to find fitness centers. These are smaller than the sport health centers but offer many of the same services. Here you will be able to take aerobics classes, enjoy the sauna, lift weights, indulge in a massage, and practice different forms of the martial arts.

Outside the Stadiums and Health Centers

You need not go to these designated facilities to find a game of soccer or volleyball. Soccer, volleyball and frisbee are played on all of the beaches (ПЛЯЖИ). A warning: if you are out to sunbathe, pick a spot not too near an ongoing soccer match. Although it may be a joy to watch, you may find yourself participating too often when you would rather not. In addition to the beaches, there are soccer balls (ФУТБÓЛЬНЫЕ МЯЧЍ) flying to and fro in the streets, parks, school yards, fields and woods.

Swimming (ПЛÁВАНИЕ) is another popular sport. If you cannot make it to the beach but would like to take a dip, go to a sport health center or visit a public pool. Some public pools, even the ones outdoors, are open year-round and have very long hours.

Bicycles (ВЕЛОСИПÉДЫ) can be rented from facilities called "ПУ́НКТЫ ПРОКÁТА" for an hour or a week or any period in between. Unfortunately, there are no designated bike paths along the roads, so you should stick to cycling in the parks if you are in a large city.

Winter Sports

Winters are long in this northern land but the activity never stops during these cold spells. In fact, many Russians thrive on the bitter cold and display this love for low temperatures by bathing outdoors in icy waters! (НЫРЯ́НИЕ В ПРÓРУБЬ) If this is not your idea of enjoying the cold, skiing (КАТÁНИЕ НА ЛЫ́ЖАХ) (cross country and slalom) and sledding (КАТА́НИЕ НА СА́НКАХ) may be more up your alley. Slalom (СЛА́ЛОМ) or downhill is best in the Northern Caucasus at the resorts Dambai and Terinkol of the Preelbrus Mountains. All equipment can be rented. You can make arrangements for a tour there through Intourist or other tourist bureaus (ТУРИ́СТСКИЕ БЮРО́). Cross country skiing is very popular and you need not travel to far away mountains to enjoy it. Rental offices (ПУ́НКТЫ ПРОКА́ТА) offer skis (ЛЫ́ЖИ), boots (БОТИ́НКИ) and poles (ПА́ЛКИ) as well as other sporting equipment (СПОРТИ́ВНЫЙ ИНВЕНТА́РЬ). Another spectator sport, or one you may choose to participate in if your are extremely hearty, is the ice swimming competition (СОРЕВНОВА́НИЕ ПО ЗИ́МНЕМУ ПЛА́ВАНИЮ). Miraculously enough, most of the competitors are women!

Hunting and Fishing

Both hunting and fishing are permitted in Russia with restrictions. There is really no place to rent out fishing tackle (РЫ́БНЫЕ СНА́СТИ) but you can buy any equipment you need at a fish tackle store where you will find poles (У́ДОЧКИ) and bait (НАЖИ́ВКА). Hunting trips (ПОЕ́ЗДКИ НА ОХО́ТУ) can be arranged through Intourist. The game is usually deer (ОЛЕ́НЬ) but who knows, you may get yourself a Russian bear! (МЕДВЕ́ДЬ)

We wish those who are in a hunting fever to return with a good bag
(С ПО́ЛНОЙ СУМКОЙ).

If you are a fisherman for hobby, these words should ring a bell:
fishing РЫ́БНАЯ ЛО́ВЛЯ
poles У́ДОЧКИ
bait НАЖИ́ВКА
May you return with a good bag! С ХОРО́ШИМ УЛО́ВОМ!

Spectator Sports

The three most popular spectator sports in Russia are soccer (ФУТБÓЛ), ice hockey (ХОККÉЙ) and figure skating (ФИГУ́РНОЕ КАТÁНИЕ). Soccer and ice hockey matches (ФУТБÓЛЬНЫЕ И ХОККÉЙНЫЕ МÁТЧИ) are held at the Olympic stadiums. The soccer season lasts from late March to October and the ice hockey season goes from November through March. Figure skating (ФИГУ́РНОЕ КАТÁНИЕ) is held in special sport complexes during the winter months. Sports events (СПОРТИ́ВНЫЕ НÓВОСТИ) are listed on the back page of local newspapers. You reserve and pick up tickets at the ticket office (СПОРТИ́ВНАЯ КÁССА) before the event. These СПОРТИ́ВНЫЕ КÁССЫ are located at the olympic stadiums. You should reserve tickets (ЗАКАЗÁТЬ БИЛÉТЫ) a few days in advance. When other countries' teams come to visit and play against the national team it is almost impossible to get tickets. Check with ИНТУРИ́СТ or СПУ́ТНИК to see if you can get tickets through them. The lines in front of the cashier's window for tickets to international games are not only long but can also be quite unpleasant due to pushing and shoving by those desperate for tickets.

Stadium Etiquette

There is some stadium etiquette you should be aware of before going to a game. First of all, unlike in America, you do not whistle when cheering for your team; whistling is considered a negative gesture such as booing. Cheering (ВООДУШЕВЛÉНИЕ), clapping (АПЛО- ДИСМÉНТЫ) and chanting "bravo" (БРÁВО!) are most common. Climbing through people to get in and out of your seat is considered very impolite.

Once you sit down, try to stay there until the breaks (ПЕРЕ- РЫ́В). People do not usually leave their seats during the matches because food is only sold during the breaks at the "БУФÉТ".

131

The Dative Case

The expression СОРЕВНОВА́НИЕ ПО (competition in) requires the DATIVE. The dative can be used with or without prepositions. It denotes the person or object to or for whom/which the action is performed. The preposition "ПО" (in) in this case denotes the cause of action:

СОРЕВНОВА́НИЕ ПО ПЛА́ВАНИЮ (neut.)
СОРЕВНОВА́НИЕ ПО БО́КСУ (masc.)
СОРЕВНОВА́НИЕ ПО ГРЕ́БЛЕ (fem.)

The endings of the masculine and neuter dative are: –У, –Ю:

ПО ВОЛЕЙБО́ЛУ (masc.)
ПО ХОККЕ́Ю (masc.)
ПО КАТА́НИЮ (neut.)

The ending of the feminine dative is: –Е:

ПО ГРЕ́БЛЕ
ПО ГИМНА́СТИКЕ
ПО АТЛЕ́ТИКЕ

Other examples of the use of the dative with the preposition "ПО":

ВЫСТУПЛЕ́НИЯ ПО ФИГУ́РНОМУ КАТА́НИЮ (neut.)
ТРАНСЛИ́РУЕТСЯ ПО ТЕЛЕВИЗОРУ (masc.)
СООБЩИ́ТЬ ПО ТЕЛЕФО́НУ
But: ТРАНСЛИ́РУЕТСЯ ПО РА́ДИО (neut.) (does not change its form like many other foreign words in О such as: ПАЛЬТО́, МЕТРО́)

Besides ПО, the other prepositions which take the dative are as follows:

1. "К" (denotes movement towards and addition to something):

go to the doctor ИДТИ́ К ВРАЧУ́ (masc.)

stick a stamp on an envelope ПРИКЛЕ́ИТЬ МА́РКУ К КОНВЕ́РТУ (masc.)

2. "БЛАГОДАРЯ" (thanks to"):
thanks to the help of БЛАГОДАРЯ́ ПО́МОЩИ (fem.)

3. "ВОПРЕКИ́" (against, in spite of): against the advice ВОПРЕКИ́ СОВЕ́ТУ (masc.)

Use of the Dative without Prepositions:

ДАТЬ СЕСТРЕ́ (femin.), БРА́ТУ (masc.) give to sister, brother
ПОМОГА́ТЬ НАСЕЛЕ́НИЮ (neut.) help people
СКАЗА́ТЬ ДРУ́ГУ (masc.) say to the friend
ПИСА́ТЬ МА́МЕ write to mother

The dative without the prepositions is widely used in the impersonal expressions. The dative denotes the person who experiences some need or feelings:

I need МНЕ НУ́ЖНО (the dative from I)
I may МНЕ МО́ЖНО
I must not МНЕ НЕЛЬЗЯ́

I need rest. МНЕ НУ́ЖНО ОТДОХНУ́ТЬ.
May I rest here? МОГУ́ Я ЗДЕСЬ ОТДОХНУ́ТЬ?

МНЕ is the dative of the first personal pronoun Я (I).
НАМ is the dative of the first personal pronoun МЫ (we).
ТЕБЕ́ is the dative of the second personal pronoun ТЫ (you, sing.).
ВАМ is the dative of the second personal pronoun ВЫ (you, the plur. and the polite forms).

The dative masculine and neuter from the third person ОН and ОНО is ЕМУ́.

133

The dative feminine of OHA is ЕЙ.
The dative plural of ОНЍ (they) is ИМ.

You already know the expression "I don't feel well." МНЕ
ПЛÓХО.
The impersonal expressions take the dative case:

МНЕ СКУ́ЧНО. I am bored.
МНЕ ГРУ́СТНО. I am sad.

These two lines sounds almost like the first lines of one of
Lermontov's poems:

И СКУ́ЧНО, И ГРУ́СТНО
И НÉКОМУ РУ́КУ ПОДА́ТЬ

I am bored, I am sad,
And nobody is near
to whom I can give my hand

Here the personal pronoun in dative "МНЕ" is ommited.

But in another poem the expression "МНЕ ГРУ́СТНО" ("I am
sad") is given in full:

МНЕ ГРУ́СТНО ОТТОГÓ,
ЧТО ВÉСЕЛО ТЕБÉ.

I am sad
Because you feel merry.

Ear training:

Contemporary literary norms of pronunciation in Russian
language which are based on the Moscow pronunciation requires that
the combination -ЧН should sound like -ШН: КОНÉЧНО, СКУ́ЧНО.
People from Petersburg incline to keep -ЧН in their pronunciation.

Whenever you want to talk about the age of a person in Russian, you use the dative.

Answer the question: How old are you? (the sing. polite form)
СКОЛЬКО ВАМ ЛЕТ?

МНЕ 18 ЛЕТ.
МНЕ 20 ЛЕТ.

СКОЛЬКО ТЕБЕ́ ЛЕТ?
МНЕ 12 ЛЕТ.

How old is he?
СКОЛЬКО ЕМУ́ ЛЕТ?
ЕМУ́ 19 ЛЕТ.

How old is she?
СКОЛЬКО ЕЙ ЛЕТ?
ЕЙ ТО́ЖЕ 19 ЛЕТ.

How old is your sister?
СКОЛЬКО ЛЕТ ТВОЕ́Й СЕСТРЕ́?
МОЕ́Й СЕСТРЕ́ 12 ЛЕТ.

How old is your brother?
СКОЛЬКО ЛЕТ ТВОЕМУ́ БРА́ТУ?
МОЕМУ́ БРА́ТУ 6 ЛЕТ.

Note that the word лет is the genitive plural of ЛЕ́ТО (summer).

The Coming of Spring

Although Russians take advantage of the bitterly cold winter months as best they can, they do celebrate the coming of spring o r МА́СЛЕНИЦА. It is celebrated one week before Lent and meant as a preparation of this event. On the last day of the МА́СЛЕНИЦА, people go to the parks to listen to free concerts, sled (КАТА́ЮТСЯ НА САНЯ́Х) and stroll (ПРОГУ́ЛИВАЮТСЯ). There, warm crepes or "БЛИНЫ́" are sold. It is an active day that brings to life everyone who was hibernating for the winter.

Russian Bathhouses

The БАНЯ—a Russian tradition that must not be missed! The Russian bathhouses are special in many respects. Here people come to relax, meet with friends, spend an enjoyable weekend afternoon indulging in baths and saunas and invigorating birch branch (БЕРЁЗОВЫЕ ВЕ́НИКИ) slappings as well as massage. It's a place many go to increase their resistance to diseases and sickness. You will find them unique and lots of fun and will hear the most interesting tales. Here not only do your pores open up but true emotions and feelings come out as well. Politics, problems of daily living, and adventure stories are popular topics of discussion.

The bathhouse has four sections:

1. the "ДУШЕ́ВАЯ КАБИ́НА" or shower cabinet
2. the "О́БЩЕЕ ОТДЕ́ЛЕНИЕ" or the basic facility.
3. the "О́БЩЕЕ ОТДЕ́ЛЕНИЕ С БАССЕ́ЙНОМ" or the basic with a pool
4. the "ЛЮКС" or the deluxe.

You should buy your ticket or make reservations ahead of time especially for the ЛЮКС and the ОБЩЕЕ ОТДЕ́ЛЕНИЕ С БАССЕ́ЙНОМ. As you enter the bathhouse, you tell the administrator which facilities you would like to use or if you have a reservation. The prices for all of the above are different. The ДУШЕВА́Я КАБИ́НА is simply an individual shower and changing space. The О́БЩЕЕ ОТДЕЛЕ́НИЕ has a changing area (РАЗДЕВА́ЛКА), a Russian sauna (РУ́ССКАЯ СА́УНА), a Finnish sauna (ФИ́НСКАЯ СА́УНА), a relaxation room (КО́МНАТА О́ТДЫХА), and a shower area (ДУШЕВО́Е ОТДЕ́ЛЕНИЕ).

The key to this facility is the Russian bath. This is a very humid and hot room where you use your birch branch to slap yourself all over. It sure does get the blood circulating! The Finnish sauna (ФИ́НСКАЯ СА́УНА) is a hot version of the American sauna (АМЕРИКА́НСКАЯ СА́УНА). Because of the extreme heat you will need your sheet, flip flops, and your cap. After this experience you will make your way into the resting room (КО́МНАТА О́ТДЫХА). Here people recuperate from the baths. All rooms are separate for men and women. There is no bar (БАР) or cafe (КАФÉ) available but you may bring your own snacks.

In the О́БЩЕЕ ОТДÉЛЕНИЕ С БАССЕЙНОМ, you have the extra of a swimming pool. Here men and women swim together. It also often has a bar where they serve beer (ПИ́ВО), snacks (ЗАКУ́СКИ), tea (ЧАЙ) and coffee (КО́ФЕ) and juice (СОК).

The ЛЮКС is rented out to small groups of 3, 6 or 7. The same facilities are provided and even a small private pool is included. Here there is no bar but you may bring your own snacks and non-alcoholic drinks (БЕЗАЛКОГО́ЛЬНЫЕ НАПИ́ТКИ).

Be sure to visit a БА́НЯ. You will be happy you did. The memories will be with you for a long time.

Some expressions:

give a massage ДÉЛАТЬ МАССА́Ж
go to the public baths ПОЙТИ́ В БА́НЮ
wash oneself МЫ́ТЬСЯ
wash oneself in the public baths ПОМЫ́ТЬСЯ В БА́НЕ
take a shower ПРИНЯ́ТЬ ДУШ
slap oneself all over with a birch branch ХЛЕСТА́ТЬ БЕ-РЁЗОВЫМ ВÉНИКОМ

Resorts

The "САНАТÓРИИ" and "ПРОФИЛАКТÓРИИ" were originally only available to the sick and needy. Today, through Intourist, foreigners are able to take advantage of many these facilities in hotel resorts. Through these hotels you can enjoy horseback riding, mineral baths, mud baths, massages, scuba diving and water skiing. Of course, the hotels do demand hard currency but it may very well be worth it. Check with Intourist for information on the different resorts.

Add to your vocabulary these words of leisure and pleasure:
КАТÁНИЕ НА ЛОШАДЯ́Х - horseback riding
МИНЕРÁЛЬНЫЕ ВÓДЫ - mineral water
ГРЯЗЕВЬ́Е ВÁННЫ - mud baths
ВÓДНЫЕ ЛЬ́ЖИ- water skiing

New Expressions:

play a sport
ЗАНИМÁТЬСЯ СПÓРТОМ

track and field
ЛЁГКАЯ АТЛÉТИКА

go water skiing
КАТÁТЬСЯ НА ВÓДНЫХ ЛЬ́ЖАХ

ride a bike
КАТÁТЬСЯ НА ВЕЛОСИПÉДЕ

relax at the resort
ОТДЫХÁТЬ НА КУРÓРТЕ

take a mud bath
ПРИНИМÁТЬ ГРЯЗЕВЬ́Е ВÁННЫ

138

So travelers, do not forget your gym shoes and bathing suits and have a good time!

Remember:

В ЗДОРО́ВОМ ТЕ́ЛЕ ЗДОРО́ВЫЙ ДУХ!
Mens sana in corpore sano (Lat.)
Healthy body, healthy mind.

CHAPTER NINE

SHOP SMART!

Some cognates you may find at Russian stores:

СУВЕНИ́Р
И́МПОРТ
ЭКСПОРТ
САМОВА́Р
ВО́ДКА
БАЛАЛА́ЙКА
ВИ́ДЕО
КО́ФЕ

From reading the newspapers and hearing about the endless lines in front of shops in Russia, you may have written shopping out of your itinerary. But remember, the scenes pictured in the Western papers depict the difficulties of the Russian citizens, not the foreign visitor. With dollars in hand, and very different shopping intentions, you will not find yourself in the same predicament as the Russian consumer. You will discover the dynamic markets and innovative cooperatives abundant with different foods and the fabulous treasures. Shopping is also a fantastic way to interact with Russian people, to observe daily life and become a part of it too. This chapter will give you some pointers on shopping in Russia which should make it less confusing.

What to Buy?

You may be wondering what kind of souvenirs to bring home from Russia. Or you may already have a list of requests from family and friends ranging from black caviar (ЧЁРНАЯ ИКРА́) to amber earrings (ЯНТА́РНЫЕ СЕ́РЬГИ).

In any case keep the following items in mind when shopping. Black caviar, a delicacy all around the world, is a good buy in Russia. Sometimes it is difficult to find outside of the hard currency shops. Fur hats (МЕХОВЫ́Е ША́ПКИ) are a favorite of young and old Russians alike. You may have thought that they are worn only in the movies. But if you spend any time in Russia in the winter, you will see that fur hats are a staple needed for these cold months.

On the more artistic side is the guitar (ГИТА́РА) or balalaika. The БАЛАЛА́ЙКА is a Russian national three-stringed instrument. If you do get inspired to buy one and get it home somehow, don't forget instructions on how to use it and sheet music as well.

Children's books are delightful and the illustrations fantastic. Even if you don't read Russian the pictures make them worth buying. Posters (ПЛАКА́ТЫ), reproductions (РЕПРОДУ́КЦИИ), and maps (КА́РТЫ) make good gifts.

Probably the most common gift is the matroyshka doll. These are the colorful wooden dolls that fit one inside the other, inside the other, inside the other.... Cloth dolls portraying a variety of nationalities are also good gifts.

141

Samovars are bulky but make a unique addition to any Western household. Lacquer boxes are also quite popular. Palekh (ПА́ЛЕХ) and Mstera (МСТЁРА) lacquer boxes are the finest kind, but beware the many Mstera and Palekh pretenders! Embroidered shawls (КРУЖЕВНЫ́Е ША́ЛИ) and table cloths (СКА́ТЕРТИ) are nice gifts, as are chess sets. Jewelry made with precious and semi-precious stones and amber (ИЗДЕ́ЛИЯ ИЗ ДРАГОЦЕ́ННЫХ И ПОЛУДРАГОЦЕ́ННЫХ КАМНЕ́Й И ЯНТАРЯ́) is also a wonderful purchase.

Five Ways to Buy!

Changes in Russia have been tremendous over the past ten years and nowhere is it more evident than in the shopping sphere. The introduction of the ideas of profits and competition into Russian society has made for a variety of shopping options. But not all of the ideas of Western competition have taken hold yet. You will probably still find that the salespeople in most stores, especially the state stores, veer far from the American stereotype of the used car salesman. If you inquire about an item and it is not visible from the salesperson's seat, they probably "don't have it." Do not expect salespeople to get out of their seat for the sake of searching for an item for you. State stores are not run on a commission basis and you will find that the markets and cooperatives are more Western in this regard. The more they sell the more money they make.

There are five types of stores you should be aware of:

"Beriozkas" Магазины "БЕРЁЗКА"
Department stores УНИВЕРМА́ГИ
Co-op stores КООПЕРАТИ́ВНЫЕ МАГАЗИ́НЫ
Markets РЫ́НКИ
Street trade ТОРГО́ВЛЯ НА У́ЛИЦЕ

Beriozkas

The "Beriozka," which literally means birch tree, is the hard currency shop (ВАЛЮТНЫЙ МАГАЗИ́Н) where you will inevitably end up spending some of your dollars. Some "Beriozkas" sell only souvenirs, records (ПЛАСТИ́НКИ), jewelry (ЮВЕЛИ́РНЫЕ ИЗДЕ́ЛИЯ) or food items (ПРОДУ́КТЫ) while others sell the above plus dishwashers, video recorders, fur coats and much more. You will often find your essentials there: razors, camera parts and beer. You will also find a large variety of very high quality gifts (ПОДА́РКИ): lacquer boxes and trays, matryoshka dolls and amber jewelry. Because many of these items can be found in other ruble stores and markets and cooperatives, it is a good idea to shop around. Items such as jewelry, embroidered shirts and shawls can be found in ruble stores. Nevertheless some very special items can only be found in the "Beriozkas." Cash, credit cards and travelers checks are all accepted. Another plus is that at the "Beriozkas" most of the sales people speak some English. Most Intourist hotels have their own "Beriozkas;" others are scattered throughout the city usually near large, Intourist hotels. "Beriozkas" are usually open all day, even on Sundays.

Department Stores

Here the adventure begins! Now that you have left the comfort of the "Beriozka", it's time to move on to the jungle of state stores. Your trips to the state stores, especially the large department stores, will be more of a social experience than anything else. Here you will see the dwellers of the city at their best, determined to get a piece of that scarce item that will be gone in a matter of hours. Department stores are called УНИВЕРМА́ГИ. The main one in Moscow is ГУМ; in St. Petersburg it is "ГОСТИ́НЫЙ ДВОР". Here you will find everything from dishes (ТАРЕ́ЛКИ) to socks (НОСКИ́), to toys (ИГРУ́ШКИ). Besides the department stores, visit the bookstores (КНИ́ЖНЫЕ МАГАЗИ́НЫ), record stores (МАГАЗИ́НЫ ПЛАСТИ́НОК) and souvenir shops (МАГАЗИНЫ "СУВЕНИ́РЫ"). A very curious and fun store is the huge "Childrens' World" ("ДЕ́ТСКИЙ МИР") in Moscow.

State run food stores are either almost empty or have lines in front of them. The grocery store is called "ГАСТРОНО́М". Russian food stores are not large or well stocked and usually have only meat (МЯ́СО), bread (ХЛЕБ), and cheese (СЫР). Univermags (УНИВЕРМА́ГИ) sell food ("ПРОДУ́КТЫ") and wine ("ВИНО́") and may run on a self-service system (САМООБ-СЛУ́ЖИВАНИЕ). There are also smaller shops that sell specific items usually named after what is sold there, for instance: dairy ("МОЛОКО́"), meat ("МЯ́СО"), and bread ("ХЛЕБ").

Although there are self-service shops such as УНИВЕР-СА́МЫ, most state-run stores including the department stores operate on a system of tickets. You will feel like you are forever standing in lines, which you will, in actuality, be doing. Your first line will be to select the item. Tell the salesperson behind the counter what you would like. He or she will write you a bill (ТОВА́РНЫЙ ЧЕК) for the item which you will then take to the cashier (КАССИ́Р). There you give the cashier your slip and tell the number of the department (ОТДЕ́Л) the item comes from and pay for it. The cashier then gives you a receipt (ЧЕК) which you will take back to the salesperson, who will give you your purchase. It is very common to save places in lines for others.

One more thing to note about the state stores—no free bags! You must buy it or bring your own. But once again, even for this bag you will have to go through the three line process again. For the tourist, however this adventure can be quite amusing and educational; a chance to learn firsthand how the system works. By the way, don't take it personally if the salespeople are not amused by your intrigue or curiosity. There is little that amuses them at all.

The following describes a typical scene in a state store:
Since often the sales ladies are young women one may address them with the general term: "Де́вушка."

An unlucky day:

A. Madam, please show me this box.
ДЕ́ВУШКА! ПОКАЖИ́ТЕ МНЕ, ПОЖА́ЛУЙСТА, ЭТУ ШКАТУ́ЛКУ.

B. Wait a minute. Can't you see that I'm busy?
ПОДОЖДИ́ТЕ. НЕ ВИ́ДИТЕ, Я ЗАНЯТА́?

A. Excuse me but it's now my turn in line.
ПРОСТИ́ТЕ, НО СЕЙЧА́С МОЯ О́ЧЕРЕДЬ.

B. So what? I need to place the products in order. When I will finish placing them in order, then I'll show it to you.
НУ И ЧТО? МНЕ НУ́ЖНО РАЗЛОЖИ́ТЬ ТОВА́Р. ВОТ КО́НЧУ РАСКЛА́ДЫВАТЬ, ТОГДА ПОКАЖУ́.

A. But I'm in a hurry.
НО Я СПЕШУ́.

B. Everybody is in a hurry. You are not the only one.
ВСЕ СПЕША́Т. НЕ ВЫ ОДНА́ (ОДИ́Н).

A. But it won't be long. Give me the box and then you can continue placing the products around.
НО ЭТО ЖЕ НЕДО́ЛГО. ДА́ЙТЕ МНЕ ШКАТУ́ЛКУ И РАСКЛА́ДЫВАЙТЕ ТОВА́Р.

B. (Keeps placing the products around.)

A. But I don't have any time to wait.
НО У МЕНЯ́ НЕТ ВРЕ́МЕНИ ЖДАТЬ.

145

B. You're giving me a headache. Here is your box. Well, are you taking it? Wait, I'll write out a bill for you. Pay at the cash register.

У МЕНЯ́ ГОЛОВА́ ОТ ВАС РАЗБОЛЕ́ЛАСЬ. ВОТ ВАМ ВА́ША ШКАТУ́ЛКА. НУ, БЕРЁТЕ? ПОДОЖДИ́ТЕ, СЕЙЧА́С ЧЕК ВЫ́ПИШУ. ПЛАТИ́ТЕ В КА́ССУ.

An even more unlucky day:

A. Madam! Please show me that box.
ДЕ́ВУШКА! ПОКАЖИ́ТЕ МНЕ, ПОЖА́ЛУЙСТА, ЭТУ ШКАТУ́ЛКУ.

B. Which box?
КАКУ́Ю ШКАТУ́ЛКУ?

A. That one, Palekh.
ВОТ ЭТУ, ПА́ЛЕХСКУЮ.

B. That' s not for sale. It's the last one.
ЭТА НЕ ПРОДАЁТСЯ. ОНА́ ПОСЛЕ́ДНЯЯ.

A. Can I speak to the person in charge?
МО́ЖНО ПОГОВОРИ́ТЬ С ЗАВЕ́ДУЮЩИМ?

B. The person in charge isn't here today.
ЗАВЕ́ДУЮЩЕГО СЕГО́ДНЯ НЕТ.

A. Who is taking his place?
А ВМЕ́СТО НЕГО́ КТО?

B. I am replacing him.
ВМЕ́СТО НЕГО́ Я.

A lucky day:

A. Madam! Show me that box please.
ДЕ́ВУШКА! ПОКАЖИ́ТЕ МНЕ, ПОЖА́ЛУЙСТА, ШКАТУ́ЛКУ.

B. Which one do you want? Palekh?
ВАМ КАКУ́Ю? ПА́ЛЕХСКУЮ?

A. Yes, yes, Give me the Palekh box please. That one.
ДА-ДА, МНЕ ПА́ЛЕХСКУЮ, ПОЖА́ЛУЙСТА. ВОТ Э́ТУ.

B. I also like this one. It's fine handicraft. Take it. Tomorrow they might all be sold out. Are you taking it? Wait a minute, I will write out a bill for you. Please pay at that cash register.
МНЕ Э́ТА ТО́ЖЕ НРА́ВИТСЯ. ХОРО́ШАЯ РАБО́ТА. БЕРИ́ТЕ. ЗА́ВТРА ИХ УЖЕ́ НЕ БУ́ДЕТ. ВОЗЬМЁТЕ? ПОДОЖДИ́ТЕ, Я ВАМ СЕЙЧА́С ЕЁ ВЫ́ПИШУ. ПЛАТИ́ТЕ, ПОЖА́ЛУЙСТА, ВОН В ТУ КА́ССУ.

The Commision and Antique Stores

The Commision stores (КОМИССИО́ННЫЕ МАГАЗИ́НЫ) sell things from abroad and things from the state stores that were not sold there. In the antique stores (АНТИКВА́РНЫЕ МАГАЗИ́НЫ) you will find, among other things, crystal (ХРУСТА́ЛЬ), jewelry, samovars, and furniture (МЕ́БЕЛЬ). In order to export items bought at the antique stores a special declaration must be obtained from the store and a large duty is levied.

Store Hours

State store hours vary. Usually they open at 10 or 11 am and close at 7 pm. Grocery stores and some other individual food stores usually open earlier in the morning. Most people take a lunch break between 1 and 2 p. m. or 3 and 4 p. m. when the stores will be closed. But if you go right after the official lunch hour (ОБÉДЕННЫЙ ПЕРЕРЫ́В) you may wait an extra 20 minutes until someone actually returns and opens up shop again. УНИВЕРМÁГИ are open from 9 am and do not close for lunch. Some food shops are the only ones that remain open on Sundays.

Co-op Stores

An increasing number of cooperatives are opening up all over the country. Most Western joint ventures (СОВМÉСТНЫЕ ПРЕДПРИЯ́ТИЯ) are still concentrated in Moscow and St. Petersburg. There are ruble and dollar (or Western joint ventures) cooperatives including Stockmann's Grocery Store, a Finnish-Russian joint venture which accepts payment only by credit card. Stockmann's sells all sorts of food items as well as cleaning supplies and knickknacks. A second popular grocery store cooperative is Sadko, a Swiss-Russian joint venture also in Moscow. Unlike Stockmann's, it accepts cash and is therefore often crowded. Do beware, pick-pocketing has been known to occur there. If the "Beriozkas" don't have what you are looking for, try the joint venture co-ops.

The more typical cooperatives are the ruble cooperatives which have been around now for quite some time. Many of these sell original crafts. Others sell more useful items that are difficult to find in state stores. For Russians the prices charged at cooperatives are rather high but for foreigners they will be more than reasonable.

Markets

As are most markets all over the world, the Russian markets (РЫ́НКИ) are very busy and well stocked. Here you will find quality fruits (ФРУ́КТЫ), vegetables (О́ВОЩИ), meats (МЯ́СО), dairy products (МОЛО́ЧНЫЕ ПРОДУ́КТЫ) and anything that can be grown on a farm. Products are sold for rubles, but their high prices put them beyond the reach of many Russians. Crafts and toys, hand knit and woven items and quality souvenirs are also sold at the markets. Over the years the markets have been growing due to the legalization of more private farming. In every city you will now find a number of booming markets.

Markets are usually open all day and close around 6 p. m. It is best to get there early for the better products.

Buying Flowers and Art Work on the Street

More now than ever, the streets of Russia have opened themselves to all sorts of selling and buying activity. Most notable for any visitor are the beautiful flowers sold on the streets. Russians love flowers and most Russian homes are never without them. There are state run flower shops (ЦВЕТÓЧНЫЕ МАГАЗЙНЫ), but most flowers sold on the streets today are sold by flower cooperatives so the prices will vary a great deal. You can often bargain for flowers.

You will often be surprised at the beautiful and imaginative works of art that you will pass while strolling down НÉВСКИЙ ПРОСПÉКТ in St. Petersburg or elsewhere. Naturally, the artists prefer dollars for their works, but usually will also sell them for rubles.

Shopping Basics

In Russia just a few years ago, your clothes shopping would probably have been limited to the necessities. You would most likely want to pick up an ethnic costume or a fuzzy fur hat or a beautiful shawl. But today, with the development of a strong entrepreneurial spirit, it is possible to put together a stylish and complete Russian wardrobe. The t-shirts sold in cooperatives are especially creative and definitely worth buying.

Sizes in Russia conform in most cases to the European sizes, using the metric system for measuring units. In the United States there are different scales for women's, men's and children's sizes, but in Russia there is only one scale which is used for everyone. All shoes are measured in centimeters.

The following is a list of size equivalencies:

Men shoes:

US sizes:	Russian equivalent:
5	36
6	37
7	38
8	39
9	40
10	41
11	42
12	43
13	44
14	45
15	46

Women and children should simply try to judge from the above table their approximate sizes. For example, a woman who wears a nine will wear about a 7 in mens and in turn a size 40.5 by Russian standards. A child who wears a children's size 2 should try a size 18 on in Russia. A child's size 8 in the United States would be about 24.

Before going for shopping for clothes you have to check the Russian CLOTHING SIZES (РАЗМЕРЫ ОДЕЖДЫ).

The following list will give you at least a reference point from which you will be able to approximate your own size for some articles of clothing:

Shirt collars:

US = 14   Russian = 36
US = 15   Russian = 38
US = 16.5 Russian = 42
US = 17.5 Russian = 44

Dresses:

US = 8   Russian = 40
US = 10   Russian = 42
US = 12   Russian = 44

Slacks:

US = 33   Russian = 44
US = 34   Russian = 46

Useful expressions:

go shopping ИДТИ́ В МАГАЗИ́Н

Do you sell. . . here? У ВАС ПРОДАЁТСЯ (У ВАС ЕСТЬ. . .)?

How much does it cost? СКО́ЛЬКО СТО́ИТ. . .?

What are your hours? КОГДА́ ВЫ РАБО́ТАЕТЕ?

I need. . . МНЕ НУ́ЖНО...
Have you got any. . . НЕТ ЛИ У ВАС?

I want to look at some. . . Я ХОТЕ́Л(А) БЫ ПОСМОТРЕ́ТЬ . . .

I want to buy Я ХОТЕ́Л(А) БЫ КУПИ́ТЬ. . .
I want size number МНЕ НУ́ЖЕН. . . РАЗМЕ́Р

May I try this on? МО́ЖНО ПРИМЕ́РИТЬ?
Please bring me the other size. ДА́ЙТЕ МНЕ, ПОЖА́ЛУЙСТА, ДРУГО́Й РАЗМЕ́Р.

What else do you have? ЧТО ЕЩЁ ВЫ МО́ЖЕТЕ ПРЕД-ЛОЖИ́ТЬ?

I don't like it. ЭТО МНЕ НЕ НРА́ВИТСЯ.

It does not fit me. ЭТО МНЕ НЕ ИДЁТ.

In Clothing:

Use the pattern:

fem. МНЕ НУЖНА́ РУБА́ШКА. I need a shirt.
neut. МНЕ НУ́ЖНО КАШНЕ́. I need a scarf.
masc. МНЕ НУ́ЖЕН ПИДЖА́К. I need a jacket.
plur. МНЕ НУЖНЫ́ ДЖИ́НСЫ. I need jeans.

I need... МНЕ НУ́ЖНО:

1. coat ПАЛЬТО́ (neuter)
What kind of a coat? КАКО́Е ПАЛЬТО́?

2. dress ПЛА́ТЬЕ
Which one? КАКО́Е ПЛА́ТЬЕ?

3. underwear БЕЛЬЁ
What kind of underwear? КАКО́Е БЕЛЬЁ?

4. scarf КАШНЕ́
Which one? КАКО́Е КАШНЕ́?

I need... МНЕ НУ́ЖЕН:

1. raincoat ПЛАЩ (masc.)
What kind of raincoat? КАКО́Й ПЛАЩ?

2. suit КОСТЮ́М
What kind of a suit? КАКО́Й КОСТЮ́М?

3. jacket ПИДЖА́К
What kind of a jacket? КАКО́Й ПИДЖА́К?

4. sweater СВИ́ТЕР
What kind of a sweater? КАКО́Й СВИ́ТЕР?

5. tie ГА́ЛСТУК
What kind of tie? КАКО́Й ГА́ЛСТУК?

6. scarf ШАРФ
What kind of a scarf? КАКО́Й ШАРФ?

7. handkerchief НОСОВО́Й ПЛАТО́К
Which one? КАКО́Й НОСОВО́Й ПЛАТО́К?

I need... МНЕ НУЖНА́:

1. jacket КУ́РТКА
What kind of a jacket? КАКА́Я КУ́РТКА?

2. hat ШЛЯ́ПА
What kind of a hat? КАКА́Я ШЛЯ́ПА?

3. cap ФУРА́ЖКА
What kind of a cap? КАКА́Я ФУРА́ЖКА?

4. hat ША́ПКА
What kind of a hat? КАКА́Я ША́ПКА?

5. skirt ЮБКА
What kind of a skirt? КАКА́Я ЮБКА?

6. blouse БЛУ́ЗКА
What kind of a blouse? КАКА́Я БЛУ́ЗКА?

7. shirt РУБА́ШКА
What kind of shirt? КАКА́Я РУБА́ШКА?

8. nightgown НОЧНА́Я РУБА́ШКА
What kind of a nightgown? КАКА́Я НОЧНА́Я РУБА́ШКА?

8. pajamas ПИЖА́МА
What kind of pajamas? КАКА́Я ПИЖА́МА?

I need... МНЕ НУЖНЫ́:

1. trousers БРЮКИ
What kind of trousers? КАКИ́Е БРЮКИ?

2. shorts ТРУСЫ́
Which ones?

4. socks НОСКИ́
Which ones? КАКИ́Е НОСКИ́?

5. stockings ЧУЛКИ́
What kind of stockings? КАКИ́Е ЧУЛКИ́?

6. gloves ПЕРЧА́ТКИ
Which ones? КАКИ́Е ПЕРЧА́ТКИ?

Now choose the matching adjective from this list for the nouns:

winter ЗИ́МНИЙ
autumn ОСЕ́ННИЙ

summer ЛЕ́ТНИЙ
long ДЛИ́ННЫЙ
sports СПОРТИ́ВНЫЙ
warm ТЁПЛЫЙ
cotton ХЛОПЧА́ТОБУМА́ЖНЫЙ
flannel ФЛАНЕ́ЛЕВЫЙ
wool ШЕРСТЯНО́Й
knitted ТРИКОТА́ЖЫЙ
silk ШЁЛКОВЫЙ
linen ЛЬНЯНО́Й
synthetic СИНТЕТИ́ЧЕСКИЙ
nylon НЕЙЛО́НОВЫЙ
evening ВЕЧЕ́РНИЙ
light СВЕ́ТЛЫЙ
dark ТЁМНЫЙ
black ЧЁРНЫЙ
short КОРО́ТКИЙ
narrow У́ЗКИЙ
straight ПРЯМОЙ
polyester ПОЛИСТЕ́РОВЫЙ
plain СТРО́ГИЙ
white БЕ́ЛЫЙ
colored ЦВЕТНОЙ
checked КЛЕ́ТЧАТЫЙ
fur МЕХОВОЙ
felt ФЕ́ТРОВЫЙ
straw СОЛО́МЕННЫЙ
lace КРУЖЕВНО́Й

Sometimes it is Worth it to Bargain. The Antonyms

There are common antonyms which can be used when you do your shopping: ДО́РОГО expensive – ДЁШЕВО cheap.

ЭТО ДО́РОГО ДЛЯ МЕНЯ́ [éa-ta dó-ro-ga dlya me-nyá].
It is expensive for me.

ЕСТЬ ЛИ У ВАС ЧТО-НИБУ́ДЬ ДЕШЕ́ВЛЕ [yést lii uu vas shto nii-bút' de-shyév-le]?

Do you have something cheaper?

In this example the adverb ДО́РОГО is given in the main form. ДЕШЕ́ВЛЕ is the comparative degree of the adverb ДЁШЕВО. The comparative form of ДО́РОГО is ДОРО́ЖЕ. There is the alternation of consonants Г - Ж which frequently takes place in the Russian language in the formation of the new words.

A Tongue Twister

This is a good exercise in pronunciation of the Russian consonants: Р, П and К. Do not forget that the Russian letters П and Р are pronounced with no respiration, they should sound more sonorous than their American and British counterparts. The Russian pronunciation of Р is rather closer to the Scottish 'R':

РАССКАЖИ́ТЕ ПРО ПОКУ́ПКИ. ПРО КАКИ́Е ПРО ПОКУ́ПКИ? ПРО ПОКУ́ПКИ, ПРО ПОКУ́ПКИ, ПРО ПОКУ́ПОЧКИ МОИ́.

Tell me about your purchases. About what purchases? About the purchases, about the purchases, about the purchases of mine.

CHAPTER TEN

BON APPETIT!

RUSSIAN CUISINE

Practice your gastronomical vocabulary with these cognates. Use these familiar words with no hesitation when you eat in or out:

МЕНЮ
БУЛЬО́Н
СУП
ОМЛЕ́Т
САЛА́Т
ЛИМОНА́Д
ШОКОЛА́Д
КАКА́О
ДЕСЕ́РТ
СЕ́РВИС
КАФЕ́
БУФЕ́Т
РЕСТОРА́Н
БАР

If you ask a Muscovite, "On a special occasion, where do you go to dine in Moscow?", you may get the response "Why, McDonalds!! Where else?"

Don't panic! Just because McDonalds is the latest hot spot in Moscow does not mean that it is the best food available in the city. Russian cuisine can be delicious.

Russian cuisine (РУ́ССКАЯ КУ́ХНЯ) features many unique offerings. Fragrant black bread (ЧЁРНЫЙ ХЛЕБ), high quality black caviar (ЧЁРНАЯ ИКРА́), fresh and sour cabbage soup (СВЕ́ЖИЕ И КИ́СЛЫЕ ЩИ), scrumptious crepes (БЛИНЫ́), and satisfying kvass (КВАС) are some of the traditions you will be exposed to.

Vegetarians (ВЕГЕТАРИА́НЦЫ) may find it difficult to meet their dietary requirements if they do most of their dining in restaurants because meat (МЯ́СО) is a basic staple. And dieters may lose their resolve when confronted with Russian pancakes (БЛИНЫ́) smothered in sour cream (СМЕТА́НА). You won't find weightwatcher sections on any menu.

Over the past few years many cooperatives and Western influences have found a place in the food sector in Russia and are growing rapidly. Chinese restaurants (КИТА́ЙСКИЕ РЕСТОРА́НЫ), American style pizzerias and fast food joints have taken hold in many of the larger cities. Fortunately, these invasions have not completely overrun the country and you will find that the Russians cling to the familiar.

Restaurants

In the past, restaurants were not out to make a profit in Russia. More customers simply meant more work. This attitude was reflected in the service and the hours. Today restaurants must make money to stay in business. However, many of the attitudes and former traditions persist. For example, some restaurants even close for a lunch break (ОБЕ́ДЕННЫЙ ПЕРЕРЫ́В)! Most restaurants close at 11:30 p.m. (23 часа 30 минут European time) and stop admitting diners at 11 p.m. (23 часа).

Cafes close earlier, around 10:00 p.m. (22 часа). For late meals you will be out of luck. There are almost no all-night diners or cafes.

If you are staying at the central hotels, most of your meals will be eaten at the hotel and will be paid for through the package plan. This is not necessarily bad, since some of the best food is found in the hotel restaurants. These restaurants are popular not only because the service and food quality is higher but also because many of them provide a buffet or what is sometimes referred to as the "Sweden table" "ШВЕ́ДСКИЙ СТОЛ". This can be a great relief from playing the guessing game of what on the МЕНЮ is available and what is not.

If you choose to eat out, make reservations (ЗАКАЗА́ТЬ) ahead of time (ПРЕДВАРИ́ТЕЛЬНО) to avoid the tremendously long waits of every cafe and restaurant. If you do not manage to make reservations, try acting foreign and offering a tip to speed up the waiting process.

Dialogue:

A. I want to make a reservation for this evening.
Я ХОЧУ́ ЗАКАЗА́ТЬ НА ВЕ́ЧЕР СТО́ЛИК.

B. All the tables are taken tonight.
НА СЕГО́ДНЯ ВСЕ СТОЛЫ ЗА́НЯТЫ.

A. But I have a very important meeting.
НО У МЕНЯ О́ЧЕНЬ ВА́ЖНАЯ ВСТРЕЧА.

B. Speak to the manager.
ПОГОВОРИ́ТЕ С АДМИНИСТРА́ТОРОМ.

A. I have a very important meeting today. I want to make a reservation for this evening.
У МЕНЯ СЕГО́ДНЯ О́ЧЕНЬ ВА́ЖНАЯ ВСТРЕЧА. Я ХОЧУ́ ЗАКАЗАТЬ НА ВЕ́ЧЕР СТО́ЛИК.

C. You have to make reservations in advance. You are not alone. What time is your appointment?

НÁДО ЗАРÁНЕЕ ЗАКÁЗЫВАТЬ СТÓЛИК. ВЫ ЖЕ НЕ ОДИН! ВО СКОЛЬКО У ВАС СЕГОДНЯ ВСТРЕЧА?

A. At seven o' clock.

В СЕМЬ ЧАСОВ.

C. Come at 6:45, we will try to do something for you.

ПРИХОДИ́ТЕ В 6:45 ПОПРОБУЕМ ДЛЯ ВАС ЧТО-НИБУДЬ СДЕЛАТЬ.

A. But can I be certain that a table will be available? I will not be alone.

НО МОГУ́ ЛИ Я ПОЛАГÁТЬСЯ, ЧТО СТÓЛИК БУ́ДЕТ? Я ЖЕ БУ́ДУ НЕ ОДИ́Н.

C. Don't worry, if I told you to come, the table will be available.

НЕ БЕСПОКÓЙТЕСЬ, ÉСЛИ Я СКАЗÁЛА ПРИХОДИ́ТЕ, СТОЛИ́К БУ́ДЕТ.

A. Thank you.

СПАСИ́БО.

Once in the restaurant, do no expect to gobble down your meal and zip out. Service is often very slow. The whole dining experience is often quite long and the atmosphere rather than the food is the main attraction. Many of the fancy restaurants offer dance, music and Las Vegas type productions. Sometimes there is even a dance floor for dancing to the music of a few live musicians.

If you are taken out to a restaurant by a native of Russia, you will find that eating a meal is more that just a process, it's a communal event that brings people closer together. Lots of toasting is essential. It's a time to savor and enjoy.

A Place Setting

The tables at the restaurants are usually equipped with:
knife НОЖ
fork ВЍЛКА
dinner spoon СТОЛО́ВАЯ ЛО́ЖКА
teaspoon ЧА́ЙНАЯ ЛО́ЖКА
napkin САЛФЕ́ТКА
glass СТАКА́Н
cup ЧА́ШКА
saucer БЛЮ́ДЦЕ
dinner plate ГЛУБО́КАЯ ТАРЕ́ЛКА
dessert plate ДЕСЕ́РТНАЯ ТАРЕ́ЛКА
wine glass РЮ́МКА
glass СТАКА́Н

Once you are seated you will be given a МЕНЮ. Open it only if you want to practice reading in Russian; the items listed often do not reflect the items available. While dozens of entrees (БЛЮ́ДА) may be listed only two or three dishes may be available. Russians never "order" (ЗАКА́ЗЫВАТЬ), they "inquire" (УЗНАВА́ТЬ). Whereas in America you would say, "I'll have the leg of lamb," in Russia you would ask, "Do you have the leg of lamb?" Even more likely you would ask, "What do you have today?"

Food for Breakfast

a glass of apple juice СТАКА́Н Я́БЛОЧНОГО СО́КА
orange juice АПЕЛЬСИ́НОВЫЙ СОК
grape juice ВИНОГРА́ДНЫЙ СОК
oatmeal ОВСЯ́ННАЯ КА́ША
farina МА́ННАЯ КА́ША
hard boiled egg КРУТО́Е ЯЙЦО́
omelette ОМЛЕ́Т
fried eggs ЯИ́ЧНИЦА-ГЛАЗУ́НЬЯ

161

open faced sandwich with butter, cheese, sausage, fish, caviar БУТЕРБРÓД С МÁСЛОМ, СЫ́РОМ, КОЛБАСÓЙ, РЫ́БОЙ, ИКРÓЙ

toast ПОДЖÁРЕННЫЙ ХЛЕБ

preserves ВАРÉНЬЕ

jam ДЖЕМ

butter МÁСЛО

tea ЧАЙ

coffee КÓФЕ

hot chocolate КАКÁО

A Typical Dinner Menu

Appetizers and salads ЗАКУ́СКИ И САЛÁТЫ

The first course ПÉРВОЕ БЛЮ́ДО

The main course ВТОРÓЕ БЛЮ́ДО

Dessert ДЕСÉРТ

Appetizers and Salads

Appetizers may be deli assortments, such as salmon (ЛОСОСИ́НА), smoked salmon (СЁМГА), caviar (ИКРÁ), cheese (СЫР) or sauteed mushrooms (ТУШЁНЫЕ ГРИБЫ́).

Salads are usually not the green leafy kind served in many American restaurants, but rather cucumber/tomato salads (САЛÁТЫ ИЗ ОГУРЦÓВ/ПОМИДÓРОВ) or radish and scallion salads (САЛÁТЫ ИЗ РЕДИ́СА/ЗЕЛЁНОГО ЛУКА) served with sour cream. Other salads resemble our potato salads (КАРТÓФЕЛЬНЫЕ САЛÁТЫ) and coleslaw (САЛÁТ ИЗ СВÉЖЕЙ КАПУ́СТЫ). There are cheese and egg salads. The Russian favorite Olivier or Stolichny salad consists of potato, peas, meat, pickles all cut into small pieces with added mayonnaise.

The First Course

Popular Russian soups are the Russian "shchi" (ЩИ) or cabbage soup with meat and the Ukrainian borscht (БОРЩ). Okroshka (ОКРО́ШКА) is a cold soup made from vegetables on a "kvass" base. It is served mostly in hot weather with sour cream and cut boiled eggs. The kvass gives the soup a very distinctive flavor. Others soups are:

meat soup МЯСНО́Й СУП
meat soup with pickles РАССО́ЛЬНИК
noodle soup БУЛЬО́Н С ЛАПШО́Й
milk soup МОЛО́ЧНЫЙ СУП
hot vegetable soup ОВОЩНО́Й СУП
cold beet soup СВЕКО́ЛЬНИК
fish soup УХА́

The Main Course

The main course in the restaurant will often be dictated to you. Fried pork (ЖА́РЕНАЯ СВИНИ́НА), beef cutlets (ТЕЛЯ́ЧЬИ КОТЛЕ́ТЫ), and chicken (КУ́РИЦА) will be honored specialties of the evening. Sometimes, fish (РЫ́БА) is also available. Some of the more traditional offerings are beef Stroganoff (БИФ-СТРО́ГАНОВ), chicken Kiev (ЦЫПЛЯ́ТА ПО-КИ́ЕВСКИ), crepes БЛИ́НЧИКИ and "pelmenii". ПЕЛЬМЕ́НИ are a Russian version of ravioli or dumplings. They are generally served with butter (МА́СЛО) and sour cream (СМЕТА́НА) —fattening but very tasty.

Meats:

beef ГОВЯ́ДИНА
veal ТЕЛЯ́ТИНА
lamb БАРА́НИНА

Poultry:

chicken КУ́РИЦА
duck У́ТКА
goose ГУСЬ
turkey ИНДЕ́ЙКА
partridge КУРОПА́ТКА
quail ПЕРЕПЁЛКА

Fish:

carp КАРП
pike СУДА́К
cod ТРЕСКА́
perch О́КУНЬ
cambala КАМБАЛА́
mackarel СКУ́МБРИЯ

You may need a few important words if you are concerned with the way your dish is done:

boiled ВАРЁНЫЙ, ОТВАРНО́Й (potato)
grilled, roasted ЖА́РЕНЫЙ
fried ЖА́РЕНЫЙ (potato)
stewed, steamed ТУШЁНЫЙ
stuffed ФАРШИРО́ВАННЫЙ
smoked КОПЧЁНЫЙ
salty СОЛЁНЫЙ
fresh СВЕ́ЖИЙ
frozen МОРО́ЖЕНЫЙ

The Garnish:

potatoes КАРТО́ФЕЛЬ
mashed potatoes ПЮРЕ́
rice РИС
pasta МАКАРО́НЫ

164

peas ГОРÓШЕК
sauerkraut КЍСЛАЯ КАПУ́СТА
pickles СОЛЁНЫЕ ОГУРЦЍ

Desserts

For dessert you are always safe with the ice cream (МО-
РÓЖЕНОЕ). Other desserts include layer cakes (ТÓРТЫ),
pies (ПИРОГЍ), pastries (ПИРÓЖНЫЕ), chocolate candy
(ШОКОЛÁДНЫЕ КОНФÉТЫ), custards and compotes (fruit in
syrupy liquid) and fruit drinks (ФРУКТÓВЫЕ НАПЍТКИ).

Fruits

apples Я́БЛОКИ
pears ГРУ́ШИ
plums СЛЍВЫ
apricots АБРИКÓСЫ
peaches ПÉРСИКИ
grape ВИНОГРÁД
watermelon АРБУ́З
melon ДЫНЯ

Berries

cherry ЧЕРÉШНЯ
wild strawberry ЗЕМЛЯНЍКА
strawberry КЛУБНЍКА
raspberry МАЛЍНА
sour cherry ВЍШНЯ
blackberry ЕЖЕВЍКА
blueberry ЧЕРНЍКА

You will have to order mineral water (МИНЕРÁЛЬНАЯ
ВОДÁ) because it is not automatically served with the meal.

165

The following is an example of a conversation you may have with your waiter or waitress:

А. ДЕ́ВУШКА, МО́ЖНО ВАС?
Waitress, could you come here?

В. ПОДОЖДИ́ТЕ МИНУ́ТКУ. Я ЗАКО́НЧУ ОБСЛУЖИ́ВАТЬ ДРУГО́Й СТО́ЛИК.
Wait a minute. I will finish serving the other table.

А. ДЕ́ВУШКА, ВЫ ПРО НАС НЕ ЗАБЫ́ЛИ?
Waitress, you haven't forgotten about us?

В. СЛУ́ШАЮ ВАС.
I am ready (literally: I am listening to you).

А. ЧТО У ВАС ЕСТЬ НА СЕГО́ДНЯ.
What do you have for today?

В. ЖАРКО́Е, ТЕЛЯ́ЧЬИ КОТЛЕ́ТЫ, ЦЫПЛЯ́ТА ПО-КИ́ЕВСКИ.
Stew, veal cutlets or young chicks in Kiev style.

А. ЧТО ВЫ РЕКОМЕНДУ́ЕТЕ?
What would you recommend?

В. ВОЗЬМИ́ТЕ ТЕЛЯ́ЧЬИ КОТЛЕ́ТЫ. ОНИ СВЕ́ЖИЕ.
Take the veal cutlets. They are fresh.

А. ТОГДА́ ПРИНЕСИ́ТЕ НАМ ДВЕ ПО́РЦИИ КОТЛЕ́Т. КАКО́Й ГАРНИ́Р?
Then bring us two servings of the cutlets. What side dishes do you have?

В. КАРТО́ФЕЛЬНОЕ ПЮРЕ́ И ЗЕЛЁНЫЙ ГОРО́ШЕК.
Mashed potatoes and green beans.

A. ХОРО́ШО. ДА́ЙТЕ НАМ ПЮРЕ И ДВОЙНУ́Ю ПО́РЦИЮ ЗЕЛЁНОГО ГОРО́ШКА.
Very good. Give us the mashed potatoes and a double portion of green beans.

B. ЗАКУ́СКУ БУ́ДЕТЕ БРАТЬ?
Will you order appetizers?

A. ДА, САЛА́Т ИЗ ОГУРЦО́В.
Yes, a cucumber salad, please.

B. ЕСТЬ САЛА́Т ИЗ ПОМИДО́Р И ЛУ́КА.
There is tomato and onion salad.

A. ПРИНЕСИ́ТЕ НАМ КРА́СНУЮ ИКРУ́ И САЛА́Т ИЗ ПОМИДО́Р.
Bring us some red caviar and tomato salad.

B. ЧТО БУ́ДЕТЕ ПИТЬ?
What will you drink?

A. 200 ГРА́ММОВ КОНЬЯКУ́.
200 grams of cognac.

B. А ЧТО НА ДЕСЕ́РТ?
What will you have for desert?

A. МОРО́ЖЕНОЕ И КОФЕ ПО-ТУРЕ́ЦКИ.
Ice cream and Turkish coffee.

Paying the Bill:

With the ruble/dollar exchange so favorable for foreigners, it will not hurt your pocketbook too much to leave a 20% (20 ПРОЦЕ́НТОВ) tip.

When you get your bill, check it carefully. If it seems exorbitant, inquire. Count your change as well. Unfortunately, foreigners are sometimes shortchanged (ОБСЧИ́ТЫВАТЬ).

167

Cafes

Cafes are quite different from restaurants. There are КАФЕ-КОНДИ́ТЕРСКИЕ, cafes that specialize in pastries (ПИРО́ЖНЫЕ), cakes (ТО́РТЫ), crepes (БЛИ́НЧИКИ) and chocolate. Ice cream cafes (КАФЕ́-МОРО́ЖЕНЫЕ) serve fantastic ice cream and juice. Some cafes provide service over the counter or in the form of a cafeteria line. Parks also have outdoor cafes where you can enjoy a snack after an afternoon stroll.

Co-op Restaurants and Cafes

The basic differences between the cooperatives and state run restaurants and cafes are prices and often quality of food and service. Cooperatives try to be different and creative. They often specialize in ethnic cuisine. They may also offer goods that come from the West. As in the case of cooperative stores, there are hard currency cooperatives as well as ruble cooperatives. The hard currency menu will be far more extensive and may include alcohol where the ruble menu does not. When making a reservation, specify whether you are paying in rubles or dollars. Sometimes there are separate dining rooms for the ruble customers and the hard currency customers.

In some cities five star joint venture restaurants have opened. Here you will discover exquisite cuisine such as baked stuffed flounder with broccoli florets or filet mignon and sauteed zucchini. German beer and Stolichnaya and fine French wines are available as well. The service and quality of the food is excellent. These are not Russian restaurants and do not charge Russian prices nor accept rubles. These are foreign businesses that charge hard currency prices that reflect true five star quality as judged by Western standards. For the best, be prepared to spend between $35 to $50 per person. Tipping is expected in all cooperative restaurants and cafes.

Other Types of Restaurants

If you are down to your last ruble and very hungry, you may decide to venture into a СТОЛО́ВАЯ or ЗАКУ́СОЧНАЯ. Notwithstanding the less than scrumptious meals sold there, the lines are often long because the food is cheap. СТОЛО́ВАЯ is usually open from the early morning until about six or seven in the evening. Its offerings include oatmeal, milk (МОЛОКО́), КЕФИ́Р which is a thick sour milk, eggs (ЯЙЦА́), cheese (СЫР), КОЛБАСА́ (sausage), juices (СО́КИ), prepared salads (ГОТО́ВЫЕ САЛА́ТЫ), soups (СУПЫ́), noodles (ЛАПША́), some prepared meat dishes (МЯСНЫ́Е БЛЮ́ДА) and desserts (ДЕСЕ́РТЫ).

In ПИРОЖКО́ВАЯ one can buy warm buns with filling (ПИРОЖКИ́), bouillons, and franks. They always serve coffee, tea and compotes.

In ПЕЛЬМЕ́ННАЯ there are dumplings (ПЕЛЬМЕ́НИ), sour cream, juices and coffee.

In БЛИ́ННАЯ you will find pancakes (БЛИНЫ́), salads, coffee, compotes.

Street Vendors

"Penguin" ice cream has made a big hit in Russia and its little vending trucks are at almost every corner. They offer exotic flavors such as kiwi, papaya, and banana, an exciting contrast to the typical Russian ice cream natural flavors: chocolate and vanilla. Other items sold in the streets are fruit flavored soda water (ГАЗИРО́ВАННАЯ ВО́ДА), juices (СО́КИ), kvass (КВАС) and pirozhki (ПИРОЖКИ́). Avoid ПИРОЖКИ́ sold on the street. These are attractive little fragrant buns with meat fillings. Some have mushroom fillings as well, but the ones sold on the streets are usually filled with old or rotten meat. It is quite likely that you will get sick from them; this is confirmed by many students who have had bad experiences from their encounters with pirozhki sold on the street. But do not be afraid of the Russian ice cream—it's tasty and the only thing it could harm is your girth.

Useful Words:

be hungry ХОТЕ́ТЬ ЕСТЬ
be thirsty ХОТЕ́ТЬ ПИТЬ
sit down СЕСТЬ
table for two СТОЛ НА ДВОИ́Х
order ЗАКАЗА́ТЬ
eat ЕСТЬ
drink ПИТЬ
tasty ВКУ́СНО
not so tasty НЕВКУ́СНО
breakfast ЗА́ВТРАК
eat breakfast ЗА́ВТРАКАТЬ
dinner ОБЕ́Д
have dinner ОБЕ́ДАТЬ
supper У́ЖИН
eat supper У́ЖИНАТЬ
bite ПЕРЕКУСИ́ТЬ
pay ПЛАТИ́ТЬ
"toast" ТОСТ
change МЕ́ЛОЧЬ, СДА́ЧА
to change РАЗМЕНЯ́ТЬ

Useful Expressions:

Do you have a table for two?
У ВАС ЕСТЬ СВОБО́ДНЫЙ СТО́ЛИК НА ДВОИ́Х?

I would prefer a table near the window.
Я ХОТЕ́Л(А) БЫ СТОЛ У ОКНА́.

Where can I wash my hands?
ГДЕ БЫ Я МОГ(ЛА) ВЫ́МЫТЬ РУ́КИ?

What do you recommend?
ЧТО ВЫ СОВЕ́ТУЕТЕ (РЕКОМЕНДУ́ЕТЕ) ВЗЯТЬ?

We are in a hurry. Please serve us as quickly as possible.
МЫ СПЕШИ́М. ПОЖА́ЛУЙСТА, ОБСЛУЖИ́ТЕ НАС ПО-БЫСТРЕ́Е.

Could I have the check please?
МО́ЖНО ЧЕК?

Idiomatic Expressions

The idiomatic expression БЫТЬ НЕ В СВОЕ́Й ТАРЕ́Л-КЕ means (literally) "not to be in one's plate" or to be not quite oneself.

The expression "ХЛЕБ ДА СОЛЬ ВАМ" means "You are welcome".

The words you say people when you see them eating:
ПРИЯ́ТНОГО АППЕТИ́ТА!
Bon appetit!

171

CHAPTER ELEVEN

DRINKS

WINES AND LIQUORS

Imbibe these cognates:
АЛКОГО́ЛЬ alcohol
КОКТЕ́ЙЛЬ cocktail
ВИНО́ wine

The Strong Drinks

ВО́ДКА vodka
КОНЬЯ́К cognac
РОМ rum
ВИ́СКИ whiskey
ДЖИН gin
БРЕ́НДИ brandy

The Natural and Dessert Wines

ШАМПА́НСКОЕ champagne
ВЕ́РМУТ vermouth
МАДЕ́РА Madeira

172

ПОРТВЕ́ЙН port wine
БУРГУ́НДСКОЕ burgundy
БОРДО́ Bordeaux
ШЕ́РРИ sherry
ШЕ́РРИ-БРЕ́НДИ sherry brandy
ПУНШ punch

While reading Russian literature you will frequently run into these words. This is how Russian poet Alexander Pushkin praised Bordeaux:

А ТЫ БОРДО́, ПОДО́БЕН ДРУ́ГУ,
КОТО́РЫЙ В ГО́РЕ И БЕДЕ́
ТОВА́РИЩ ЗАВСЕГДА́, ВЕЗДЕ́
ГОТО́В НАМ ОКАЗА́ТЬ УСЛУ́ГУ
ИЛЬ ТИ́ХИЙ РАЗДЕЛИ́ТЬ ДОСУ́Г,
ДА ЗДРА́ВСТВУЕТ БОРДО́, НАШ ДРУГ!

And you, Bordeaux, are similar to a friend
who in both sorrow and distress
is always a comrade, who is ready everywhere
to render us a service
or to share with us the quiet leisure,
Long live, Bordeaux, our friend!

The selection in Russian liquor stores (ВИ́ННЫЕ МАГА-ЗИ́НЫ) is not as rich as the wine lexicon of Russian literature. But, nevertheless, you may encounter such drinks as ВЕ́РМУТ, ПОРТВЕ́ЙН, МАДЕ́РА, ЦИНАНДА́ЛИ.

Vodka and wines can be found in wine departments of big supermarkets and sometimes in odd places, such as milk stores or newspaper stands. For hard currency, there is a rich variety of European, American, and Russian liquors in the "Beriozkas."

173

The latest news is an assortment (АССОРТИМЕ́НТ) of Western liquors and strong drinks on the street stands and in various co-op stalls. But be cautious about buying them on the street. There are many fake drinks sold over there in bottles from Western liquors. A small, motley assortment of Western drinks is sold in the stores: French whiskey, German vodka, and sweet Amaretto can be found in many places. Sometimes you may run into "Teacher's" whiskey or find a bargain: a large bottle of Scandinavian pure alcohol for a very good price.

Champagne in Russia has always been a treat. It is traditionally served on special occasions such as weddings, birthday parties and anniversaries. Pushkin captured the Russians' passion for champagne in *Eugene Onegin:*

ВДОВЫ́ КЛИКО́ ИЛИ МОЭТА
БЛАГОСЛАВЕ́ННОЕ ВИНО́
В БУТЫ́ЛКЕ МЁРЗЛОЙ ДЛЯ ПОЭТА
НА СТОЛ ТОТЧА́С ПРИНЕСЕНО́.
ОНО́ СВЕРКА́ЕТ ИПОКРЕ́НОЙ
ОНО СВОЕЙ ИГРИВОЙ ПЕ́НОЙ
(ПОДО́БИЕМ ТОГО–СЕГО)
МЕНЯ́ ПЛЕНЯ́ЛО: ЗА НЕГО́
ПОСЛЕДНИЙ БЕ́ДНЫЙ ЛЕПТ БЫВА́ЛО,
ДАВА́Л Я. ПО́МНИТЕ, ДРУЗЬЯ?
ЕГО ВОЛШЕ́БНАЯ СТРУЯ́
РОЖДА́ЛА ГЛУ́ПОСТЕЙ НЕ МА́ЛО,
А СКО́ЛЬКО ШУ́ТОК И СТИХО́В,
И СПО́РОВ, И ВЕСЁЛЫХ СНОВ!

The blessed wine
of Widow Clicault or Moette
in a frozen bottle
is brought at once
to the table for the poet
It flashes as if it were from Hippocrene
It charms me with its wanton froth
(resembling this or that):

174

I used to give for it the only mite I had,
Do you remember, friends?
Its enchanting stream gave birth
to many foolish things
and a great many jokes and verses,
and arguments and merry dreams!

Gatherings at home reveal a second side to the Russian character. Often celebrations or get togethers at homes involve guitar playing, singing, and long conversation. The reserved Russians from the streets can be quite loud and boisterous at home among family and friends.

One thing all get-togethers have in common is alcohol, usually lots of it. Along with the alcohol come snacks; no, not pretzels and Doritos. Even for the most informal of gatherings, a variety of foods (breads, vegetables, cold cuts, cheeses, pickles, pastries) will accompany the drinks. Parties in Russia are much more communal than in the West. Generally, everyone sits around the refreshments: there is little scattering of guests or private conversation. When one person proposes a toast, all must participate. And toasts come one right after the other over there! By the end of the evening, several empty bottles will be standing on the table. Parties also last quite a long time. If you are invited to "drop by for a drink," expect to spend a few hours at the least at your host's place. Rushing out is considered impolite.

Whether at a party or elsewhere, "long Russian conversations" among friends often center around literature, art, history, religion, philosophy. Lately, however, politics and social ills have captured a more prominent role in daily conversations. Most Russians love to talk and when the topic of conversation is of great significance, time is of no essence.

ПОДНИ́МЕМ БОКА́ЛЫ, СОДВИ́НЕМ ИХ РА́ЗОМ!
ДА ЗДРА́ВСТВУЮТ МУ́ЗЫ, ДА ЗДРА́ВСТВУЕТ РА́ЗУМ!

Let us raise our goblets, let us clap them together!
Long live the Muses, long live reason!

These lines of Pushkin's *Bacchanalian Song* (ВАКХИ́ЧЕСКАЯ
ПЕ́СНЯ) express the spirit of the Russian table (ЗАСТО́ЛЬЕ).
Toasting is a traditional feature of such gatherings. In Russian feasts,
drinking wine is the most essential part. Generally Russians drink to
enhance a conversation, to warm-up the atmosphere at the table and,
in winter, literally to warm themselves up.

In Russian tradition, once a bottle of vodka is opened, it is
never left unfinished. The bottle tops resemble the original soda pop
caps that, once removed, do not fit back on the bottle. The thought
of mixing vodka with something odd such as orange juice is simply
out of the question. It is shot after shot after shot over there. Do not
try to outdo your Russian friends. Remember the old saying: Know
your limit (ЗНАЙ СВОЮ́ МЕ́РУ).

Different kinds of Russian vodka:

РУ́ССКАЯ Russian
МОСКО́ВСКАЯ Moscow
ОХО́ТНИЧЬЯ Hunter's
ПЕРЦО́ВАЯ Pepper
ЛИМО́ННАЯ Lemon
ПШЕНИ́ЧНАЯ Wheat

Brandies in Russia are often called cognacs. There are many
kinds of cognac-brandies Crimean, Dagestanian, Azerbaijanian,
Kazakh, Armenian, Georgian, Moldavian. The latter three are
considered the best. But even among those you should look for better
brands. Sometimes quality and strength are marked by stars on the

176

labels. The more stars, the better the quality and the higher the price.

Avoid Azerbajanian cognac that is exceptionally stinky.

Look for Armenian, Georgian, Crimean, and Moldavian wines. They come as natural white, rosé, or red wines; or domestic port, madeiras, sherries, and champagne. You can look for Kvanchkara, which, they say, was Stalin's favorite wine. Try Zhinandalii, Mukuzanii, Mariulii, and other famous Georgian wines. Try the Crimean wines made by Abraw Durso, they are among the best.

Sample Balzam, Zubrovka, which were popular liqueurs in Russia not long ago.

The choice of alcoholic drinks (АЛКОГО́ЛЬНЫЕ НАПИ́ТКИ) is limited in restaurants. Sometimes, you will not be able to get a КОКТЕ́ЙЛЬ but will have to resort to wine (ВИНО́), champagne (ШАМПА́НСКОЕ), cognac (КОНЬЯ́К), vodka (ВО́ДКА) or beer (ПИ́ВО). ВИНО́ and ШАМПА́НСКОЕ are ordered by the glass (СТАКА́Н), carafe (РЮМКА) or bottle (БУТЫЛКА). The ВО́ДКА can be ordered by the bottle or by the gram. 100 grams is the standard for one person. Officially, the drinking age in Russia is 21, but this is never enforced.

Bars

The concept of a bar is quite different than the Western one. They simply are not very popular and are not that much fun. But once again, things are changing. There have been a number of Western style bars popping up in Moscow and St. Petersburg in the past few years. Some demand hard currency. In ruble bars, stick to the basics; an order for an Alabama Slammer may get you some pretty odd looks especially when menu consists of a generic "cocktail" and juice. As of today, your best bet in bars may still be foreign hotel bars.

Tipping is not absolutely necessary but is becoming more and more common.

Nightclubs and Discos

There are a few nightclubs and discos, but most are not like their Western counterparts. Buy tickets ahead of time or call and make a reservation. There are a few that are open all night (ВСЮ НОЧЬ) but most close at midnight (ПОЛНОЧЬ) or 1 a. m. Nightclub dancing is simply not a big fad in Russia yet. Restaurants are still the most popular places for entertainment.

NON-ALCOHOLIC DRINKS

Besides different kinds of mineral water (МИНЕРАЛЬНАЯ ВОДА), including Moskovskaya, Slavyanskaya, Essentuki, Borzhomi, other non-alcoholic drinks (БЕЗАЛКОГОЛЬНЫЕ НАПИТКИ) generally available are Pepsi, Coke, lemonade (ЛИМОНАД), fruit flavored drinks available in pear, raspberry, orange, mandarin, and cherry flavors and juices (СОКИ). Kvass (КВАС) is a unique Russian drink made from fermented black bread. Its flavor and quality vary greatly from place to place.

CHAPTER TWELVE

RUSSIAN ETIQUETTE

Now that you can read the names of the streets, stores and hotels, have an idea of Russian cuisine and a knowledge of some Russian liquors, you are almost equipped for the journey to Russia. If you familiarize yourself with at least a few greetings in Russian, you will feel even more confident.

When we visited Russia recently, we met one man who did not speak English at all. He knew just two phrases which he pronounced with a good American accent. To the first question: "Do you speak English?" he would confidently answer "Yes, of course." His second and last English sentence was, "I don't believe you," followed with a smile of an American movie star. And nobody could believe that he didn't speak English. The same way, you should rather play up your ignorance of Russian than take it seriously. And use any situation in Russia as an opportunity to improve your language skills. Russian may seem like Greek to you, but it is nevertheless an Indo-European language, like English.

Expressing Lack of Comprehension:

Sorry, I don't understand Russian. Do you speak English?
ИЗВИНИ́ТЕ, Я НЕ ГОВОРЮ ПО-РУ́ССКИ. ВЫ ГОВОРИ́ТЕ
ПО-АНГЛИ́ЙСКИ? [iz-vii-ní-te ya ne ga-va-rú pa-rús-kii. Vy
ga-va-rí-te pa-an-glís-kii?]

Sorry, I didn't catch that.
ПРОСТИ́ТЕ, Я НЕ ПО́НЯЛ (masc.), НЕ ПОНЯЛА́ (femin.)
[pras-tí-te ya ne pó-nyal (ne pa-ne-lá)].

Please repeat that.
ПОВТОРИ́ТЕ, ПОЖА́ЛУЙСТА. [paf-ta-rí-te pa-zhá-lus-ta].

Speak slower, please.
ГОВОРИ́ТЕ, ПОЖА́ЛУЙСТА, МЕ́ДЛЕННЕЕ. [ga-va-rí-te
pa-zhá-lus-ta myéd-le-nee].

Continue, please.
ПРОДОЛЖА́ЙТЕ, ПОЖА́ЛУЙСТА. [pra-dal-zháy-te
pa-zhá-lus-ta].

Greetings and Introductions:

I am glad you came here.
РАД ВА́ШЕМУ ПРИЕ́ЗДУ [pat vá-she-muu prii-yéz-duu].

Welcome
РАД ВАШЕМУ ПРИХО́ДУ [rat vá-she-muu prii-chó-duu).
or
РАД, ЧТО ВЫ ПРИШЛИ́ [rat shto vy prii-shlí].

May I introduce you to...
РАЗРЕШИ́ТЕ ПРЕДСТА́ВИТЬ ВАС ... (КОМУ? + dat.)
[raz-re-shí-te pret-stá-vit' vas]

Allow me to introduce myself. My name is Maria Petrova.

РАЗРЕШИ́ТЕ ПРЕДСТА́ВИТЬСЯ. МЕНЯ́ ЗОВУ́Т МАРИ́Я
ПЕТРО́ВА. [raz-re-shí-te pret-stá-vi-tsya me-nya za-vút ma-rí-ya
pet-ró-va]

I am pleased to meet you.
РАД(А) С ВА́МИ ПОЗНАКО́МИТЬСЯ [rat (rá-da, fem.) s
vá-mii paz- na-kó-mii-tsya].

I am glad to see you.
РАД С ВА́МИ ВСТРЕ́ТИТЬСЯ [rat s vá-mii fstryé-tii-tsya].

How are you?
КАК ЖИВЁТЕ?
[kak zhii-vyo-te?]

Quite well, thank you.
СПАСИ́БО, НЕПЛОХО.
[spa-sí-ba ne-pló-kha]

I am pleased to hear it.
РАД ЭТО СЛЫ́ШАТЬ.
[rat éa-ta slý-shat']

*Expressions of Thanks, Begging Pardon and
Answering the Thanks:*

Thank you.
СПАСИ́БО.
[spa-sí-ba]

Thank you very much.
БОЛЬШО́Е СПАСИ́БО.
[bal'-shó-ye spa-sí-ba]

Excuse me
ИЗВИНИ́ТЕ.
[iz-vii-ní-te]

Pardon me.
ПРОСТИ́ТЕ.
[pras-tí-te]

I beg your pardon.
ПРОШУ́ ПРОЩЕ́НИЯ.
[pra-shú pra-shchyé-nii-ya]

May I interrupt you?
ПОЗВО́ЛЬТЕ ПЕРЕБИ́ТЬ ВАС.
[paz-vól'-te pe-re-bít' vas]

I am sorry.
ЖАЛЬ, СОЖАЛЕ́Ю. ПРОСТИ́ТЕ.
[zhal' sa-zha-lyé-u pras-tii-te]

It is my pleasure.
НЕ СТО́ИТ БЛАГОДА́РНОСТИ.
[ne stó-it bla-ga-dár-nos-tii]

Don't mention it.
НЕ́ ЗА ЧТО.
[né za shta]

You are very kind.
ВЫ О́ЧЕНЬ ДОБРЫ́.
[vy ó-chen' dab-rý]

Very kind of you.
О́ЧЕНЬ МИ́ЛО С ВА́ШЕЙ СТОРОНЫ́.
[ó-chen' mí-la s vá-shey sta-ra-ný]

Very generous of you.
ВЫ О́ЧЕНЬ ЛЮБЕ́ЗНЫ.
[vy o-chen' lu-byéz-ny]

Much obliged to you.
ÓЧЕНЬ ВАМ ПРИЗНÁТЕЛЕН (masc.), (ПРИЗНÁ-
ТЕЛЬНА) (fem.)
[ó-chen' vam priz-ná-te-len (priz-ná-tel'-na)]

That's quite all right.
ПОЖАЛУЙСТА.
[pa-zhá-lus-ta]

If you please.
ЕСЛИ БЫ ВЫ БЫЛИ СТОЛЬ ЛЮБÉЗНЫ
[yés-lii by vy bý-lii stol' lu-byéz-ny]

Can you do me a favor?
БÝДЬТЕ ДОБРЫ́.
[but'-te dab-rý]
БÝДЬТЕ ЛЮБÉЗНЫ
bút'-te lu-byéz-ny]

I hope I was not intruding.
НАДÉЮСЬ, НЕ ПОМЕШÁЛ(А).
[na-dyé-us' ne pa-me-shál(a)]

The Forms of Polite Response:

That is all right.
ВСЁ В ПОРЯ́ДКЕ. ВСЁ ХОРОШÓ.
[fsyo f pa-ryát-ke fsyo kha-ra-shó].

Don't mention it.
НЕ ОБРАЩÁЙТЕ ВНИМÁНИЯ.
[ne ab-ra-shchán-te vnii-má-nii-ya]

Don't worry!
НЕ БЕСПОКÓЙТЕСЬ!
[ne bes-pa-koy-tes']!

183

With pleasure.
С УДОВО́ЛЬСТВИЕМ.
[s uu-da-vól'-stvii-em]

Don't hesitate.
НЕ СТЕСНЯ́ЙТЕСЬ.
[ne stes-nyáy-tes']

Make yourself at home.
РАСПОЛАГА́ЙТЕСЬ КАК ДО́МА.
[ras-pa-la-gáy-tes' kak dó-ma]
ЧУ́ВСТВУЙТЕ СЕБЯ́ КАК ДО́МА.
[chúst-vuy-te se-byá kak dó-ma]

Regards and Kind Wishes:

Remember me to
ПРИВЕ́Т ОТ МЕНЯ́...
[prii-vyét ot me-nyá]

Give my love to (give my regards to)
ПЕРЕДА́ЙТЕ СЕРДЕ́ЧНЫЙ ПРИВЕ́Т...
[pe-re-dáy-te ser-dyéch-ny prii-vyét]

Daily Greetings:

Hello
ЗДРА́ВСТВУЙТЕ [zdrást-vuy-te]

Hi
ПРИВЕ́Т [prii-vyét]

Good morning
ДО́БРОЕ У́ТРО
[dób-ra-e út-ra]

Good day
ДО́БРЫЙ ДЕНЬ
[dób-ry dyen']

Good evening
ДО́БРЫЙ ВЕ́ЧЕР
[dób-ry vyé-cher]

Good night
СПОКО́ЙНОЙ НО́ЧИ
[spa-kóy-nay nó-chii]

Leave-taking

Good-bye.
ДО СВИДА́НИЯ.
[da svii-dá-nii-ya]

So long.
ПОКА́. БУ́ДЬ ЗДОРО́В(А).
[pa-ká but' zda-róf(va)]

Good night.
ДО́БРОЙ НО́ЧИ (while departing in the evening).
[dób-ray nó-chii]

See you later.
ДО ВСТРЕ́ЧИ.
[da fstryé-chii]

I'll be seeing you.
УВИ́ДИМСЯ.
[u-ví-dim-sya]

Good luck!
СЧАСТЛИ́ВО!
[shches-lí-va]

All the best!
ВСЕГО ХОРОШЕГО!
[fse-vo kha-ró-she-va]
ВСЕГО ДОБРОГО!
[fse-vó dób-ra-va]

Have a good time.
ПРИЯТНОГО ВРЕМЯПРОВОЖДЕНИЯ.
[prii-yát-na-va vryé-mya-pra-vazh-dyé-nii-ya]

Hope to see you soon.
НАДЕЮСЬ, СКОРО УВИДИМСЯ.
[na-dyé-us' skó-ra uví-dim-sya]

See you soon.
ДО СКОРОГО СВИДАНИЯ.
[da skó-ra-va svii-dá-nii-ya]

Do not forget us!
НЕ ЗАБЫВАЙТЕ!
[ne za-by-váy-te]

Greetings for Special Occasions:

Happy Birthday!
С ДНЁМ РОЖДЕНИЯ!
[z dnyom pazh-dyé-nii-ya]

Happy Holiday!
С ПРАЗДНИКОМ!
[s práz-nii-kam]

Happy New Year!
С НОВЫМ ГОДОМ!
[s nó-vym gó-dam]

Merry Christmas!
С РОЖДЕСТВО́М!
[s razh-dest-vóm]

Some Other Greetings:

Cheers!
ЗА ВА́ШЕ ЗДОРО́ВЬЕ!
[za vá-she zda-róvye]

Bon appetit!
ПРИЯ́ТНОГО АППЕТИ́ТА!
[prii-yát-na-va ape-tí-ta]

Pleasant dreams!
ПРИЯ́ТНЫХ СНОВИДЕ́НИЙ!
[prii-yát-nych sna-vii-dyé-niy]

God bless you (after sneezing) БУ́ДЬТЕ ЗДОРО́ВЫ!
[but'-te zda-ró-vy]
The answer is: СПАСИ́БО.
[spa-sí-ba]

Be well!
ВЫЗДОРА́ВЛИВАЙТЕ!
[vyz-da-ráv-lii-vay-te]

Welcome!
С ПРИЕ́ЗДОМ!
[s prii-yéz-dam]

С НОВОСЕ́ЛЬЕМ!
[s na-va-syél'-yem]
on occasion of moving into a new
apartment

Rest well!
ХОРОШО́ ОТДОХНИ́ТЕ!
[kha-ra-shó a-dakh-ní-te]

Expressions of Invitations:

The different ways to invite, to accept or to reject an invitation of a person to dance:
A. May I invite you to the dance?
МОГУ́ Я ПРИГЛАСИ́ТЬ ВАС НА ТА́НЕЦ?

B. Yes, of course.
ДА, КОНЕ́ЧНО.

B. No, thank you.
НЕТ, СПАСИ́БО.

The pattern of the polite form of an invitation consists of auxiliary verbs: may, permit, allow plus the infinitive of the verb ПРИГЛАСИ́ТЬ with a pronoun (ВЫ) in the genitive (ВАС):

МОГУ́ Я + ПРИГЛАСИ́ТЬ ВАС
МО́ЖНО + ПРИГЛАСИ́ТЬ ВАС
РАЗРЕШИ́ТЕ + ПРИГЛАСИ́ТЬ ВАС
ПОЗВО́ЛЬТЕ + ПРИГЛАСИ́ТЬ ВАС

The form Я ПРИГЛАША́Ю ВАС requires use of the infinitive of the verb (ТАНЦЕВА́ТЬ, ГУЛЯ́ТЬ walk, ИГРАТЬ play) or the noun in accusative with the preposition "НА" or "В": НА ВАЛЬС, НА ТА́НЕЦ, НА КОНЦЕ́РТ, НА ПРОГУ́ЛКУ
ПРИГЛАША́Ю ВАС НА КОНЦЕ́РТ (But ПРИГЛАША́Ю ВАС В КИНО, В ТЕАТР).

The noun ПРИГЛАШЕ́НИЕ also requires use of a noun in the accusative with the preposition "на" or "в":
ПРИГЛАШЕ́НИЕ В ГОСТИ
ПРИГЛАШЕ́НИЕ НА ПРОГУ́ЛКУ (invitation for a walk)
ПРИГЛАШЕ́НИЕ НА СВА́ДЬБУ (an invitation to a wedding ceremony).

The title of the famous novel of Vladimir Nabokov is ПРИГЛАШЕ́НИЕ НА КАЗНЬ ("Invitation to an Execution").

The accusative with the prepositions "НА" or "В" denotes the direction of the action. It is translated with the preposition "to" and answers the question "where?" (КУДА?). In the accusative feminine the endings are: -У,-Ю. In the masculine and neuter accusative and in the accusative plural the nouns keep a form of the nominative case: НА ВАЛЬС, НА ТАНЕЦ, НА КОНЦЕРТ, В ТЕАТР, В КИНО, В ГОСТИ.

The Russian Character

Now equipped with everyday phrases for communication, let us look into the Russian character itself. Generalizations and stereotypes are not always the best way to describe people and culture, nevertheless they may be useful to a point for a visitor. We will simply try to provide you with a few distinguishing features which may help you to react appropriately to certain people's behavior and avoid some awkward situations.

Russians are known to be soulful and emotional yet reserved. This is not a contradiction. Their music, poetry and other arts exude powerful emotions, but the people seem to be quiet in their manners. On the streets they feel it is best not to be noisy and importunate.

Conversations are not carried on loudly; clothing is mostly gray, dark and unsensational. Raucous behavior, screaming and loud laughing and gesturing are not appropriate for public display. Americans in Moscow or St. Petersburg sometimes stick out like a sore thumb simply because they carry on converstions louder than others while walking down the street.

At the same time, you will rarely hear words of apology when you are pushed and shoved during rush hour on the street, in a store or on public transportation. Do not be offended. For some reason, it's not customary to apologize for pushing. Do not take it personally. It coexists with otherwise polite and friendly behavior.

You will find that Russians are more open in communication than many Western people. You might be addressed more often on the street by a passerby or conversation might suddenly begin in a store line or in a bus.

You might also find that Russians are culturally oriented people. Operas, ballets, concerts and museum exhibitions all play an important role in the life of the average Russian. Don't miss the opportunity to get involved in Russian cultural life.

Family and Friends

The family unit is quite strong in the Russian tradition. Children leave home much later than in America and often newlyweds move in with one of the couple's parents. The scarcity of housing is one factor that plays a role here of course, but it is also true that Russians like to keep the family together. Because both spouses work in most households, grandmothers are needed members of the family. Unlike in America, where society is centered on young adults and the middle aged, in Russia the focus is on children and elderly people.

Daily living for the average Russian family is very difficult. Most households have no a dishwasher, washer and dryer, or any of the amenities of the typical Western household. Shopping is difficult and time consuming. Buying food for dinner may require visiting three or four stores and standing in three or four lines. TV dinners and fast food (except of course McDonald's) have not caught on over there; everything is prepared from scratch.

Personal Space

Russians are accustomed to more physical contact than are Americans. You will notice a large percentage of women and girls walking down the street arm in arm. Men too are more affectionate to each other and will often put their arms around each others' shoulders. When greeting one another, hugs and kisses are exchanged liberally.

Many Americans often feel uncomfortable about the close contact that is customary in Russia. It is common for an American to feel awkward speaking with a Russian face to face because Russians allot much less personal space than Americans when they converse. If you really feel uncomfortable and would like to inconspicuously widen the gap between you and the person with whom you are conversing, you can always try sitting down at a table.

A Look at Women in Russia

Women have the dual responsibility of both housework and professional work. Household work in Russia is not an easy task, and most of it is usually done by the woman of the house. However, there are some families that do divide housework between the husband and wife evenly.

Many woman from the West are startled by the behavior of Russian men toward them. Women have expressed utter dismay over conducting business with Russians who show little respect for their capabilities in the business arena. But women visitors will notice doors being opened for them and hands being stretched out to them every time they step out of a cab or off the bus. Some American women take offense at such behavior, others find it rather refreshing.

Holidays

The holidays celebrated since 1991 in Russia are quite different from those celebrated not long ago. The pre-Soviet holidays have returned to the spotlight. The New Year is still the most important holiday of the year. It is a time to decorate the Christmas tree (ЁЛКА) at home and exchange gifts. The celebration of the New Year for children lasts for two weeks overtaking Russian Christmas which is celebrated January 7. During this time Christmas trees are decorated in the biggest concert halls, special shows for children are being performed, and gifts in bright packages are given to the children's audience by Father Frost (ДЕД МОРО́З), his granddaughter Snow White (СНЕГУ́РОЧКА) and their friends, the good animals.

The other holidays that have emerged, or rather re-emerged, are Maslenitsa (МА́СЛЕНИЦА) and Easter (ПА́СХА) in spring, Troitsa (ТРО́ИЦА) and Spas (СПАС) in summer for Christians, as well as Hannukah (ХА́НУКА) for Jews and Ramadan (РАМАДА́Н) for Muslims.

You will no longer witness military parades on November 7, the holiday of the October Revolution and May 1, the International Labor Day. But they are official holidays. May 1 has become more the celebration of spring. March 8, which was the International Women's Day, is still observed but has turned into a cross between American Mother's Day and Valentine's Day. It is rather a time to give women flowers, perfumes and chocolates than to spend hours at official meetings listening long reports about the solidarity of woman all over the world in their political struggle.

Attitudes Towards Traveler from the West

Russians always have been intrigued and fascinated with foreigners. They were always curious about Western life, music, television, business, literature and more. Western culture has had strong impact on their culture. The business sector turns continuously to the West for advice and examples. The government too is taking bits and pieces of Western governmental laws and structures and integrating them into the new system. So today, more than ever before, Russians are interested in learning more about the West from visitors. The atmosphere on the streets is mostly of friendship and you will find that Russians are fabulous hosts to Westerners.

CHAPTER THIRTEEN

MOSCOW

RUSSIA: A HISTORICAL PERSPECTIVE

The history of the Russian state began with the "coming of the Varangians" in 862 A.D. These bold Scandinavian navigators, known in the West as Vikings, were called in Russia the Varangians. The Chronicle of the 11th century writes about the Russians inviting three Varangian Dukes to the "Great Northern city" on the banks of Lake Ladoga. The oldest among them, the Varangian Duke Rurik, founded the first ruling dynasty in Russia, the Rurikovichi.

In 878-882, the Varangians, while searching for important trade routes, moved to the South and made Kiev their capital. In 882, during the reign of Great Duke Oleg (878-912), the name of the country first appeared: Kievan Rus'. While some historians believe Rus', or later Russia, comes from the old name of the Volga River, Ros or Rha, the majority maintain that it is derived from the word РУ́СЫЙ, the blond or light-brown color of the Slavs' hair. The Greek and Roman authors called this land Roxolania, Rutenia, Rus', Russia, and Rossia.

George Florovsky, one of the most significant authorities in the history of Russian thought, divided the history of Russia into five periods:

1. The Pre-Christian period
2. The Kievan period
3. The Moscovian period
4. The St. Petersburg or the Imperial period
5. The Soviet period

And now one could add a sixth period, the post-Soviet period.

Pre-Christian Rus'

The Slavs came to Europe in the 1st-3rd centuries A.D. at the time of the Great Migration of the peoples. They settled in the territory between the White and Black Seas, from the Danube to the Volga. They shared a common heritage with other people who came from the East and settled in Europe, namely, the Indo-European language and mythology. You can easily recognize the common roots in the English, German and Russian languages:

Mother - Mutter - МАТЬ
Son - Sonne - СЫН
Brother - Bruder - БРАТ
Sister - Schwester - СЕСТРА́

The Pre-Christian Slavs were not differentiated from the other Slavic tribes. They shared a common territory and lived in the west, east, north and south of Eastern Europe.

194

The Kievan Rus'

Christianity was known to penetrate into the territory of Russia during the time of the early Apostles. In 945, in the treaty made by the Kievan Duke Igor with the Greeks, his troops were already described as consisting of Christians and non-Christians. In 955, Igor's widow, the Duchess Olga, was baptized by the Byzantine emperor and the Patriarch in Constantinople. In 988, the whole of Rus' was baptized by the grandson of Olga, the Kievan Duke Vladimir.

The Baptism of Russia meant its subjection to the spiritual influences of the Byzantine Empire. Strong influences came as well from Bulgaria which already had the Bible, and rich liturgical literature in Old Slavonic, the common literary language of all Slavs.

In the beginning of the 13th century, a great trial fell on Russia. For almost two and a half centuries it remained under the rule of the Tartar-Mongolians. During that time, the faithfulness of Russia to the newly-acquired spiritual heritage was tested. This period was colored as well by other influences. Russia met face to face with the syncretic culture of the nomadic people who brought along their own traditions and involved Russia into the sphere of its action.

The Moscow Period

Moscow led in organizing the resistance to the Tartars, which ultimately led to the defeat of the Golden Horde in 1480 under the reign of Ivan III (1462-1505). By that time the gathering of the Russian lands had been completed. Moscow became the established seat of leadership and the center of all political, cultural and commercial activity of the country. The idea of Moscow as the "Third Rome" (Byzantium being "the

Second Rome") was coined in the dramatic time after the fall of the Byzantine Empire in 1453. It was reinforced by a marriage link: in 1472 Ivan III married Sophia, the niece of the last Byzantine emperor. It was at that time that the Grand Duke of Moscow assumed the Byzantine titles of "autocrat" and "tsar" (an adaptation of the Roman "Caesar") and adopted the two-headed eagle of Byzantium as a state emblem. Fond of Italian architecture, he brought the best Italian masters to build cathedrals and palaces in the Kremlin. Ivan the Great was actually the first who, according the famous Russian historian Nicholas Karamzin, "tore open the curtains between Europe and us."

In 1547, his grandson Ivan the Terrible (1533-1584), became the "Tsar of All Russia." He was the last heir of the old Ruric dynasty. He acquired his title for a good reason. Although deeply religious, he was very cruel; he persecuted many of the unloyal members of old Russian nobility, the boyars (БОЯРЕ) [ba-yá-re]. Ivan the Terrible conquered the lands of the Tartars and became the heir to the territory and people of the Golden Horde. The Kingdoms of Kazan (1552) and Astrakhan (1556) were annexed to the growing empire. Russia became a Eurasian country.

The Imperial Period

In the time of Peter the Great (1673-1725), Russia turned radically toward the West. In 1689, Peter the Great (ПЁТР ВЕЛИКИЙ) became tsar and was set on rapidly westernizing Russia. Both Rationalism and Enlightenment were imported from the West and implanted into the Russian soil. The new fashions, manners and style of life were foisted upon traditional Russian society. Peter forced the boyars to shave their beards, put powdered wigs on their heads and made them dance in balls. He founded St. Petersburg on the shores of the Gulf of Finland and declared it the capital of Russia in 1712. It meant breaking off with the Russian past and entering into the European scene. St. Petersburg was a new European city and quite different from the traditional Russian city Moscow. Its buildings, gardens, canals, and the splendid style of its architecture made it an enchanting European capital with a Russian character, yet the ancestral importance of Moscow made it forever the heart of Russia. As a result, Russia was balanced by the two great and very distinct cities.

The victory in the Great Northern war with Sweden (1720–1721) gave Peter the title "Emperor."

Developments kept drawing Russia closer to Europe. In 1812 during the reign of Alexander I, Russia entered into a direct confrontation with Napoleonic France, the mightiest European power of that time. Napoleon brought Europeans into Russia in attempt to conquer it, after which the Russians in turn came to Europe to help defeat Napoleon. The idea of the Holy Union of Europe was coined in the intellectual circles around Alexander I, but the defeater of Napoleon failed to materialize this idea.

The 19th century is rightfully considered the Golden Age of Russian civilization. It was marked by a flourishing of art and literature, music and architecture, and it gave to the world such renowned writers as Alexander Pushkin, Leo Tolstoy and Feodor Dostoyevsky and composers such as Modest Mussorgsky, Peter Tchaikovsky, Alexander Scriabin and many others.

The Soviet Period

This period began in 1917 after the Bolshevik Revolution. It marked the destruction of the old Russian society and the creation of a new state built on the basis of the Marxist ideology, with the Communist party leaders on top of this bureaucratic system. This system formally ended in 1991.

A WALK THROUGH MOSCOW

Moscow's setting

МОСКВА is seated on the banks of the Moskvá River. One of the largest cities in the world, it consists of approximately 5,000 streets and plazas.

Its concentric circles moves out from its old center where the the Kremlin (КРЕМЛЬ) stands. What is now Boulevard Ring (БУЛЬВÁРНОЕ КОЛЬЦÓ) and the Garden Ring (САДÓВОЕ КОЛЬЦÓ) used to be the furthest boundaries of the city. The Outer Ring is designated as a beltway (ОКРУ́ЖНАЯ ДОРÓГА) around the city. The Outer Ring stretches 25 miles from north to south and 22 miles from east to west.

It is not only the capital of Russia (СТОЛИ́ЦА РОССИ́И), but also the center of Russian culture and history. The population of Moscow is over 10 million.

The Kremlin

The word Kremlin means citadel. Here you will find the finest architecture, the grandest museums and the monuments of a long and distinctive history.

In the beginning there was a wooden citadel, the original wooden Kremlin (КРЕМЛЬ) built by the founder of Moscow Duke Yury Dolgoruky (КНЯЗЬ ЮРИЙ ДОЛГОРУ́КИЙ). In 1156, КРЕМЛЬ was surrounded by wooden walls. This Kremlin was destroyed by Tartar forces, but soon after its walls and buildings were restored. In 1367 the walls and towers of white stone were erected.

In the time of Ivan III (1485-1516), a great red brick defense wall was built, enforced by large pillars (arch. Mark and Anton Fryazin, Antonio Solari, Alevsis Fryazin). A few of these pillars serve as entrance gates to the Kremlin.

In the 15th–16th century КРЕМЛЬ became one of the strongest citadels in Europe. In the 17th century, the watchtowers were embellished with stone tents, and on the Spassky tower the clocks were installed. Its southern wall was rebuilt in the 18th century. There are 20 towers on the Kremlin walls, including Spasskaya, Tsarskaya, Senatskaya, Petrovskaya, Taynitskaya. With the addition of several buildings in the nineteenth century, it acquired the look it maintains to this day.

Inside the Kremlin walls you will see history unfold before your eyes. Outside the northwestern side of the Kremlin wall is the *Alexandrovsky Garden* (АЛЕКСА́НДРОВСКИЙ САД) named after tsar Alexander I. Next to the Arsenal tower of the Kremlin, you can see the Tomb of the Unknown Soldier memorializing the defeat of the Nazis.

The *Square of the Cathedrals* (СОБО́РНАЯ ПЛО́ЩАДЬ) is the center of the Kremlin. After the concept of Moscow as the "Third Rome" was established, the architecture of the Kremlin acquired a majestic style. СОБО́РНАЯ ПЛО́ЩАДЬ is surrounded by three large impressive cathedrals.

The *Cathedral of the Assumption* (УСПЕ́НСКИЙ СОБО́Р, 1475–1479, arch. Aristotle Fioravanti), with its somber monumental forms, is an interesting blend of architecture of the Italian Renaissance and the traditional forms of Russian architecture. In the interior of this cathedral one may see frescoes by the famous Russian painter Dionisy.

In the *Archangel Cathedral* АРХА́НГЕЛЬСКИЙ СО-БО́Р (1505–1508, arch. Alevsis Novy) you can see the tombs of the Russian tsars and Grand Dukes before Peter the Great.

The *Cathedral of the Annunciation* (БЛАГОВЕ́ЩЕНСКИЙ СОБО́Р) (1484-1489, the architects from Pskov) represents in its composition and decor the architectural traditions of Northern Russia. Its chapels were built in the second half of the 16th century. There are many icons from the 14th-16th centuries and murals of the 16th century inside the cathedral.

The *Church of the Rizpolozhenia* (ЦЕРКОВЬ РИЗ-ПОЛОЖЕ́НИЯ) (1484-1489, the Pskov architects) resembles the Cathedral of the Annunciation. It has many frescoes from the 17th century.

The 197-foot tall *Belltower* named after Ivan the Great (КОЛОКО́ЛЬНЯ ИВА́НА ВЕЛИ́КОГО) was built by the Italian architect Bon Fryazin in 1505-1508 and grew another 69 feet under Boris Godunov. For a long time, it served as a watchtower in the middle of the Kremlin and once was the tallest building in Moscow.

The festive *Terem-Palace* (ТЕРЕМНО́Й ДВОРЕ́Ц) (1635-1636, arch. Ushakóv, Konstantínov and others) with its white-stone thread and its brightly-colored tiles was built on the foundation of a two-story palace of the 16th century. It includes chambers of the tsars with 11 domes of the private chapels.

The *Patriarchian Palaces with the Church of the 12 Apostles* (ПАТРИА́РШИЙ ДВОРЕ́Ц, ЦЕ́РКОВЬ 12 АПО́СТОЛОВ) (1652-1656) has similar ornamentation as the Cathedral of the Assumption.

The *Hall of Facets* (ГРАНОВИ́ТАЯ ПАЛА́ТА) (1487-1491, arch. Mark Ruffo, Pietro Antonio Solari) contains the Throne Hall of the Russian tsars and emperors, traditionally used for receptions and banquets. It is the home of many valuable Russian icons and frescoes.

The *Armory Palace* (ОРУЖЕ́ЙНАЯ ПАЛА́ТА) houses old regalia, costumes, gold and silver treasures, rare arms, and a collection of coaches. It was built between 1844-1851 (arch. K. Ton, N. Chichágov, V. Bákarev) and decorated in the Russian style of the 17th century.

The other group of buildings are of later origin. Relatively small in size for their power significance, they were the centers of state activity. One of the most monumental museums of the Kremlin is the *Armory* (АРСЕНА́Л (1702-1736, arch. M. Tchoglokóv, M. Rémezov, Kh. Konrad, I. Schumacher) founded by Peter the Great as a military storage and a museum at the same time. It was rebuilt at the end of the 18th century by Matvéy Kazakóv. In 1812, during Napoleon's invasion, it was partially destroyed. Now, it houses many of the arms, armor and valuable gifts of ambassadors starting from the 16th century.

The *Grand Kremlin Palace* (БОЛЬШО́Й КРЕМЛЁВСКИЙ ДВОРЕ́Ц) (1838-1849, arch. K. Ton, N. Chichágov, V. Bákarev, F. Richter) built in a pseudo-Russian style. It resembles the Terem-Palace in its exterior. This group of several buildings includes the remnants of a palace of the 15-16th century and the oldest church in Moscow (from 1393-1394). The luxurious interior of the palace was built in a mixture of the baroque and classical styles. Originally these were the palaces of the Grand Dukes of Russia. The main halls were decorated with different Russian military orders. The St. George Hall and others located here are the most splendid and opulent halls in all of the Kremlin. During the Soviet period they were the headquarters of the Supreme Soviet of the USSR. The palace is used for formal diplomatic receptions, for government meetings and for the New Year's celebrations for children during the winter school break.

The *Senate* (СЕНА́Т) (1776-1790, arch. M. Kazakóv) is one of the best examples of Russian classicism. Its main entrance is mounted with a solemn portico.

Red Square

Ever since the 15th century, Red Square has been the center of activity in Moscow. It has taken on many faces over the centuries. It was first mentioned in the Russian Chronicles in 1434 as a market place (ТОРГ). In the 16th century it was named ТРО́ИЦКАЯ ПЛО́ЩАДЬ (Trinity Plaza) after the ТРО́ИЦКАЯ ЦЕ́РКОВЬ (Trinity Church). There was a huge round stone pediment (ЛО́БНОЕ МЕ́СТО) created in 1534 upon which the tsar's and patriarch's decrees were announced to the people.

After the big fire of 1571 the place was called ПОЖА́Р (fire). In the 17th century it was renamed КРАСНАЯ (beautiful). For many years Red Square was a ceremonial center. In our century it became a place for military parades and official demonstrations in front of Lenin's Mausoleum, where the embalmed body of the first Soviet leader lies. The Mausoleum (1929–1930, arch. Alexey Shchúsev), according to the goal of its creators, was meant to be the focus of Red Square. It is made of dark red granite combined with dark marble, labradorite, and porphyry. The Soviets have been known to wait in unbelievably long lines in order to pay tribute to their leader. Today, there are a very few lines and it is not certain how long Lenin's body will remain in there. He may soon join the other Soviet leaders in the cemetery located behind the Mausoleum.

The backdrop of the square is the *Pokrov Cathedral* (ПОКРО́ВСКИЙ СОБО́Р) or *St. Basil's Cathedral* (СОБО́Р ВАСИ́ЛИЯ БЛАЖЕ́ННОГО), named after the Russian holy fool. It was built in the colorful Byzantine style in the time of Ivan the Terrible (1555-1561 arch. Póstnik Yákovlev and Bárma), as a sign of the victory over the Kazan Khanate. It houses nine churches with fanciful cupolas which vary in design and are arranged at different levels. Completed in 1561, it is the oldest building on Red Square. The chapel of Saint Basil was joined to the Cathedral in 1588. The bell-tower and gallery on the second floor were built in the second half of the 17th century. The outer murals are of the 18th century. It is a showcase for three centuries of distinctive architectural styles—a sight to behold! Many visitors find it very beautiful, while others liken it to something that belongs in Disneyland, but all agree that it is quite an architectural achievement. The cathedral is now a museum, featuring crypts, vaults and galleries.

In front of it is the *Monument of Minin and Pozharsky* created in the style of classicism (1818, sculptor I. Martos), which commemorates the two leaders of the resistance movement against the Polish invasion in 1612.

The red brick building in the northern part of Red Square is the *Historical Museum* (ИСТОРИ́ЧЕСКИЙ МУЗЕ́Й) (Krásnaya plóshchad', 1/2). Built between 1874–1883, it was designed by the architect Vladimir Sherwood in a pseudo-Russian style with tents and kokoshniks (a word used for the female hair decorations). With its twenty rooms full of archeological objects, maps, documents, costumes, paintings, it traces the history of Russia from antiquity.

The three story white-stoned building of the same style which faces the Kremlin walls is the department store *GUM*, the former Upper Trade Stalls built between 1886–1894, (arch. A. Pomerántzev). It has numerous small shops carrying a wide range of goods. (Krásnaya plóshchad', 3/2)

As you leave the Kremlin you will enter a bustling city full of energy. Exploring the city of Moscow is great fun. Sightseeing by foot is a great way to see things that you might miss if you ride public transportation.

"Downtown" Moscow: The Merchant District

КРА́СНАЯ ПЛО́ЩАДЬ is surrounded by the oldest part of Moscow, КИТА́Й-ГО́РОД (not quite Chinatown, КИТА́Й in this case relates to the old Russian word КИ́ТА which means "wall"). It is the former trading center (or in Old Russian ТОРГО́ВЫЙ ПОСА́Д) with many beautiful architectural monuments. It was fenced by thick walls with towers (1535–1538). The remnants of its mighty walls you may see on Tretyakóvsky proyézd next to one of the first Moscow buildings in the Modern style, the "Metropol" hotel (1899–1903, arch. V. Valkotte, A. Erichson, the ceramic panel "The Princess Reverie" by the famous Russian artist M. Vrubel) (Teatrál'naya plóshchad', 1). This bold coexistence of different times and styles is one of the charming features of Moscow architecture.

On the streets surrounding the Kremlin those who love the old Moscow will make many interesting discoveries.

Zaryádye

ЗАРЯ́ДЬЕ is a charming part of Moscow next to the hotel "Rossiya" (úlitsa Rásina, 6) containing the monuments of architecture of the 15–18th centuries.

The Old Gostíny Dvor (СТА́РЫЙ ГОСТИ́НЫЙ ДВОР) (1791–1830, arch. O. Bovet, S. Kárin on the project by D. Kvarenghi) on Rázin street, 3, is a monumental merchant building with a colonnade and embrasures. The Palace of the Old English Yard (ПАЛА́ТЫ СТА́РОГО АНГЛИ́ЙСКОГО ДВОРА́) of the 16–17th century, with the festive halls was for a while a center for diplomatic and economic relations with foreign countries. Later, Peter I opened up the School of Mathematics (úlitsa Rázina, 4) in it. The one-domed Church of St. Maxim (1698) is next to The Old Sovereign Yard (СТА́РЫЙ ГОСУДА́РЕВ ДВОР), the old mansion of the 16th century belonged to Michael Romanov, the first tsar of Romanov dynasty. The second floor was built in 1674. The porch and the upper wooden floor were added in the middle of the 19th century by F. Richter. It houses the exhibition of the art and everyday life of the 17–19th centuries known as "Paláty 16-17 véka v Zaryádie" (úlitsa Rázina, 8–10).

The *Známensky Convént* (ЗНА́МЕНСКИЙ МОНАСТЬ́ІРЬ) was established in the 17th century. The five domed Znamensky Cathedral (1679-1684, arch. F. Grigóriev, G. Anísimov) has excellent acoustics and nowadays holds concerts. The cells for monks were built in 1675-78. The bell-tower was erected in the 18th century. The Trinity Church in Nikitnikakh (ЦЕ́РКОВЬ ТРО́ИЦЫ В НИКИ́ТНИКАХ) (1631-34) is one of the best examples of the pillarless churches of the 17th century with rich decor and assymetrical composition. The interior is decorated with murals of the 17th century. Some of the icons were painted by the famous Russian painter Simon Ushakóv. Now the church is a branch of the Historical Museum (Nikítnikov pereúlok, 3).

One of the most beautiful streets of old Moscow is Nikol'-skaya úitsa next to Red Square. Here one can see some of the best examples of the early St. Petersburg Baroque, the building of the *Slavic-Greek-Latin Academy* (1701-1709), the first higher educational establishment in Russia. It was located here, on the territory of a former monastery between 1687-1814. Some of its graduates include Lomonósov, Bazhénov and Kantemír, among other significant cultural minds of the 18th century. In the cathedral of the academy the reformer of Russian verse, Semeón Pólotsky, is buried (Nikólskaya úlitsa, 7-9).

The building of the *Historical-Archival Institute* (1814, by arch. A. Bokaryóv, I. Mironóvsky), was built on the territory of the former Tsars' Printing Yard (16-19th centuries). Its facade copies the old gate of the first Russian Printing Yard. In the courtyard, there is the Palace "Teremók" (1678) (Nikol'skaya úlitsa, 15).

On Istoríchesky proézd, 1, next to GUM, there is the *Mint Establishment* of the 17-18th centuries, a rare monument of an industrial building of Old Moscow. In its courtyard is a richly decorated baroque building of the end of the 17th century with carvings and tiles.

The building of the former *Gosudárstvennaya Dúma* (1890–1892, arch. D. Chichágov) was built in a pseudo-Russian style reflecting the style of the Historical Museum. Now it houses the Central Museum of Lenin. Its exposition occupies 22 halls and covers the main periods of the life and work of this political leader. Open daily 11–7. Closed Mon. (plóshchad' revolútsii, 2)

Inside the Boulevard Ring: White City

The Boulevard Ring (БУЛЬВА́РНОЕ КОЛЬЦО́) encircles the center of Moscow, the Kremlin, the Kitay gorod and what is known as White City. Located in downtown Moscow, White City (БЕ́ЛЫЙ ГО́РОД), is the site of mansions and buildings of the Russian nobility, state officials, intellectuals and artists, as well as the center of cultural life with many theaters, concert halls and museums.

The Ring, actually more of a horseshoe, is formed by a chain of ten boulevards, which took the place of the city's old fortress walls with 27 mighty towers in the 19th century. Ten towers, such as the Nikítskaya, Pokróvskaya, Yáuzskaya, Petróvskaya, Prechístyenskaya were thoroughfare. Their names are preserved in the names of some Moscow plazas and streets carrying the word "gate" (ВОРО́ТА) in their names.

The first boulevard appeared in Moscow in 1796 between Strastnáya plóshchad' and Nikítskiye Gates was Tverskóy Boulevard (ТВЕРСКО́Й БУЛЬВА́Р). It was decorated with flowerbeds, fountains and statues. In 1880, a statue of Pushkin was placed here (sculp. A. Opekúshin). Here Dostoevsky delivered his famous speech on Pushkin in 1880.

It is the oldest and the largest throughfare on the ring. There are a few traces of that time along Tverskoy. The former mansion of Herzen, which now houses the Literary Institute, is one of them. For a few years, another famous Russian author, Andrei Platonov, lived in one of the wings of this mansion in a small room while working as a yard-keeper in this institute. Tverskoy Boulevard is also a home to the theater district, which includes the Moscow Art Theater (the new building), the Pushkin

Drama Theater and the Museum-Apartment of the actress Maria Ermolova. The theater named after her is located on Tverskaya.

The Boulevard Ring starts at Prechístyensky Gates, goes towards *Gogolevsky Boulevard* (ГОГОЛЁВСКИЙ БУЛЬВАР) (former Prechístensky) with a statue of Gogol (1952, sculp. N. Tomsky) in the beginning of it to úlitsa Prechístenka, with many mansions of the 17-19th century along it which belonged to the Moscow nobility.

Suvórovsky Boulevard (named after Alexander Suvórov, the famous General of the time of Catherine the Great) continues this chain which is interrupted by Arbat Plaza from the other side. *Strastnóy Boulevard* (СТРАСТНОЙ БУЛЬВАР) with the mansions of the 18-19th century begins on the other side of Tverskáya Street. Further along the ring, from Petróvskiye Gates (ПЕТРОВСКИЕ ВОРОТА) comes *Petróvsky Boulevard* (ПЕТРОВСКИЙ БУЛЬВАР) with the remnants of the *Vysokopetróvsky Convent* (úlitsa Petróvka, 28). Founded in the time of Dmitry Donskoy, the first defeater of the Tartars at the Kulikovskaya Battle in 1380, this convent was a part of the cloisters which formed a defensive ring for the northern entrance of Moscow. Its cathedrals were built in the 16th century. Most of the later convent buildings were erected with the support of the boyars Naryshkins in a style which was called the "Naryshkin baroque" (НАРЫШКИНСКОЕ БАРОККО).

Petróvsky Boulevard leads to *Tsvetnóy Boulevard* and Trúbnaya Plaza (ТРУБНАЯ ПЛОШАДЬ), from where *Chistoprúdny Boulevard* (ЧИСТОПРУДНЫЙ БУЛЬВАР) brings us to the bustling Myasnítskaya street. The name of this boulevard means "clean pond." During the winter, its large pond is used for ice skating. The theater "Sovreménnik" faces Chistoprúdny Boulevard.

There are a lot of attractions inside the Boulevard Ring. The old building of Moscow University founded in 1755, (1776-1793, arch. M. Kazakov, D. Gellardi) is on Mokhováya úlitsa. Two monuments to its former graduates, the Russian writers Alexander Herzen and Nicholas Ogaryov (1922, scul. N. Andreyev) stand in its courtyard. The "new" building of the University (1833–1836, arch. E. Túrin, rebuilt in 1905 by arch. K. Bykóvsky) with a monument of its founder Lomonósov (1957, sculp. I Kozlóvsky) in the center of a courtyard, is located across the street from the old building. The science library of the university is located in the rotunda in its left annex. The university church was dedicated to St. Tatiana, the benefactress of students.

The *Manezh* (МАНЕ́Ж) (Mokhováya, 1/9), the former Imperial Riding School, was built in the Empirial style in 1817 by arch. A. Betancure (decorated by Bovet, 1824–25) in honor of the victory over Napoleon. It now holds the Central Exhibition Hall.

The *House of the Noble Assembly* (1793–1803) (Púshkinskaya úlitsa, 1/6) called the Column Hall (КОЛО́ННЫЙ ЗАЛ) and the House of the Governor-General (1775–1778) (Tverskáya, 13) were built by the famous Moscow architect Matvéy Kazakóv. КОЛО́ННЫЙ ЗАЛ is one of the largest concert halls in Moscow. It holds concerts and conferences. During the winter break there are celebrations of the New Year for children.

The *Moscow Conservatory named after Tchaikovsky* (КОНСЕРВАТО́РИЯ И́МЕНИ ЧАЙКО́ВСКОГО) is on Hérzen street, one of the oldest streets in Moscow. In front of its main building, is a statue of Peter Tchaikovsky (1954, sculp. V. Múkhina). Further down, at Hérzen street 36, there is the Church of the Grand Ascension (ЦЕ́РКОВЬ БОЛЬШО́ГО ВОЗНЕСЕ́НИЯ) (1820–1840) with its noble structures of late classicism. Here in 1831 Pushkin married one of the first beauties of Moscow, Natália Goncharóva.

The part of Moscow from the Kremlin to Arbat was filled by palaces, chambers and mansions of nobility from the time of

Ivan the Terrible to the second part of the 19th century, when the rich merchants began to settle there.

The majestic *House of Pashkóv* , or the old building of the *Rumyantsev Museum and Library* (1784-1786, arch. V. Bazhénov), is one of the best examples of Russian classicism (Mokhováya, 24). Next to it is the complex of new buildings (1929-41) of the Russian State Library, sometimes referred to as Rumyantsev Library, one of the biggest libraries in the world (Vozdvízhenka, 3). Formerly called Lenin Library, it contains about 30 billion books in 247 languages.

The *Museum of Architecture named after Shchúsev* (1773, arch. M. Kazakov), is located in the city mansion of Talyzin. It was rebuilt after the fire of 1812 (Vozdvízhenka, 5). The building has a portico with pilasters of the Corinthian style. The interior is well preserved. Its exposition contains rare manuscripts, sketches, drawings, and engravings of famous architects.

The exotic building in pseudo-Mooresque style with cupolas and the rounded colonnade (arch. V. Mazurin) belonged to the merchant-millionaire Alexander Morozov famous for patronizing Russian literature and art. Now it houses the *House of Friendship.* Lectures, exhibitions, concerts are held here.

The busy shopping district of Moscow includes *Kuznétsky most, Petróvka, Neglínnaya,* and *Stoléshnikov pereúlok.* In the 19th century, Kuznétsky most was the center of fashion with many French shops and fancy stores. The TSUM (ЦУМ), or Central department store is a popular shopping center of 12 shops on Neglínnaya and Petróvka streets, Stoléshnikov pereúlok and Kuznétsky most. Its main building, the former "Mure and Merilise" (1908-1910, arch. R. Klein), is a modern construction in pseudo-gothic style (the store is open Mon-Fri, 11 a.m.-9 p.m. Sat. 8 a.m.-9 p.m. Closed Sun.)

Among the historical monuments in this part of the city, is the *Rozhdéstvensky Convent* founded in the 14th century. Its cathedral was built in the beginning of the 16th century. It has a pyramidal composition. The Church of Ivan the Golden Mouth (ЦЕ́РКОВЬ ИВА́НА ЗЛАТОУ́СТА) is of the 17th century, the bell-tower was built by arch. I. Kozlóvsky (1835) (Rozhdés-tvenka, 20).

Ménshikov Tower (МЕ́НЬШИКОВСКАЯ БА́ШНЯ) or the Church of Archangel Gabriel, was built in 1704-1707 by the architect Zarúdny commissioned by Peter the Great's friend Ménshikov. The tower with its wooden spire and a figure of Archangel Gabriel was the tallest monument in Moscow at that time (almost 3 feet taller than the tower of Ivan the Great.) But in 1723 the wooden spire was burned by lightning and then replaced by a short cupola. The richly decorated Church of Archangel Gabriel is considered one of the best constructions of the Russian baroque. It combines elements of Moscow architecture and St. Petersburg baroque (Telegráfny pereúlok, 15a).

Another example of Moscow baroque is the *Church of the Sign* (ЦЕ́РКОВЬ ЗНАМЕ́НИЯ) of the late 17th century. Its bright red and white colors are typical for this festive style (úlitsa Granóvskovo, 2).

The former *Palace of the Boyar Troyekurov* (ПАЛА́ТЫ БОЯ́РИНА ТРОЕКУ́РОВА) built in the 16th and rebuilt at the end of 17th century incorporates the elements of different styles and shows the influence of European architecture (Geórgievsky pereúlok, 4).

Inside the Garden Ring

What is now the *Garden Ring* (САДО́ВОЕ КОЛЬЦО́) used to be the borders of the city. A five-yard high wooden wall with more then 100 towers was built on the high earth rampart. The names of some of these towers were preserved in the names of some streets, such as Tverskáya, Sadóvo-Triumphál'naya. The wall was built between 1591-1592, during the reign of Boris Godunov and was destroyed during the Time of Troubles and rebuilt in the 17th century. After the war with Napoleon, it was torn down, the moat was covered, streets were built over it and buildings were erected. The Garden Ring, which encircles Moscow, incorporates 16 streets, including Sadóvaya and Samotyóchnaya.

Earth City

The most colorful part of Moscow inside of the Garden Ring is *Earth City* (ЗЕМЛЯНО́Й ГО́РОД). Here you will see the structures of the 17th century, among them, one of the most festive Moscow constructions, the Church of the Birth of Our Lady in Putínki (ЦЕ́РКОВЬ РОЖДЕСТВА́ БОГОРО́ДИЦЫ В ПУТИ́НКАХ, 1649-1652) (úlitsa Chékhova) and the two-story palace of Avérky Kirílov connected with the church (ПАЛА́ТЫ АВЕ́РКИЯ КИРИ́ЛОВА, (1656-1657) (Bersénevskaya náberezhnaya, 20).

Several houses in Earth City are worth seeing. The house of Úshkov (1793, arch. V. Bazhénov), is considered one of the masterpieces of Russian classic architecture (Myasnítskaya, 21). The house of Lobánov-Rostóvsky which features a spectacular arch (1790's) (Myasnítskaya, 43), the mansion of Batashóv, with its triumphant Corinthian portico and the mansion of Barýshnikov were built by Matvéy Kazakóv in the late 18th century. They represent a combination of intimacy and majesty common to Moscow classicism (Myasnítskaya, 42). In the latter, Alexander Griboyedov wrote his famous play "Sorrow from Intellect." There is one exotic building on Myasnitskaya street, the building with the roof-pagoda, dragons, and lanterns in a pseudo-Chinese style (1896, arch. R. Klein, K. Gippius). It is an old store named "Tea" where one can buy both tea and coffee. Across the street from it is the Main Post Office (1912, arch. Munts), which has always

211

been the point of measurement of the distance from Moscow to any place. Further down, on Myasnítskaya, 39 is a notable building with a bold combination of a pinkish-purple tufa with a bluish glass, a rare example of Constructivist architecture by the famous French architect Le Corvoisier (1929-1936).

The *Mansion of Ryabuschínsky* (ulitsa Kachálova, 6/2) with its free planning, expressive facade, big windows of different shapes, and elaborate ornaments, is one of the best examples of the Moscow modern style (arch. F. Schechtel, 1902-1906). Now it houses the Museum-apartment of Gorky. The House of Pertzóv (1905-1907, arch. S. Malútin) with its bold use of assymetrical composition, is an original example of the Neo-Russian modernism (Sóymonovsky proyézd, 1).

The new architectural complex on the *Novy Arbat* includes the festive five-domed Church of Simeon Stolpnik with a tent-style bell-tower (from the 17th century). The Old Arbat, a street for pedestrians only, attracts many tourists.

Zamoskvoryéchie

The old districts of Moscow where merchants and impoverished nobles once lived is a lively part of the city. With its richly decorated churches and cozy mansions, Zamoskvoryéchie maintains the unique aura of Old Moscow.

The *Tretyakóv Gallery* (ТРЕТЬЯКÓВСКАЯ ГАЛЕРÉЯ) named after its founder Pavel Tretyakov, is one of the main attractions of this part of Moscow. Built in the pseudo-Russian style (1899-1906, the facade by the famous Russian artist V. Vasnetzov, 1902), it houses 58,000 works of Russian art, including ancient icons, paintings and sculptures. (Lavrúshinsky pereúlok, 10)

The *Church of our Lady of all Mourning for Joy* (ЦÉР-КОВЬ БОГОМÁТЕРИ ВСЕХ СКОРБЯЩИХ РÁДОСТИ) (1828-1836, arch. O. Bovet) is one of the best examples of Moscow classicism. Its bell-tower and the dining room were built by the prominent architect of Russian classicism V. Bazhénov between 1783 and 1791 (Big Ordynka, 20). The Mansion of Dolgorúkovy is also a creation of Bazhénov (1770) and Bovet (1820) (Bolsháya Ordýnka, 21/16). The festive Church of Nikóla in Pyzhí (1657-1670) has a lot of decorations made of bricks (Bolsháya Ordýnka, 27a).

The brightly colored five-domed *Church of Clement* (1762-1770) with its tall bell-tower (1758) (Pyátnitskaya 26/7) combines the decorative traditions of old Russian architecture with the late baroque style. The *Church of John the Warrior* (1713, ЦÉРКОВЬ ИОÁННА ВÓИНА) (úlitsa Dimítrova, 46), a construction of the 18th century, was commisioned by Peter the Great in honor of the victory of Poltava. The *Church of Gregory Neokessaryisky* (1667-1669) on Bolsháya Polyánka, 29a has a well preserved tile frieze, a part of an outer painting made by Stepan Polubes.

Outside the Garden Ring

Outside the *Garden Ring,* there is a prominent monument of the 15th-17th centuries, the festive *Krutîtskoye podvórye* (КРУТЍЦКОЕ ПОДВÓРЬЕ). It includes the Cathedral of the Assumption (УСПÉНСКИЙ СОБÓР) of the 15th century (rebuilt in the 17th century) and the Metropolitian Palace (1665). The stone passages connecting the buildings are decorated with bright tiles (Pérvy Krutítsky pereúlok, 4).

The *Church of Nikóla in Khamóvniki* (1676-1682) is decorated with three layers of kokóshniki. Its colored tiles and carved decor are very picturesque. The tiled bell-tower has a tent construction.

The *Church of Pokróv located in Medvédkovo* (ЦÉРКОВЬ ПОКРОВÁ В МЕДВÉДКОВЕ, 1634-1635) was built in the mansion of the defender of Moscow against the Polish invasion, Duke Pozharsky. It has a tent construction resembling St. Basil's Cathedral on Red Square.

The three-domed *Church of the Trinity in Khoroshévo* (1596-1598) is a part of what used to be Boris Godunov's estate. It is decorated with half-rounded kokóshniki. Its bell-tower is of a later origin (1840) (Karámyshevskaya náberezhnaya, 15).

The *Church of Pokrova v Rubtsóve* (1619-1626) was built in honor of the victory over Polish King Ladislaus (Bakúninskaya úlitsa, 36).

The small *Church of the Trinity* in Tróitse-Lýkovo (ЦЕ́РКОВЬ ТРО́ИЦЫ) (1690-1695, arch. Ushakóv, Konstantínov) with its three-layered construction, richly decorated with carved ornamentation, is one of the best monuments of Naryshkinsky baroque.

The *Church of Pokrov in Fili* (ЦЕ́РКОВЬ ПОКРОВА́ В ФИ́ЛЯ́Х, 1691-1693) is famous for its original layered construction, one of the best of its kind. The interior of the late 17th century is well preserved and contains a curved iconostasis and icons by painters who worked in the Armory Palace in the Kremlin (Novozavódskaya úlitsa, 47).

The monumental *Bogoyávlensky Patriárshy Cathedral* (the end of the 18th century, arch. E. Túrin, Spartákovskaya úlitsa), the *Church of Nikita the Martyr* (1751, arch. D. Ukhtómsky, úlitsa Karla Marxa, 16) and the *Church of Pokrová* (Kutúzovsky prospéct, 38) are good examples of Moscow baroque.

Pokróvskie voróta, Razgulyáy, úlitsa Chernyshévskovo, Lefórtovo are noteworthy for constructions of baroque and classicism. The majestic *Palace of Catherine*, or *Golovín Palace*

(ГОЛОВИ́НСКИЙ ДВОРЕ́Ц), was built in the second half of the 18th century by D. Kvarenghi and D. Rinaldi. It has 16 pillars of the festive Corinthian style. It is the biggest colonnade in Moscow (Pérvy Krasnokursántsky proyézd, 3).

The *Slobodskóy Palace* (СЛОБОДСКО́Й ДВОРЕ́Ц) (Vtoráya Báumanskaya, 5) was built by Matvey Kazakóv on the project of D. Kvarenghi. It was rebuilt by another prominent architect D. Gilliardi in 1826. Its red facades with the two-columned loggias are of the late origin. The park of the palace with ponds and bridges is partially preserved. Now it houses the Moscow Technical University. Next to it is *Lefórtovsky Palace* which belonged to the closest friend of young Peter the Great, Franz Lefort. After the death of his friend, Peter moved here from the Kremlin and it became for a short time a residence of the young Russian Tsar. Here his famous first assemblies took place. (Vtoráya Báumanskaya, 3).

There are a few other buildings by Matvéy Kazakóv, including the *Mansion of Demîdov* (ОСОБНЯ́К ДЕМИ́ДОВА) (80's of the 18th century) with the monumental Corinthian portico (Gorókhovsky pereúlok, 4) and the former *Golitzyn's Hospital* (1796-1801) (ГОЛИ́ЦИНСКАЯ БОЛЬНИ́ЦА), a building of majestic composition. The latter was one of the best public constructions of that time. The tomb of D. Golitzyn is located in the church of the hospital (Léninsky prospéct, 8).

The *Mansion of Razumóvsky* (1801-1803, arch. A. Menelas), is a rare example of a wooden mansion which survived the fire of 1812 (úlitsa Kazakóva, 18). The *Mansion of Usatché-vykh-Naydénovykh* (1829-1831, arch. Gellardi) is a well preserved city mansion with garden pavillions (úlitsa Chkálova, 53).

An ensemble of architecture of a later period can be seen on Komsomol Plaza with its three railroads: the yellow and white building of the *Leningrad Railroad Station* (former Nikoláevsky)

(1851, arch. K. Ton) where the first train from St. Petersburg arrived almost one hundred and fifty years ago. Next to it, the *Yaroslávsky Railroad Station* (ЯРОСЛА́ВСКИЙ ВОКЗА́Л, 1902-1904, arch. F. Schechtel) has an asymmetrical construction in the Neo-Russian modern style. The *Kazan Railroad Station* (КАЗА́НСКИЙ ВОКЗА́Л, 1913-1926, arch. A. Shchúsev, artists Kustódiev, Lanceret, Roérich) is located across the plaza. Its main tower resembles the tower of Suyumbéki in Kazan but it is decorated with old Russian ornaments. The Central House of the Railroad Workers (1925, arch. A. Shchúsev) and the 26-story hotel "Leningradsky" (1954) are also a part of this ensemble.

The *Kievan Railroad Station* with its asymmetrical construction (1913-1917, arch. I. Rerberg) was done in the Neo-classical style (Kievan Railroad Plaza). The hotel "Ukraina" is on the corner of Kutúzovsky prospéct.

The *Museum of the Borodin Battle* (1962, arch. A. Korabélnikov) is located on Kutúzovsky prospéct. Its main building has a cylindric construction and is decorated with colored glass showing a decisive episode of the Battle in Borodino. In front of it stands the statue of Michael Kutuzov and his comrades-in-arms, Generals Bagration and Ermolov.

At the end of Kutuzovsky prospect is the *Triumphal Arch* erected in honor of victory Russia in the war of 1812 and the successful foreign campaign of the Russian troops in 1813-1814 (1827-1834, sculp. I. Vitali, arch. O. Bovet).

The *Rusakov House of Culture* (ДОМ КУЛЬТУ́РЫ И́МЕНИ РУСАКО́ВА) is one of the best examples of Russian constructivism (arch. Mél'nikov, the late 20's). It has a dynamic composition and its auditorium has an unusual architectural layout which gives a visual effect of transformed space (Stromýnka, 6).

216

The *Planetarium* (1927-1929, arch. M. Barshch) with its laconic forms is another example of the constructivist style of that time (Sadóvo-Kúdrinskaya, 5).

The *Television Center* (1964-1969, arch. L. Batalóv) has a tower almost 541 feet high. In the tower is the famous revolving restaurant *Sed'móe Nyébo* (The *Seventh Heaven*) (úlitsa akadémika Koroléva, 15).

In the southwest of Moscow, there are many new streets. In this region are the new complex of Moscow University, the new buildings of the *Circus,* of the *Children's Musical Theater,* and of the Central Stadium *Luzhniki* (built in 1955-1956). The stadium seats over 100,000 people, has 130 halls and a large park with training courses. Near the stadium, stands the hotel Yunost'.

The complex of the new buildings of Moscow University, (1949-1953, arch. L. Rúdnev, S. Chernyshóv) is centered around one of the few skyscrapers in Moscow. Its main building contains a few departments of the university, the assembly hall, the scientific library, the museum, and the House of Culture. It has 50,000 rooms, including dormitories for students in its annexes. Altogether 37 buildings belong to the university. In front of the university is a park with a statue of Lomonósov, the founder of Moscow University. There is a lookout tower on the highest point of Léninskiye (former Vorobiévy) Mountains (ГО́РЫ) which offers one of the best views of Moscow. "One who wants to understand Russia must come here and look at Moscow from here," Chekhov had once said when climbing up the mountains. One may recall here the description of a panorama of Moscow from Poklónnaya gorá by Leo Tolstoy in *War and Peace* : "Seeing this strange city with unprecedented forms of unusual architecture, Napoleon felt the blend of a slight envy and disturbing curiosity which is felt by people upon seeing alien life unaware of them."

MOSCOW OPERA, BALLET, DRAMA AND CONCERT HALLS

Russians are avid theater and concert goers. Theaters stage both domestic and foreign productions. You might compare a Russian staging of Shakespeare, Moliere, Ibsen, Maeterlinck, Arthur Miller or Tennesee Williams with Western productions. During your trip, don't miss the chance for you to see and hear Pushkin, Gogol, Tolstoy, Dostoyevsky, Chekhov or Bulgakov in the original language.

The Theaters of Opera and Ballet

The *Bolshói Theater* БОЛЬШОЙ ТЕАТР (Teatrálnaya plóshchad', 2), once called the Great Imperial Theater, is by far the most famous in all of Russia.

Its ballet troupe, orchestra and opera productions are world renowned. There are many Russian and foreign operas and ballets in its repertoire. Its orchestra is also remarkable. Tickets are often hard to come by for popular performances. Try to get tickets for rubles on your own at the theater to avoid paying hard currency at a tourist bureau.

The Bolshoi is not only famous for its fabulous performances, but also for its exquisite architecture. Built between 1821 and 1824, by design of the famous architect O. Bovet in the empire style, it is one of the best examples of Moscow architecture. It was rebuilt after a fire in 1856 by Kavos. Its monumental portico with 8 columns has a pediment with a figure of Apollo, the benefactor of art (sculptor P. Klodt). The seating capacity of the Bolshoi is 2,155.

The Bolshoi also presents performances on the stage of the pompous Kremlin Palace of Party Congresses (6,000 seats), the accoustics of which are more suited to political debates than operatic voices. The entrance is through the Kutáfia Gate, by the Manezh which leads to the Trinity Gates.

The *Stanislavsky and Nemirovich-Danchenko Musical Theater* АКАДЕМИ́ЧЕСКИЙ МУЗЫКА́ЛЬНЫЙ ТЕА́ТР О́ПЕРЫ И БАЛЕ́ТА И́МЕНИ К.С. СТАНИСЛА́ВСКОГО И В.И. НЕМИРО́ВИЧА-ДА́НЧЕНКО (Púshkinskaya, 17) was founded in 1941 and holds 1,400 people. Its repertoire includes classical and modern operas and ballets. It is located in a very pleasant area.

Moscow Chamber Opera Theater КА́МЕРНЫЙ МУЗЫ-КА́ЛЬНЫЙ ТЕАТР, (Leningrádsky prospéct, 71) is a rather young theater, founded in 1971. It has many experimental productions.

The *Operetta Theater* ТЕА́ТР ОПЕРЕ́ТТЫ (Púshkinskaya, 6). Founded in 1927, it holds 2,000 people. Its interior is surprisingly similar to that of Carnegie Hall, except in miniature. It hosts productions of many classical and modern operettas including Lehar, Kalman and Johann Strauss.

The *Children's Musical Theater* ДЕ́ТСКИЙ МУЗЫКА́ЛЬНЫЙ ТЕА́ТР (prospéct Vernádskogo, 5). Built in 1979 by Krasílnikov and Velikánov, it has an unusual construction, a cylindrical tower with 5 sculptured portals. The building is decorated with the figure of Blue Bird, the subject of the well-known play by Maeterlinck.

The Drama Theaters

The *Maly Theater* ГОСУДА́РСТВЕННЫЙ АКАДЕМИ́ЧЕСКИЙ МА́ЛЫЙ ТЕАТР, the former Little Imperial Theater, is one of the oldest drama theaters in Russia. Founded in 1824, it became famous for its staging of the Russian classics, especially of the famous "playwright of Zamoskvoréchie" Alexander Ostróvsky, who was the creator of the realistic trend in the Russian theater and whose plays were once called "the university for the Russian people." The repertoire includes productions of classical and contemporary Russian and Western plays. The major stage of the Maly is at Teatrál'naya plóshchad' 1/6 and its branch in Zamoskvoréchie, at Bolsháya Ordýnka, 69. The main building was constructed by Bovet and reconstructed in 1838-40 by arch. Ton. The statue of Ostrovsky was placed in front of it in 1929 (sculpt. N. Andreyev).

Moscow Art Theater (MKHAT) (arch. Chichágov, Shechtel, sculptor Golúbkina) (proézd Khudózhestvennogo teátra, 3). Founded in 1898 by Konstantin Stanislavsky, the theater became famous for its productions of Chekhov's plays. Its emblem is a seagull after the successful staging of Chekhov's play "The Seagull" in the 1898-99 season. The theater works in the tradition of "psychological realism" according to the system of Stanislavsky disclosing the "drama of everyday life." The old building keeps the atmosphere of Chekhov's time. The modern building of Moscow Art Theater was opened on Tverskoy Boulevard in 1973. The repertoire includes productions of classical and contemporary Russian and Western plays.

Be sure to visit MKHAT, especially if you are concerned with good Russian. The pronunciation of the actors of this theater is considered to be the literary norm of contemporary Russian language.

Ermolova Theater (ТЕА́ТР ЕРМО́ЛОВОЙ) (Tverskáya, 5) named after Maria Ermólova who was, in the words of Konstantin Stanislavsky, "a whole epoch for the Russian theater." Founded in 1937, it stages classical and contemporary Russian and Western plays.

Vakhtángov Theater (ТЕА́ТР ВАХТА́НГОВА) (Arbat, 26) named after Stanislavsky's pupil, Evgeny Vakhtángov (1883-1922). Founded in 1921, it is an excellent experimental and fine traditional theater.

Moscow Drama Theater named after Pushkin (МОС-КО́ВСКИЙ ДРАМАТИ́ЧЕСКИЙ ТЕА́ТР И́МЕНИ ПУ́ШКИНА) (Tverskoy boulevard, 23) was founded in 1950 on the basis of the well known Tairov Chamber Theater Classical and contemporary plays are performed on its stage.

The *Theater named after Mayakovsky* (ТЕА́ТР И́МЕНИ МАЯКО́ВСКОГО) (úlitsa Hérzena, 19) became popular between 1943 and 1967 under the direction of Nicholas Okhlópkov. It houses a wide range of productions, from Shakespeare's *Hamlet* to Mayakovsky's The *Bug*.

The *Theater of Drama on Málaya Brónnaya* (ДРАМА-ТИ́ЧЕСКИЙ ТЕА́ТР НА МА́ЛОЙ БРО́ННОЙ) was founded in 1946. It hosts productions of domestic and Western playwrights. The theater is located in a charming area near the Patriarch ponds (ПАТРИА́РШИЕ ПРУДЫ́), the area of the setting of Bulgakov's novel "The Master and Margarita."

The new building of the *Theater of Drama and Comedy on Taganka* (ТЕАТР ДРА́МЫ И КОМЕ́ДИИ НА ТАГА́НКЕ) with a brick facade is located on úlitsa Chkálova, 76 (1974-81, arch. A. Anísimov). Its hall faces the landscape of Old Moscow. The production of the theater is lively and experimental. Many foreign plays are performed here.

The *Theater "Sovremennik"*(ТЕАТР "СОВРЕМЕ́ННИК") develops the theatrical school of MKHAT with productions for both young and adult audiences.

The *Theater of the Red Army* ТЕА́ТР КРА́СНОЙ А́РМИИ (plóshchad' Kommúny, 2) was built between 1934-1940 by arch. K. Alabyán, V. Simbírtsev). A pompous building with a pentacle in its plan has two theatrical halls. Its repertoire includes classical and modern plays, both Russian and Western.

The *Gypsy Theater "Romen"* (ЦЫГА́НСКИЙ ТЕА́ТР "РОМЭН") (Leningrádsky prospéct, 32-2) is a professional Gypsy theater founded in 1931. Its production can sometimes be melodramatic, but it is worth seeing since many Gypsy songs and dances are performed. The performances are held in Russian, songs are performed in the Gypsy language.

The *Central Children's Theater* (ЦЕНТРА́ЛЬНЫЙ ДЕ́ТСКИЙ ТЕА́ТР) (arch. Bovet, 1821, Teatrál'naya plóshchad', 2) was founded in 1921 and presents performances for children and young people. The theater stages many favorite children's fairy tales and plays.

The *Theater of The Young Spectator* (ТЕА́ТР ЮНОГО ЗРИ́ТЕЛЯ) (pereúlok Sadóvskikh, 10). Founded in 1941, the theater hosts performances mostly for teenagers.

The building of the *Central Theater of Puppets named after Obraztsov* ЦЕНТРА́ЛЬНЫЙ ТЕА́ТР КУ́КОЛ (Sadóvaya-Samotyóchnaya, 3) was built in 1971 by arch. Yu. Sheverdyáyev, A. Mélikhov and decorated with a "puppet cuckoo clock" with moving figures of some of the heroes of children's fairy tales. Although primarily a children's theater, it also puts on plays for adults.

The *Theater of Puppets* ТЕА́ТР КУ́КОЛ (Spartákovskaya, 26) was founded in 1930 as the *Children's Books theater*. It holds performances for children and adults.

The *Theater of Mimics and Gesture* (ТЕА́ТР МИ́МИКИ И ЖЕ́СТА) (Izmáylovsky Boulevard, 39–41) was founded in 1963. It is probably especially good for those who are tired of "Words! Words! Words!"

Dúrov's Theater of Animals (ТЕА́ТР ЗВЕРЕ́Й И́МЕНИ ДУ́РОВА) was founded in 1912 under the name "The Corner of Dúrov." Its performances feature well-trained animals. The new building was built in 1980 by G. Savich. It has a cylindrical form and richly decorated with forged bronze sculpture. An adjoining elephant stable is a part of the theater (úlitsa Durova, 4).

The *Circus on Tsvetnoy Boulevard, 13* is a charming, well-equipped circus. One thing we can say about the Moscow Circus is: "Do not miss it!" You may very well have seen the Moscow Circus at home, but remember that when a troupe travels it can only bring along about a third of its equipment, performers and animals. The perfectly trained animals, amazing acrobats, and agile contortionists are just a few of the fabulous acts you will witness. The trained bear is one of the unique attractions of this circus.

The *New Circus* (prospéct Vernádskogo, 7) was built in 1971 by the architects Belopólsky, Vulých, Feoctístov. Its ring can be transformed into a swimmimg pool or a skating rink. For those traveling in the winter, there is also a circus on ice by the Moscow Ice Ballet.

Orchestras, Ensembles and Concert Halls

The *State Symphonic Orchestra* (ГОСУДА́РСТВЕННЫЙ СИМФОНИ́ЧЕСКИЙ ОРКЕ́СТР) has series of performances every year. The other prominent musical ensembles and choirs are: the *Orchestra of the Bolshoy Theater*, the *Orchestra of Radio*, t h e *Barshay Chamber Orchestra, Beethoven's Quartet*, the *Yuriev Choir Capella,* and the *Pyatnitsky Choir.*

The *Grand Hall of the Conservatory* (БОЛЬШО́Й ЗАЛ КОНСЕРВАТО́РИИ) (Hérsten Street, 13) was opened in 1901. It houses symphony orchestra concerts, choirs, musical recitals and festivals. Its organ is one of the biggest in the world. The hall has excellent acoustic. Its walls are decorated with portraits of famous composers.

The *Small Hall of the Conservatory* (МА́ЛЫЙ ЗАЛ КОНСЕРВАТО́РИИ) is a part of the building of the Conservatory. It was open in 1898. Its acoustics are quite good. The hall is very cosy. Its organ was placed in 1954.

Tchaikovsky Concert Hall (КОНЦЕ́РТНЫЙ ЗАЛ И́МЕНИ ЧАЙКОВСКОГО) (Bol'shắya Sadóvaya úlitsa, 20) was built in 1935-40). This well constructed hall has one of best organs in the country. It holds series of musical concerts and literary performances.

The *Hall of Columns* (КОЛО́ННЫЙ ЗАЛ ДО́МА СОЮЗОВ) (Púshkinskaya, 1) holds many concerts and holiday events. Since 1935, the New Year celebrations for children around the Christmas tree have been held in this festive hall.

The *Hall of the Gnesins Music Institute* (КОНЦЕ́РТНЫЙ ЗАЛ МУЗЫКА́ЛЬНО-ПЕДАГОГИ́ЧЕСКОГО ИНСТИТУ́ТА И́МЕНИ ГНЕ́СИНЫХ) úlitsa Voróvskogo, 30/36) holds many good concerts.

The *Concert Hall in Známensky Cathedral* (úlitsa Rázina, 8a) holds concerts of old and sacred music. It has excellent acoustics.

Museums of Art and Architecture

The *Tretyakóv Gallery* ТРЕТЬЯКО́ВСКАЯ ГАЛЕРЕ́Я (Lavrúshinsky pereúlok, 10, near the subway station "Novokuznetskaya") has the finest collection of Russian art dating back from the 11th century. The gallery is named after two brothers who were art collectors in the 19th century, Sergei and Pavel Tretyakov. Within 40 years they amassed 1,850 works of Russian artists of the 19th century such as Peróv, Kramskói, Vasnetsóv, Polénov, Répin, Súrikov, Levitán, Seróv. In 1892, after Sergey died, Pavel Tretyakov gave the entire collection to the city of Moscow.

The museum has over 50 halls, each devoted to either a period of time, a subject, or an artist or group of artists. There is an excellent collection of Russian icons by the famous painters Andrey Rublev and Feofan the Greek, as well as a collection of portraits by such notable Russian portrait-masters of the 18-19th centuries as Fyodor Rókotov, Vladimir Borovikóvsky, Dmitry Levítsky, Orest Kiprénsky.

Look for the works of one of the most elegant Russian painters of the 19th century, Carl Brulóv, especially his complex multifigured composition "The Last Day of Pompeii" ("ПОСЛЕ́ДНИЙ ДЕНЬ ПОМПЕ́И"). You will likewise be impressed with the lofty visionary work of the famous Russian academist

224

painter Alexander Ivánov, "The Appearance of Christ before the People" (ЯВЛЕ́НИЕ ХРИСТА́ НАРО́ДУ"), a huge bright canvas. You will be equally touched by the sharp dramatism of expression of Vassiliy Súrikov in his painting "Boyárynya Morózova" and by the tragic overtones of Nikolay Ge's canvas "Peter I and Tsarevitch Alexei," depicting the split and conflict in Russian history. The most noticeable work by Ilia Répin in the gallery is "Ivan the Terrible Slaying his Son" ("ИВАН ГРО́ЗНЫЙ УБИВА́ЕТ СВОЕГО́ СЫ́НА"). Based on historical fact, this painting carries in itself the deep despair of the artist in the face of evil coming from human deeds. In one of the next halls your attention will be caught by a "Christ in the Desert" ("ХРИСТО́С В ПУСТЫ́НЕ") by Ivan Kramskói which displays the different mood. It shows an understanding of the tragedy of human history and a readiness to overcome it.

The works of the other painters such as Vassily Tropínin, Vassiliy Polénov, Alexey Savrásov, Issak Levitan give us a warm and sharp view of Russia of the 19th century—its life, its people, and its nature. In the gallery are well-represented works of painters of the Realist trend and the modernist painters of the 19-20th centuries. It displays the works of painters deeply immersed in national substance, such as Konstantin Koróvin, Kustódiev, Malyávin, Ryábushkin, Michael Nésterov, on the one side, and the canvases of the "Russian Europeans" featuring in their works the main trends of European art, on the other, including the imaginative paintings by a master of color Borísov-Musátov, the melancholic retrospectives of Alexander Benois, the nostalgic images of Konstantin Sómov and the syncretic style of work by Mikhail Vrubel.

Russian avant-garde art is represented, among the others, by the group "Bubnóvy Valét" (1910), including Mikhail Lariónov, Natalia Goncharóva, Alexander Lentúlov, Pavel Konchalóvsky, Ilia Mashkóv, Alexander Kuprín, and others.

Much of the Tretiakov collection consists of Russian paintings of the late 20th century. It also houses regular exhibitions, both contemporary and retrospective.

The *Pushkin Fine Arts Museum* МУЗЕ́Й ИЗОБРАЗИ́-
ТЕЛЬНЫХ ИСКУ́ССТВ И́МЕНИ ПУ́ШКИНА (ulitsa Volkhonka, 12,
ph. 221-20-56), first known as Alexander III's Museum, was
founded by prof. Ivan Tsvetaev, the father of Marina Tsvetayeva
(1895-1912, arch. R. Klein). The architecture of the museum is
based on antique subject matter since the museum was designated
for collections of replicas of antique sculptures. Now the museum
has the second largest collection of European art in Russia after
the Hermitage in St. Petersburg. It houses works of Western art
from all over the world. You will see works by Boschus, Breugel,
Botticelli, Van Dyck, Rembrandt, Watteau, Poussin, David,
Delacroix, Courbet, Constable, Lawrence, Cezanne and other
notable European artists. The museum boasts one of the best
collections of the French impressionists, including works of
Bonnard, Renoir, Monet, Pissarro, and Degas. Paintings by
post-impressionists Matisse, Van Gogh and Gauguin are also
well-represented. Open daily (11-5). Closed Tues.

Other Art Museums

The *Museum of Art of the Peoples of the East* (МУ́ЗЕЙ
ИСКУ́ССТВА НАРО́ДОВ ВОСТО́КА, (Suvórovsky Boulevard,
12a) contains a rich collection of Roerich's visionary works.
Exhibitions represent the traditional and contemporary art of
China, Japan, Korea, Vietnam, the Near East and the Far East.
Its collection of Persian art, the richest in Russia, goes back to
the fourth millenia B.C. It includes antique ceramics and Luristan
bronzes, the Iranian ceramics from the Middle Ages (bowls, jugs,
vessels, tiles), the Iranian miniatures of the 15-16th centuries, old
manuscripts, Iranian textile of the 16-17th centuries and valuable
carpets of the 17-18 centuries.

The *Museum of Decorative and Applied Art* ВСЕРОС-
СИ́ЙСКИЙ МУЗЕ́Й ДЕКОРАТИВНО-ПРИКЛАДНО́ГО ИСКУ́ССТВА
(Delegátskaya úlitsa, 5). Located in the former Palace of Oster-
man, the museum contains works of art of the 17-19th centuries,

including lacquered miniature, Zhostov trades, Bogorodsky and Dymkovsky toys and Gzhel ceramics.

The *Museum of Tropinin and the Moscow Painters of his Time* МУЗЕЙ ТРОПЙНИНА И МОСКОВСКИХ ХУДОЖНИКОВ ЕГО ВРЕМЕНИ (Shchetíninsky pereúlok, 10). Located in Zamoscvorechie, the mansion belonged to professor Petukhóv. It welcomed many famous Russians, the composer Alexander Scriábin, the artsists Borísov-Musátov and Pável Kuznetsóv. It was bequeathed by the owner to F. Vishnévsky, a collector of works of Tropínin and other Moscow painters. In 1968, Vishnévsky gave the mansion and about 200 pieces of art, including 40 works of Tropínin, to the future museum. In 1971 the museum was opened. Its first hall represents the portrait art of the 18th century. In the second hall are portraits by Tropínin, including the version of his famous "The Lacemaker." In the third, the chamber hall, there are portraits in watercolor. In the fourth room, there is "Self-portrait with Brushes and Pallete in the Studio next to Lenivka River" (1844) by Tropínin, and other painters of his time.

The *Museum-Studio of the Sculptor Golúbkina* (МУЗЕЙ-МАСТЕРСКАЯ СКУЛЬПТОРА ГОЛУБКИНОЙ) (úlitsa Shchúkina, 12). Presents sculptural works, cameos, and drawings by the sculptor.

The *Museum of Victor Vasnetsóv (*МУЗЕЙ ВИКТОРА ВАС-НЕЦОВА*)* (pereúlok Vasnetsóva,12). The former home of the artist in which he lived for 30 years. Based on his drawing, this a Russian style village house in the center of Moscow containing many works by Vasnetsóv.

Literary, Musical and Theatrical Museums

Tolstoy's Moscow Mansion (МУЗЕЙ-УСАДЬБА ЛЬВА ТОЛСТОГО "ХАМОВНИКИ") is a favorite visiting spot for Tolstoy readers (Leo Tolstoy Street, 21). The sixteen rooms of the house built in 1808 are preserved just as they were when Leo Tolstoy and his family lived there between 1882 to 1909. Here he wrote his last novel "Resurrection," and the plays "The Living Corpse," "The Power of Ignorance" and "The Fruits of Enlightenment."

There is also the *Leo Tolstoy Museum* which houses his manuscripts, personal writings, paintings and sketches of Tolstoy. It is located in the former house of the Lopukhíns (1817-1822, arch. A. Grigóriev). A typical mansion in the classical style, it has yellow-white walls and a portico with a pediment. The interior of the mansion is well preserved. (Prechístenka, 11)

The *Pushkin Museum* МУЗЕ́Й ПУ́ШКИНА. Born in Moscow, Pushkin never lived in this house. But he may have visited this charming mansion belonging to the Khruschóvs-Seleznyóvs (1814, arch. A. Grigóriev). Besides the main building, it included the church, the garden with pavilions and the annex buildings. To this day, only the fence with the entrance and some of the interior are preserved. The museum has a rich exposition connected to the life and work of Pushkin. Open for excursions and individual visits. Literary and musical recitals are held here. (Prechístenka, 12/2)

Pushkin's Apartment on the Arbat КВАРТИ́РА ПУ́ШКИНА НА АРБА́ТЕ is located in the mansion where in January 1831 Pushkin rented an apartment for himself and his future wife, Natalia Goncharóva. Here he had a party before the wedding and invited his friends, the poets Denis Davýdov, Peter Vyázemskiy, Nicholas Yazýkov and Eugene Baratýnsky. The Pushkins spent the winter here. Do not forget to visit this museum when strolling down the Arbat. (Arbat, 53)

The *Chekhov Museum* МУЗЕ́Й ЧЕ́ХОВА. The museum was opened in 1954 in the building where Chekhov lived between 1886-1890. The front door still bears his original brass plate. Here he wrote his short novels "The Tedious Story," "The Steppe," and the play "Ivanov." In this house, he was visited by Tchaikovsky, the painter Levitan, and the writer Korolenko. He called this building the "house-tallboy." The exhibition recreates the atmosphere of the writer's life and work. (Sadóvo-Kúdrinskaya úlitsa, 6)

The *Museum-Apartment of Dostoyevsky* МУЗЕЙ-КВАРТИРА ДОСТОЕ́ВСКОГО. Opened in 1928, the museum is located in what used to be the suburbs of Moscow, Máryina Róshcha, in the former Mariinsky hospital, where Michael Dostoyevsky worked as a doctor. Born on October 30, 1821, Fyodor Dostoyevsky lived here between 1823-1837. A monument of the great Russian writer (1918, S. Merkúrov) stands next to the museum. The museum preserves the surroundings and atmosphere of Dostoyevsky's rooms. His desk, chair, bookcase, manuscripts, books, magazines, wooden pen, and even glasses are all in his study. Above the desk, hangs a copy of Raphael's "Madonna and a Child," his favorite painting. The museum contains manuscripts of "Crime and Punishment," "The Idiot," "Demons," "Adolescent," and "Brothers Karamazov" with Dostoyevsky's notes and sketches. There is a rich iconography of the famous Russian writer, including a sketch by I. Kramskoi, an etching by Dmitriev-Kavkazsky, a portrait by Shcherbátov and many other pictures. Dostoyevsky's personal library is also kept here. (úlitsa Dostoyévskogo, 2)

The *House-Museum of Lermontov* ДОМ-МУЗЕ́Й ЛЕ́РМОН-ТОВА. Lermontov studied at the Noble Boarding-School of Moscow University between 1828-1830 and then at Moscow University for the following two years. He lived on Molchánovka with his grandmother Arsenieva. Here he wrote "The Strange Person" and about a hundred poems. Lermontov's sketches and his musical instrument are among the many artifacts that recreate the poet's surroundings. (Málaya Molchánovka, 2)

The *Museum of Bryúsov* МУЗЕ́Й БРЮСОВА. The museum of the poet, theoretician and publisher Valery Bryusov, one of the founders of Russian Symbolism, who was connected to Moscow throughout his life. The museum was opened in 1949 in the building where Bryúsov lived between 1910-1944. He was visited here by the Russian symbolist poets, Alexander Blok, Maximillian Volóshin, Konstantin Bal'mont and by the Belgian poet Emile Verchairne. The museum traces the literary work of one of the most prolific Symbolist writers. (prospéct Míra, 30)

The *Memorial Study-Museum of N.V. Gogol* МЕМО-РИА́ЛЬНЫЙ КАБИНÉТ-МУЗÉЙ Н.В. ГО́ГОЛЯ was opened in 1979 in the house of A. P. Tolstoy where Gogol lived between 1848-1852. Here he worked on the second volume of his novel "Dead Souls" and read his famous play the "Inspector-General" to the actors of the Maly Theater. The most influential minds of that time, Alexander Turgénev, Sergei and Ivan Aksákovs and the well-known playwright Alexander Ostrovsky visited him here. And here in this fireplace, in 1852, he burned the second volume of the manuscript for "Dead Souls." The tragic figure of the stooping Gogol, the work by the prominent Russian sculptor N. Andryeyev and architect F. Shechtel (1909) stands in the courtyard. (Suvórovsky Boulevard, 7)

Theatrical Museums:

Most of them are attached to the theaters, such as the Bolshoi, Maly, Art, and Vakhtangov.

Bakhrúshin Central Theatrical Museum ЦЕНТРА́ЛЬНЫЙ ТЕАТРА́ЛЬНЫЙ МУЗÉЙ И́МЕНИ БАХРУ́ШИНА. Founded by the Russian theatrical activist Bakhrúshin (1865-1929) on the basis of his private collection, this is the first Russian theatrical museum. It exhibits the history of the world theater. In its depository are more than one billion items, including documents, portraits, sketches of costumes and facsimiles of plays. (úlitsa Bakhrúshina, 31/12)

The *Museum of the Central Theater of Puppets* МУЗЕ́Й ЦЕНТРА́ЛЬНОГО ТЕА́ТРА КУКОЛ is the third largest puppet museum in the world, after the Munich and Dresden museums, with about 2,000 puppets. The rare collection includes puppets from 40 countries and goes back to the 15th century. (Sadóvo-Samotéchnaya, 3)

Musical Museums

Besides the *Museum-Apartments of A.N. Scriabin* (úlitsa Vakhtángova, 11) and *A.B. Goldenweiser* (Tverskáya, 17), there is the *Central Museum of the Musical Culture named after M.I. Glinka.*

Glinka Museum of Musical Culture ЦЕНТРА́ЛЬНЫЙ МУЗЕ́Й МУЗЫКА́ЛЬНОЙ КУЛЬТУ́РЫ И́МЕНИ ГЛИ́НКИ holds the personal archives of Russian composers, the letters by Beethoven, Wagner, Liszt, Tchaikovsky, facsimiles of scores, as well as drawings, pictures and recordings. It has a rare collection of musical instruments (1,500 items). Many concerts, rehearsals, musical conferences and lectures are held in the concert hall of the museum. (úlitsa Fadyéyeva, 4)

Economic, Technical and Scientific Museums

Planetarium (Sadóvo-Kúdrinskaya úlitsa, 5) was built at the end of the 1920's (arch. Barshch, Sinyávsky). Its round hall is covered with a cupola with a half-spheric screen. It features the map of the sky, the disposition of stars and planets. Popular scientific film shows and lectures take place here.

The *Polytechnical Museum* (ПОЛИТЕХНИ́ЧЕСКИЙ МУЗЕ́Й) is one of the oldest educational centers. Built in 1870, the museum occupies a huge block with 55 halls and more than 20,000 items on display, including a large exhibition on the history of science. Its library is one of the largest technical libraries in Russia. Lectures are held there on a regular basis. (Nóvaya plóshad', 3/4)

The *Zoological Museum* (ЗООЛОГИ́ЧЕСКИЙ МУЗЕ́Й). The old museum of Moscow University has a valuable exposition of animals from all over the world. (úlitsa Gértsena, 6)

Paleontological Museum (ПАЛЕОНТОЛОГИ́ЧЕСКИЙ МУЗЕ́Й). Bones, bones, and bones... Well organized and systematized, it is one of the oldest paleontological museums in the country. It features fossils of past geographical epochs. (Profsoúznaya úlitsa, 123)

The *Mineralogical Museum* МИНЕРАЛОГИ́ЧЕСКИЙ МУЗЕ́Й И́МЕНИ ФЕ́РСМАНА holds a rare collection of precious gems. (Léninsky prospéct, 18, corpus 2)

The *Main Botanical Garden of the Academy of Sciences* ГЛА́ВНЫЙ БОТАНИ́ЧЕСКИЙ САД АКАДЕ́МИИ НАУ́К holds many specimens of plants from different parts of the world. (Botanícheskaya úlitsa, 4, and prospéct Míra, 26)

The *Exhibition of Economic Achievements* ВДНХ was built in the heavy, pompous style typical of the Stalin era. Most of the 80 exhibitions show the achievements in the areas of agriculture, industry, and science. Nevertheless, it is also a place to enjoy the fresh air. There is a circus there, as well as cinemas and performances. There are also plenty of cafes and restaurants on the grounds. Open: Mon.-Fri.9.30 a.m.-10 p.m. Sat.-Sun. (9.30a.m.-11p.m.) From Sept. to May (10 a.m.- 6 p.m.) (prospéct Mira, subway station: "VDNKH")

Cathedrals and Monasteries/Cloisters

Saint Danílovsky Monastery СВЯ́ТО–ДАНИ́ЛОВСКИЙ МОНАСТЫ́РЬ. Founded in 1282 by Duke Danila, the son of Alexander Nevsky as a fort against the Tartars' raids, it is the oldest monastery in Moscow. It was recently restored as a residence of the Russian Metropolitan. Here the celebration of the 1,000th anniversary of Christianity in Russia took place in 1988. (Danílovsky val)

Donskói Monastery ДОНСКО́Й МОНАСТЫ́РЬ. Founded by Tsar Fedor in 1591 in celebration of the defeat over Crimean Khan Kyzy-Girey. It was built on the former site of the camp of the Russian troops who fought against the Khan. The Small Cathedral (1591-93) is the first brick building of the convent. The Big Cathedral was built at the end of the 17th century. The church and bell-tower were erected in the beginning of the 18th century. In the Big Cathedral there is an exposition of the Museum of Architecture. The Necropol of the Monastery is unique. Many famous Russian writers, artists and political leaders are buried here. (Donskáya plóshchad', 1)

Novodévichy Monastery НОВОДЕ́ВИЧИЙ МОНАСТЫ́РЬ is one of the most fascinating architectural achievements and significant historical monuments of the 17th-19th centuries in Moscow. It was founded in 1524 by Grand Duke Vasili in memory of the liberation of Smolensk from 100 years of Polish occupation. It used to be a convent for noble ladies and the home of many relatives of powerful leaders. Its wall of the 16-17th century is about 900 yards long and has 12 towers and two gates. The one to the north faces the Kremlin, and the other to the south, the Vorobyóvy góry. The bell-tower (КОЛОКО́ЛЬНЯ) is about 72 yards. The mighty fortress of the monastery withstood two raids on Moscow by the Crimean Tartars in 1571 and 1591. It contains 14 buildings from the 16-17th centuries in the Russian baroque style. Its oldest building is the Cathedral of Our Lady of Smolensk (СОБО́Р СМОЛЕ́НСКОЙ БОГОМА́ТЕРИ), from the first part of the 16th century. The cathedral contains a carved gilded iconostasis and many great works of art. It was here that Boris Gudonov was elected tsar in 1598. The same year the convent was the abode of Tsarina Irina, widow of Tsar Fedor Ioanovich who had taken the veil. After her death, her chambers were called the Godunov's chambers. Tsarina Sophia, the sister of Peter the Great resided here for 14 years, beginning in 1689. Under Peter the Great the convent became a home for abandoned babies and later a shelter for veterans. In 1812, Napoleon's troops tried to blow it up, but it was saved by the Russian nuns. Many famous Russian writers, artists and political leaders are buried in the Novodevichy cemetery located by the convent. (Novodévichy proyézd, 1, near the subway station "Sportívnaya")

The *Andrey Rublév Museum of Old Russian Culture and Art* МУЗЕ́Й ДРЕВНЕРУ́ССКОЙ КУЛЬТУ́РЫ И ИСКУ́ССТВА И́МЕНИ АНДРЕ́Я РУБЛЁВА, the former Spaso-Andrónikov Monastery was founded by Andronic, a pupil of St. Sergéi Rádonezhsky. The white stone Spassky Cathedral dates from the beginning of the 15th century (1410-1425). The dining room of the convent was built in 1504, the many-layered church from the end of the 17th century and the other buildings are from the 17th-19th centuries. The Andrey Rublev Museum is the home of a tremendous collection of Russian icons. The famous icon painter Andrey Rublev is buried on the monastery grounds. (plóshchad' Pryámikova, 10)

The *Símonov Monastery* СИ́МОНОВ МОНАСТЫ́РЬ was founded at the end of the 14th century. The architectural ensemble dates back from the 16th-17th centuries. (Vostóchnaya úlitsa, 4)

The *Novospássky Monastery* (НОВОСПА́ССКИЙ МОНАСТЫ́РЬ) is located on Krestyánskaya plóshchad', 9. It was moved to this place from the Kremlin in the 15th century. Its impressive architectural ensemble was built in the 16th-18th centuries.

Parks

Gorky Park is one of the most popular parks in Moscow. It stretches along the right bank of the Moskva River for about 12 miles. Here you can find rides, sports facilities, restaurants, cafes, chess boards, and an open air theater. In the summer, boats are rented out and in the winter the paths of the park are watered down for skating (Krýmskiy val, subway station "Park cul'túry").

Izmailovo Park ИЗМА́ЙЛОВСКИЙ ПАРК is the most attractive parks of the city and the ideal place to relax. The park includes a bowling alley, a playground, a theater, a cinema, a library, and a billiard room. In winter, a skating rink and ski rentals are available (subway station "Izmáylovsky park).

Izmáilovo Estate ИЗМА́ЙЛОВО (Ismáilovo, gorodók ímeni Báumana). The former tsars' estate of the second part of the 17th century, located on an island. Here Peter the Great spent his childhood. The remains of the estate consist of the five-domed Pokrov Cathedral (СОБО́Р ПОКРОВА́, 1679) decorated with tiles, a massive bridge tower and two festive gates (1682). Izmailovskii forest-park is one of the biggest in Europe. A sports complex with a swimming pool, sauna, stadium, the Institute of Sports and the Museum of Sports are located here. One of the biggest hotel complexes is situated on the shores of Serébryano-Vinográdny ponds. (Izmáylovskoye chaussee, 71)

Sokolniki Park ПАРК "СОКО́ЛЬНИКИ" is the old park named after the tsar's falconers who used to live here. It contains an open air theater, bicycles for rent, the restaurants, cafes. It is a good site for cross-country skiing. (Rusakóvskaya, 62, subway station "Sokól'niki")

Hermitage Garden САД "ЭРМИТА́Ж". A small but very pleasant and elegant park in the center of Moscow. (Karyétny ryad)

Swimming Pools

"Moscow" БАССÉЙН "МОСКВÁ" (subway "Kropótkinskaya").
A heated pool that functions year-round.

The *Moscow Olympian Center for Aquatics* МОСКÓВСКИЙ
ОЛИМПЍЙСКИЙ ЦЕНТР ВÓДНОГО СПÓРТА (Mirónovskaya
úlitsa, 27, subway "Izmaílovo") offers almost everything in this
attractive area of activity.

The Surroundings of Moscow

Although you will have plenty to do and see in Moscow
proper, there are also some very interesting and beautiful places
on the outskirts of Moscow. Ask your tour guide or Intourist
about visiting these areas.

The Estate Museum *Arkhangelskoye* МУЗÉЙ-УСÁДЬБА
АРХÁНГЕЛЬСКОЕ is located in a small village about 16 miles
from Moscow. It used to be the palace of Prince Nicholas
Yusúpov. The central complex was constructed at the end of the
18th century for the former owner prince Golítsyn by the French
architect Chevalier de Huerne in the style of classicism. Bought
in 1810 by Prince Nicolai Yusúpov, one of the former favorites
of Catherine the Great, the director of the Imperial theaters and
of the Hermitage Museum, it became the home for his private
collection of European paintings, antiques, furniture and china. It
contains paintings by such prominent European painters as
Bouchet, Tiepolo, Van Dyck, Rotari, Caravaggio and architectural
landscapes by Hubert Robert. On the second floor, in the library,
next to a window is the figure of J. J. Rousseau in full size made
of papier-maché sitting in an armchair and pointing towards the
park. The park with pavilions surrounding the area is laid out in
both French and English styles. Its alleys are lined with copies of
Italian marble statues, allegorical figures, and monuments. There
is a monument of Pushkin, who was a friend of the old
Catherinian nobleman Yusúpov, to whom he dedicated the poem,

"To a Nobleman." In the western part of the park, there is a monument to Catherine the Great depicting her as Themis, the Goddess of Justice. The famous private theater of Yusupov was built in 1817. The famous Italian artist Gonzago made its stage decorations.

To get there by car, drive along the Leningrádsky prospéct, then the Volokolámsky chaussee (highway), taking a left turn onto the highway to Petróvo-Dál'neye.

The *Kuskóvo Palace Museum* МУЗЕ́Й-УСА́ДЬБА "КУСКО́ВО" (úlitsa Yúnosti, 2). The palace КУСКО́ВО (1740-70, arch. de Vailly, Argunóv, Mirónov, Dikúshin) was formerly the summer residence of Prince Pyotr Sheremétyev. Located on the outskirts of Moscow, on the banks of a pond, it is a picturesque ensemble built in the style of early classicism. The museum houses a rich collection of Russian and European porcelain and ceramics (more than 800 objects). The most impressive rooms are the White ballroom with large windows and many mirrors, the drawing room, the dining hall, the oak-paneled study, and the gallery of tapestries. Other smaller buildings are in the garden, laid out in the French style. Open May 15-Sept 15 (11-7). Closed Tues. and during the cold season.

The *Palace-Museum "Ostankino"* ДВОРЕ́Ц-МУЗЕ́Й "ОСТА́НКИНО" (1792-98, arch. Comporezzi, Argunóv, Mirónov) built in the style of late classicism, is a former suburban estate of Prince Nicholas Sheremétiev. The ensemble consists of the mansion and the theater building in the center. The theater was often transformed into a ballroom. In Sheremetiev's theater there were 200 actors, including musicians, singers, and dancers. He married one of them, the daughter of a blacksmith Kovaléva-Zhemchugóva. One of Ostankino's streets is named after her. The Palace, the collection of Russian art of the late 18th century and the park in French style with many marble sculptures are the main tourist attractions. The church of Trinity dates back to the 17th century. (Pérvaya Ostánkinskaya úlitsa, 5)

237

Kuzminki КУЗЬМИНКИ (Kuz'minskaya úlitsa) was built by Kazakóv, Gillardi, Egótov. A former estate of the late 18th century and beginning of the 19th century, this ensemble is a historical landmark of Russian classicism.

The *Museum "Kolomenskoye"* МУЗЕЙ "КОЛОМЕНСКОЕ" (Proletárskiy prospéct, 31, subway station "Kolómenskoye"), overlooking the Moskva River, has a rich history. It was the favorite summer residence of the Grand Dukes of Moscow. In 1380, Dmitriy Donskoy passed it on his way to fight against the Tartars. On return from the battle, he celebrated his victory of the Kulikovskaya battle here. The oldest building, the Cathedral of Resurrection (1532), was built in honor of the birthday of Ivan the Terrible. Later Kolomenskoye was a favorite summer resort of tsar Alexei Mikhailovich, the father of Peter the Great. Peter visited it frequently in his youth.

The pride of Kolomenskoye is the Cathedral of the Ascension, the first and the best example of the "tent" style architecture in stone. Hector Berlioz, who visited Kolomenskoye in the middle of the 19th century, described the impressions of this Cathedral: "Nothing staggered me more than the Russian monument in the village Kolomenskoye . . . Everything wavered in me. That was the mysterious calmness. The harmony of the perfect forms . . . I saw the striving upwords and for a long time I stood stunned." Next to this unique monument, there are the church-bell of St. George from the 16th century and the water tower from the 17th century. The other prominent monuments from the 16th century are the Church of John the Baptist (ЦЕРКОВЬ ИОАНА ПРЕДТЕЧИ) in Diakovo and the impressive five-onion-domed Kazan Church (КАЗАНСКАЯ ЦЕРКОВЬ). The only remains of the original tsars' estate are the Main Gate, the Clock Tower and the Water Tower. The estate exhibits much old Russian wooden architecture (ДЕРЕВЯННАЯ АРХИТЕКТУРА).

Tsaritsino ЦАРИЦЫНО was Catherine's estate of the late 18th century. It was one of the best works by V. Bazhénov and M. Kazakóv. Bazhenov built the two pavilions for Catherine the

Great and her son Pavel I, and the buildings for guards, the Small Palace (МА́ЛЫЙ ДВОРЕ́Ц), the Opera House, the Bread House, the gates and the bridges in pseudo-Gothic style. But Catherine did not like it. After 10 years of intensive work, the ensemble was destroyed and Bazhenov was replaced by Kazakov. Kazakov began to build the palace but did not finish it due to the death of Catherine. In the beginning of the 19th century architect Egotov built the garden pavilions. Even though it is unfinished, the ensemble makes a strong and unforgettable impression. (úlitsa Bazhénova)

CHAPTER FOURTEEN

ST. PETERSBURG

A HISTORICAL PERSPECTIVE

Moscow and St. Petersburg - the rival cities

Moscow and St. Petersburg represent two poles, two periods in Russian history tradition and innovation, emotion and reason. They are very different. Moscow, a "big village" as it used to be called, organically expanded outward from its center and grew up as a living organism. Like Rome, it was built in concentric circles. Its beginning goes far back and it has a long and rich history.

St. Petersburg is logical and irrational at the same time. It is a new city, a "foreigner city" among Russian swamps, a "European-American colony," as Gogol put it. Gogol expressed the difference between these two cities very astutely: "Moscow is needed by Russia. Petersburg needs Russia."

1991 marked the third time this enchanting city on the Gulf of Finland (ФИНСКИЙ ЗАЛИ́В) was renamed. In 1914, in order to rid the name of its German suffix "burg," St. Petersburg was named Petrograd, the Russian word "ГРАД" (the old form of the word ГОРОД) replacing the German "burg." While still in the spirit of changing names, the Soviet government chose to call the city Leningrad in 1924 after the death of Lenin. Now St. Petersburg has returned to its original name.

This relatively young city founded in 1703 is considered one of the most beautiful cities in the world. It was the influence, care and strength of Peter the Great (ПЁТР ВЕЛИКИЙ) that made its creation possible. It was the courage and perseverance of the people that kept it alive. The planning of the city was an architectural feat in itself, but the actual construction of the grand city was a physical miracle. Situated on what many called a swamp (БОЛОТО) on the mouth of the Neva River (УСТЬЕ РЕКИ НЕВЫ) at the Gulf of Finland (ФИНСКИЙ ЗАЛИВ), the city, made up of a number of islands, spans an area of over 350 square miles. Floods and harsh weather conditions made the construction of the city, with its canals and bridges, very difficult. Peter the Great intended to make the city a "window onto Europe" (ОКНО В ЕВРОПУ). He wanted to integrate Russia into the European community. The transfer of the capital from Moscow to St. Petersburg was not well received by the people. Nevertheless, Peter brought in peasants and ordered the construction of houses and government buildings. Wood was plentiful but stones had to be brought in from elsewhere. Many perished for the sake of Peter's city; some say the city was built on the bones of the thousands who died while building it.

However, Peter was far less extravagant than his successors. He commissioned modest buildings and was most interested in creating a vast shipyard and developing strong military and commercial structures for the city. Most of the grand palaces were built after his reign. After Peter's death, the city was given less attention. The Moscow tradition was still strong in the memories of the Russian people. Peter II (ПЁТР ВТОРОЙ) moved his court back to Moscow and many others deserted the unfinished city. Yet Empress Anna (ИМПЕРАТРИЦА АННА) restored the court to St. Petersburg and, along with Empress

Elizabeth (ИМПЕРАТРЍЦА ЕЛИЗАВЕ́ТА), continued the advancement of the capital. During the reign of Catherine the Great (1762-1796), it received its finishing touches. The best architects from all over Europe came in to beautify the streets and squares.

It went through the flood and the war with Napoleon, the tragedy of the Decembrists (ДЕКАБРЍСТЫ) and the terrorism of the so called "People's Will" organization (НАРОДОВО́ЛЬЦЫ). This fantastic city, which suddenly sprang up among the northern swamps through the powerful will of its creator, cultivated the sweet poison of idealism and mystical anarchism. It went through the severe experience of World War I (ПЕ́РВАЯ МИРОВА́Я ВОЙНА́), the following revolutionary fever and euphoria of 1917 and the bitter soberness of the following years of hunger and disruption. It went through the despair of the Civil War (ГРАЖДА́НСКАЯ ВОЙНА́), when "brother went against brother," then years of political repressions, arrests and the strictly organized enthusiasm of workers.

The next disaster that struck the great city was in 1941. For three years it withstood a siege by the Nazis. 107,000 bombs and 255,000 shells were dropped on it. Over 650,000 inhabitants died during those years from starvation, cold and bombings. Thousands of buildings were destroyed, supplies were cut off and transportation was stopped. But the Leningraders never surrendered and by 1943 the blockade had ended. Immediately after World War II (ВТОРА́Я МИРОВА́Я ВОЙНА́), the reconstruction of Leningrad began, and its industry and commercial activity were restored quite quickly.

Today СА́НКТ-ПЕТЕРБУ́РГ is the most beautiful city in Russia, and is one of the most important cultural centers. It has been the centerpiece of many famous novels and poems as well as the home of a great number of Russian novelists, poets, musicians, artists. Its inhabitants hold its history, inspiration and tradition dear to their hearts. One of the greatest charms of St.

Petersburg is the White Nights (БЕ́ЛЫЕ НО́ЧИ), when the northern sky lights up the streets at night. It never really gets dark so people stroll along the streets until the wee hours of the night. They last approximately from June 10 through July 3.

A WALK THROUGH ST. PETERSBURG

Palace Square

At the end of St. Petersburg's main street, Nevsky prospect (НЕ́ВСКИЙ ПРОСПЕ́КТ), is *Palace Square* (ДВОРЦО́ВАЯ ПЛО́ЩАДЬ). When St. Petersburg was capital, it was a site of one of the tsar's residences.

At the center of the square stands the Alexander Column (АЛЕКСА́НДРОВСКАЯ КОЛО́ННА) topped by an angel of peace (1829–1834, arch. Auguste Montferrand, sculpt. B. Orlóvsky). One of the tallest memorial columns in the world, it was put up by Nicholas I (НИКОЛА́Й I) in 1832 to celebrate the victory over Napoleon. By far the most impressive structure of the square is the *Winter Palace* (ЗИ́МНИЙ ДВОРЕ́Ц, Dvortsóvaya náberezhnaya, 36). This three-story former imperial residence is part of the architectural ensemble of the famous museum known as the Hermitage (ЭРМИТА́Ж). Built during the reign of Elizabeth (ЕЛИЗАВЕ́ТА) and completed by Catherine the Great (ЕКАТЕРИ́НА ВЕЛИ́КАЯ), it is one of the finest examples of Russian baroque (РУ́ССКОЕ БАРО́ККО). Constructed by the famous Italian architect Bartolomeo Rastrelli (1754–1762), it was reconstructed by Russian architects V. Stásov and A. Brulóv (1838–39) after the great fire of 1837. The palace spans four entire blocks. It has 1,047 rooms and halls and 117 staircases. The Main Staircase, built of white marble, is preserved from the 18th century. The St. George Hall or Large Throne Room with 48 Italian marble columns, the Heraldic Hall, the Petrovsky Hall or Small Throne Room were constructed in the classical style. Many of the halls were decorated with Ural stones. For the columns of the Malachite Hall more than two tons of Uralian malachite were used. The Heraldic Hall is decorated with the coats of arms of

Moscow, St. Petersburg and other cities of Russia and is illuminated by splendid chandeliers.

The *Small Hermitage,* (МА́ЛЫЙ ЭРМИТА́Ж) with figures of Flora and Pomona in front of it, was built between 1764-1775 to house the first private art collection of the Russian tsars (arch. Zh.-B. Vallenes-Delamotte). Its facade with the six-columned Corinthian portico and the attic with the sculptural group were constructed in the style of early classicism. Built later, the central Pavilionny Hall is illuminated by two rows of high windows. It is richly decorated with white columns, chandeliers, fountains and a mosaic on the floor. Between 1783 and 1787, the Imperial Hermitage Theater (ЭРМИТА́ЖНЫЙ ТЕА́ТР) in the classical style with a Corinthian colonnade was built by G. Kvarenghi. Its Teatralny Hall is richly decorated with a Corinthian columns, medallions and statues of Apollo and the Muses (arch. K. Albani).

The *New Hermitage* (НО́ВЫЙ ЭРМИТА́Ж), notable for its portico decorated with ten granite Atlases, was built between 1839-1852 by L. von Klentse, V. Stasov, N. Efimov. It was the first building in Russia designed to be a museum. Among its halls one can find the Hall of Twenty Columns made of Karelian granite and a white marble Roman courtyard. It is linked to the main building by a system of corridors.

On another side of the square is the General Staff (ГЛА́ВНЫЙ ШТАБ), the location of the military headquarters and Ministries of Foreign Affairs and Finance. Built in the classical style, this immense convex building was brilliantly designed by Carlo Giovanni Rossi (1819-1829). In its center is a huge Triumphal Arch topped by a chariot commemorating the victory of 1812 (arch. S. Pímenov, V. Demut-Malinóvsky). Slightly off to the east side of the square is the *Main Admiralty* (ГЛА́ВНОЕ АДМИРАЛТЕ́ЙСТВО) (1806-1823, arch. A. Zakhárov, I. Kórobov). It occupies the area that was originally the location of the moated fort and symbolizes the fame of the Russian navy, one of Peter the Great's most cherished treasures. The tower with the gilt spire is decorated with a group of sea nymphs carrying the earth's sphere (1812-1813, arch. F. Shchedrín). On its attics, on different levels, stand four heroes of antiquity and 28 statues, the allegories of the seasons of time, forces of nature and winds. Its three-story wings are adorned with 12-columned Doric porticos.

Before we go further, here is a little hint to help you identify the architecture of St. Petersburg. The Russian baroque, exemplified by the exterior of the Winter Palace is generally identifiable by its blue shades. The classical style is characterized by a golden or yellow tone. Of course, those of you who are architects will be appalled by this oversimplification, yet it is quite helpful for the laymen among us.

The Peter-and-Paul Fortress

Originally an important military structure, the Peter-and-Paul Fortress (ПЕТРОПА́ВЛОВСКАЯ КРЕ́ПОСТЬ (1703-1740, arch. Domenico Trezzini) later became a prison, then an arsenal and is now a museum. Located on the banks of the Neva River (РЕКА́ НЕВА́) on Záyachi Ostrov (ЗА́ЯЧИЙ О́СТРОВ), it was built in 1703 and marked the birth of the city. Peter's Gates built in the shape of a triumphal arch, were decorated with statues of Belona and of Minerva (1717-1718). The Peter-and-Paul Cathedral (ПЕТРОПА́ВЛОВСКИЙ СОБО́Р) (1712-1733) is the central architectural work in the fortress. It was built in the Dutch tradition. Its bell tower has a needle-like spire covered with golden leaf with a swinging angel at the top. The clock strikes every quarter of an hour. The wooden carved iconostasis was made in a shape of a triumphal gate in the tradition of Moscow baroque (1722-26, arch. I. Zarúdny). The bodies of Peter the Great and all of his successors except Peter II and Nicholas II are buried here.

Be sure to take a tour through the old prison cells of the fortress. Peter the Great's son Alexei was tortured to death here. At the end of the 18th century it became a political prison where Alexander Radíshchev and Decembrists, and later Nikolay

Chernýshevsky, Feodor Dostoyevsky and Alexander Morózov languished behind the 65-foot thick fortress walls.

Near the Fortress, on the shores of the Neva river, a house for Peter I's boat was built in a style which can be considered as transitive from baroque to classicism. It has severe Doric porticos and high rectanglular windows. A richly decorated roof crowned with a figure of a woman with an oar, a symbol of navigation.

Smolny

On the east side of the city is one of Rastrelli's master-pieces, the Smolny Convent (СМÓЛЬНЫЙ МОНАСТЫ́РЬ), commissioned by the Empress Elizabeth as a nunnery for orphan girls (Smól'ny proyézd, 1). The building replaced the summer Elizabethian palace. It is built in the baroque style and its center is commanded by a richly decorated five domed cathedral (1748-64, arch. Rastrelli). The interior was constructed later in a more strict classical style.

The Smolny Institute, or the Institute for the Noble Young Ladies, is located in two buildings which originally served as a school for the daughters of nobility and a widow's house. Designed by Giacomo Kvarenghi (1806-1808), this huge construction, represents the typical features of Russian classicism. Its Assembly Hall with two rows of Corinthian columns is very festive. During the revolution, Smolny was the central head-quarters of the Bolshevik party.

Along the Neva River

The Neva (50 miles long) is a very short river. It crosses the city, and falls into the Gulf of Finland. There are a lot of bridges across the river, including the bridge of Alexánder Névsky, Dvortsóvy, Ánichkov, Litéyny, Birzhevóy, Kámenny, Grenadérsky and others. At night the bridges are opened and some are raised. The finest view of the Neva is from the Kirov Bridge (former Elagin) from where Vasil'evsky Island, the Peter-and-Paul Fortress and many palaces may be viewed. The Decembrists' Square (ПЛО́ЩАДЬ ДЕКАБРИ́СТОВ) with the Bronze Horseman is on its left shore.

The Bronze Horseman

This statue depicts Peter the Great mounted upon a rearing stallion whose hooves trample on a wild snake. Pushkin and Dostoyevsky were among those who wrote about this famous monument. All Russians have at some point memorized the lines of Pushkin's famous poem "МЕ́ДНЫЙ ВСА́ДНИК" ("The Bronze Horseman"):

КУДА́ ТЫ СКА́ЧЕШЬ, ВЕ́РНЫЙ КОНЬ?
И ГДЕ ОПУ́СТИШЬ ТЫ КОПЫ́ТА?

"Where are you galloping, faithful horse,
And where will you lower your hoofs?"

Built by the French sculptor Étienne-Maurice Falconet (1768-1782), the Bronze Horseman is one of the best equestrian statues in the world.

The Senate and the Synod

Two three-story buildings of the Senate and the Holy Synod (СЕНА́Т И СИНО́Д), with their eight-columned Corinthians loggias and courtyards, were constructed in 1829-34 by Carlo Rossi in the classical style. They are connected with the Triumphal arch and are richly decorated with reliefs and statues by S. Pímenov, V. Demut-Malinóvsky, N. Ustínov. The attic is crowned with a sculptural group "Justice and Piety" (plóshchad' Dekabrístov, 1, 3).

247

The Manezh

The Cavalry Guards Manezh (КОННОГВАРДЕЙСКИЙ МАНЕ́Ж) (1804–1807, arch. G. Kvarenghi) is a rectangular building with an eight-columned Doric portico and a pediment with the statues at its corners. Two marble groups (1817, arch. P. Triscorni) were made after the marble statues in front of Quirinal Cathedral in Rome. The Manezh now houses the exhibition hall (Isaákievskaya plóshchad', 1).

St. Isaac's Cathedral

Not far from the Bronze Horseman is the largest cathedral in САНКТ-ПЕТЕРБУ́РГ and one of the largest cathedrals in the world, St. Isaac's Cathedral. Designed in the empire style, this impressive edifice is made of 43 varieties of gray marble and bedecked with 112 red granite columns (1818–1858, arch. O. Montferrand, sculptors I. Vitali, N. Klodt, A. Loganovsky). It has a golden dome supported by thirty giant pillars. By climbing 262 steps, you can reach the dome. Inside are beautifully polished columns, reliefs, sculptures and numerous paintings and mosaics made by C. Brulov, F. Bruni and P. Basin.

Many Americans compare its structure to the Capitol building in Washington D.C. It is open as a museum 11a.m.-5p.m. Closed Tues.

The Isaakievskaya Plaza

The main entrance of St. Isaac's Cathedral faces Isaac's Square (ИСАА́КИЕВСКАЯ ПЛО́ЩАДЬ). It is decorated with a statue of Nicholas I (sculp. N. Klodt.) On the banks of the Moyka River there is Mariinsky Palace, a wedding gift of Nicholas I to his daughter Maria (1839–1844, arch. A. Stackenschneider). It housed the Provisional Government (ВРЕ́МЕННОЕ ПРАВИ́ТЕЛЬСТВО) in 1917 and then was the headquarters of the City Soviet of the Working People's Deputies.

248

Nevsky Prospect

The main street of central St. Petersburg runs for about three miles and is interrupted only near the Moscow Railroad Station where the Old Nevsky begins.

On the odd-numbered side of Nevsky, at the corner of Gogol Street, stands the former building of the Waverly Banking House (1912), now the Aeroflot office. Further on, there is one of the finest examples of the Russian baroque, the *Stroganoff Palace* by B. F. Rastrelli (1752-54).

On the even-numbered side of Nevsky, stands the Romanesque-style *St. Peter Evangelical Church* (ЛЮТЕРÁНСКАЯ ЦÉРКОВЬ СВ. ПЕТРÁ), built between 1833-1838 by A. Brulóv for Petersburg's German artists.

Next to Griboyedov Canal, there is the *Kazan Cathedral,* featuring mighty portals and porticos, a colonnade of Corinthian columns, bronze doors and bronze statues in the niches (1801-11, arch. Andrey Voroníkhin, sculp. I. Martos, V. Demut-Malinóvsky, S. Pímenov). Since 1932, it has been the Museum of the History of Religion and Atheism. From the cathedral cupola hangs a 325-foot-long Foucault pendulum (МÁЯТНИК) demonstrating the rotation of the earth. The tomb of General Michael Kutuzov is placed in the cathedral. The statues of two famous defeaters of Napoleon, Michael Kutuzov and Michael Barklay-de-Tolli (1829-36, sculp. B. Orlóvsky) stand by the cathedral. A mighty iron fence (1810-12) is in front of the cathedral. (Kazánskaya plóshchad', 2)

The *Church of Christ on Blood,* also known as the *Church of the Resurrection of Christ* (ЦÉРКОВЬ ХРИСТÁ НА КРОВЍ или ЦÉРКОВЬ ВОСКРЕСÉНИЯ ХРИСТÓВА, 1883-1907) stands on the spot where the terrorists from the "People's Will" organization assassinated tsar Alexander II (náberezhnaya kanála Griboyédova.) It features the Byzantine style of the Moscow central Cathedral of St. Basil but is more dramatic in mood (arch. Alfred Porland, painters V. Vasnetsóv, M. Nésterov, A. Ryábushkin).

Further down Nevsky Prospect, there is the former *House of Engelhardt*, where Berlioz, Liszt and Wagner performed their music. Now it is the *Small Hall of the Philarmonia*. Next to it stands the *Church of St. Elizabeth* (arch. Vallenes-Delamotte). Built between 1763–1783, it contains elements of baroque and classic architecture.

The building of the former *City Duma* (City Council) on Duma Street was designed by G. Kvarenghi between 1784–1787 as a commerce building with an open arcade. It has been rebuilt several times. Next to it stands the Tower of the City Duma (arch. D. Ferrari, 1799–1804).

Across the street from the Duma building, stands the *Europeyskaya Hotel*. Reconstructed in 1910 in the art nouveau style and recently renovated, it is now an Intourist hotel.

Square of Arts

The central building of this Square is the former *Michael Palace* built for Grand Duke Michael, one of the sons of Paul I, by Carlo Rossi between 1819–1825. The main three-story building and two-story wings are enclosed within a fence. The festive staircase of its lobby is surrounded by a columned gallery. The majestic White Column Hall was decorated by Carlo Rossi, the other halls, by V. Demut-Malinovsky, A. Vigi, B. Medichi, Scotty. The *Russian Museum* (РУ́ССКИЙ МУЗЕ́Й) was founded here in 1898. Its west building was built in 1916 by L. Benois and S. Ovsyanikov. There are Russian icons, paintings, drawings, engravings and handicraft on display.

On the opposite side of the street, there is the *Philarmonia named after Shostakovich* (formerly the *Noble Assembly* , 1834-39) and the building which now hosts *Brodsky's Memorial Museum*

On the northwestern part of the square between these two buildings there is the *Small Opera and Ballet House* designed by Alexander Brulóv and Carlo Rossi (1831–33). (plóshchad' Iskússtv, 1)

There are several large department stores next to the *Nevsky Prospekt* subway station. Bol'shóy Gostíny Dvor built in the forms of early classicism between 1761–1785 by Rastrelli and Vallenes–Delammotte. It stretches under the arcades for almost a mile and has a lot of small shops (Nevsky prospect, 35). The large department store *Passage*, built between 1911–13 by N. Vasíliev, features elements of the new constructivist style. Its facade is made of glass and stone. (Nevsky prospect, 48)

On the corner of Nevsky prospect and Sadovaya street is *Saltykov–Shchedrin Library* located in three buildings. The corner building with the semi-circular facade with the Ionian portico was built between 1796–1801 by E. Sokolov. Between 1828–34, Carlo Rossi constructed the second building with the large Ionian loggia decorated with 18 columns and statues of Homer, Plato, Virgil, Tacitus and the other writers and philosophers of antiquity (V. Demut-Malinovsky, C. Pimenov, S. Galberg.) The third, three-story building added between 1896–1901 (arch. E. Vorotylov) was built also in the strict classical forms. This library holds the second largest collection of books in Russia and houses unique manuscripts, first edition books, the correspondence of Peter the Great, the library of Voltaire and other rare collections.

Rossi Street

The Teatral'naya ulitsa, or Rossi street (ýЛИЦА РÓССИ), was made up between 1828–1834 of two identical columned buildings of yellow and white, the colors of the classical style. This is one of the best examples of Petersburg classicism.

One building houses the *Theatrical Museum and Library*, the other, the *Ballet School* whose graduates include Anna Pavlova and Vatslav Nijinsky.

Anichkov Palace (АНИЧКОВСКИЙ ДВОРЕЦ) with a garden built by Elizabeth for Count Razumovsky (1740–1750) is located between Ostrovsky Square and the Fontanka River. Its festive White Hall with Ionian columns, mirrors and chandeliers and a gallery for musicians was decorated in the style of late classicism (1809–1810, arch. L. Russka).

Anichkov Bridge (АНИЧКОВСКИЙ МОСТ) across the Fontanka River (1839–1841) designed by A. Gotman with four bronze statues by N. Klodt is one of the finest in Petersburg.

Toward Yelagin Island, Kirov prospect leads the way with the stylish house of Lindvale (1902–1904) and some other buildings in the modern style. Not far from the Peter–Paul Fortress there is the *Moslem Mosque* (1910, arch. N. Vasiliev, A. Gauguin) modeled after the mausoleum of Tamerlan Gur–Emir at Samarkand. The interior of the mosque is very impressive.

On Kirov prospect are the buildings of the *Film Studio Lenfilm* and the 945-foot-high *Tower* of St. Petersburg Television.

Mansions and Palaces of St. Petersburg

The two-story *Palaces of Kikin* (ПАЛАТЫ КИКИНА) built in the beginning of the 18th century by A. Schluter, is typical of the early St. Petersburg style of architecture. (Stavropól'sky pereúlok, 9)

Men'shikov Palace (МЕНЬШИКОВСКИЙ ДВОРЕЦ), is one of the first stone buildings in the city. It was built between 1710 and 1730 (arch. D.-M. Fontana, G. Schedel) and rebuilt at the end of the 18th century. The interior, decorated at the beginning of the 18th century, is preserved in the lobby, staircase, and various tiled halls. (Universitétskaya náberezhnaya, 15)

Sheremetiev's Palace or *Fontaines House* (ШЕРЕ-МЕ́ТЬЕВСКИЙ ДВОРЕ́Ц or "ФОНТА́ННЫЙ ДОМ") was built between 1750-1755 by S. Chevakínsky in the baroque style. The richly decorated iron fence with gates was made between 1837-1840 by I. Corsini. (náberezhnaya Fontánki, 34)

Stroganoff's Palace (1752-1754, B.-F. Rastrelli), the three-story building with richly decorated facades is one of the best examples of the Russian baroque. The early interior was decorated by Rastrelli in the baroque style and the late interior was made by Andrey Voroníkhin in the classical style (the Painting Gallery, The Mineral Hall). (Névsky prospéct, 17)

Shuvalov's Palace (ШУВА́ЛОВСКИЙ ДВОРЕ́Ц) (1753-1755, arch. S. Chevakinsky) rebuilt many times, has a facade in the baroque style. The famous Russian poet and scientist Michael Lomonosov frequently visited this house. The lobby is well preserved. (úlitsa Rákova, 25)

The three-story building of *Yusupov Palace on the Moyka River* (ЮСУ́ПОВСКИЙ ДВОРЕ́Ц НА МО́ЙКЕ) was rebuilt in 1760's by J. B. Vallene-Delamotte. The facade is decorated with the mighty Doric portico; the gates were made like a triumphial arch. The second building was built in 1830's after the project of A. Mikháilov. The rooms of the second level, including the majestic White Columned Hall decorated in the classical style, are well preserved. The private theater, a part of the palace construction, is richly decorated with gild stucco molding in the baroque style. The rooms of the first level were rebuilt in the neoclassical style in 1910 (náberezhnaya Móyki, 94).

Yusupov's Palace on the Fontanka River (ЮСУ́ПОВСКИЙ ДВОРЕ́Ц НА ФОНТА́НКЕ) with loggias, the six-columned Ionian portico has strict classical proportions. It was rebuilt by G. Kvarenghi in the 1790's. (náberezhnaya Fontánki, 112)

The *Marble Palace* (МРА́МОРНЫЙ ДВОРЕЦ, 1768-1785, arch. A. Rinaldi) was built by Catherine the Great for her favorite Count Grigóry Orlóv. Built in the style of early classicism, it is incrusted with marble of different hues. The festive staircase and the Marble Hall with reliefs by F. Shúbin and I. Kozlóvsky are well preserved. (Dvortsóvaya náberezhnaya, 6)

Tavrichesky Palace (ТАВРИ́ЧЕСКИЙ ДВОРЕ́Ц, 1783-1789, arch. I. Stavróv) was built by Catherine the Great for the defeater of Crimea, Count P. Potyómkin Tavríchesky. The main two-story building is decorated with a six-columned portico. The suite of the majestic halls includes a rotunda with a cupola and the White Columned Hall with two rows Corinthian columns. In the beginning of the 20th century, the Palace was reconstructed for the State Duma. (úlitsa Vóinova, 47)

The *Mansion of A. Lobánov-Rostóvsky* (ОСОБНЯ́К ЛОБА́НОВА-РОСТО́ВСКОГО, 1817-1820, arch. O. Montferran) faces the Admiralty. Its main facade has a majestic eight-columned Corinthian portico placed on the arcade of the first level. Its two marble lions next to the entrance were depicted by Pushkin in his poem, "The Bronze Horseman" (Admiraltéysky proyézd, 12).

The three-story *Mansion of A. Lavale* (ОСОБНЯ́К ЛАВА́Ль, 1806-1810, arch. J. Thomas de Tomond) with its ten-columned Ionian attic, three balconies, reliefs decorating festive windows is famous for its notable visitors. Russian poets Vassily Zhukóvsky, Alexander Pushkin, Michael Lermontov were among them. (náberezhnaya Krásnogo flóta, 4)

The *House of N. Rumyantsev* (ДОМ РУМЯ́НЦЕВА) (rebuilt in 1826-1827 by V. Glinka) with the mighty twelve-columned

Corinthian portico is decorated with the sculpture group "Apollo on Parnassus" by I. Martos. Between 1831-1861 it housed the Rumyántsevky Museum with its rare art collection and library. Now, the Museum of St. Petersburg is located here. (náberezhnaya Krásnogo flóta, 44)

Shuvalov's Palace on the Fontanka (ШУВÁЛОВСКИЙ ДВОРÉЦ НА ФОНТÁНКЕ) was rebuilt between 1844-1846 by B. Simon. Its facade reflects the forms of the Italian Renaissance architecture. The White Columned Hall is decorated in the classical style. The interior of the Golden Room was done in the eclectic style of the late 19th century. (náberezhnaya Fontánki, 21)

The huge three-story *Nicholaev Palace* (НИКОЛÁЕВСКИЙ ДВОРÉЦ) was built between 1853-1861 by A. Stackenschneider for the Great Duke Nicholas. Its facade is decorated with many pilasters and a four-columned portico. There are three courtyards in this palace. The columns, reliefs and chandeliers in the lobby and in the festive staircase are very impressive. (úlitsa Trudá, 64)

The *Palace of the Grand Duke Vladimir* (ДВОРÉЦ ВЕЛЍКОГО КНЯ́ЗЯ ВЛАДЍМИРА АЛЕКСÁНДРОВИЧА, 1864-1872, arch. A. Rezánov) was built in the style of a Florentinian Renaissance palazzo. Its marble majestic staircase is decorated with sculpture. Paintings in the palace are by Victor Vereshchágin. The Banquet Hall is decorated in the Russian style. (Dvortsóvaya náberezhnaya, 26)

The *Mansion of M. Kschesinskaya* (ОСОБНЯ́К М. КШЕ-СЍНСКОЙ) was built between 1904-1906 in a very innovative manner with some elements of the neo-antique style in its decor. (úlitsa Gór'kogo, 1)

The *House of M. Savina* (ДОМ М. СÁВИНОЙ) was built in 1900's in the modern style. It is decorated with big windows, stucco moulding and majolica. (Aptékarsky óstrov, úlitsa Literátorov)

The *Mansion of S. Abamelec-Lazareva* (ОСОБНЯ́К АБАМЕЛЕ́К-ЛАЗАРЕВА, 1913-1915, arch. I. Fomin) is one of the best examples of the architecture of neoclassicism. (náberezhnaya Moyki, 21-23)

The Ensemble of Alexándro–Névskaya Lávra

Alexándro-Névskaya Lávra (АЛЕКСА́НДРО-НЕ́ВСКАЯ ЛА́ВРА) was the cloister founded by Peter the Great in 1710 in honor of Alexander Nevsky, the defeater of the Teutonic Knights in 1240 (úlitsa Alexándra Névskogo, 1). The Church of the Annunciation (БЛАГОВЕ́ЩЕНСКАЯ ЦЕ́РКОВЬ) (1717-1722, arch. D. Trezzini) is a monument of the early classical style, typical of the early days of St. Petersburg. The three-story building with high windows and a high roof crowned with a lantern houses the upper and lower churches. In the upper church was the silver tomb of Alexander Nevsky, now kept in the Hermitage. In the lower church, there is a tomb of General Alexander Suvórov. Now the church is a branch of the City Museum of Urban Architecture. Works by I. Martos, F. Shchedrin, and F. Gordeyev are displayed there.

The two-story Cloister buldings were built in the gallery-style. The oldest construction is the Dukhovskóy building (ДУХОВСКО́Й КО́РПУС) (1717, arch. Trezzini). The Archbishop's house (МЕТРОПОЛИ́ЧИЙ ДОМ) (1755-1758, arch. M. Rastorgúev) is richly decorated. The Trinity Cathedral (ТРО́ИЦКИЙ СОБО́Р) (1776-1790, arch. I. Staróv) is the center of this ensemble. It contains two bell-towers and the main building, with its heavy cupola and six-columned portico. The cathedral is richly decorated with Corinthian columns, gilt caps and doors of the holy gates, and rich stucco moulding and paintings (by Kvarenghi) that are well illuminated through large windows.

Next to the cloister, there are the *Lázorevskoye Cemetery* and *Tíkhvinskoye Cemetery* where many Russian writers and artists are buried. The necropolis of the Alexander Nevsky Monastery is well preserved. It holds one of the best collections of memorial sculptures of the 18th and 19th centuries. Among the best are the tombs of E. Gagárina (1803) and M. Kozlóvsky (1802) by Kozlovsky's student V. Demut-Malinóvsky. (plóshchad' Alexándra Névskogo)

Art and Architecture Museums

САНКТ-ПЕТЕРБУ́РГ is simply a treasure trove of all forms of art and architecture, even in comparison with Moscow and its 150 museums. It is most famous for its collections at the *Hermitage* (ЭРМИТА́Ж). The first collection of European art was placed there in 1764. Now the Hermitage collection consists of over two million items and occupies more than a thousand rooms in several buildings. It traces remnants of pre-historic culture on the territory of Russia, including Scythian culture and art and evidence of the prehistoric nomads in Siberia as well as the ancient civilizations of Egypt, Babylon, Assyria, the Near and Middle East, Greece and Rome, Byzantia, China, India and Japan. Most museum-goers are particularly impressed by the fabulous collection of Western European art. The vast holdings of French, Dutch, Spanish, English, German, and Italian art are simply amazing. Here you will find works by Leonardo da Vinci, Michelangelo, Titian, El Greco, Velasquez, Rubens, Van Dyck, Rembrandt, Poussin, Gainsborough, Renoir, Matisse, Gauguin, Van Gogh, Degas, Picasso, Monet, Cezanne, Rodin, to name a few. And this is only one section of the entire museum! For those who are in numismatics' fever, there is a big section in the Hermitage collection dedicated to Russian and foreign medals, badges and orders. Foreign visitors have been known to take 3 or 4 trips to the ЭРМИТА́Ж during their stay. Open: every day 11-8, Wednes. 11-3. Closed Thurs. (Dvortsóvaya náberezhnaya, 34)

The *State Museum of Russian Art* is located in two buildings, one is the former Mikháilovsky Palace, the central building in the Square of Arts; the other was built in 1916 for the museum collection. The collection represents the main periods and movements in the development of Russian art. It includes a valuable collection of Russian folk art and Russian ancient icons, as well as handicraft works, engravings, drawings, and paintings by the most outstanding Russian masters. (Inzhenérnaya, 4/2)

Brodsky Memorial Museum МУЗÉЙ-КВАРТЍРА БРÓДСКОГО, contains about 80 of his own works and more than 500 paintings of his contemporaries. Open daily 11–8. Closed on Thurs. (plóshchad' Iskússtv, 3)

Permanent Exhibition of St. Petersburg Artists (ПОСТОЯ́ННАЯ ВЫ́СТАВКА ПЕТЕРБУ́РГСКИХ ХУ-ДÓЖНИКОВ) holds various exhibitions of contemporary artists. Open every day (10 a.m–9 p.m.). (Névsky prospéct, 8)

Museum of City Sculpture МУЗÉЙ ГОРОДСКÓЙ СКУЛЬПТУ́РЫ is located in the architectural complex of the Alexander Nevsky monastery founded in 1710. Displays works by Martos, Shchedrin, Gordeyev and others. Open daily 11–7. Closed on Thurs. (úlitsa Alexándra Névskogo, 1)

Cemeteries:

Piskarevskoye Memorial Cemetery (ПИСКАРЁВСКОЕ МЕМОРИÁЛЬНОЕ КЛÁДБИЩЕ). This is the burial ground for the Leningraders who perished during the Nazi siege of World War II. It is an immense plot of land which contains the graves of over 500,000 people who died during the three–year blockade. Masses of flowers are laid on the graves every day by the citizens of St. Petersburg. A trip to the Piskarevskoye Memorial Cemetery is a must for truly experiencing the tragic history and brave spirit of the Leningraders. The cemetery is on the outskirts of the city.

Historic Museums

The *Museum of the History of St. Petersburg* (МУЗЕЙ ИСТОРИИ САНКТ-ПЕТЕРБУРГА). Founded in 1918 by the Society of Lovers of Old Petersburg, the museum has a rare collection of manuscripts, printed maps and plans of the city beginning with the first projects of Peter the Great and original designs by Bartolomeo Rastrelli, Giacomo Kvarenghi, Carlo Rossi, Andrey Voronikhin. It contains paintings, pictures of Petersburg, historical relics and documents, including the history of different monuments, the statue of the Bronze Horseman among them. It includes displays depicting the three-year blockade. Open Mon, Thurs., Sat., Sun., (11-7), Tues., Fri. (1 p.m.-9 p.m.); closed Wednes. (náberezhnaya krásnogo flóta, 44)

Peter I's Cottage ДОМИК ПЕТРА, the summer residence of Peter the Great, was built from pine logs in 1703 within three days. It has two rooms and a studio. The windows are glazed with special "moon" glass. Since 1784, it has been enclosed within a stone building to protect it. A boat built by Peter himself is inside the cottage. Open May-Nov. (noon-7 p.m.). Closed Tues. (Petrográdskaya storoná, Petróvskaya náberezhbaya, 5)

The Central Navy Museum ЦЕНТРАЛЬНЫЙ ВОЕННО-МОРСКОЙ МУЗЕЙ was founded by Peter I for display of the models of constructed vessels, and covers history of the Russian fleet since its beginning to the present day. It has over 1,500 items on display, including paintings, sculpture, pictures, battle flags, medals, decorations. It is housed in the building of the former Stock Exchange (1805-1810, arch. Zh. Toma de Tomona, scupt. I. Prokofiev, F. Shchedrin.) Open weekdays (12-7), Sun. (11-6). Closed Tues. (Vasíl'evsky óstrov, Púshkinsky square, 4)

Suvorov's Military-Historical Museum ВОЕННО-ИСТОРИЧЕСКИЙ МУЗЕЙ СУВОРОВА. The history of the legendary victories and vicissitudes of Generalissimus Suvórov are thorougly traced in the museum's display. (úlitsa Saltykóva-Shchedriná, 43)

Museum of the October Revolution МУЗЕЙ ОКТЯБРЬСКОЙ РЕВОЛЮЦИИ is housed in the mansion of the ballerina Mathilda Kschesinskaya (1904-1906, arch. A. Gauguin) and covers Russian revolutionary history between 1861-1921. (úlitsa Kúibysheva, 4)

Technical and Scientific Museums

The *Museum of Anthropology and Ethnography* (МУЗЕЙ АНТРОПОЛОГИИ И ЭТНОГРАФИИ ЙМЕНИ ПЕТРА ВЕЛИКОГО, is the home of the Academy of Sciences (АКАДЕМИЯ НАУК). The building was erected between 1718-1734 for holding a library and a scientific collection. It contains two wings connected with a multilayered tower with a cupola. It is more commonly known as the Kunstkammer after Peter the Great's Exhibition of Rarities, Curiosities and Oddities, which is located in the gallery of the upper floor. It is quite an exotic place. Here you will see a display of Peter the Great's surgical instruments as well as a globe from 1754. The highlight of the museum, however, is its collection of deformed human and animal embryos.

Other sections show collections gathered by Russian explorers and scientists during expeditions and archeological excavations all over the world. The culture and life of the people of Asia, Africa, Oceania, Polynesia and native people of North and South America are featured here. It contains a unique collection of costumes of the noblemen of China of the 17th century as well as national costumes of other Far Eastern nations, including a rich selection of garments, theatrical costumes and masks of India. Open Thurs., Sun. (11-5). (Vasílievsky óstrov, Universitétskaya náberezhnaya, 3)

Other Museums

The *Museum of Ethnography* (МУЗЕЙ ЭТНОГРАФИИ) features works of the craftsmen Palekh and Khokhloma, toys from Vyatka, Russian embroidery and lace, Turkmenian carpets, Georgian leatherwork, Armenian jewerly, and more. Lectures and documentary films are held here on a regular basis. Open daily (11-6). Closed Mon. (Inzhenérnaya úlitsa, 1/4)

The *Arctic and Antarctic Museum* (МУЗЕЙ АРКТИКИ И АНТАРКТИКИ) features the natural complex of these continents and the history of their exploration. Open daily (11-7), Sun. (11-5). Closed Mon. (úlitsa Maráta, 24)

The *Zoological museum* (ЗООЛОГИЧЕСКИЙ МУЗЕЙ) features about 100,000 exhibits. The Hall of Mammoths is unique. Open daily (11-5). Closed Mon., Tues., Thurs. (Universitétskaya náberezhnaya, 1)

Literary Museums

The *Literary Museum* (ЛИТЕРАТУРНЫЙ МУЗЕЙ ИН-СТИТУТА РУССКОЙ ЛИТЕРАТУРЫ) is better known as Pushkin's Home, or ПУШКИНСКИЙ ДОМ. The museum was founded in 1899, what would have been Pushkin's 100th birthday. It contains rare manuscripts, archives and letters of famous Russian writers. Recorded legends, folk tales and traditional songs are available to listen to. The museum traces the history and growth of Russian literature, a source of great pride to the Russian people. Personal items of writers such as Gogol, Tolstoy and Dostoyevsky are also on display. Its collection contains a million items. (náberezhnaya Makárova, 4)

The *Pushkin Museum* (МУЗЕЙ-КВАРТИРА ПУШКИНА) is the actual home of the famous poet. The rooms have remained unchanged since his death and many of his original belongings can be seen here.

Notice that the "museum" is Pushkin's home and the "home" is the literary museum! (náberezhnaya Móiki, 12)

The *Museum of Dostoyevsky* (МУЗЕ́Й ДОСТОЕ́ВСКО-ГО) features the Petersburg period of life of the writer. (Kuznéchny pereúlok, 5/2)

The *Museum-Apartment of Blok* МУЗЕЙ-КВАРТИ́РА БЛО́КА (úlitsa Dekabrístov, 57) gives you a feeling for the life of this true Petersburg poet. As you visit this museum you probably will think of a stanza of Akhmatova's poem:

Я ПРИШЛА́ К ПОЭ́ТУ В ГО́СТИ
РО́ВНО В ПО́ЛДЕНЬ, В ВОСКРЕСЕ́НЬЕ.
ТИ́ХО В КО́МНАТЕ ПРОСТО́РНОЙ
И ЗА О́КНАМИ МОРО́З.

I went to visit the poet
At midday sharp, Sunday.
There was a quiet spacious room
and frost behind the windows.

The *Museum of Anna Akhmatova* (МУЗЕ́Й АННЫ АХМА́-ТОВО́Й) is devoted to one of the best Russian Acmeist poets, features the history of dramatic life of Akhmatova in the intensive literary scene of Petersburg. (náberezhnaya Fontánki, 34)

Theatrical and Musical Museums

The *Museum of Theatrical and Musical Art* (МУЗЕ́Й ТЕАТРА́ЛЬНОГО И МУЗЫКА́ЛЬНОГО ИСКУ́ССТВА) features drawings, sketches and documents covering the history of great performances. (plóshchad' Ostróvskogo, 6)

262

The *Exhibition of Musical Instruments* (ВЫ́СТАВКА МУ-ЗЫКА́ЛЬНЫХ ИНСТРУМЕ́НТОВ) contains a rare collection of musical instruments from all over the world. (Isaákievskaya plóshchad', 6)

Libraries:

The *Academy of Science* БИБЛИОТЕ́КА АКАДЕ́МИИ НАУ́К. (Bírzhevaya líniya, 1)

The *Academy of Art* БИБЛИОТЕ́КА АКАДЕ́МИИ ХУДО́ЖЕСТВ. (Universitétskaya náberezhnaya, 17)

The *Saltykov-Schchedrin Public Library* ПУБЛИ́ЧНАЯ БИБЛИОТЕ́КА И́МЕНИ САЛТЫКО́ВА-ЩЕДРИНА́ is one of the largest libraries in the world. (Sadóvaya úlitsa, 18)

The *Pushkin Children's Library* ДЕ́ТСКАЯ ЦЕНТРА́ЛЬНАЯ ГОРОДСКА́Я БИБЛИОТЕ́КА ИМЕНИ ПУ́ШКИНА (úlitsa Gértsena, 33).

Opera, Ballet, Concerts, Drama and Cinema

The *Mariinsky Theater of Opera and Ballet* (МАРИ́ЙНСКИЙ ТЕАТР О́ПЕРЫ И БАЛЕ́ТА) is by far the most famous in САНКТ-ПЕТЕРБУ́РГ. The theater burned down in the middle of the 19th century. It was rebuilt by Kavos in 1860. The theater was named Mariinsky Theater after the Empress Maria (ИМПЕРАТРИ́ЦА МАРИ́Я), wife of Alexander II. The Mariinsky was the center stage of Russian Opera and of the Russian ballet. Here Pavlova and Shalyapin performed. It was renamed Kirov's Theater Opera and Ballet after the revolution but recently regained its original name. (Teatrál'naya plóshchad', 2)

The *Maly Theater of Opera and Ballet* (АКАДЕМИ́ЧЕСКИЙ МА́ЛЫЙ ТЕА́ТР О́ПЕРЫ И БАЛЕ́ТА И́МЕНИ МУ́СОРГСКОГО) was originally called Mikhailovsky, built by Alexander Brulov and Carlo Rossi and rebuilt in 1859 by Kavos. In 1918, it became an opera house; in 1933, a ballet company was founded. (ploshchad' Iskusstv, 1)

The *Theater of the Music and Drama Institute* УЧЕБНЫЙ ТЕА́ТР ИНСТИТУ́ТА МУ́ЗЫКИ И ДРА́МЫ presents dramas and musical performances. (Mokhováya, 35)

The *Musical Comedy Theater* ТЕА́ТР МУЗЫКА́ЛЬНОЙ КОМЕ́ДИИ was opened in 1929 and has always been popular. Lots of operettas. (ulitsa Rákova, 13)

The *St. Petersburg Philharmonic Concert Hall* КОН-ЦЕ́РТНЫЙ ЗАЛ ПЕТЕРБУ́РГСКОЙ ФИЛАРМО́НИИ was formerly the Leningrad Philharmonic Concert Hall. The former Nobles' Club, built in 1834-39 by P. Jaquet with a facade made by Carlo Rossi, has housed the Philharmonic since 1921. (úlitsa Bródskogo, 1)

The *Glinka Capella* (АКАДЕМИ́ЧЕСКАЯ ХОРОВАЯ КАПЕ́ЛЛА И́МЕНИ ГЛИ́НКИ, is one of the finest choral groups in Russia. The Choir Hall was built in 1880 by L. Benois, but the choir, which was founded by Peter the Great, has been around since 1713. Many famous musicians have performed here, including Michael Glínka and Nicholas Rímsky-Kórsakov. (náberezhnaya Móiki, 20)

The Drama Theaters

The *Pushkin Drama Theater* (АКАДЕМИ́ЧЕСКИЙ ТЕАТР ДРА́МЫ И́МЕНИ ПУ́ШКИНА) was originally named the Alexandrinsky Theater (АЛЕКСАНДРИ́НСКИЙ ТЕА́ТР) in honor of the wife of Nicholas I. This richly decorated building with a chariot of Apollo topping it was designed in the empire style (1828-1832, arch. Carlo Rossi, sculp. Pimenov and Demut-Malinovsky). The statues in the niches were made by Russian sculptors after Rossi's drawings. The theater was renamed after the revolution. Performances of classical and modern dramas are often held there. (plóshchad' Ostróvskogo, 2)

The *Theater named after Komissarzhévskaya*. Blok wrote that the great Russian tragic actress Komissarzhévskaya was an embodiment of "the revolt of search" in art. Meyerhold was once a producer of this theater. From its founding, its stage saw the plays by Ibsen, Maetherlink and Chekhov. (úlitsa Rákova, 19)

The *Akimov Comedy Theater* ТЕА́ТР КОМЕ́ДИИ И́МЕНИ АКИ́МОВА is one of the best. (Nevsky prospect, 56)

The *Gorky Theater* БОЛЬШО́Й ДРАМАТИ́ЧЕСКИЙ ТЕАТР И́МЕНИ ГО́РЬКОГО was founded by Gorky in 1919. Lately, it has become quite popular under the director Tovstonogov. (nábyeryezhnaya Fontánki, 65)

The Circus

The *St. Petersburg Circus* ЦИРК is one of the oldest in all of Russia. The building in which shows are held to this day was designed in 1876 by V. Kennel. (nábyerezhnaya Fontánki, 3)

Movie Theaters

There are movie theaters all over St. Petersburg and most of the key ones are on Nevsky Prospect (НЕ́ВСКИЙ ПРОСПЕ́КТ). If you take a stroll down Nevsky, you will pass a number of theaters and you can get all the information on shows right there. There are buffets in the movie theaters to have a bite before the film begins.

Parks and Gardens

One of the several islands located in the delta of the Neva, *Yelagin Island,* (ЕЛА́ГИН О́СТРОВ) was used for summer residents by tsars, aristocrats, and rich merchants. It was named after its owner, a nobleman of the late 18th century, I. Yelagin. The largest park in St. Petersburg was laid out there (arch. Carlo Rossi). The old Yelagin Palace was built by Carlo Rossi between 1818-1822 in the style of Russian classicism for Empress Maria Fedorovna, the widow of Paul I. It rises behind a white stone terrace. Its festive facade is decorated with a six-columned Corinthian portico. The suite of the halls of different colors is decorated with stucco moulding (V. Demut-Malinovsky, S. Pimenov) and murals (D.-B. Scotti, A. Vigi, B. Medichi). Especially majestic is the Oval hall with caryatids, columns of Ionian style and stucco moulding on a cornice. When going to this island, inevitably Blok's poem "On the Islands" (1909) comes to mind:

ВНОВЬ ОСНЕЖЁННЫЕ КОЛОННЫ,
ЕЛА́ГИН МОСТ И ДВА ОГНЯ.
И ГО́ЛОС ЖЕ́НЩИНЫ ВЛЮБЛЁННОЙ,
И СКРИП ПЕСКА, И ХРАП КОНЯ́...

Once again the snow-covered columns
of Yelagin Bridge and its two lights.
And the voice of an enamoured woman,
And the snort of a horse
and the crunch of sand...

In 1932 the park was named Kirov Park. Recreation facilities in the park include: boating, summer theater, cinema, beach, and exhibition halls. In June and July, celebrations of the White Nights are held there.

Known as *Tsaritsin Lug* (meadow), the *Field of Mars* (МА́РСОВО ПО́ЛЕ) received its name at the end of the 18th century after the statue of the famous Russian General Alexander Suvórov was placed there. As the site of many military displays and parades it was very bare and dusty. Today flower beds have been laid down which make the garden a pretty sight.

The *Summer Garden* (ЛЕ́ТНИЙ САД) was founded by Peter the Great. His Summer Palace (ЛЕ́ТНИЙ ДВОРЕ́Ц ПЕТРА) was built here between 1710-1714 by Domenico Trezzini and A. Schluter. This two-story house was only occasionally used by the tsar. It is well preserved and now holds a museum. The entrance hall with the statue of Minerva, the Green Study, the ceiling frescos and tiled stoves are very attractive. In the garden, marble sculptures of the 18th century stand among old oaks, linden and elms. The Coffee House (КОФЕ́ЙНЫЙ ДО́МИК, 1826, arch. C. Rossi) was built on the place of a grotto from Peter's time. Its walls and attic are decorated with masks, garlands and wreaths (V. Demut-Malinovsky). The festive terrace with fences and iron vases by Rossi faces the Swan Canal. The impressive iron fence (ОГРА́ДА) along the Neva River was installed between 1771-1784 by arch. Yu. Felten; the majestic fence from the Moyka was installed later. Since the 19th century, the Summer Garden has been a favorite place for people to stroll and for children to play. Pushkin wrote about the childhood years of Eugene Onegin whose main daily routine was to go for a walk around ЛЕ́ТНИЙ САД. Museum open May-Nov. (12-8), closed Tues. (Dvortsóvaya náberezhnaya, Lyétny sad)

The *Komaróv Botanical Garden* БОТАНИ́ЧЕСКИЙ САД (ulitsa proféssora Popova, 2). Open daily May-October; the greenhouses open 11 a.m.-6 p.m. Closed Fri.

The *Zoo* ЗООПАРК covers 20 acres. It contains about 250 species, including panthers, rhinos and aurochs. Open May-August (10 a.m.-10 p.m.); September-November (10 a.m.-6 p.m.); December-February (10 a.m.-4 p.m.); March-April (10 a.m.-7 p.m.). (Petrográdskaya storoná)

THE SURROUNDINGS OF ST. PETERSBURG

САНКТ-ПЕТЕРБУРГ is surrounded by parks and former summer residences of the members of the Imperial family and their friends. The palaces and parks are extraordinary in their architecture and elegance. Most were destroyed during World War II but have been restored and are open to visitors.

Petrodvorets

The creation of this most fabulous park on the Gulf of Finland can be attributed to both the work of Peter the Great (ПЁТР ВЕЛЙКИЙ) and his daughter Elizabeth (ЕЛИЗАВЕ́ТА). In Peter's time the estate was designed by the French architect, Alexander Jean-Baptiste (1704) and was completed by Rastrelli during Elizabeth's reign. It is 18 miles from St. Petersburg. The best way to get to Petrodvorets is by speedy hydrofoil which you can board on the banks of the Neva in St. Petersburg.

Petrodvorets (formerly Peterhof) has upper and lower French style parks. The lower seaside park, the oldest one, includes fountains and waterways, the *Monplaisir Palace* and the *Alexandria Park* of the 19th century.

Located in the upper park, the *Big Palace*, otherwise known as the Russian Versailles, was built between 1714-23. In 1747-1752, the Palace was rebuilt by B.-F. Rastrelli in the baroque style. From the former interior, he kept only the Study of Peter I with its carved oak panels. The Portrait Hall with 368 sentimental portraits by the Italian painter Pietro Rotary is one of the most notable in the baroque interior. The grounds by the palace feature the Big Cascade (БОЛЬШО́Й КАСКА́Д), the Blue Grotto and a two-stepped cascade of fountains. The main fountain is "Samson tearing open the jaws of a lion," symbolizing Russia's victory over Sweden in 1709 (1802, sculp. M. Kozlóvsky). The spur of its water rises up to 69 feet. There are many whimsical fountains, including a pine tree which squirts water out each of its branches and another which sprays water when people touch certain stones. The Sea Canal with 22 fountains on its banks links the park with the Gulf of Finland. The Big Cascade ensemble was decorated with 129 statues of the 18-19th centuries done by the masters of that time.

The *Monplaisir Palace* (1714-22, project by A. Shluter, arch. I.-F. Braunstein), another attraction of Petrodvorets, is a one-story building with two galleries and pavilions. In the Lacquered Study, decorated in the Chinese style with lacquerd panels, there is a large collection of Dutch paintings. In the festive Big Hall, there is a decorated ceiling and the sculptured relief, "The Seasons."

In the *Hermitage* (1721-25, arch. Braunstein), the works of Western European painters cover the walls of the dining room like one precious carpet. The other park constructions include the Open-air Cage (ВОЛЬЕ́Р) (1721) covered with shells and the Green hat (ОРАНЖЕРЕ́Я) (1721-24).

In the *Alexander Park* there is the fantastic Gothic Chapel dedicated to the defeater of the Teutonian Knights, Alexander Nevsky, and the Palace-Cottage with elements of Gothic style in its decoration.

The Petrodvorets park, with its statues, pavilions, and fountains, is the perfect place for a stroll.

Pushkin

The town *Pushkin*, or ЦА́РСКОЕ СЕЛО́, was the former home of the imperial family until 1917. Located about 15 miles from Petersburg, it was founded during the reign of Peter the Great (1710). Its two parks were named after the emperors

Catherine and Alexander. The prominent structure of Catherine's park is *Catherine Palace* (ЕКАТЕРЍНЕНСКИЙ ДВОРЕ́Ц) designed by Bartolomeo Rastrelli (1752-1756) in the reign of Elizabeth I. Its facade is large and impressive with blue walls, grand white columns, and pilasters of gold. The inside of the palace is very extravagant. It has a suite of halls of a transitive, from baroque to classical style. The Cavalier's Dining Room (КАВАЛЕ́РСКАЯ СТОЛО́ВАЯ) and the Painting Hall (КАРТЍННЫЙ ЗАЛ), with two layers of windows lighting up 139 paintings of Western European artists, were designed by Rastrelli. The other rooms, such as the Green Dining Room (ЗЕЛЁНАЯ СТОЛО́ВАЯ), the Festive Bedroom (ПАРА́ДНАЯ ОПОЧИВА́ЛЬНЯ), and the Chinese Blue Living Room (КИТА́ЙСКАЯ ГОЛУБА́Я ГОСТЍНАЯ), were constructed by Ch. Cameron. Some halls, including the Festive Study of Alexander I (ПАРА́ДНЫЙ КАБИНЕ́Т), were built in the empire style.

The two-story pavilion with the *Agate and Jaspers Rooms* built on the project Cameron (1780-1785) links Catherine's Palace with *Cameron Gallery* (1783-86, arch. Cameron), a two-story building made for Italian sculpture.

Among the other park constructions are the *Pavilion Hermitage* with a cupola (1743-53, arch. M. Zemtsov, S. Chevakinsky, B.-F. Rastrelli), the *Upper Bathroom Pavilion* (1777-1779, arch. I. Neyélov) and the *Pavilion Grotto* (1753-1757, arch. Rastrelli), both facing the lake. The five-arched *Marble Bridge* with columned gallery and porticos was built between 1770-1776. In the middle of the lake on a granite base stands the *Chesmenskay Column* (1771-1778, project A. Rinaldi). The *Chinese,* or *Squeaking Pavilion* (1778-1786, arch. Yu. Felten) acquired its second name because its weather vane squeaks. In the park, you can see the fountain, *Girl with a Vessel* (1810, sculp. P. Sokolóv). When studying in the *Lyceum*, Pushkin wrote a poem inspired by this fountain:

ýРНУ С ВОДÓЮ НЕСЯ́,
ОБ УТЁС ЕЁ ДÉВА РАЗБИ́ЛА
ДÉВА ПЕЧÁЛЬНО СИДИ́Т,
ТИ́ХИЕ СЛЁЗЫ ЛИЯ́.

Carrying the urn with water
The girl broke it at a reef.
The girl sits sorrowfully
Shedding quiet tears.

The former annex of *Catherine's Palace*, a four-story building, was built between 1788-1792 (arch. I. Neyélov) and rebuilt for the *Lyceum* in 1810-1811 (arch. V. Stásov). The walls of the Actovy Hall are decorated with pictures of war attributes. Here Pushkin read his poem to his literary mentor, one of the best Russian poets, Gavriil Derzhavin.

Alexandrovsky Palace (1792-96, arch. D. Kvarenghi), *Alexandrovsky Park* with the *Chinese Bridge* (1783, project Ch. Cameron), the *Gothic Chapel* (1827) and the *Egyptian Gates* (1828, arch. A. Menelas, sculp. Demut-Malinovsky) are other notable constructions of *Tsarskoye Selo*.

Pavlovsk

Less than 5 miles from Pushkin and 25 miles from Petersburg is a park which was once the site of the tsar's hunting parties. It was the residence of Paul I, the son of Catherine the Great. An iron gate stands at its entrance. The three-story yellow *Grand Palace* (1782-1786) overlooks the river Slavyańnka. In 1797-1799, the gallery and wings were raised and additional annexes were added. It has 64 large columns and is the dominant structure of the park. The masters of that time worked in this palace.

The interior of the palace is in the classical style, only the Festive Bedroom was decorated in the style of Louis XVI (arch. V. Brenna). It consists of the Throne Hall richly decorated with stucco moulding, the Italian Hall with the original Italian sculpture, the Greek Hall with columns and antique lamps, the Gallery of Gonzago, the Palace library, the study room "Lantern" with a semi-circular glass wall and caryatids and the dining room in its refined colors. Most of the park pavilions were made by Cameron: the *Open-air Cage, Three Graces* (the marble scultural group by P. Triscorni), the *Memorial of Parents* (the sculpture by I. Martos), the pavilion *Musical Hall*, the *Colonnade Apollo* with a cast iron copy of Apollo of Belvedere and the *Rotunde Temple of Friendship*. The *Pill Tower (1797)* was made by V. Brenna and decorated by Gonzago. The *Mausoleum to the Husband-Benefactor* (1808-1809, Zh. Toma de Tomon) looks like an antique temple inside.

The French style park covers over 1,500 acres which are filled with ponds, waterfalls, and strolling areas. It was laid out by two prominent masters, Cameron and Gonzago. The slow river Slavyanka crosses it and calls to mind Zhukóvsky's lines:

СЛАВЯ́НКА МИ́ЛАЯ,
КОЛЬ ТОК ПРИЯ́ТЕН ТВОЙ

Slavyánka, dear,
how pleasant is your
slow flow.

Lomonosov

The town of *Lomonosov,* on the shore of the Gulf of Finland about six miles from Petrodvorets and 25 miles from Petersburg, was the location of the summer palace of Peter the Great's friend, Alexander Ménshikov, the first Governor-General of St. Petersburg in the 1700s. The palace (1719-25) was named

Oranienbaum (ОРАНИЕНБА́УМ) after the orange trees that grew there. The *Grand Palace*, with a Japanese pavilion, was the work of architects G. Fontana and G. Shedel (1710-1727). In 1727, Menshikov was exiled and the palace became the Imperial Building Administration. It was then given to tsar Peter III. The Palace was reconstructed by Rastrelli. Two wings were added to the main building. The *Palace of Peter III* with entering gates was built between 1758-62 by A. Rinaldi. Catherine also made Oranienbaum her summer residence and built herself the *Chinese Palace* (1762-74, arch. A. Rinaldi), with 17 main halls including the Hall of Muses, Blue Drawing Room, a Chinese Room and Bugles Cabinet decorated with a panel of bugles. Paintings were done by Venetian masters. The large French style park is divided into lower and upper parts. The town is named after the famous poet and scholar Michael Lomonósov who often visited the area. In the park, there is a monument in honor of him.

CHAPTER FIFTEEN

OTHER RUSSIAN CITIES

ADDITIONAL RUSSIAN CITIES WORTH A VISIT!

Some of the Russian cities outside Moscow and St. Petersburg have a great deal to offer both historically and aesthetically.

Many are quite near one another, which will make it easy to hit a number of them in a relatively short period of time. The cities are grouped under three headings: The "Golden Ring" cities, the cities of northwestern Russia, and the cities to the east of European Russia.

The Golden Ring

The Golden Ring is a group of historic and important cities covering the territory surrounding Moscow. Some of the key cities of this ring are listed below.

NORTHEAST TO MOSCOW

Sergiev Posád

СЕ́РГИЕВ ПОСА́Д sits on the rivers Koshúra and Glímitza, 44 miles from Moscow. It is the home of one of the most significant monasteries in Russia, the Monastery of Trinity—St. Sergius (СВЯТО–СЕ́РГИЕВСКАЯ ЛА́ВРА), founded in 1340. It grew into a massive complex of buildings. Destroyed by the Tartars in 1408, the complex was rebuilt after their departure. The monastery became a very important and well protected center from then on. It was surrounded in 1540–1550 by great white fortress walls with 11 towers. In the early 1600s, when the Poles threatened the city, it remained steadfast and did not submit to the invaders.

Inside of the monastery walls there is the white-stone Trinity Cathedral (ТРО́ИЦКИЙ СОБО́Р) with shining domes. It was erected in the year of the canonization of its founder, Sergius of Radonezh in 1422. His relics are buried in a silver sarchophagus inside the cathedral. It once housed icons by Andrey Rublev, including his legendary "Trinity," but they have been replaced by copies, and originals were placed in the Tretiakov Gallery.

The Church of the Holy Ghost (ХРАМ СОШЕ́СТВИЯ СВЯТО́ГО ДУ́ХА) was built of brick in 1476. In 1554, a second large cathedral with five great bulbous towers was erected there. The work began during the reign of Ivan the Terrible in 1559 and completed in 1584 under the father of Peter the Great, tsar Fyodor Ioanovich, who frequently visited the Trinity-Sergius Monastery. This is called the Cathedral of the Assumption (УСПЕ́НСКИЙ СОБО́Р) with the iconostasis done by Símon Ushakóv. You cannot miss its celestial towers because they are brightly painted in blue and gold and covered with stars. There are 13 other churches in the town.

Sergiev Posad is also the location of the tomb of Boris Godunov, one of the tsars of Russia. For five hundred years this monastery has been a place of pilgrimage in Russia. The Theological Seminary is located here. The town is the hub of the toymaking industry (ПРОИЗВО́ДСТВО ИГРУ́ШЕК) and is also famous for its woodworking (РАБО́ТЫ ПО ДЕ́РЕВУ).

A day trip to Sergiev Posad is simply a must! Take the local train from Yaroslávsky railroad station, or Yaroslávsky chaussée (highway), if you go by car.

Yaroslavl

ЯРОСЛА́ВЛЬ, located on the banks of the Volga River, was founded by Duke Yaroslav the Wise of Kiev. It is the oldest recorded town on the river, mentioned in writings from 1071. It is one of the most beautiful old Russian towns. Because of its location on the Volga River, Yaroslavl was a very important commercial center engaged in trade with Western Europe during the reign of Ivan the Terrible. Today this ancient town is quite a prosperous industrial center, but when in 1937 the Volga-Don Canal was created, Yaroslavl lost much of its significance as a trading port.

The most impressive structure of the main square is the Church of Elija the Prophet. It is filled with 17th and 18th century murals and icons. The Spáso-Preobrazhyénsky Monastery is also a very important historic spot of the town. Founded in the 12th century, it was later converted into a palace for the archbishop. One of the best known cathedrals, the Transfiguration Cathedral (1516) is located inside the walls of the monastery. It was in this monastery where the only copy of the "Lay of Igor's Campaign" was first found, but then it was lost again during Napoleon's invasion of Moscow.

ЯРОСЛА́ВЛЬ is 150 miles from Moscow. Get to Yaroslávl by train from Yaroslávsky railroad station, by car on the Yaroslávsky chaussée or by boat down the Volga.

Hotels: "Volga" (with Intourist office), Kirov street
Gostínitsa "Tsentrálnaya," Vólkov Square
"Yaroslávl'," Square Svobódy
Sites: Local Museum and Art Museum (Spaso-Preo-
brazhyénsky Monastery, Plóshad' Podbél'skogo, 25)
Museum in the Church of Elija the Prophet (úlitsa
Sovétskaya)
Historical and Local Museum (Sovétskaya plóshchad', 19/1.
Open 10-5. Closed Sat.
Art Museum (plóshchad' Chelúskintsev, 2). Open 10-5.
Closed Tues.
Planetarium (plóshchad' Tréfoleva, 20). Open 11-7. Closed
Tues.

Vladimir

ВЛАДЍМИР, situated on the river Klyazma, is yet another
ancient town near Moscow. It was founded in 1108 by Vladimir
Monomakh, the Grand Duke of Kiev as a fortress to guard his
kingdom. The son of Duke Dolgoruky (the founder of Moscow),
Andrey Bogolubsky was the next ruler of "Vladimir na Klyazme."
When he defeated his opponents in Kiev in 1169, he made
Vladimir a politically powerful city. In 1238 it was destroyed by
the Tartars and came under Moscow's rule in the 15th century.
All political power moved to the city of Moscow and remained
there.
The main attractions of Vladimir are the golden entrance
gate to the town, which dates back to 1164 and the five-domed
Cathedral of the Assumption (УСПЕ́НСКИЙ СОБО́Р) of the 12th
century. The icons of Andrey Rublév, Daniil Chérny and their
pupils (1407) can be seen here. УСПЕ́НСКИЙ СОБО́Р was the
home of the 12th century Byzantine icon of the Virgin of
Vladimir (ИКО́НА ВЛАДЍМИРСКОЙ БОГОМА́ТЕРИ). Now it is in
the Tretyakov Gallery. Three hundred years later, the Italian
architect from Bologna, Aristotle Fioravanti, copied the
decorations of the Cathedral of Assumption and used them for
the Kremlin Cathedral of the Assumption.

Another noteworthy cathedral is one-domed St. Dmitrius Cathedral (ДМИ́ТРОВСКИЙ СОБОР). Completed in 1197, is said to be one of the most spectacular churches in all of Russia. Its lofty reliefs display an array of subjects relating to the Scriptures and to Russian history as well. King David, Alexander Makedonsky and the benefactor of this cathedral Duke Vsevolod are depicted on its walls.

The Assumption Cathedral of the Princess' Convent founded in the 12th century by the wife of Vsevolod was famous for its magnificent frescoes. On the north and south walls there are scenes from the life of the Virgin Mary to whom this cathedral was dedicated. For a long time, the cathedral was the burial place of the Grand Princesses. Alexander Nevsky, the defeater of the Teutonic Knights was buried in another remarkable cloister, Rozhdéstvensky monastery, in 1263.

Vladimir is home of many beautiful churches and monuments of the 17-19th centuries. There is the lovely little Church of the Assumption built in 1642 on the shores of Klyazma river and two eighteenth-century churches (of Nikóly and Nikítskaya) with their graceful silhouettes.

Vladimir is 60 miles from Moscow. You may get to it from Kúrsky Railroad Station (direction to Nízhny Nóvgorod).

Hotels: "Vladimir" (with Intourist office) úlitsa Trétiego Internatsionála

"Klyazma" (úlitsa Lénina)

Suzdal

Suzdal is known to be an entire museum in and of itself. Archeological excavations show evidence of its existence as early as the tenth century. The Kievan architecture in it is a result of the legacy of the Grand Duke Vladimir Monomakh. Tartar invasions almost destroyed all of Suzdal. Invasions by the Poles and Crimean Tartars as well as fires and plagues further challenged the survival of the town. Remarkably, Suzdal withstood those troubled times and is now a bundle of ten centuries of powerful history. Outside of the town center is the Kremlin, where the primary building is the white-stone Cathedral of the Nativity of the Mother of God (СОБО́Р РОЖДЕСТВА БОГОРО́ДИЦЫ) which dates back to the time of Vladimir Monomakh, to the 11th century. Its frescoes are of the 13th century, the iconostasis is of the 17th century. Noteworthy are the Golden Gates of the southern and western portals of the cathedral.

The center of the city is actually dominated by the ТОРГ, or market, which is the heart of the main square. However, its key structure is the Church of the Resurrection (ЦЕРКОВЬ ВОСКРЕСЕ́НИЯ) (17th century). Around the main square stand a number of smaller churches. Two large monasteries are found in Suzdal, the Monastery of the Lament of Christ, sometimes referred to as the Spaso-Efimievsky Monastery (13th century) and the Monastery of the Intercession of Mary of Pokrovsky Convent (founded in 1364, most structures were built in the 16th century). The Spaso-Efimievsky, the largest monastery in the town, stands on the banks of the Kamenka river. Its wall with 12 towers is over two miles long! The most incredible structure is the five-domed Cathedral of Spaso-Preobrazheniye. The Pokrovsky Convent was the home (or truly the prison!) of the wives of both Vassilii III and Peter I. There are the graves of two exiled tsarinas, Solomonia Saburova and Evdokia Lopuchina in the cathedral of the convent. Among three other convents in Suzdal, the most notable is the Alexandrovsky Convent which was founded in the 13th century by Alexander Nevsky. The Voznesénsky Cathedral in it was built by the mother of Peter I, Natalia Naryshkina.

Suzdal houses the museum of wooden architecture. The town is 75 miles from Moscow and 18 miles from Vladimir. You may get there by local train from the Yaroslavsky railroad station or by car on Yaroslavsky highway. Hotel: Suzdal Intourist.

Uglich

This ancient city is mentioned in legends that date back to 937. It is located on the Volga River and takes its name, which is an old form of the the Russian word У́ГОЛ, meaning corner, from the sharp bend in the section of the river on which it sits. It too was destroyed by the Tartars and remained theirs for over 150 years until 1375, when Ivan Kalita bought it from them. It was in the palace courtyard of this town that the nine year-old body of tsarevich Dmitri, the only son of Ivan the Terrible, was found dead with his throat cut. The murderer was never caught and much unrest resulted from the incident. During the Time of Troubles (СМУ́ТНОЕ ВРЕ́МЯ), the town bounced back and forth between Russian and Polish leadership. In 1612, it finally became a definitive city of Russia. Today the city is an industrial center concentrating on metal working and machine building. It is also a center of dairy farming.

Although little is left in the kremlin of the town, some of its structures have been nicely restored, including the Palace of tsarevitch Dmitri. It was commisioned in the 15th century by the young brother of the Ivan the III, Duke Andrei the Big, who died in prison as a result of a feud with his older brother. The Spaso-Preobrazhénsky Cathedral with its five domes is the largest of the kremlin buildings. It was built in the 18th century and is part of a museum.

The Monastery of the Resurrection (1674, ВОСКРЕСЕ́НСКИЙ МОНАСТЫ́РЬ) and the Church of the Nativity of John the Forerunner (1689-1700, ЦЕ́РКОВЬ РОЖДЕСТВА́ ИОА́ННА ПРЕДТЕ́ЧИ) are two of the most representative buildings of 17th century Russian architecture in Uglich. The latter was depicted by N. Roerich in his painting "Uglich." The finest example of Russian architecture of the late 16th and early 17th centuries is the Church of the Assumption (1628) (УСПЕ́НСКАЯ ЦЕ́РКОВЬ) or "Marvelous" (ДИ́ВНАЯ) of the old Alexian Monastery (АЛЕКСЕ́ЕВСКИЙ МОНАСТЫ́РЬ) famous for the three octagonal spires which hold onion shaped cupolas.

Rostov the Great

РОСТО́В ВЕЛИ́КИЙ is not to be confused with the city Rostov on Don, which is located further south on, you guessed it, the River Don. РОСТО́В ВЕЛИ́КИЙ sits on Lake Nero and is another ancient town on the "Golden Ring." Records date this ancient city back to 862! At that time it was an important port used as a place to trade with Scandinavian merchants. In the 12th century it became the "Great" because it was of equal size and might to Kiev and Novgorod. Like many cities it remained under Tartar rule after the invasion for quite some time. In 1474, however, Dmitri Donskoi became ruler of the city. In the 17th century, it was once again invaded, this time by the Lithuanians and Poles.

The city has an ancient kremlin which exhibits late 17th century architecture. Inside the kremlin sits the palace of the former Archbishop Ion Sisoyevich (МЕТРОПОЛИЧЬИ ПАЛАТЫ). Yet, unlike most Russian cities, most of the more interesting architectural achievements of РОСТОВ ВЕЛИКИЙ are found outside of the kremlin. The stately Cathedral of Assumption (УСПЕ́НСКИЙ СОБО́Р), for example, which was built with the same design as УСПЕ́НСКИЙ СОБО́Р in Moscow, is quite impressive. There are a few graceful churches of the second part of the 17th century in Rostov: the Church of Resurrection (1670, ЦЕ́РКОВЬ ВОСКРЕСЕ́НИЯ) and the Church of St. John the Divine (1683, ЦЕРКО́ВЬ ИОАННА БОГОСЛО́ВА) with the silken shine of the aspen tiles of round towers flanking these two churches. The Church of Gregory the Divine is built on the place of the old monastery, where one of the first colleges of Northeastern Russia was opened in 1214.

There is the Church of the Savior on the Marketplace next to the kremlin with noteworthy frescoes of the 17th century.

You may get there by train from Yaroslavsky Railroad Station.

CITIES IN NORTHWESTERN RUSSIA

The towns of the Golden Ring lie closer to Moscow than to St. Petersburg and it is probably best to travel to them from the capital. The following three cities, however, which are also very important historical centers, are situated a bit closer to St. Petersburg outside of the ring. Novgorod is actually located between the two cities on the main route from Moscow to St. Petersburg. The following is a sketch of these northern cities.

Pskov

Pskov has a rich history spanning over 10 centuries. In ancient times it was an important military post for the Eastern Slavs in their push towards Estonia and Livonia and against the Teutonic Knights. It was ruled by the Novgorod Republic, but also had its own Dukes from time to time. In 1348 an independent republic was established. It was forever at war with the Grand Duke of Lithuanian and the Teutonic Knights but managed to withstand the many attempted sieges until it finally fell to Moscow in the 15th century. More recently, Pskov was the location where Nicholas II abdicated in March of 1917.

Pskov's kremlin is the most interesting site in the city. Surrounded by large limestone walls, it sits up high on the banks of the Velikaya and Pskov Rivers. The Trinity Cathedral was built in 1699. Inside the church is the tomb of the First Duke of Pskov and a second token tomb in honor of the Great Duke Dovmont, the most famous Duke of the city.

To go to Pskov, take the train from Moscow to St. Petersburg, from Peterburgsky Railroad Station, change at Chudovo.

From Novgorod, by train to Pskov.

By boat on the Volga

Hotels:

Gostínitsa "Oktyábr'skaya" (prospect Oktiabriá)

Gostínitsa "Touríst" (Krasnoznámenskaya úlitsa, 4)

Sites: the Historical Museum in the former Pogánkin Court

Novgorod

A bit further out from St. Petersburg on the route to Moscow is the great city of Novgorod, "New Town." It has a history that extends over 11 centuries. The soil of the city can tell the history of Russia better than any other in the land. It was in this city that the famous Norse settlers arrived under the leadership of Rurik. Throughout the years, Novgorod grew and prospered until 1471. In 1570, Ivan the Terrible slaughtered 60,000 of its citizens in fear of a plot to assassinate him. The Swedish occupation of 1611 to 1617 wrought further havoc on Novgorod, reducing the population of 400,000 to a mere 8,000. A series of terrible fires further destroyed the city and confirmed its ruin.

Much has been reconstructed and there is a lot to see and feel in this great city. An oval citadel is enclosed by a huge stone wall, the kremlin, on the west bank of the Volkhov. Within this well-preserved kremlin is the six-domed St. Sophia Cathedral (СОФИ́ЙСКИЙ СОБО́Р), built by the Greeks in 1052. Its central dome is said to resemble an ancient warrior's helmet. Within the kremlin you will also find the palace of the Archbishop (ВЛАДЫ́ЧНЫЙ ДВОР), the Historical Museum (ИСТОРИ́ЧЕСКИЙ МУЗЕ́Й) and the Granovitaya Palata (ГРА-НОВИ́ТАЯ ПАЛА́ТА). ИСТОРИ́ЧЕСКИЙ МУЗЕ́Й has over 80,000 exhibits dating back to the 11th century. Outside of the kremlin walls you will encounter many other churches which will give you a good account of the architectural history of Russia.

You may go there by train from Moscow and St. Petersburg.
Hotels:
"Sadko"
"Vólkhov," (úlitsa Floróvskogo)
"Il'men'," (úlitsa Górkogo)
Sites:
Historical Museum (inside the kremlin, over 80,000 exhibits in 35 halls including unique Russian letters dating from 11th to 15th centuries written on birch-bark
Church Art Museum in the Granovitaya Palata in the kremlin
History Museum of the Revolution.

Kizhi

The island of Kizhi is located about 250 miles northeast of
St. Peterburg on the northern tip of Lake Onega. It is one of the
most ancient inhabited places in Russia. The island is now an
open air museum and tours of it are given by boat or train. Its
wooden architecture is the highlight of the island, but oddly
enough most of the structures were brought in from other parts
of Russia. Kizhi has now become famous for its Church of the
Transfiguration built in the early 18th century. What makes the
church so original and spectacular is that it is made entirely of
wood, even its 22 domes! Due to its location and design, the
effects of the changes in the light that falls on it during the day
is very enchanting and provide for a wonderful viewing of the
many icons in the church. The sites of Kizhi are not limited to
churches; there are also barns, houses and water and windmills.

To get there by train go to Petrozavodsk and then from the
Ozernaya river station take the pleasant journey through the
rivers and lakes.

CITIES TO THE EAST

Not many travelers to Russia venture east of the Ural
Mountains—possibly because there is so much to see west of the
mountains! Nevertheless, many wonderful trips are available
through Siberia, where some of the most breathtaking sights in
the world are found.

Novosibirsk

НОВОСИБИ́РСК, the largest Siberian city in Russia and an
important industrial center, is on the banks of the river Ob.
Novosibirsk is best known for its research center,
Akademgorodók (АКАДЕ́МГОРОДОК) or "Academy Town,"
located about 20 miles south of the city. With the best facilities
and finest scientists in all of Russia, Akademgorodok attracts
many foreign researchers and scholars and is therefore well
supplied and very accommodating to foreigners. One of its main

attractions is the Museum of History and Architecture (МУЗЕЙ ИСТОРИИ И АРХИТЕКТУ́РЫ) which is an open air museum that displays old architecture from all over Siberia. The best way to get there from Novosibirsk is by taxi.

The city of Novosibirsk is quite modern, dating back only to 1893, and is said to have remnants of all styles of 20th century architecture. It was founded at the time of the building of the Trans-Siberian Railroad. It is the third largest city in Russia, after Moscow and St. Petersburg. It is also a respected cultural center with a grand opera house, a very fine conservatory, and many theaters and museums. Novosibirsk, however, is not as popular as it would appear because of its harsh climate. Winter temperatures often fall to negative 50° F and summer temperatures can reach a scorching 90°!

To get there, go by train to Vladivostok on the Trans-Siberian Railway (6 days journey) or by air.

Vladivostok

Like Novosibirsk, Vladivostok is a very young city. Founded in 1860, it immediately became a large city and a very important strategic base of Russia. Its name in translation means "rule the East." It was the key naval point for the Russian navy during the Russo-Japanese War. Since then it has remained an important base for the fleets. It was closed to foreigners in the Soviet period but is now open. It is a center for whaling and fishing fleets.

CHAPTER SIXTEEN

GEOGRAPHICAL HORIZONS

Russia is a bi-continental, Eurasian country. It is surrounded by two oceans, the Arctic and the Pacific. It is a country of a great variety of natural zones.

THE NORTH OF EUROPEAN RUSSIA

Compared to the United States, Russia is a more northern country with a cooler climate. The North of Russia takes up one third of the territory of the European part of Russia. One quarter of this part lies behind the polar circle, where the polar night lasts for two months in the winter and the polar day, with its white nights, lasts for two months in the summer.

The Russian North is the region of the tundra with swamps and the taiga with rich forests. Three quarters of the territory of the Russian North is covered by coniferous and mixed forests of different varieties of trees which span East to West, approaching the borders of European and Asian Russia. One may have an exotic experience when traveling to the Russian tundra, where the people ride on dogs and deer sleds as well as on cars and trains. The image of Rudolph the red-nosed reindeer is pretty common in the tundra. The reindeer are not only a convenient means of transportation here but also a good source of food and medicine.

The Russian North is rich with rivers and lakes. The Northern Russian rivers are: Northern Dviná which empties into the North sea, Nevá which comes from Ládoga Lake, Vólkhov which flows into Ladoga Lake, Onéga which falls into the White Sea, and Pechóra.

Remember the names of the two last rivers when you read two of the most significant works of Russian literature, "Eugene Onegin" by Alexander Pushkin and "A Hero of our Time" by Mikhail Lermontov. Their main characters, Onegin and Pechorin, have names derived from the names of these rivers. One hundred years later in the same literary tradition, the pen-name Lenin was derived from the name of one of the biggest rivers in Siberia, the Lena.

The main cities of the north are Múrmansk, Arkhángelsk, Vorkutá, Petrozavódsk, St. Petersburg. Three of these cities are ports. St. Petersburg is a big Russian port on the shores of the Gulf of Finland. Arkhangelsk at the mouth of Northern Dviná is the other important port of this region. Múrmansk on the sea coast is the third port of Northern Russia.

The primary occupations of the population of the Russian North are industry, hunting, and fishing on the sea coast, and agriculture in the river valleys.

"ALONG THE MOTHER VOLGA" – THE VOLGA RIVER REGION

The Vólga, one of the largest and longest Russian rivers, crosses the whole territory of European Russia from the swamps in the northwest to the steppes of the southeast and empties itself into the Caspian sea. The name Volga in the Sarmat language means "navigable." Its old name "Ra" means "plentifulness," "spaciousness." Many Russian rivers flow into the Volga on its downstream, including Oká, Moscow, and Káma.

The Volga is the oldest means of transportation between the south and north of Russia. On the other side, different nomadic people crossed the ВОЛГА from the east on their way to the west. The Asiatic nomads made their fierce raids crossing this river. After capturing Russia in 1240, the Tartar headquarters were established at Saray on the Lower Volga. The Volga always has been a crossroads of different interests, influences and cultures.

This river witnessed many events in Russian history, including the decisive battles with the Tartars in 1552. Such Russian cities as Samára and Tsarítsyn were established since that time in order to protect this area against raids of the Tartars. In the 17th century in the Time of Troubles, the Povolzhye withstood the Polish invasion. From Nizhny Novgorod, the city on the banks of Volga, the regiments of the Duke Pozharsky and Minin came to Moscow.

Two centuries later, Volgograd, the city on the banks of the Volga river, was the place of a decisive victory over the Nazi troops. Today the Volga plays an important role in trade.

The territory along the Volga River is called the Povólzhie (ПОВÓЛЖЬЕ). It stretches for about 700 miles from the mixed forests of the north taiga, with its coniferous and broad-leaved trees, to the south, where the forest-steppe with alternating glades and the steppe appear.

The landscape of the Povólzhye ranges from mostly low and flat areas of the Eastern European and the Prikaspíyskiye plains to the high Privólzhskiye heights and Zhiguli Mountains.

The key industries in this region include livestock, fishing, agriculture, timber, automobiles and petroleum. The main cities of the Povolzhye are Sarátov, Kazán and Ástrakhan.

THE DOORWAY TO THE EAST – THE URAL

The Urals in translation from Tartar means "belt." The old writers called the Ural mountains the Reefian belt. The Ural mountains are the natural boundary between the continents of Europe and Asia. Its western side faces Europe and its eastern side turns toward Asia. It is here where the landscapes of the East, West, South and North come closely together.

Its western heights, Predurálye (which means in front of the Urals) comes down to the Eastern European Plain in the European part of Russia. The eastern heights, Zaurálye (which means behind the Urals) run down into the Western Siberian Plain in Asia.

The landscape of the Urals holds a treasury of various geographical features: mountains, forests, valleys, and rivers.

Mainly mountainous with waves of foothills, sharp cones of mountain ridges, sloping cliffs, and deep caves of cliffs, it contains a lot of fertile meadows and fields in its low part.

The natural zones of the Urals include the tundra, the taiga, the coniferous and wide-leaved forests, the glades, the steppe, and the half-desert.

On the North Ural there is the taiga with the coniferous forests. The landscape of the central and southwest Urals resembles the landscapes of the Lower Povólzhye. It is a region of wide-leaved forests and the forest-steppe.

The climate of the Urals is continental. There are snow storms in the winter and plenty of hot days in the summer. The dry climate of the central Asia influences the climate of the Southern Urals.

To get a flavor for this part of Russia, read Pushkin's "The Captain's Daughter" "КАПИТÁНСКАЯ ДОЧЬ," partially set in the Urals.

The Urals is the one of the centers of developed industry and agriculture, known for its metallurgy, coal and semi-precious stones. The main cities of the Urals are Orenbúrg, Pyerm' and Ekaterinbúrg. The last city was named in honor of Empress Catherine the Great. Here the last Russian Tsar Nicholas II and his family were murdered by the Bolsheviks in 1918 during the Russian civil war.

"DEEP IN THE HEART OF ASIA" - WESTERN AND EASTERN SIBERIA AND THE FAR EAST

According to some sources, the name of Siberia derived from the Tartar word Senbir, which means the first or the chief. It was the name of one of the Tartar cities on the Irtysh River, a residency of the Tartar Khans. Siberia became a part of Russia in the second part of the 16th century after the forces of the Russian cossack Yermak defeated the well-organized resistance of the Western Siberian Khanate. The Far East was explored by Russians beginning in the 17th century.

Siberia is a vast territory from the Ural mountains to the mountain ridges dividing the Arctic and the Pacific oceans. The western part of it is covered by the Western Siberian plain which stretches from north to south for 2,500 km and covers 9/10ths of the territory of Western Siberia.

The landscape of Western Siberia has flat contours crossed by a number of large flowing rivers. In the southeast of Western Siberia the Altay Mountains rise. They stand out in sharp contrast to the flat plateau and sharp cliffs. The mixed forests grow along the mountainside, where the soil is fertile. In the forests the grass grows 8-10 feet height. The border of the forests ends at the height of 8,000 feet. Above it high alpine meadows and the high-mountain tundra appear. In the Altay mountains begin two big Siberian rivers, the fully-flowing navigable river Ob about 16 miles wide and the Irtysh River which begins in the Mongolian Altay. The main cities of Western Siberia are Novosibírsk, Omsk, Tomsk, Barnaúl and Toból'sk.

Eastern Siberia stretches from the Yenisey River to the mountain chains dividing the basins of the Arctic and Pacific Oceans. Its territory exceeds the territories of all the countries of western Europe. Eastern Siberia has a cold climate. Its winter is long and chilly. Its summer is dry and hot. In contrast to Western Siberia, Eastern Siberia has mainly mountainous territory. It is covered with the Central Siberian plateau (СРÉДНЕ-СИБИ́РСКОЕ

ПЛОСКОГОРЬЕ) which stretches to the Far East. Its highest peak lifts up to 1.25 miles. Here the largest river of Siberia, the Lena, begins. It crosses the Central Siberian plateau from the south to the north and connects Eastern Siberia with the ocean. Its length exceeds 280 miles.

The Central Siberian Plateau occupies the majority of Eastern Siberia. To the south are the mountains the Western and Eastern Sayány. They are crossed by the Yenisey, one of the largest and the most important Siberian rivers. In the Stanovóy Ridge in the northeastern part of Eastern Siberia, there are basins of the north Siberian rivers, Kolymá (the shores of which for many years were the place of deportation of prisoners) and Indigírka where the remnants of mammoths were found.

Lake Baikal, in Eastern Siberia, is one of the deepest lakes in the world. It contains hot springs.

In the Zabaykalskie Mountains, there is an alternation of mountain chains and plateaus with deep low river valleys. The forest-steppe and the steppe of Zabaikalia with its black-earth soil is an important agricultural zone. The climate here is warm, although winter lasts more than five months. One of the most beautiful Russian rivers, the Lena, begins near the Baikal. It crosses the Central Siberian Plateau and connects Eastern Siberia with the ocean. The Angara, a full-flooded river, is a tributary of the Yenisey, drawing its source from Lake Baikal.

The Yenisey is longer than the Volga and it crosses all the natural zones of Eastern Siberia.

The Siberian territory of the Arctic coast is occupied by the tundra. Above the polar circle there is the polar tundra with sparse modest trees and mossy bogs. It is covered with rivers, lakes, valleys and mountain ridges with cliffs. In the far north the forests disappear. Towards the south, on the border between the tundra and taiga, is the forest-tundra with its large marshy zones. Then the Siberian taiga begins with a tremendous variety of trees. The majority of Eastern Siberia is occupied by either gloomy, "black" taiga with dark coniferous forests, or light with pine-trees. The virgin forests of Siberia are an essential source of fresh air and an oasis of health for the whole planet.

Industry, agriculture, hunting and fishing are the primary occupations of the population. The main cities of Eastern Siberia are Yakútsk, Irkútsk, Verkhoyánsk, Krasnoyársk, Ulán-Udé and Chitá.

THE FAR EAST

The boundary between the continents of Asia and North America passes in the Far East. In 1728, the Russian Captain Bering discovered the Bering Strait, which separates Asia from America. The border between the United States and Russia goes through the Bering Strait.

The Far East is located more than 5,000 miles from Moscow. When it is midnight in Moscow, it is already morning in the Far East. The natural boundary of the Far East on the north are the mountain ridges dividing it from Eastern Siberia. On the south, its boundaries go along the rivers Amúr and Ussúri. The Amúr, a large full-flowing river, and its tributaries Ussúri and Zeya are the primary rivers of the Far East.

The landscape of the Far East is extremely varied. It includes the ridges of the north, the volcanos of Kamchátka and the Kurílian Islands and the fertile plains of the South-Ussurian territory. The climate is cold and dry in winter and humid and warm in summer.

The natural zones of the Far East are very different. A zone of the tundra includes the Anadýr territory, Chukótka, the northern part of Sakhalín island and the Kamchátka Peninsula. It goes very far to the south. Priamúrie, Primórye, the Kurílian Islands, the south of Sakhalín and Kamchátka are all zones of the taiga. The natural resources of the South Ussúrian taiga are extremely rich and beautiful. The area contains 150 different kinds of trees and bushes. The Amur steppes are covered with grass as tall as a human being.

292

The main cities of the Far East, besides Vladivostok, are Blagovyéshchensk which means "good message," Petropávlovsk, the name of which is derived from the names Peter and Paul, and Khabárovsk, named in honor of the Russian General Khabárov who successfully led the expeditions to the Amur River.

Since 1903 the Far East has been connected with the European part of Russia by the Trans-Siberian Railroad.

So go ahead and do some traveling. As you have read, there is a lot to see and experience in Russia!

Have a good trip! СЧАСТЛЍВОГО ПУТЍ!